THE
SUMMONING

HEATHER GRAHAM

THE
SUMMONING

mira

mira

ISBN-13: 978-0-7783-6991-2

The Summoning

For Robert Rosello, one of the best friends possible, and his wife, Yesenia, and beautiful kids, Victoria and Anthony. For years and years of the ups and downs in life, support at all the right times, and laughter. With Dennis, half of our family "Waldorf and Statler team." Sometimes Slush Pile bassist.

Thank you.

All the love in the world.

CAST OF CHARACTERS

At McLane House Bed-and-Breakfast

Kristi Stewart—recently inherited her great uncle's property

Jonah Whitney—household manager

Genie Turner—chef and housekeeper

Sydney Gary—young assistant to Genie

Shelley Blake—medium who conducts popular séances

Jedidiah McLane—Kristi's great uncle

Ian Murphy—old friend of Jedidiah's

Jamie Murphy—Ian's grandson who lived with him

Keith Hollis—handyman and groundskeeper

FBI and Law Enforcement

Dallas Wicker—new agent assigned undercover

Joe Dunhill—detective with the Savannah police

Adam Harrison—founder and director, Krewe of Hunters

Jackson Crow—field director, Krewe of Hunters

Angela Hawkins—Krewe agent, married to Jackson Crow

Dr. Bill Perry—medical examiner

Dr. Colleen Horvath—forensic anthropologist

Guests

Carl Brentwood—young up-and-coming actor

Claire Danson—Carl's manager

Murray Meyer—Carl's agent

Granger and Janet Knox—a contractor and his wife

Lacey Knox—their daughter

THE
SUMMONING

PROLOGUE

Twenty years ago

Dallas ran, far from the house. He could hear his aunt Betsy calling to him, but he needed to escape. Betsy was kind; she was trying. But she didn't understand that sometimes he needed to be alone, away from piano lessons, Little League and all the things she tried to make him do to forget. He hated the house now. His father, who'd been given leave for the funeral, was back overseas, a lieutenant in the army—dousing his own grief in the deserts of the Middle East.

A ten-year-old boy didn't forget that easily that he'd lost his mother—piano lessons didn't ease the pain.

At least his aunt's old house was far from Savannah—out past the old section and the new section, on the outskirts, in an area rife with hills and hummocks and streams. And the old cemetery.

Once upon a time, there had been a great plantation up on the hill, and near it, the remnants of the old church remained. He loved the ruins; he loved to go and wander around the remaining walls of the building and down the stairs to the catacombs and then back up to the graveyard. He liked to read what he could on the old gravestones and tombs, and imagine the rest. He preferred one grave especially. It had belonged to Louis Falmouth, a soldier during the revolution. Louis had become something of a friend for him—a made-up friend, he guessed—but he talked to the grave. He imagined Louis telling him fantastic tales about running with the Swamp Fox, a hero of the revolution, a man who dared cross enemy lines, dodged Redcoat bullets and brought desperately needed information to the American troops.

The sun was setting as he ran. At first, it shot glorious beauty across the sky. Then it created a purple and gray gloom, and a mist slowly settled on the ground.

Dallas wound through the overgrown bracken and brush, through the oaks and toward the creek, right by the church. He paused at a lichen-covered weeping angel. She seemed exceptionally lovely and sad in the growing foggy darkness.

"Hello, ma'am," he said politely. He looked around; he was near Louis's tomb, and all around him there was statuary, more angels guarding what had been family plots, the little gates and brick fences broken and jagged now, forgotten as the lives that had been lived. Death's heads adorned many stones, and the mist made them seem to grin.

Bowing to the angel, he turned, and almost tripped over another old stone, one that was broken down beyond recognition of name, date or any other identifying numbers or words. This one was beneath a giant statue, an avenging angel with wings outspread, and for a moment, Dallas was afraid.

Soon it would be completely dark.

He steadied himself on a stone. "Excuse me, sir," he said to the angel, for that one didn't look sad or forlorn, but rather fierce. His imagination played tricks with him; the angel might come to life, begin to move. It seemed to stand against the mist and the coming night and the rising moon as if it were a warrior—ready to take on a young boy with the swipe of one wing.

"Here, this way! Over here!" a voice suddenly demanded.

Real? Imagined?

He turned, frightened and uneasy, but he ran toward the sound of the voice. In his haste, he tripped. He fell over a broken stone, flat down on the ground. He rolled to rise to his feet, but froze instead.

He was lying next to a body.

It was an old man with worn clothing, a gray beard, time-marked face.

It wasn't the body of the long-dead, nor a haunt of his imagination.

The man was bleeding.

"Sir!" Dallas cried, rolling to a knee by the man's side. "Sir?"

But the bleeding man did not respond.

That was when he heard words come out of the mist—real words. "Son, what are you doing? Don't just sit there—go for help."

Dallas looked up in terror, certain that the avenging angel had indeed awakened.

But it was not a statue who had spoken.

In front of Dallas stood Louis Falmouth, hero of the revolution, just as he'd been depicted in the book about the war at his aunt's house: beige breeches, cotton shirt, green vest and earth-colored frock coat, his brown hair tied back. He was stern as he looked at Dallas, and for a moment, the boy just stared, open-mouthed.

Had he lost his mind, gone a little crazy, as the doctors had feared after the attack on his mother had left her dead?

"Boy!" his hero said. "Move, now, get help. Those ruffians, the wretched crew that killed your mother, they did this to old Mr. Polk. It was a lark to steal his piddling belongings. Just as it was a lark to torment your mother. He may live. *This man could live, and bring them to justice.* Right this! Go, get help—now!"

Dallas stumbled to his feet. He stared, and blinked hard, but Louis Falmouth remained.

"Go!"

Dallas ran. As hard and as fast as he could to his aunt's house.

He forced himself to be coherent, afraid no one would believe him, that no one would help.

At first, Aunt Betsy did not. She and her friend Michael looked at him with sympathy.

"I'm not seeing things because of Mom! I'm begging you—get help!"

He must have sounded sure; Aunt Betsy called 911 while Michael grabbed the first aid kit and his shotgun and headed out with Dallas.

They ran back through the trees and the bracken, finally coming to the stones of the graveyard.

Dallas looked around; there was no sign of the Revolutionary War hero Louis Falmouth.

And he feared there would be no Mr. Polk, and then they would lock him up in some hospital for people gone crazy with grief.

But the old man was there, still down on the ground, bleeding from a deep wound on his leg.

Michael set to work with the emergency kit, ordering Dallas to help with a tourniquet, stop the bleeding.

EMTs arrived, and Mr. Polk was carried out on a stretcher to an ambulance parked on a nearby road.

"You did good, kid. You did good," Michael told him, ruffling his hair. "It's a miracle that you found that man. How the hell did you see him there, behind stones, with all that overgrown bracken and grass?"

Dallas started to answer—but he couldn't tell the truth. "Just lucky, I guess."

Mr. Polk lived. He went on to identify the three drifters who had beaten him to a pulp.

★ ★ ★

The same men who had attacked Dallas's mother as she was out for a run one night, and had left her to die.

Dallas went back to the cemetery to thank his hero; Louis Falmouth just nodded gravely, and then smiled, turning and disappearing as he did so. Dallas knew, however, that he would see him again.

In another three months, his father got his honorable discharge from the military and he and Dallas moved back to Fredericksburg, Virginia.

They began life anew. In time, life became something...almost normal. There was school for Dallas, the football team, and his dad's new girlfriend and then wife, Susan. She was kind and decent, and rather than ask Dallas to forget his mom, she would ask him to talk about her.

But Dallas never stopped visiting graveyards when he needed some time for himself.

And he never stopped talking to the dead.

CHAPTER ONE

Savannah, Georgia

"Yes, I feel him—I feel his presence. He is here, among us."

Shelley Blake—who was possibly the worst medium in the world—spoke softly and bowed her head. "Keep holding hands!" she said to the small group gathered at the foldout table. "Hold tight, for the spirits may be strong and the living must stay strong, as well."

The "he" the *so-called* medium was summoning was Monty McLane, who supposedly killed his wife, Trinity, and his father, Samuel McLane—the entrepreneur who had built the McLane House in 1828. The story went that Monty had slain them in a fit of rage in 1864, when Savannah had surrendered to General Sherman when the Union general's infamous March to the Sea threatened the city with the wrath of destruction the army had brought to three hundred miles of countryside as he'd headed to the Atlantic. On Christmas day that year, General William Tecumseh Sherman had given the city of Savannah to President Abraham Lincoln—and Monty McLane, his father and his wife had been buried in the back of the house by the surviving family member, young Josiah McLane, a boy of fourteen, too young to have made his way into the fighting.

He had hastily buried them there—without marker, pomp or circumstance, to save their bodies from what well might have been the wrath of the enemy.

The house had been hosting Confederate injured; it soon became a hospital for Union soldiers and the headquarters for Colonel Albert Huntington, one of Sherman's most trusted officers.

So of course, the house was haunted. Like most of Savannah. Every respected old building—the cemeteries, churches and so on—hosted a few ghosts.

Ghosts were good business.

Kristi Stewart stood in the doorway to the parlor of the McLane house—*her* house now—watching the séance. After all, she was the hostess here. At the insistence of one the guests— Carl Brentwood, a twenty-something actor from LA—she had arranged for tonight's event.

Kristi only continued the séances here because they were such an established part of staying at the house. Visitors came because the house had a reputation for being so very haunted—and the guests seemed to love what Kristi considered to be the absolute ridiculousness of the séance. They ate up every bit of Shelley's over-the-top performance.

Similarly, neighborhood tours went by the so-called haunted house every night, pointing out the grand Victorian porch that now swept around what had once been a federal-style home, and still boasted a double stairway to the entrance. As a media consultant with a city tour group, Kristi had made sure tours went by the house. And, as the owner, she kept a mannequin of Monty McLane in the upstairs window—well-lit for the amusement of the tourists that went by.

Kristi loved the house and its history, and especially Savannah history. But most of the people who came to stay at McLane House were more interested in hearing only the grisly legends.

"Monty, are you here with us?" Shelley asked.

Kristi had to hand it to Shelley—she could make her voice become a bizarre whisper that was entirely chilling. And she dressed the part: she wore a flowing black caftan and carried a crystal globe that she'd set in the center of the table. Her dark hair was swept neatly behind her ears beneath a crimson scarf. Shelley had been conducting her séances in the city for about twenty years. She was in her mid-forties, attractive, with huge, dark eyes that added to her look of mystery. She was quite able to play up her "abilities" to a perfect T.

The table rocked suddenly, and Kristi had to swallow back a groan. Shelley had knocked the table herself, with her knee. Kristi had clearly seen her do it.

Soft gasps went around the table.

"The spirits are among us!" Shelley proclaimed. "Monty— you're here, you're with us."

Shelley had the habits of the house down pat; she'd timed her words to go with the flow of a whispery breeze that arrived each time the air conditioner kicked in. Naturally, the lights in the parlor were turned off, and the candles that were set on the table and the mantel flickered with that tiny bit of air.

Kristi heard a quiet voice—it was coming from the kitchen, from the computer she kept there.

She quickly hurried over, ready to turn off the screen. She'd left a local news website open, and a video had started playing automatically. An anchorman was talking, his face grave. "The police have reported no new leads on the disappearance of Simon Drake, last seen before a meeting with a number of his supporters. They are asking anyone with any information to call the number on your screen. The situation is reminiscent of the disappearance of prominent businesswoman Eliza Malone, who disappeared without a trace two years ago, a case that remains open on the books today. Any help…"

"Another one!"

Startled, Kristi turned. Jonah Whitney, her great-uncle's old friend who had stayed on to manage the house, was in the room, holding a paper cup of coffee—he could drink coffee day and night without missing a wink of sleep.

"Jonah," she said and smiled.

"Sorry, I was about to turn off the news and head up to my room."

"You don't want to come to the séance?" she teased. Jonah hated the séances, and always had; he was delighted that now that she was the owner, he was no longer obliged to be around for them in any way, shape or form.

"Heard them saying that man was missing. Don't know what the hell is going on around this place, people disappearing." He shook his head.

"I'm going to turn off the sound, okay? Don't want it to disturb Shelley. They're dumb and ridiculous, yes, but hey, you're the one who told me the séances are the bread and butter around here."

"Yes, I know. I'm out of here!" He grinned, heading for the back stairs.

Shaking her head, Kristi turned off the computer and walked back to the archway separating the rooms to watch over the séance. It seemed especially silly to her, pretending to dredge up past wrongdoings when bad things were happening in their world now. Savannah was not without its crime, but it was a good city with good police, and she prayed their most recent problem would be quickly solved.

Shelley was calling out, "Spirits of the McLane house, I summon you!"

"Oh!" One of the guests, Lacey Knox, the teenaged daughter of a contractor from Ohio—gave out a soft little gasp. "Yes, I can feel...a presence!"

"Something, yes!" her mom, Janet, wife of the contractor, agreed.

Yes, you feel air-conditioning! Kristi thought.

Shelley's eyes were closed, and she was muttering something of a chant. "Keep holding hands, close your eyes. I must feel... I must feel the spirits!" she said. And then, after several seconds of closed-eyed silence, she murmured, "It isn't Monty. I believe that it's... Trinity, Monty's poor wife, doomed to roam the house!"

Kristi wasn't supposed to speak during the séance—she wasn't even at the table. She couldn't help herself, though. She kept her voice a hushed and eerie whisper. "Monty," she said, "was blamed because Trinity was a Yankee, and at that time, North-South relations were so tense that it didn't matter that they'd been married for a long time. Monty had met her in New York—he had been there years before with Jefferson Davis, future president of the Confederacy, who had been giving a speech *against* secession at Cooper Union."

Other eyes remained closed. Shelley looked over at Kristi, shooting her a very evil glance.

"Sorry," Kristi mouthed.

"Yes, Trinity! We are here, we are seeking the truth! We wish to know the truth. History says that you tried to return home, that you longed to meet with the Union soldiers and to have them get you back to New York City. Some say you sneaked out at night when you knew that the Union troops were near, that you were falling in love with Colonel Huntington. That you led them here. You were a patriot—or a traitor—depending on point of view. But the war is long over... Is it true? Did you bring Colonel Huntington to McLane House? I know this is hard for you...but please, give us a sign! One rap for *yes*, two raps for *no*."

Once again, Kristi *saw* Shelley's leg move. A single knocking sound rocked the table again, drawing gasps from the assembled group.

Again, Kristi groaned inwardly. Eyes around the table had opened.

Carl Brentwood seemed genuinely surprised and awed. At his side, pretty Lacey Knox, eighteen years old and, apparently, an object of the young actor's attention, was equally amazed.

Even Granger Knox, the older bulldog-faced, no-nonsense contractor from Brunswick, a smaller city south of Savannah, seemed impressed. His wife, Janet, plump and sweet-looking, was clutching his hand tightly and glancing nervously around the darkened room.

Attractive, thirtyish Claire Danson and white-haired, dignified Murray Meyer, Carl Brentwood's media manager and agent, respectively—the only other two guests at the table—were visibly shaken, as well.

They had appeared far too sophisticated to be so taken. Claire had such a chic appearance with her short, very fashionable red hair, perfect makeup and mile-long nails. Murray, too—always dressed immaculately, even when casual, his silver-white hair brushed back smoothly as if he had been a star of the distant past himself.

"You simply couldn't turn your back on your beliefs!" Shelley said.

Another rap sounded. Carl Brentwood let out a gasp.

Okay, he was young—maybe twenty, an up-and-coming young heartthrob. But the parental Knox duo and either Claire or Murray had to have seen that jerk of the knee!

And Kristi found herself speaking again. "Trinity never embraced the Southern cause. She believed, always, in the sanctity of the Union and she was a die-hard abolitionist, but she kept to herself in Savannah, and she loved her husband dearly. The McLane family were into business, not agriculture, and they owned no slaves."

She saw Shelley's jaw tighten as the woman clenched her teeth.

But before anyone could react, it seemed that the entire house shook.

Kristi frowned, but she saw Shelley smiling—and she realized that a large tram, bearing tourists on one of the city's many ghost tours, had just rattled on by, hitting one of the potholes in the old road outside the house.

"Dearest Trinity!" Shelley proclaimed, "you were innocent—your evil husband simply suspected you of infidelity and, in his mind, treason! I can see him, now, Trinity, such a handsome man, tall and dark-haired and light-eyed. I can see him so clearly."

Well, of course Shelley could see him; they were in the back parlor, by the stairway to the second floor and a photograph of Monty—possibly taken by *the* Matthew Brady—held a place along the stairway wall with other McLane men and women who had lived in the house. Though the room was dark, a nightlight offered a pale illumination of the stairway, and Kristi could see Monty McLane easily enough herself.

The light seemed to waver; it was almost as if the man moved in the photograph, almost as if he tightened his jaw with anger.

"Dear Trinity, yes! I feel you!" Shelley cried dramatically.

Again, as if on cue, the house rattled.

Let it end! Kristi thought.

Shelley let out an exhausted sigh, as if communing with Trinity had drained her of all possible energy.

"She's gone now. Trinity is gone," Shelley said. "Poor thing, she tried so hard to tell us the truth, she can no longer manifest. But, oh, she was so strong for several minutes!" Shelley turned and looked at Kristi. "You may hit the lights now, Kristi."

Kristi was more than happy to oblige.

Light flooded the room.

"That's it?" Granger Knox said. He looked at his wife. "I thought we were going to try to contact my mother?"

"Mr. Knox," Shelley said, "the ghosts in this house are strong—and territorial. I'd be delighted to contact your mother for you, but I'll need you to come to my shop. It's right down on the riverfront. I'll give you my card. Please let me know when you'd like an appointment."

Janet Knox reached out to accept the card.

"Wow! That was amazing!" Carl Brentwood said. He saw Kristi across the room and smiled. "Thank you—thank you for setting this up." He turned to Claire and Murray. "See—we can sell this! I can host a show, and we can hire Shelley again and... oh, Kristi, we'll naturally book the entire house for a few days, and we'll make you famous!"

Kristi smiled weakly and said, "I'm so glad you all enjoyed yourselves."

She excused herself and escaped into the kitchen, heading for the coffeepot.

Her guests, she knew, would continue talking, all certain they had really spoken with one of the ghosts of the house.

Shelley came into the kitchen, seeing that the door that separated the kitchen from the rear parlor was closed.

"Kristi!" she said. "What were you trying to do to me out there?"

"Sorry—I just don't like to see the poor woman condemned for something I don't think she did."

"Well, I have to change my story now. She spoke! She really spoke."

"Shelley, a tram went by," Kristi said.

Shelley shook her head. "You never have believed I really contact the dead. But that—that *shake* of the house? I really didn't do that."

"Sure," Kristi murmured. She offered Shelley a forced smile.

"You're new here," Shelley said. "But you've been working with tourists forever—you have to know that the city *and* this *house* are really haunted. I mean, it was your great-uncle who left it to you, right?"

"That's right," Kristi agreed. She'd always loved the house—she'd never expected to own it. Her family tree was complicated. Josiah McLane had survived the war and even regained his house after the Union troops had left the city and the era of Reconstruction had begun. But he, in turn, had fallen in love with a New Yorker, and she'd come with the funds to restore the house. Josiah and his bride had two children, a son and a daughter, and the daughter had married a Scottish immigrant, Ian Stewart, and he'd left three sons, and through the following years, they'd procreated a lot. But her great-uncle, who had inherited the house through the family line, hadn't had any offspring.

There were other nephews and nieces, scattered around the country.

Kristi, however, had been the one who had fallen in love with Savannah. And Kristi had been the one who had hung on to every word of Uncle Jed's stories. Eventually it was she who had seen to his care at the assisted living facility where he'd spent his last days.

She'd imagined the house would have been put up for sale at his death, and he'd have left all his earthly treasures to a home for cats—he'd adored cats. Jedidiah had in fact left everything *except* the house to a facility just outside the historic district that cared for abandoned pets. It was fitting, she had thought.

The house had been a bed-and-breakfast for years, hanging on with the help of Jonah Whitney as manager—who, being just twenty years younger than her great-uncle Jedidiah, had basically determined on retiring, but remained now to help Kristi out. He'd been delighted that Kristi had inherited the house. And while he still maintained his apartment in the attic, and was a great help, he was pleased that she was taking over most of the management.

Running and maintaining the house was expensive, and she was keeping her business as a designer and media consultant to make sure that the bills always got paid, including those for the house and Jonah Whitney's small salary.

It was Jonah who had told her that she had to keep up with the séances. He was glad that she loved Savannah so much, and that she was fond of facts. "But don't you go being a snob," Jonah had warned her. "We need the income! Shelley gives us twenty percent of the take, so while you may not think it's much, those hundreds come in handy."

Kristi knew he was right, and she thanked his wisdom again as Shelley handed her a small stack of cash.

"Anyway," Shelley told Kristi happily. "It was a great night. I do believe we summoned someone. Not only that, the actor guy—sweet kid, surprisingly—gave me a hundred-dollar tip!"

"Nice," Kristi said. She smiled again, hoping Shelley was leaving. "The actor guy" had asked that they have the séance at midnight, and so it was very late, and she needed to be awake at six in the morning to let her breakfast staff in and get going for the day.

"Well, good night, and thank you for calling on me," Shelley told her.

"You're welcome, and thank you," Kristi said.

Shelley waved and headed down the little hall that went by the narrow back stairway and to the old servants' entrance. An old Savannah gray brick walkway led out to the sidewalk and the street.

The path also led to the backyard—which was a nice size, considering just how close the houses were in the historic district, many of them flush to one another. The McLane house had a patio courtyard directly behind the house, accessed by a third door, one that was kept locked from midnight to sunrise, and beyond that there were two structures that were once the stables and the smokehouse; today they housed all manner of supplies that might be needed for the business. The old buildings were well-maintained as they were the backdrop for the courtyard. Right behind them were flower beds and the memorials erected by Josiah McLane for his family members in 1901, when, at last, some of the fury, hatred and bitterness of the Civil War and the era of Reconstruction were finally beginning to become a part of the past.

Some people said an earlier McLane—Lieutenant Justin McLane, Revolutionary spy, who had actually been the first to own the property—was buried out there, on the grounds where he'd been hanged for his activities against the British.

No one knew if he'd actually died there—they only knew he'd been hanged by the British, having surrendered out in the nearby swamps so that others could disappear.

Kristi was proud that in a long-distant way the man had been her ancestor.

She didn't believe for a minute that anyone was buried in the back of the house. A few years back, Jonah had caught two "ghost-hunters" digging up the backyard in hopes of discovering the patriot's bones, and he'd seen to it that they had been arrested. Jonah was a good guy—he hadn't continued to prosecute the pair; he had asked that they be let off with a stern warning after their initial night in jail.

Kristi locked the door behind Shelley and walked through the house, picking up the last cups and glasses left about by the guests. She paused in the front parlor. Back in the day, the large room at the front of the house had been where the family greeted guests; the rear parlor, where they'd had the séance, would have been the family room. They were extremely lucky that ownership of the property had come down with the family through the decades. The old McLane piano, a Duncan Fife sofa and a period daybed remained in the back parlor. Refurbishing had been done now and then during various times in the years gone by, but much was original—including the portraits of the family that lined the grand stairway that led up to the second floor and the eight bedrooms that graced the house.

When he'd built the house, McLane had thought he'd have many children, and his children would have many children.

He hadn't imagined war would tear his world apart.

Cups and other leftovers from the evening all tidied up, Kristi passed through the back parlor one more time, then went through to the small, now-screened back porch that led to the courtyard. She checked the door; it was securely locked. Outside, Spanish moss dripped from old oaks that skirted the courtyard. The moon wasn't quite full, but the glow it cast down on the yard gave the space an aura of nostalgic beauty.

Climbing the stairs, Kristi couldn't help but look at the portraits of the McLane family that lined the stairway.

She paused in front of the Civil War–era photograph of Monty McLane—he of infamy, who had supposedly slain his family when they had so traitorously welcomed Union injured into the house and allowed it to become the headquarters for a Federal colonel.

He'd been a striking young man. While someone in the family had seen to it that all the old photographs in the house had been properly preserved and maintained with special preservation materials, they hadn't added color. But through the black-and-white contrast of the photograph, it seemed that his eyes had been light and his hair dark. He made a handsome figure, not smiling, but staring seriously into the lens. He had been cut down in a hail of bullets from the Union troops who had discovered him after the alleged murders.

"Well, good night, old boy," she told him. "Until later. Thank you, of course, for being here."

She went on up the stairs, almost forgetting the séance.

Jonah's apartment was up in the attic; despite the many stairs, the septuagenarian preferred the relative quiet of the attic space. He had a small fridge and a microwave up there, and loved his quarters in the house. He had a large-screen TV and soaked up certain programs in his free time. He was a huge fan of old sitcoms and sometimes—when she was in her own room, working on various flyers, radio spots and ad scripts—she could hear him laughing at the same *I Love Lucy* shows he had watched a dozen times over.

She smiled. Jonah was a great guy—spry, and all there. If he loved "Lucy," more power to him. She was of a mind herself that Lucille Ball had been one of the greatest comediennes the country had ever produced.

Her room was at the end of the second-floor hallway—the largest room, once the master quarters, and it stretched from the front of the house to the back, allowing her a large work space by a window overlooking the square, and a bedroom area, where she had her bed, an old wardrobe and a dresser set, all to the side of the hearth corresponding with that in the back parlor. She glanced over at her worktable. She needed to finish a mailing with an advertisement for a chain hotel's local Christmas activities. She'd get to it right after breakfast in the morning. It might be barely summer, hot and humid in Savannah, but winter was always on the way—in advertising, at least.

For a moment, she hesitated. The large upholstered chair where she had sat when her Uncle Jed had still been alive remained where she had kept it, by the wall, but close to the bed, ready to be drawn up when they had talked and laughed and exchanged stories.

The chair was a haunting reminder of a very good man. She often told herself that he had lived nearly a hundred very good years, but still…she missed him. That was always the case—no matter how old someone was, and no matter what the reason for their passing—if you loved that person, you missed them when they were gone.

Maybe she should move the chair.

Tomorrow.

Donning a nightgown, she plunged into bed, not even bothering to take her makeup off. Absolutely exhausted, she quickly fell into a deep sleep.

Alexandria, Virginia

Dallas Wicker was accustomed to strange hours and stranger work situations. He'd graduated from the academy just a year ago, and, after his first assignment out at a murder site in rural Virginia, he'd found himself being interviewed by Assistant Director Adam Harrison and his supervising field director, Jackson Crow.

But it wasn't quite 1:00 a.m. when he received a call from Crow that morning, and it was barely 2:00 a.m. when he found himself sitting in front of Adam Harrison at the man's handsome town house in Alexandria—his bag packed, ready to go.

"An assignment?" he asked. He was curious; there was a young man there as well, who'd been introduced to him as Josh.

He'd gone to shake the young man's hand before he realized that Josh wasn't among the living, but rather, an accomplished ghost, quite capable of making himself easily seen.

By those who could see.

And, of course, Dallas could *see*, which apparently he'd revealed to those who shared the gift when he'd solved the abduction of a woman out near Richmond. It had been the spirit of an old soldier hanging around a historic tavern who had led Dallas to the kidnapper's van. He'd explained his lucky break by saying he'd only followed tracks and broken branches and other clues in his hunt.

Someone was watching, of course, always watching, for those who were suited for the special unit of the FBI known informally as the Krewe of Hunters.

"Sorry to bring you out so late—or so early… You're going to be flown down to Savannah as soon as we're through here, and a car will be waiting for you at the airport. I'd like you to get where you're going by breakfast time."

"Yes, sir," he said. He was still somewhat in awe of the older gentleman who had created the Krewe. Harrison ran his agents through his number one man, Jackson Crow, and he also had his hands in a dozen philanthropic projects. He was a highly respected man whose position in the government agency was not known by many. The charity projects that he both worked himself and donated to were legendary.

"Dallas, let me start with this. Have you ever heard of the Whaley House?"

"No, sir, I have not."

Adam handed him a picture. It was of a house, most probably built in the mid to late 1800s.

"Well, interesting fact here. A United States agency—the US Department of Commerce—according to area records, keeps track of what they call 'officially' haunted places."

"Officially haunted. Interesting."

"And there are others with that designation."

Adam handed him another picture. It was of another beautiful dwelling, this one with an intriguing mix of styles. It appeared as if he had been begun, at least, in the early 1800s, in the Federal style, but had been added to in the Victorian era, at which time a wraparound porch had been put up to grace the second story. A majestic dual stairway led to the front door of the house, while a fine brick path led around the side. It was all framed by oaks, with haunting wisps of Spanish moss sweeping down from the branches.

"That's the McLane house, in Savannah. It's off a beautiful square, in the oldest area of the town."

"I'm guessing it's haunted, too?"

"Not officially, but as I've said, there are others, and we've been asked to investigate a number of places that might be... officially haunted."

"And we've agreed to do this?" Dallas asked, surprised. The Krewe didn't tend to advertise its specialty, and definitely not to agencies outside the FBI.

"Only when it coincides with other...events. Such as mysterious deaths and disappearances."

"Ah—hmm. Was this house built on a gallows site or a grave-yard?"

Adam shrugged. "There could be bodies. There's an infamous story about a Confederate soldier who slipped in after Sherman took the city and killed his wife and father for either politely asking the Union troops in—or perhaps because the wife was sleeping with a Yankee colonel. May or may not have happened, and may have happened in a variety of ways. A Revolutionary Patriot could be there, too. The house isn't known for a grave-yard." Adam shrugged. "Hey, it's Savannah. It's haunted."

Dallas frowned, curious—and worried.

He'd worked hard to become an agent, and as soon as he'd heard rumors about the Krewe of Hunters he'd known he wanted that assignment.

But now...he was just to investigate old ghosts?

And in Savannah.

Adam was studying him, maybe reading his mind.

The man handed him another picture. Dallas looked down at the image of a man in his midfifties to sixties.

"Simon Drake," Dallas said quietly.

Adam nodded, waiting.

"About to run for the state senate in Georgia. He was sup-porting a new 'crackdown on crime' in the city. He disappeared two nights ago."

"We believe he was—kidnapped?" Dallas asked.

"We believe he's dead," Adam said flatly.

"But we're not sure."

"Mr. Drake was last seen speaking at a square in the city. He was heading on to a meeting with a group of his supporters, toward the riverfront. You'll be supplied with maps, although I understand you are familiar with Savannah."

Yes, he was familiar with Savannah.

"I'm at a loss, sir. Haunted houses and a disappearing politi-cian..."

"His disappearance took place near the McLane house."

"And near others, I imagine."

Dallas was handed another picture. This was of a woman with graying hair and an open smile.

"Eliza Malone. Prominent businesswoman, outspoken on improving the city. She also disappeared—near the McLane house. Two years ago."

"Still…"

"Thing is," Josh said, speaking up, "And trust me, I know," he added, smiling ruefully, and as if reading Dallas's mind, "most of the dead are kind. They were as they were in life, usually seeking justice, or seeking to touch a loved one, trying to find a way to say goodbye. But some remain as well to watch over places—to help. But you are aware of that."

"No one really knows what happened at the McLane house in December of 1864," Adam said. "I've given you two names of people who were last seen in the area of the house. There have been other disturbing incidents occurring nearby… Almost as if there's a strange Bermuda Triangle situation there. A supposed suicide occurred recently—an older man, a Savannah native named Ian Murphy. And then there was another death from a fall—this one a young and very healthy man, Lachlan Plant, a personal trainer. I've emailed all the information we have to you, and have physical files for you to review. Other government agencies are involved who don't wish to have official association with the investigation. You won't go in as a federal agent, but rather as a friend of the young man who died from a fall. You'll be a licensed private investigator, of course, to give you some of the access you'll need to get into certain places, police records, and so on."

"And this friend who died from a fall…"

"Lachlan Plant—and he wasn't from Savannah."

"But his fall—was it from a height? The porch of the McLane house?" Dallas asked.

"No—from a sidewalk curb," Adam said drily.

"A curb?"

"You can read all about it on the plane. As I said, you're a PI hired by the family. In truth, he was an only child and his parents are dead, so, I'm counting myself as his family."

"Are you related—in any way?"

"In the way there is something very wrong about a young man's death," Adam said.

"Thing is," Josh put in, "these could all be unrelated incidents and tragedies—and then again, the McLane house is dead center in all that's going on."

"We were approached by a local police detective—not officially, but through some back channels. He'll be there to help you with whatever he can. But even the detective—Joseph Dunhill—will think that you're working independently. For now, we're invited in. If there's a reason to step in because the disappearances do prove to be cases of kidnapping—we'll step in. Until then, it's just you."

"I'm to find out if those deaths are related—and find the missing people?" Dallas asked.

"Dead or alive," Adam said.

It seemed she had barely slept before she was awake.

Light was coming in through a break in the curtains, but it was weak. Opening her eyes, she frowned, thinking she had awakened before her alarm had even gone off.

Confused, she started to sit up. The light in the room was very dim, but...

There was a man in the chair; the plushy upholstered wingback chair she used to sit in by the bed.

He was wearing a Confederate cavalry uniform. He had light eyes, dark hair...

And he was the spitting image of the man in the portrait on the stairway wall.

He wasn't real; she was dreaming.

Dreaming. And, in her dream, she couldn't seem to make a sound, to let her cry of fear rip through the air.

"Please, it's all right," the image said softly, standing politely.

She jumped out of bed, first backing away from the chair—and then hurrying forward to swipe her hand through the image, some speck of logic in the back of her mind trying to reason that it had to be a prop, or a puppet—someone playing a practical joke on her.

She touched nothing...

Nothing but cold air.

But the image remained.

"Stop that, Kristi, please. You are a logical woman!" the apparition said.

His words sounded cultured, as if he were well-educated, with just a slight Southern drawl.

Dreaming, she was dreaming...

She stood, getting out of bed. She could feel the hardwood floor beneath her feet.

"Kristi, forgive me—I don't make a habit of entering a lady's bedchamber unannounced and uninvited. But circumstances being what they are...well, I knew that you could see me."

"See you?" she whispered, in shock, she thought, still looking for the logic he believed that she possessed, ready to scream... yet unable to do so.

He stepped forward, taking her by the arms—and now she could feel him!

His touch was very strange and cold.

"I'm real, and I'm here," he told her.

"Oh, my God. Shelley...actually summoned you?" Kristi asked, incredulous.

"She opened one of those portals, you know," he said. "A door between the worlds of the living and dead."

"Shelley opened a portal," Kristi said. "And you came through?"

"No, not really. I've been here all along," the ghost said, grinning. He sighed. "Since the late 1700s. But tonight was the first time someone saw me. You saw me!" he said, and she could have sworn he seemed very pleased.

She worked her jaw to speak. Her words were halting and confused.

"You…you…you want me to help you, to bring out the truth of what happened so long ago, maybe…clear your name. Clear Trinity's name… I mean, if you didn't kill her…"

"Kill Trinity? She was the love of my life, and to clearing me…well, that would be nice, but…what I really want you to do is help me figure out what the hell is happening now." His eyes met hers. "No, Kristi, right now."

It was as if she could feel his words, feel the passion in them, a searing heat against that strange, strange, cold!

"You understand? You'll help?" he demanded.

She nodded, terrified.

He released her.

She fell back onto the bed.

She was losing it, losing it entirely. Too much pressure, work, the house…and Shelley's wild séances!

She stood, stared at him, praying he would disappear.

He didn't. His ghostly eyes bored into hers.

She ran. Dashing down the hallway and the stairs, through the back parlor, the front parlor and out the mudroom, frantically working at the lock to open the front door and get the hell out.

She burst out of the house—and right into a man on the doorstep.

He was tall and solid, flesh and blood; she could feel the muscles in his chest, she could almost feel his heart, *really beating.*

His hands were real, strong as they caught her, and his eyes were hazel and amused as he smiled down at her with curiosity. Something electric seemed to stream from his touch, and a tremor ripped through her, something different, but almost as strong as the terror that had seized her upstairs.

"I heard that McLane House had a wonderful and welcoming staff," he said, "but really—this just goes beyond all expectations!"

CHAPTER TWO

Great, Dallas thought, being hit by a whirlwind.

Not only was he on something of a wild goose chase, but the woman he was steadying—who had exploded out of the house like a bat out of hell—obviously had something wrong with her.

She was staring at him with huge, wild, blue eyes.

Something had truly frightened her.

For a moment, those eyes of hers were on him in sheer panic; then she blinked, and stepped back, as if coming to the conclusion that he was just flesh and blood, and not something surreal and terrifying. The change in her was mercurial—despite the short, silky nightgown she was wearing, she suddenly had an air of control and casual dignity.

"Ah, hello. I'm so sorry—I'm at a disadvantage. Are you a— guest?"

"That was what I was assuming," he told her.

She was a very attractive woman. Her blue eyes were enhanced, made even bluer by the deep, burnished-gold color of her hair, cascading wildly around her shoulders.

"Are you all right?" he asked her. "The way you flew out here... Is someone threatening you in there?"

"Oh, no, no… I just ran out for air and…to have a minute to myself!" she said.

Lying. Definitely.

But he'd have to get inside to figure out just what was happening.

The short silky thing she was wearing certainly enhanced her appeal. Her legs were perfectly curvy, and the way the material fell over the rest of her…

He forced himself to keep his eyes on hers as he shifted his backpack on his shoulder and offered her a handshake. "My name is Dallas. Dallas Wicker. A reservation was made for me last night—this is McLane House, right?"

"Right, right, yes…of course. And I am sorry—you're most welcome here. I just—I hadn't known we had another reservation for today."

"Oh—I have a confirmation number," Dallas said.

"That's fine. I'm sorry. The reservation must have gone through Jonah—the manager here," she said quickly, and then, realizing she still held his hand, she shook it quickly and released it. "I'm Kristi Stewart, proprietor," she told him. "And forgive me, please… I thought I saw a friend going by on the sidewalk, and wasn't expecting anyone at the door and…"

"I thought you wanted to be alone?" he said.

"Oh, yeah, well—both. Anyway, do come in. It is quite early—check-in doesn't usually happen until later. But of course, please come in. Breakfast starts in about an hour from now and…"

She stopped speaking and seemed to smile ruefully at herself. "Forgive me—I'll get out of the way, and then you can come in."

She held open the door wider, stepped inside and allowed him entrance.

He paused just a minute, looking down at the sidewalk and Johnson Square across the way; cars were beginning to move, school buses were out and the sun was beginning a nice ascent in the sky. But it was a quiet time of early morning.

He was damned sure she hadn't seen a friend out on the side-walk—or wanted a breath of fresh air.

He smiled and stepped into the house.

"This is our front parlor," she told him. "There's a back parlor, and a screened-in porch, and then a courtyard down here. Offices and a library off to the side over there—with a computer. The internet is available at any time. Or there's Wi-Fi. The stairs are right through that archway, and I believe you're going to be in room number seven...sorry, I know you'll be in seven, it's the only room that isn't taken this morning. I don't believe the room is ready. Make yourself at home in the parlor for now. The staff should be arriving any second and..." She paused, suddenly self-conscious. "I'll be right back down!" she said.

She turned and fled—departing with almost the same speed with which she'd crashed into him.

As she left, he followed her journey up the stairs. She was now showing self-consciousness about her apparel, clutching the back of her nightdress, making sure it extended below her round der-riere. He smiled, watching her go, bemused, and somewhat se-duced. Probably the stunning way they had met. He hadn't felt such a fascination in...he couldn't remember when.

His attention was drawn to the framed paintings and old pho-tographs that lined the stairway wall. They included a painting of a distinguished man in a frock coat with long hair tied at the nape of his neck, a lovely woman in an antebellum dress, and a soldier in a Confederate Calvary officer's attire—a real photo-graph from the day, he thought. There were four more framed images, all photographs, their attire indicating they had lived and perhaps died in the house in later decades, from the later 1800s up into the 2000s.

The house itself was charming, immaculate—without being so pristine that guests, even children, couldn't be comfortable.

Period furniture, tastefully restored, graced both the front parlor and the back parlor. Setting his case down and looking out to the screened porch, he saw the extent of the courtyard beyond, the outbuildings and a depth of yard behind it that was unusual, especially in the historic district. It was an exceptional piece of property, he thought. Possibly as nice as it was because it had stayed in the same family for years—the only exception being the years following the Civil War, after which—he'd learned through the massive file Adam Harrison had given him—Josiah McLane had petitioned for the property, and it had been returned to him during the waning years of Reconstruction. Even the current owner, Kristi Stewart, was a descendent, though her branch of the family tree was a bit extended. But other family had long since left the area; Miss Stewart had distant cousins in both California and New York.

An older man came down the stairs; he was tall and lean with a time-wrinkled face, a head of snow-white hair and a quick smile.

"Mr. Wicker!" he greeted. "Welcome, I'm Jonah Whitney. I was told you'd be early, but…well, you're really early! Welcome, welcome indeed! Did Genie let you in?"

Dallas stepped forward, offering his hand to the man. "No, sir. I met the owner. She was…apparently stepping out for a breath of air when I arrived."

"Ah, yes, well, Kristi does like to rise early. She helps out in the kitchen. We're renowned for our breakfasts here. Bed-and-breakfast, you know. We try to keep the beds comfortable and our breakfast excellent. Coffee? The pot is automatic—already brewed for those who come in to get the rest of world going."

"Coffee would be excellent," Dallas said.

Jonah Whitney beamed. "Come along then, and see the kitchen."

They went through an arched doorway to a large kitchen, complete with massive, state-of-the-art appliances and a large butcher-block workstation. The coffee brewed on a tile counter; the window above the sink overlooked the yard and a gray brick pathway that curved and headed into the back, skirting around the courtyard and haphazard oaks that dripped hauntingly with Spanish moss.

"Beautiful place," Dallas murmured.

"It is." Jonah poured coffee and handed a cup to Dallas. "Cream, sugar?"

"Black is fine," Dallas assured him.

"I love the house. Old Jedidiah—he just passed a few months back—and I went way back." He grimaced. "We're reenactors. Men playing at silly war games, but... I always say it's a good thing, too. We taught the past, about the inventions that led up to many tools and conveniences we have today—and the bad things about the past, too. We both did Revolutionary War and Civil War reenactments. Jedidiah was a young commissioned officer during World War II. He was a big proponent of remembering history—lest it ever be forgotten. He was a fighter in the Civil Rights movement—just a great man."

"I'm sorry for your loss."

"Oh, Jedidiah had a great run at life. He hated it when we had to move him to assisted living, but his last days were comfortable. And he had Kristi with him so much of the time. He loved her—she listened to his stories from the time she could crawl up on his lap, and enhanced his values. She's great with history and tells the truth of it—and what is assumed, and what might be true and what not, be it the good, bad or the really damned ugly. Ask her anything about the city, if you've a mind."

"That's great to know," Dallas said.

"Do you believe in ghosts, Mr. Wicker?" Jonah asked.

"Pardon?"

"Ghosts, sir, ghosts. The house is famous for them. Now, Kristi, she's a believer in facts, but...this house is well-known to be haunted. We've a very popular local woman who will come in and do a séance for you if you like. She's reasonable—price-wise, I mean."

"Do you have…current ghosts wandering in here?" Dallas asked.

Jonah seemed confused. "Current ghosts?"

"I understand a man died on the sidewalk, almost across the street."

"Sad business, that, so sad. He was a friend of Kristi's. Not a good friend, but a friend. Well, I should say that Savannah is a friendly place, but…he worked at a gym where Kristi went now and then. Good fellow—tragic, almost unbelievable. Such a loss," Jonah said, shaking his head.

As they spoke, Dallas heard a key twisting in the lock. He turned and saw a small hallway, lined with hooks for outdoor clothing, leading to a door. He imagined that, once upon a time, it would have been a servants' entrance to the house.

A woman entered and beamed as she greeted Jonah. "Morning!" She was probably in her early forties, with gray appearing in her dark hair, cheerful brown eyes and a plump body. She saw Dallas and paused. "Well, hello." She immediately extended her hand to him. "I'm Genie Turner."

"Dallas," he told her. "Dallas Wicker. A new guest."

"Well, welcome, sugar!" she said, grinning, and setting down a brown bag of groceries she had carried in. She studied him unabashedly. "And are you alone, sir? Is there a wife or a pretty miss along with you?"

"Just me," Dallas told her, unable to stop from smiling back at her.

She kept studying him. "California," she said sagely. "Blond hair, tan…"

"Genie, please, let's be polite to our new guest," Jonah said.

"I am being polite," Genie said. "I'm getting to know the man, Jonah." She looked at Dallas again. "Surfer—that tan, that hair…those muscles!"

"Genie!" Jonah protested again.

Dallas laughed. "No, ma'am. I'm down from the DC area."

He decided not to add the fact that he'd spent his first ten years of his life just on the outskirts of the city, not more than twenty miles away.

"My, my," she said. "A politician?"

There was obvious disapproval in her tone.

He smiled. "Not a politician. Actually," he told them, "I'm an old friend of that young man who died on the street near here."

"Oh!" Genie said, staring openly.

Jonah was doing the same.

"They just want me to verify some facts, that's all."

"I see," Genie said. She clearly didn't see at all.

He added, "I'm happy to be here, nonetheless. McLane House is beautiful, and there's nothing I like as much as a chance to stay in such an incredible place."

"Sure," Genie said.

"Are you a cop?" Jonah asked.

"No, sir. Private investigator, and I'm just down here to ease everyone's mind. Neither of you happened to see anything, did you? He died not a half a football field from here."

"We heard the sirens," Jonah said.

"And saw the police, the crowds, the media—the ambulance," Genie said.

"Of course," Dallas agreed.

They were all silent for a minute, and then Genie said, "Well, both of you—out of my kitchen. Breakfast is a morning meal, you know, and I need to be getting to it. Sydney will be along any second now, Mr. Wicker, and if you'll just give her a chance to run up and make sure that your room is all spick-and-span, we'll get you in there early. For now…"

"I'd love to take a walk out back—in that glorious court-yard," Dallas said.

"Please! There are monuments behind the old stable building," Jonah told him. He winked. "To our ghosts! Enjoy."

"Breakfast is from 7:30 a.m. until 9:00 a.m.," Genie said. "But we'll have your room all set within thirty, so..."

"I can go out that door and down the path?" Dallas asked.

"Yes, sir, you can," Jonah said.

"Thank you."

Dallas went out and down the steps that led to the path, fully aware that the two he left behind immediately began to speculate on his purpose in the city—and just what he thought he could find about such a tragic, and senseless, accidental death.

Only total humiliation had allowed Kristi to open the door to her room—and then close it again behind her.

She looked carefully about, even under the bed.

There was no one—in the flesh, or not.

She forced herself into the fastest shower known to man, and dressed so quickly she had to check in the mirror to make sure she was fully clothed.

She gave her hair a few swipes with her brush and promised herself to do better later.

Before leaving, she paused to look around again.

Had she been dreaming?

It had been so real.

And then, running straight into a man on the porch. A tall, blond, striking, muscle-bound stranger. Beyond attractive, with a smile that could stop her heart, and a way about him...

He was a guest. And she had literally thrown herself into his arms.

Her face reddened with the thought.

He must think that she was an idiot...or worse!

With a shake of her head, she rued the fact that he hadn't just been a delivery man—rather than someone staying here, someone she'd have to see again.

She took a deep breath and looked around the room again. It was empty. No images of anyone or anything…

No sense of anything other than being alone.

She'd been up so early, and now she was running late. It wasn't that Genie and Sydney, Genie's energetic young helper, couldn't manage without her—they could. It was just that it was her place, and she liked helping and even being the house's hostess.

She hurried out into the hallway and this time, almost crashed into Sydney. She was just twenty-one, majoring in hospitality at the university every other semester. Eventually, she wanted to manage her own house, and she was certain that her experience at McLane House was going to prove to be important.

"Sorry!" Kristi said.

Sydney was bearing a can of room freshener and a little vase of fresh flowers.

"Morning—our new guy is in seven, and it was clean, but you know Genie. Have to check, fresh sheets, no dust whatsoever and…"

"Right, right," Kristi said. "Seven…the only room left."

The door was just feet from her own. She winced inwardly, and hoped he wouldn't be horrified that he was so close to the crazy owner of the house.

"He's something, huh?" Sydney said, her brown eyes wide. "Carl Brentwood is cool—I mean, he's super famous and still so nice. So cute! But this guy…he's like…wow."

"Yeah, wow," Kristi murmured.

"A private investigator."

"What?"

"Like Veronica Mars," Sydney said.

"I…what?"

"Mr. Blond Hunk. He's a private investigator," Sydney told her. "He's here because he's some kind of a friend of the family to…"

She paused for a minute, staring unhappily at Kristi.

"To who?"

"To your friend—Lachlan Plant," Sydney said.

Kristi frowned, experiencing the little ache she always felt when Lachlan was mentioned. He'd been such a great guy—not that she'd known him that well, and not that she'd been great about showing up at the gym when she really needed more workout time.

Lachlan had been new to the city; so enthusiastic about making a life for himself there. And he'd died in the most ridiculous manner.

She still felt his loss, the disbelief and sadness that so many of his new friends had felt. He had no family; he'd come from Chicago after a stint in the military—he'd fallen in love with Savannah, and taken a job at the gym.

He'd been just settling in, and she'd been busy with Jedidiah. They had teased and flirted a few times.

His death was such a stupid accident and so sad.

She shook her head. "Investigating? What can he be investigating? Lachlan fell. Apparently, he hit his head wrong and his brain swelled and…"

"I'm sorry, Kristi, I'm so sorry. I'm just telling you what Genie told me. He—I mean, this Dallas guy—he seems really nice. I met him when I was coming in. I'm sorry."

"You don't have to be sorry. I'm just—surprised. I mean, the police were there, there was an autopsy, and… I don't know what there is to investigate."

"He's just being a friend, I think," Sydney said, hoping to improve her words or maybe even their guest himself in Kristi's mind.

"Sure," Kristi said softly. "Well, we now have a full house. I'll run down and help Genie."

She left Sydney and hurried down the stairs.

Carl Brentwood, Murray Meyer and Claire Danson were in the back parlor, sipping coffee and going over papers with one another. Carl and his retinue seemed to be an odd crew to Kristi, but he'd explained what the two did for him when they had all checked in.

Murray Meyer booked Carl's work for him, and advised him on whether a role was a good one to take—or possibly harmful to his career. Claire, on the other hand, managed his time—helping him accept the right public engagements, make all the right social media moves and keep his life and career in good shape. They all seemed to be friends, though Carl was reliant on the good advice of the other two.

Murray had been at his job forever—at the moment, he had told Kristi, he was keeping his roster of clients small and A-list. He was working only with people he liked—and he liked Carl. The young actor sincerely cared about people.

Claire was far newer at the celebrity game; she was very pretty, in a very thin way. Her features were beautifully crafted—high, defined cheekbones, big brown eyes. But she had a tendency toward nervous energy that seemed far too high-powered—especially for a small bed-and-breakfast establishment in the heart of Savannah.

The three of them greeted Kristi cheerfully.

She smiled, greeting them in return.

"Can't thank you enough for that séance last night!" Carl said.

"Who could have imagined how amazing it would be? I can't believe we didn't have a camera running last night. We're all set for tonight, though. We'll have papers for you later—permissions and payment for filming," Claire said.

"Kristi, it will be so good for the house and the city and... I promise you," Carl said earnestly, "we'll make it all good, and at the end, you'll have final approval of everything."

He was so sincere. She smiled weakly.

Maybe the new guest would protest. Maybe a private investigator wouldn't appreciate being filmed, or having his stay disrupted by a film crew.

She excused herself and went to find Genie in the kitchen, working away.

"New guy seems cool," Genie told her, and turned, her eyes wide and twinkling. "And wait until you see him."

"I've seen him," Kristi said drily.

Genie was oblivious.

"He's outside now, admiring the place."

Kristi looked out the window to the back.

He was there, tall, broad-shouldered, handsome in a casual sports coat, tailored shirt, dark jeans.

Private investigator...

He was in the far back, staring at the monuments.

She didn't know why...

Something about seeing him there oddly warmed her—and chilled her at the same time.

She was bizarrely afraid of the things that were now to come.

McLane House—beautiful, fascinating, old, historic, Dallas thought. He figured he'd heard of it at some time when he'd been young, but what he really knew stemmed from what seemed like volumes of material he'd received from Adam Harrison.

The land's original owner, Justin McLane, supposedly haunted the property that had been his when Georgia had been a Crown Colony, before anyone in Georgia had known that one day, they'd be living in what would become the United States of America. He'd been discovered with stolen documents during the short-lived and failed siege of Savannah in 1779—and hanged purposely on his own property, a warning to others who might secretly be aiding Revolutionary forces. It was assumed his body had been left on the grounds somewhere, but after being hanged as a spy, his body might have been dumped anywhere—possibly right into the Savannah River.

With the war over, the property had been regained by his

son, and then, come the early 1800s, the McLane house had been built.

Now there were handsome monuments along a garden trail that led past the old stables and smokehouse. Justin McLane was depicted as a statue in his Patriot uniform, as if he was about to stride across the yard in his passion for his cause.

There was no fine sculpture to Monty McLane—the Civil War rebel who had gunned down his father and his wife; there was a stone to him, one that declared him a casualty of the War Between the States. There were also little sculptures of deer and cherubs and praying angels, and a plaque reading, "Hearts beat loyal where they will, and our Great Maker will one day judge us all."

Apparently, the McLane family at the turn of the twentieth century didn't want to suggest their ancestor had been a good man—but that, maybe, under the circumstances, anyone could have understood his turmoil and passion.

"Doesn't excuse murder," Dallas said softly. "Whatever did happen."

"There really is no mystery," a voice said.

He was surprised to be answered—even more surprised anyone had come upon him out here without his immediately having realized it.

Dallas turned, and was somewhat taken anew by the woman who stood before him—Kristi Stewart. Now in jeans and a casual knit shirt, she was every bit as striking as she had appeared in her wild-eyed state and bedroom attire.

"You think not? There's a saying—'history is written by the victors.' Who knows what really went down here that fateful day in 1864? Maybe McLane has been maligned by those with something to hide."

She smiled. "Oh, I don't see a mystery there, either—personally, I think that Monty McLane was innocent. Get furious with your wife for supposed infidelity? Sure. But why kill your father for that? Monty was known to have been a kind husband, loyal son and loving father. I can find no suggestion that Trinity McLane was slipping in or out of the city to meet with anyone—much less becoming a traitor to her husband's cause—and cheating on him. The only witnesses to what happened were the victors. Doesn't make them bad men, but if something bad happened, they might have no choice but to cover it up. My opinion on events, that's all. But sorry, that's not actually what I was talking about," she told him.

"Oh?"

"Your friend...the man whose death you're investigating, I knew him, and we were all here the day it happened."

"You saw what happened?"

"No, no one saw him fall. But he was right by Johnson Square—it's the oldest square and first in the city, you know. Which means there's always someone around. I mean, someone called 911, and an ambulance came and..."

She broke off, letting her words end with a whispered sigh.

"I didn't know him well. I did see him now and then at the gym, and if I was asked, yes, I'd say he was a friend. He was a nice guy, always smiling, ready to help, opening doors—especially thoughtful when people were disabled in any way, doing rehab at the gym from an accident or surgery."

"And he just fell—and died."

"I know!" she said, shaking her head as if it was unfathomable to her, too. "They say he must have tripped and fallen in just the right way to hit his head the wrong way. That's what the papers said."

"Right. I know. I'm sure you can understand how his friends just can't accept that explanation without having more information—more from people who knew him here, who saw what happened."

"Yes, I just..." She paused. "I just don't know what you can find out that will help or...or change anything."

"I don't either, honestly. I just want to be able to assure the people who weren't here."

People? Adam Harrison, the one person determined to know the truth. Then again, Adam believed that there was more to the death than met the eye—or the investigation thus far.

"What about Mr. Murphy?" he asked her, smiling and shrugging apologetically.

"Ian Murphy?" she asked him, frowning. "Ian—was nearly ninety and suffering from cancer. He—he died from a fall, too, but…he was suffering. He was a good guy—friends with my great-uncle. He used to tell us that he wasn't going to be a vegetable, and we'd try to tell him all the reassuring things…a nice man, and a sad end, but…he always said that the end would be his own choice when the time came."

"A long life, well-lived, is the best that any of us gets," he murmured, feeling awkward—and a great deal like an interloper.

But what if Ian Murphy hadn't chosen his time to die?

And then again, what the hell could they all have in common: a politician, a businesswoman, a personal trainer—and an old man who had died of cancer?

He smiled at her. "So, you're a descendent of the McLane who first owned the property?"

"Yes, although the family tree swirled around a bit. Well, I just thought to tell you…your room is ready now. You met Jonah, who really runs the place, and Genie—truly, all-powerful for anything you may need—and Sydney, who is just a doll. You may see another man tinkering around the place and he's Marvin Falk, who keeps up the grounds and does minor repairs and is our magnificent jack-of-all-trades. You can ask any one of us if you need anything. There are other guests, and I'm sure you'll meet them around the breakfast tables and…well, I wish you the best in your endeavors. And… I apologize again for…colliding into you this morning."

He smiled. "It was a lovely collision," he assured her.

She flushed and quickly turned and headed back to the house. He watched her go, and thought again that she had a compelling beauty. He was intrigued.

Professionally, he was on something of a wild goose chase... but his stay here might not be so bad. He knew that Kristi McLane was not married: the extensive files he had didn't mention a fiancé, or a significant other of any kind. Then again, paper files never could fully explain what was going on in someone's heart or mind.

He smiled at himself; she was definitely distracting. And, yet, maybe distracting would be good, because it might well come with *helpful*.

Kristi Stewart knew Savannah; she had even known Ian Murphy and Lachlan Plant.

He glanced at his watch. Time to leave his things in his room, and then get to the riverfront to meet with Detective Joseph Dunhill.

He took another look at the beautiful garden. The yard was deeper than most that ringed the square. An old stone wall surrounded the property, but it wasn't high—most men would scale it easily.

It was hard to believe that once, there'd been nothing here, and a man had been hanged for his loyalty to a cause.

"Are you here, Justin?" he asked softly.

There was no reply.

But even as he turned to the house, he was certain something was there...someone? Watching, perhaps?

CHAPTER THREE

Kristi was certain she had finally begun to concentrate when she heard a soft knock at her door.

She tried to tell herself it was an irritating interruption—but she realized she was kidding herself.

She wasn't focused at all.

Not even on the fact that now she could speak to the dead.

She couldn't think about anything other than Dallas Wicker... it simply wasn't every day someone like him appeared at her door—flush against her, as she'd plowed right into him.

But he was here because he considered Lachlan's death to be suspicious. Or maybe not—just to know the truth about it. Dying because you tripped on a sidewalk did sound either completely unlucky or suspicious as hell.

She opened her door; for just a moment, she thought no one was there.

She gasped.

The ghost was back. She stared at him.

"I knocked," he said, looking at her hopefully.

"So," she whispered, "if I say you should go away, you'll do so?"

He appeared to be a very disconcerted ghost. "It would, of course, be the courteous and polite thing to do. But," he added cheerfully, "I would only come back when I wasn't asking entry to your private space, and...well, you don't seem to react very well. There are lots of people who would be delighted to have a conversation with me."

"Shelley conjured you—can't you go haunt her?"

He sighed deeply, looking downward, as if striving for patience.

"Shelley did not *conjure* me." He paused, then started humming music from the old *Twilight Zone* television series. "You know...doors, portals, time travel, whatever."

She blinked in disbelief.

"You've been here since the Civil War—but you talk about the *Twilight Zone*?"

"Saw the original. The owner back in the sixties—1960s, that is—loved the show. Now I like to catch up on Netflix."

A ghost...joking? And yet, he seemed so real, and serious as well.

He went on, "I have been here—near the house, walking the streets of Savannah—since 1864, searching, praying...hoping..."

"Hoping for what?" Kristi asked.

"Never you mind—that part of life and death are my cross to bear. I must speak with you—I fear for your life now."

"My life!" she said, stunned.

She heard a noise from the next room—number seven. The tall, blond, well-built private investigator just had to be next to her.

She reached out as if she could draw the ghost into her room, realized she'd touch nothing but air, and stepped back. "You're invited—come in!" she told him.

He stepped through the doorway; she quickly closed her door and strode deeply into the room, over to the onetime dressing area where she kept her desk, computer and work boards.

"Why would my life be in danger?" she asked the ghost of
Monty McLane.

"You loved your great-uncle Jedidiah—you listened to him.
And you would go with him to see Mr. Murphy, and you were
the one with them when the two old men talked and compared
their notes."

"I loved Uncle Jed," she said simply, confused, and wondering if she was having a psychotic break of some kind. "Ian was
his friend—they were of an era, comparing their notes—and
then arguing history, military maneuvers and more. Of course,
I cared deeply for both of them, but...they were old, and sick...
Death happens. All men who live are born to die," she said softly.

"You really are a sweet creature," Monty said. "Sadly naive.
Like Trinity."

"I'm not naive," she countered quickly. "I *am* busy. You're
welcome to haunt the house, taunt the guests...thrill Shelley to
no end when she does her séances. But guess what? This house
is expensive to maintain. We can't count on the income from
renting rooms to keep it all up. I really have to work!"

"You won't need to work—and the house will fall out of the
hands of the family and none of it will matter anyway, if you
don't listen to me."

"If I listen, will you go away?"

"As much as possible."

There was another tap at her door. She cast an evil glare at
Monty McLane, warning him. "Please do not make me look
like a fool. That might be the private investigator and—"

"It's not. But you're not going to start screaming again, or
passing out on me or anything, are you?" Monty asked.

"I don't know what—"

She broke off as she opened the door.

And then she understood.

It wasn't Dallas Wicker—or any other living guest, for that
matter—who had come to the door. It was another ghost. She

knew him, of course, from his portrait on the wall by the stairs, and, in his case, from many a local history book.

This ghost was Justin McLane—revered from his part as being Lieutenant McLane, one of George Washington's handpicked spies. He had given his Patriotic cause an incredible amount of information about troop movements and other particular details during the American Revolution—before being caught and hanged. He hadn't left behind a declaration like Nathan Hale with his statement before his execution of "I only regret that I have but one life to give for my country." Justin's words had been far more personal and quite simple: "Tell my wife I love her, and tell my son that this world will be for him."

She stared at him. And, as she did so, she suddenly found herself frozen, torn between wondering if her psychosis was becoming very deep—or if there hadn't always been something there. Something that made her feel the history of a place, the death of a place, and even something beautiful and safe about life. She had denied that ghosts could exist, of course. That's what sane and rational people did.

She didn't let out a scream and she didn't pass out.

She took a steadying breath, then stepped back to welcome him in. "Lieutenant, join the um...party. Please." Then she moved aside, let him in and closed the door. Looking over at Monty, she asked, "Just how many of you are there?"

"I think that the death of Lachlan Plant was the one that clinched it for me," Detective Joe Dunhill told Dallas. "Don't get me wrong—people do die in bizarre ways. Really bizarre, some of them. Back in the nineties, a golfer died when he got pissed off and struck a bench with his club—club broke and ricocheted back, right into his heart. Well, there's a lesson in sportsmanship, I guess. Oh, Lord, and the truly disgusting...a woman died of an allergic reaction to having sex with a German shepherd, and in New Jersey, a guy died trying to steal clothing out of a donation bin right before Christmas—got himself stuck in it and suffocated. Ah, there's more, plenty more—a little kid was killed at a zoo in Morocco when an elephant tossed a rock out of an enclosure. I looked up bizarre deaths—and there are plenty, I assure you. But still—a healthy dude dies from falling off a *curb*?"

"I agree—it sounds farfetched," Dallas told him. He liked Joe Dunhill—the guy was young, maybe in his late twenties. He'd probably just earned his detective stripes. He was tall and lanky, with short-cropped brown hair and a lean face, gray eyes and a passionate manner. "But what did the medical examiner say? What about witnesses?"

"Go figure on this—the way his head was struck, yes, it could have happened on the curb. I don't understand that much about the head, but the blow fell right where it caused an instant hemorrhage in the brain. Amazing, when you think about it—football players, boxers, others…they take massive blows to the head. The skull protects what's inside. But hit the head just right? You're gone in an instant."

"So it could have happened that way. Accidental death."

"It could have."

Dallas curled his hands around his coffee mug. They were at an outside restaurant right on the Savannah River. It was a beautiful day. Tourists were wandering along the riverfront, boats were out on the water and, in the distance, there was the shore of South Carolina.

He looked at Dunhill. "How could there have been no witnesses? You're talking the heart of the old town—there are always people walking around."

"It happened at the crack of dawn. He was found at about 7:00 a.m. by a dog walker, who hysterically called the police. She tried to wake him—she thought that maybe he was a drunk who had one too many."

"She moved the body."

"You've read the reports."

"I've read the reports—but I didn't interview the witnesses," Dallas told him.

"You said that plural—there was only one, and she wasn't a witness to the man's death. She found him, said that she tried to shake him awake—and realized he was dead. The medical examiner estimated that he hadn't been dead long—he'd probably died about an hour before being found."

"And no one was out—no other dog walkers, bus drivers, school kids…no one?"

"No one we could find. We know that he worked late. The gym stays open until midnight—he was the closer for the gym that night. But what happened to him when he left the gym—which is right near us now, off the river—we have no idea. There were no toxins in his body. He hadn't been drinking," Joe said.

"What would make you think, though, that his death might be associated with the death of an old man—an old man suffering from cancer, one who had said he was going to choose his own time of death?"

"Yeah, we were told that Ian Murphy didn't want to go through the pain at the end. But he went out his second-floor balcony. But in his medicine cabinet, he had enough morphine to do himself in a dozen times over. Why would he jump—I mean, there was no guarantee that a fall would kill him."

"I agree with the logic, but…what did the men have in common? And what did they have in common with the businesswoman—Eliza Malone—who disappeared two years ago, or the politician who just went missing now?" Dallas asked.

Dunhill sat back, frustrated. "I don't know. Apparently, no one around here sees it, but…when I was a kid, my mom was friends with Adam Harrison. He was a hell of a man—donating to the church where she went, and the group there that helped out those with illnesses. My mom had Parkinson's—Adam Harrison was big on giving. Anyway, I heard that he was with a special unit, so... I gave up on telling people that I believed something was going on. And I wrote to Adam."

Dallas was quiet.

"You think I'm seeing things that aren't there, too, right?"

"I didn't say that."

"But you're thinking it."

Dallas smiled. "It's way too early to find out. This man, Ian Murphy...if I've read everything right, he left no heirs—and in his will, stated that he wanted his home and belongings to go to a private historical society."

"Yes."

"I have tons of paperwork to read, but...what are my chances of getting in to this historical society? I'd like to find out what Mr. Murphy was doing before his death."

"Shaving. He still had shave lotion on his face."

"Sorry, I didn't mean immediately. I meant, I wonder if he was working on something, if he knew something, if he was re-searching something. Both the businesswoman, Eliza Malone, and the politician, Simon Drake, were big on cracking down on crime, right?"

"It was definitely part of Simon Drake's campaign. And Eliza... She was loved in the community. She wanted the drug pushers away from the schools. She could have been on to some-thing. As in, I was thinking that someone supposedly big in busi-ness—a respectable citizen—was actually the head of a group of pushers. The one making the big money. But... I could be wrong."

"Was Lachlan Plant into drugs in any way?"

"Not at all—he was against steroids, except, of course, when absolutely necessary medically. He was always talking against the use of steroids in the gym—he gave classes on what they could do to the human body. The guy loved vitamins—and the concept of every man treating his body like the soul temple it should be."

Dallas took a sip of his coffee thoughtfully. "Say there is something going on—let's theorize that it's the drug trade. Steroids, perhaps, painkillers and molly, cocaine, crack, whatever. I can see where Lachlan Plant might have been down on something he knew, if something was happening at his gym that he disapproved of—and the politician and the businesswoman might have known something. But how does Ian Murphy fall into this?"

Dunhill groaned. "I don't know. Thing is, with Ian Murphy, I'd met the old guy, you know? He was bright as hell. And if I'd been told he'd taken an overdose of morphine, I'd have thought, well, the old guy said that he'd die on his own time, and that's what he did. But—that fall! I just don't believe that's the way he would have chosen to go. So maybe he overheard something. Thing is, he was always researching, learning, debating with Old Jed..."

"And you think he might have learned the wrong thing?"

"It's possible."

"All right," Dallas murmured. "Old Jed...you mean Jedidiah McLane who owned the place where I'm staying—McLane House?"

Dunhill nodded. "I know that Jedidiah died peacefully, in his sleep. His friend was there—the old guy who works at the house, Jonah Whitney. And his great-niece, Kristi Stewart. Kristi loved him—she was with him. And the rest of the household, too. He just closed his eyes. Smiled—and died."

"But if he was such good friends with Ian Murphy, wouldn't he have known if Murphy had found out something that suggested criminal activity?"

"Yeah, I've thought of that, too. But maybe Ian hadn't gotten around to telling him, or talking to him. They were both old as the hills. Like I said, I could be wrong. I could wind up fired, and I do love my job. But have you ever had a hunch? Like a feeling that something is really wrong, that we're looking at a puzzle, and the pieces just have to be put together? Almost like there's a ghost, whispering over your shoulder, something like that? Have you ever had that kind of feeling?"

Dallas smiled. "Yeah, I've had that feeling," he said. "So, you have it set up for me to have a conversation with the medical examiner?"

"Yes!" Dunhill rose excitedly. "Yes, thank you...you believe me?"

"I believe that I've got to start somewhere, and the medical examiner seems as good a place as any."

"Chatham County Medical Examiner's and Coroner's Office," Dunhill clarified. "It's on 67th Street. I'll drive."

"You've gotten me here under unusual circumstances—don't you need to report to work?" Dallas asked.

"No, my captain knows I'm seeing a private eye, and he's not a bad guy. Thinks it's okay if someone goes on a chase if they're not using up resources unnecessarily—he knows I'm helping you, though, as Adam suggested, you're just here as a private investigator—privately investigating."

"All right then—I'll be glad to hear what he has to say."

"Want to hear another odd one?"

"What?" Dallas asked, frowning.

"Another weird way to die. A chef in China was chopping up a snake—a cobra. It's a delicacy. Anyway, the damned thing was decapitated—and bit him anyway."

"Reflexes, the brain being the last to die?" Dallas asked.

"Got to be some of the best revenge I've ever heard about," Dunhill said. "Now, that I'm sure a man couldn't pull off, though there was a rumor that heads fresh off the guillotine moved and even spoke. Pity—it would help if some of our dead people would speak to us."

"It definitely helps when they speak," Dallas muttered. "So, onward? Nothing like a sunny morning at the morgue."

★ ★ ★

"She appears to be quite calm," the ghost of Justin McLane informed the ghost of his great-grandson, Monty McLane.

Calm? Sure, why not be calm through one's own crazy illusion? Kristi wondered.

"She wasn't calm this morning—she was quite hysterical, I do assure you!" Monty replied.

Kristi stared from one of them to the other. The family resemblance was impressive, and she took a moment to be proud: her ancestors had been tall and straight-backed, ruggedly dark and handsome. They also seemed to have fine characters, though how she was judging that from such little contact with her new *friends*—certainly imaginary—she didn't know. She supposed if she was creating her illusions, she'd be creating them as she wanted them to be.

Kristi spoke up, "Monty seems to think that I'm in some danger."

"We're concerned," Justin said.

"Because?" Kristi asked.

The two of them looked at one another again. "At first, we rather thought it was nothing," Monty said.

"We can be quite bored upon occasion, you know," Justin said.

"Which makes it ridiculously easy to come up with conspiracy theories," Monty said.

"Did they even… I mean, conspiracy theories? Did they even think of such things back…in your day? Or days? You—you never met in life. You couldn't have."

Monty looked at Justin and grinned ruefully. "Thank the lord—our descendent knows something of mathematics."

"You're quite a wiseass, if they had such a term way back when," Kristi said irritably.

"My dear child, we do learn through the ages—in fact, the invention of the television makes us incredibly well-educated.

No, we did not know one another in life. We were born and died decades apart. We met only in death," Justin said somberly. "A tragic death for me, I'm afraid. I was never ashamed of what I did—in fact—I'm quite proud, though I'd have preferred not to have been caught. However, I was, and thus, when I found that I was between worlds, I did my best to watch over my dear wife and son. And that son came back to this very property, and in time, he built this house. The thirteen colonies were quite different from the start, so I must admit, it was not much of a surprise when war raged between North and South—and I became witness to what befell my great-great-grandson. When I realized he had remained behind as well, I was saddened by his death, but again, did my best to comfort him in that death."

"And you're still here," Kristi murmured.

"As am I," Monty added. "I have a reason, I believe."

"He did not kill his beloved Trinity," Justin said. "You see, here is the thing—history is always written by the victors. Now, don't get me wrong—there were many fine men fighting and dying for the Union. The world should know now that slavery is entirely wrong—even though it does still exist in parts of the world—"

"And you know that...how?" Kristi asked.

"Television, child, television," Justin said. He waved a hand in the air. "My point is... I tried to stop what happened to Monty... I didn't have the power. Colonel Albert Huntington was not a good man. When he came to the house, Monty had just arrived back—and Monty was caught. Trinity screamed and cried and told him to surrender. For her, he was willing to give himself up. He tried to reach her, and Huntington—who had a fool's infatuation for Trinity—shot at him. Except that at the same time, Trinity ran to Monty, and the shot hit and killed her. Then Huntington gunned down Monty and his father, Samuel. I think a number of Huntington's men were horrified, but they were also afraid of Huntington—and perhaps, shamed by what had been done. And so the story went out that Monty killed his wife and father rather than see them in the hands of the enemy."

"And I am left to haunt the place," Monty said softly. "Without the woman I loved."

Kristi let out a breath, still doubting her state of sanity. But whether her ghosts were figments of a pressured imagination or real—as real as ghosts could be—they were sympathetic ghosts.

And her family.

"I'm so sorry," she said.

"Have you seen Trinity?" Monty asked her hopefully.

"No, I have not. I didn't see either of you until after the séance."

"Well, we were not summoned by that silly woman," Justin said impatiently. "We've been here. Maybe you weren't ready to see us."

"And maybe we didn't feel such a pressing need for her to see us—until lately," Monty suggested softly.

Kristi didn't have a chance to answer him. There was a knock at her door. "Excuse me," she murmured, walking to the door. She hesitated before opening it, but when she turned around, the two had disappeared.

As if they had never been.

She opened the door. The young actor, Carl Brentwood, stood confidently in the hall. "I'm so sorry to bother you here, but I was hoping we could talk. Downstairs, of course. I didn't mean to be so rude—coming right to your door. But I didn't know how to reach you otherwise."

She smiled. "It's fine. We can head down to the back parlor."

"Thank you so much," he told her earnestly.

She didn't want to do a televised séance, but it would probably be good for the business. Everyone loved "haunted" Savannah, and, it seemed, everyone loved a haunted house.

She looked back into her room one last time; it was empty.

She closed the door, wondering what her deceased ancestors got up to when she couldn't see them.

"The brain is astounding. The finest 'computer' ever built, and such a creation that even I, a scientist, believe in God above to have made something so magnificent," Dr. Perry, the medical examiner, told Dallas with enthusiasm.

Dallas glanced over at Joe Dunhill, who had accompanied him to the morgue. Joe's shrug indicated that they just might get a lecture.

Despite the days since his death and the completion of his death certificate, the body of Lachlan Plant remained at the morgue; friends were getting the money together to claim the body and arrange for a funeral and burial.

From a distance, Plant looked as if he slept peacefully on the slab, as if he were the picture of health—despite being dead. The icy morgue temperature had kept him from decay thus far. He had been tall, lean and, as was expected for a fitness expert, well-built.

But close up, one could see the gray pallor of death upon him, nature's way of claiming its own—dust to dust, ashes to ashes.

Dr. Perry shook his head, mumbling, "Shame, shame, what a fine man he was—no family, but friends aplenty."

"And his death—" Dallas said.

"Now, in itself, the brain is incredibly fragile, and that's why we have the human skull. Good, strong, tough piece of equipment, the human skull. It can take all kinds of blows—and still protect the brain." The lecture began.

"Doc," Joe Dunhill said quietly.

"Yes, yes," Perry said, "but you're asking about my opinion right? Or you're asking about the facts that could lead to an opinion. So you must understand. The skull is a wonderful thing. Actually composed of many bones, all within the cranium and the face. But as wonderful as it is, the skull can be penetrated, and a hard blow often brings about death by damage to the brain itself, and by causing the brain to bounce around and take a vicious bruise. I'm using layman's terms, naturally—"

"Layman's terms are fine," Dallas assured him. "But could this really have happened by a simple fall?"

"Freak accident, but yes."

"What if someone struck him on the head—would the same damage occur?" Dallas asked.

"The injury was at the cranial base—a basal fracture forced splinters into the brain and brought about death. He was found on the sidewalk by the curb—no one saw any kind of violence toward him. Could he have hit his head hard enough falling? Yes. He was a big man. A medical examiner calls the method of death, but we also use what officers are able to tell us. I did label the cause of death as inconclusive—because yes, he could have been hit on the head. So..." Dr. Perry lifted his hands. "His death has been presumed accidental—fatality from an accidental fall. There are two things we are looking at—cause of death and manner of death. Manner of death was the blow to his head. Cause of his death? Presumed to be a fall. However... nothing in my expertise can give a pat answer to the *cause* for the manner of his death. I can't rule out homicide, and I can't say that what occurred wasn't an accident. No matter how absurd it seems, that does seem to be the answer."

To Dallas, a freak accident seemed on the far side of plausible.

"What about the other man?" Dallas asked.

Perry looked at Dunhill. "Another man tripped and fell on the sidewalk?"

"No, sir, I'm talking about the elderly gentleman—Mr. Murphy."

"Ian Murphy?" Dunhill seemed honestly surprised.

"Yes, sir," Dallas said.

"Well, the poor fellow...he jumped. I'm afraid I did rule that a suicide. Again, my responsibility is manner of death—broken to bits, I don't need to describe it all to you—but it was widely known that he'd decided he would choose his own time to go," he said softly.

"There are much easier ways—especially for a suffering elderly man. Overdoses of medicine—a lot of sleeping pills," Dallas said.

"Maybe he was afraid he wouldn't do the job," Perry said. "He was alone in his house at the time. Everyone was saddened, though no one was surprised."

"Was his house searched?" Dallas asked Joe.

Joe nodded. "We went in after the event. Thing is…the initial reaction was for first responders to head to the body, try to help, and then the patrol officers who came on had to control the crowd, had to call it in, get the ME out…"

"So, if someone had been in the house with him, they could have been long gone before the house was actually searched. And, since a suicide wasn't unexpected, it wasn't much of a search."

"I came in on it late—we had to investigate because of the way he was found, but it wasn't seen as a dangerous situation. No one thought that he might have been pushed."

"Pushed!" Perry exclaimed. "Why would anyone push a man already dying? Ah…a mercy killing?"

"Not really what I was thinking," Dallas murmured.

"Why the hell would anyone kill a dying man?" Perry repeated. "He would have been dead within months."

"Maybe not soon enough," Dallas said.

"Soon enough for…what?" Joe asked, puzzled.

"I don't know—but we need to find out. What is the only thing you don't leave behind after you die?" Dallas asked quietly. He turned and looked at Perry and then at Joe, who were both looking at him in confusion.

Dallas smiled grimly and said, "That which you have in the mind—in the brain, that wonderful computer you talked about. Things, papers, books—all could be stolen and destroyed. But the only way to destroy knowledge is to destroy the brain it's in—kill the carrier."

"You're suggesting that Ian Murphy knew something that got him killed?" Joe asked.

"Exactly," Dallas told him.

Kristi could well understand the star appeal of Carl Brentwood: his enthusiasm was contagious, and he seemed to really like people. He was earnest and more—courteous at every turn.

"We can be almost entirely undisruptive to the property," he told her, leaning on the arm of a chair as they spoke, making his point. "Two cameramen with self-contained rigs including lighting, two sound people working mics at two angles. Nothing would have to be removed. Other than that crew of four, you'd have no one who wasn't already here. I've already spoken with the Knox family—Kristi, they love it. Their daughter is considering a career in film, and this is flattering, of course, but she thinks that being in a video with me would help her in the future. So—"

"There's another guest in the house at the moment," Kristi reminded him.

"Yes, yes, and I will get his blessing. Please say yes? Here's what I believe it can do for you—make the house the most popular inn in Savannah. Okay, one of the most popular in Savannah."

He grinned, blond and boyish in his appeal.

She smiled tightly in return.

"A private eye may not be so happy about being in a video," she warned.

"Oh, well, he doesn't have to be in it—we'll basically be filming just in the parlor, where Shelley does her séances."

"Basically?"

"Well, if a ghost was to lead us somewhere…"

She could offer him a real smile at that.

"Trust me," Kristi told him, "there is no great treasure hidden in the house anywhere, or buried in the basement. The family was never rich. We weren't hiding Confederate gold or anything like that. The ghosts aren't going to lead us to any riches."

He lowered his head, still grinning. "I'm not after riches. But you never know. Ghosts just might lead us to...um... I don't know, ghostly secrets?"

"You can't go invading people's bedrooms."

"Never! Oh, please, Kristi—it will be just a few hours that we're actually filming. And it could be so good!"

She glanced over at the stairway; Carl's retinue—his agent, Murray Meyer, and his manager, Claire Danson—had come down just to the back-parlor landing.

She looked in the other direction; Jonah was there, nodding his approval.

Kristi shrugged. "Okay. I can call Shelley—"

"I'll take care of that."

"And you'll make sure that it's all right with our other guest."

It was her house; she could do what she wanted and just tell Mr. Dallas Wicker that he'd need to avoid certain areas if he didn't wish to become involved with the project.

"I'm assuming you're going to have waivers—or possibly pay people," Kristi said, looking over at Claire and Murray.

"Oh, you bet," Claire answered for Carl.

Carl just shook his head and shrugged at Kristi, implying he trusted his manager would look after those things.

"Speak with Mr. Wicker, and then let me know." She rose and looked around her, suddenly feeling the need to be out of her own house.

"Kristi?" Jonah called to her.

"Back soon," she said.

"Where are you going?" Jonah asked her.

"Out."

★ ★ ★

"You see what I mean?" Joe Dunhill asked. "My superiors are good at their jobs—we have good cops here. Busy cops. We're a good city, but we're also not without our violent crime. It's beautiful here—and it can also be deadly. We've a mix of locals and tourists, we have old hatreds and new crimes. When you have assaults, rapes and active murders to solve, an old man jumping out a window and a young one dying on a curb go the way of what seems most evident. But there's something wrong, something just not right."

"I agree with you—and I understand that any agency can only go as far as the investigation will lead—and in a big city, they have to move on," Dallas said, taking a long sip of coffee. They had stopped for a quick bite to eat at a counter-service restaurant on the riverfront. "It's often where we come in," he said gently.

"Are you really a licensed PI?" Dunhill asked him.

"Yes. I got my license before I went into the academy," Dallas said. "Adam Harrison sticks to the truth—and when you went to his unit for help, he thought of me."

"Because you're a PI?"

Dallas hesitated. Others in the Krewe had also been licensed as investigators—he just happened to know Savannah, as well.

Dallas shrugged. "All right. The police are still actively working the disappearance of Simon Drake. Who vanished in the same way as Eliza Malone two years ago—from the Johnson Square area."

"Of course. The investigation into the disappearance of Mrs. Malone is still ongoing, as well. It's just grown very...cold. Naturally, we're all afraid of the same with Simon Drake."

"So, by all appearances, Simon Drake was a politician hell-bent on lowering the crime rate in the Savannah area."

"Yes."

"And Eliza Malone was instrumental in forming a 'fighting

crime is big business' coalition among the business owners and operators in the city."

"Exactly. She had major chain hotels and restaurants and shops—as well as locals, you know, bed-and-breakfast inns, boutique owners and so on—all involved."

"How might they relate to a young fitness expert and an old man dying of cancer?"

Dunhill shook his head, frustrated. "Hell if I know. And all of it going on in the heart of the city—right around Johnson Square. I can't figure, but I know there's something, and it's just bugging the hell out of me that I can't quite put my finger on it. Okay, I can't get my finger close to it! But my gut is telling me that something is going on." He fumbled in his pocket and produced a business card.

Dallas already knew the name on it from the endless files that Adam Harrison had provided him—Brenda Nunez. She had been a volunteer campaign worker for Simon Drake. She'd been interviewed by the police, having been at the rally for Simon Drake on the riverfront before he had disappeared. She wasn't a family member, and she hadn't been a major player in his campaign; she had loved his politics.

"She'll meet you at four o'clock at the Colonial Park Cemetery," Dunhill told him. He rose, balling the remnants of his sandwich into the paper on which it had been served and tossing it into the trash. "Call me. I'm available anytime. Nothing official, but my superiors really know exactly what I'm doing. It's just not—"

"On the books. Gotcha. I'll be in touch."

Dallas watched Dunhill leave and then stood. He threw out his own trash, and started out.

What was the thread that connected the incidents?

Or was it that there was no thread?

It was there. Somewhere. The logic of it all seemed to be

missing, but… Joe Dunhill's gut instinct was right. Something was there, simmering beneath the surface.

Dallas had a little time. He started to wander the streets, remembering that he did love the old architecture, that there was much about the city to enjoy. History entwined with more history, and the beautiful pulse of life today.

Two people hard on crime vanished. Two other people dead, bodies left where their "accidental death and suicide" had taken place.

Dallas paused, staring at the unending flow of the river.

Because the two known deaths could be given the appearance of accident and suicide…while the others could not?

He didn't like to be a defeatist—but Simon Drake and Eliza Malone were most probably among the dead.

If they could just find the remains…

But this was a city where the Savannah River snaked through, and dense swamps were not far from the bustle and heart of the action. Lots of places to dispose of a body.

And yet this killer was possibly hiding murder in plain sight.

CHAPTER FOUR

Kristi found herself wandering down Drayton Street, away from the river. She turned down East York, and then on to Abercorn, finding she'd walked to the Colonial Park Cemetery. She hadn't particularly planned on coming this way, at least not consciously, but she did love to visit here.

The old cemetery—right in the heart of the city—was a park now. About six hundred or so old stones and tombs remained, while it was estimated that ten thousand were buried there. The cemetery had been opened in 1750 by the British and closed to burials by 1853. A yellow fever epidemic had swept through the city in 1820, bringing around seven hundred souls to rest there. It had a section specifically for "duelists," and many a Revolutionary War soldier had come to find eternity at the cemetery, as well. A handsome arch had been erected by the Daughters of the American Revolution in the early years of the twentieth century and dedicated to the Patriots of the American Revolution, and a long, curving path made its way through the old stones and offered benches for sitting, relaxing, enjoying the sway of the moss that dripped from the trees.

She found an empty bench and sat. It was peaceful, though

the cemetery was seldom empty of visitors, since tour groups came to sightsee, and locals like herself loved to wander through. Today, it seemed very relaxed. She looked up at the sun, filtering through the trees, and then closed her eyes for a moment. When she opened them, she wasn't alone.

This time, she didn't scream.

The man at her side was in a military uniform, complete with wig and tricorn, and she wondered for a moment if he might have wandered over from a historic presentation or if he might be a tour guide.

But then she realized he was one of the dead.

Great. Now they were coming out of the woodwork.

"I've seen you so many times before," he said softly. "And by the way you're looking at me now, you can finally see me, too. Begging your pardon, miss, I am Lieutenant Max Hudson, and it is an extreme pleasure to make your acquaintance."

She smiled weakly. There were other people around, studying the old headstones. She didn't speak.

"I'm glad they've made such a lovely place here—those gone are not all remembered by monuments, but in a strange way, as a park, this gives us life."

"Yes," she murmured.

"Ah, well! The dead have not always been respected! I watched during the War Between the States. The Union soldiers and their horses were camped here—men burned and weary from fighting. Sad affair—all praying to the same God, and yet bitter, of course, for the very losses they brought upon themselves. But the soldiers thought it fun to re-chisel stones, to break and move some, having very little respect for the dead. But then, war is such that you see your friends pile high atop one another in mountains of bloodied flesh, and so, playing with the stones of men and women long gone seemed like no evil at the time." He shrugged thoughtfully. "Even if Sherman did give the City of Savannah to Lincoln as a Christmas present in 1864. A little cemetery destruction was as nothing."

Kristi just nodded slightly.

"I must say, I did have some fun of my own with those destructive fellows. Oh, nothing too evil—they'd been fighting too long. I moved a few food tins, disposed of a bit of their libations and walked about knocking and wailing and freezing the old boys. Made them see the error of their ways now and then!" He was smiling. "One must do what one can, you know."

The other visitors had moved far enough away that Kristi felt she could speak without looking like she was talking to herself.

"I'm glad you were able to make them think twice about wanton destruction," she said. "But I know my history, and I love Savannah. You could haunt someone who doesn't know much about the city," she added hopefully.

"But you see me," he said. "Today, you see me. It is as if you have opened your eyes." He turned to her.

"Lucky me," she murmured.

"Not luck," he said. "Something very special. You never know, my dear, when the dead may prove themselves to be of some assistance."

His words disturbed her; she couldn't help but wonder just what was happening, causing her world to fly into chaos in so swift a manner.

He patted her hand; she didn't feel a touch, just a brush of cold air. "We'll talk again," he said, and rising, he moved on. He strode over to where a teen girl, obviously growing bored as her parents read a stone, tapped away on her cell phone, head down.

Lieutenant Hudson walked through her; the girl suddenly straightened, shivered as if chilled. She looked around anxiously, and pocketed her phone.

The cemetery wasn't providing the respite Kristi had wanted. Standing, she wandered over to the Graham tomb. It wasn't a tomb or vault such as those found in Louisiana or even in other cemeteries where families had large handsome vaults. It was brick and low to the ground. She stood reading the plaque on the tomb, although she could have recited the facts from memory.

It was then she realized that someone among the living was standing at her side. Tall, bronzed and blond, Dallas Wicker still struck her as someone who should have been a lifeguard down on a beach somewhere, not an investigator.

"Nathanael Greene rested here until his remains were moved to his monument—on Johnson Square," he said smiling at her. "Ah, death! Why would such a hero lie in the tomb of another? Died of heatstroke or exhaustion in the state and came here—and that wily turncoat Graham had run on back to England when the Patriot cause was willing, and thus his tomb was empty."

"You know Savannah," she said.

"Somewhat," he said. "You like to come here?"

"Um, yes." She took a deep breath. "Are you sightseeing?"

He laughed. "I've been out and about in the city, and wandered here, getting ready for my next move. I saw you at the tomb. Thought I'd say hi."

She smiled. "Hi. By the way, Carl Brentwood is going to be talking to you. He wants to film a séance. Friday night. I've told him that you are also a guest, and that he must get your permission."

"He wants to film a séance?"

She nodded. "His own production—for social media, to sell an idea... I'm not sure. He swears it will be good for the house. I've told him that if you object..."

For a moment, she thought he would. She realized then that there was a steel in his eyes, and he'd never be a man to be taken lightly.

"A séance," he said. "On film. Could be interesting. I don't want to be on camera, but I'd love to observe from the wings, so to speak." He shrugged. "It's fine with me. And very courteous of you to say my permission was required."

She flushed, looking away. "Well, I'm sure you're busy. And I do need to get back to work."

He nodded, but he was still studying her. She felt the heat rising to her cheeks; he was a very attractive man.

She could still feel the iron strength of his body and arms as he had caught her.

"Uh, have to go," she said, trying a small smile.

"See you back at the house," he said.

She was ridiculously afraid she would trip as she walked away. She didn't trip, but he called her back.

"Miss Stewart."

She turned to face him again, just a few feet further away.

"I'd love to talk sometime."

"Of course. I'm available," she said weakly. "I'm pretty good with history, but this city is teeming with excellent historians."

"Everyone's history is a bit different, isn't it?" he asked. "There are just so many different...perspectives one can take."

Something about his words chilled her.

He was an investigator. He was looking into a suspicious death.

Lachlan had just fallen, that's what they had said, a tragic accident... Not far from her house...

Kristi suddenly had the feeling Dallas was there for much more than a deeper investigation into an accidental death.

She waved and hurried out of the cemetery.

Brenda Nunez was a bright young woman with long black hair and flashing dark eyes—eyes that saddened when she talked about Simon Drake.

She leaned back in her café chair and sipped her tea.

"He was the nicest man," she said, and then her eyes widened as she looked at Dallas. "*Is* the nicest man—he has to be okay!"

"I understand you were one of the last people to see him after the rally," Dallas said.

She nodded. "I was handing out pamphlets—you know, on what he wanted to accomplish, about him, his family... He'd spoken to a small crowd on the riverfront. He didn't plan a big rally or anything. He was just answering questions and people gathered, and they lingered, and he was generous with his time—wanted to answer everyone. He didn't have bodyguards, or anything—maybe he should have, but, oh, Mr. Drake really just loved people and wanted the best for everyone."

"So, he was on the riverfront, surrounded by people. And then what?"

"I guess I rather hero-worshipped him. I stayed while he talked to everyone. Hours. I think he gave his speech at noon, and then it was at least four o'clock or so when the crowd began to thin. He came up to me and thanked me for staying until the end—even his campaign manager had moved to the closest restaurant. With Mr. Drake's blessing—he said, 'Henry, you go on, get something to eat. We'll meet back up at the hotel later.' You see, Mr. Drake was listening to a man who hadn't gotten any justice—his son had been murdered ten years ago, and the case had just gone cold. Mr. Drake assured him he was going to fight to have every case solved, no matter how old. He would have people work with the police and dig and investigate—all the way back to the days when Oglethorpe founded the city, if need be. People were asking him how he could manage that, and he was outlining a way of enlisting help from librarians, retired police and investigators... He had answers!"

"Interesting. And when did he leave? What did he say to you?"

"He excused himself from a group of people and came over to me and asked me specifically to give the last people a few pamphlets. He said he had an appointment at Johnson Square. And then...then he walked away. It's the last time I saw him."

"The riverfront was busy. Johnson Square is right off the riverfront...surrounded by city hall, Christ Episcopal Church, banks, houses, businesses."

She nodded solemnly. "The riverfront was busy, and I'm sure the whole area was. It was a Saturday, so banks were closed… but I think there would have been services at the church…and there are homes and…someone else should have seen him," she whispered. "He was headed to *Johnson Square*. Just about every tourist in the city winds up there…" She paused indignantly. "How could he disappear from that area?" she finished. "How could it be that no one saw anything?"

"Someone saw something," he assured her. "But possibly they don't understand what they saw."

"The police have asked for help," she said. "No one has come forward—not that I know about."

"Maybe someone still will," Dallas said. "Brenda, can you tell me anything else about Simon Drake? He was a widower," he added—more information he had received from Adam's files. "Was he seeing anyone?"

She shook her head. "Not that I knew about—he carried a picture of his wife. He really loved her. They never had children, but from everything I've heard—and from people who were always around him, not just local like me—he was a devoted husband. When she died, he threw himself into his work, to right things that had gone wrong, and to hopefully maybe make a real difference. Educated people are less likely to resort to crime to survive—he wanted to work on all kinds of education issues. He wanted to press for work programs so people wouldn't wind up on drugs or stealing because they couldn't get jobs."

"Did he have any enemies? In all of this, he might have slighted someone. Or maybe someone was against his agenda?"

"He was a politician. People disagreed with him sometimes. But he didn't attack other people in his speeches or ads or anything else. He was amazing—he said what he would do instead of tearing down what others had or hadn't done. He was…he was what I believe a lot of our founding fathers to be—really ruled by idealism. I mean, did you know that, years ago, our congressmen served their terms and then went back to work? Imagine! The taxpayers didn't support them forever and ever."

Dallas smiled at that. Brenda seemed to be a great promise of good for the future. She'd fallen in love with the politics of an ethical man.

"Idealism certainly existed. The signers of the Declaration of Independence knew they were risking their lives and everything they owned, that they would be hanged as traitors if caught. But the founding fathers were men as well—I understand they could get fiery in their debates, and that they weren't all angels. But yes, we did start out with our politicians wanting to serve more than to find reward in what they did. But, Brenda, what makes you so sure that Simon Drake made it all the way to Johnson Square when he left you?"

"I was still talking to him, and so I was with him halfway down the street until we were done talking. I watched him walk—straight toward the square."

"Did he say who he was meeting—did he tell anyone who he was meeting?" Dallas asked.

"He just said he thought he was going to get some very interesting information, that's all. He...he was really excited about whatever he was going to find out about. When I left him, he smiled and winked at me and said he had to hurry—he even raised a finger to his lips and whispered, 'Shush!' It was as if we were sharing a secret, only I didn't know what it was. I got the impression that maybe..."

"Maybe?"

"Maybe he was going to learn something that would help his campaign. I don't know, Mr. Wicker. I just don't know more. I'm so sorry!"

"Please, don't be sorry. You've been a tremendous help."

"I haven't really given you anything. I've told all this to the police. Like I said, they've had videos out, they've begged for help. It's as if he just vanished."

"No one vanishes."

Brenda looked out the café's window at the passing people. Then she lowered her head, and said softly, "No, they just wind up beneath the earth, forgotten."

"I'm going to find him, Brenda, wherever he may be," Dallas told her.

A promise.

Somehow, he was going to have to make sure he fulfilled it.

Afternoon tea at McLane House did offer tea—also coffee, sodas, pastries, beer and wine. And it was early evening, but afternoon tea was what it had always been called.

Kristi's presence wasn't required for the preparation, the service or the cleanup. Jonah, Genie and Sydney had it easily covered. As with breakfast, things were set out as a buffet in the front parlor, and guests were welcome to enjoy whatever they had chosen in either parlor or out in the courtyard.

But Kristi was restless; she'd spent an hour on actual work—without being disturbed by anyone, or so much as a breath of cold, *ghostly* air. So she decided to go back downstairs.

Genie loved to bake, and the offerings as far as pastries went were homemade creations and highly touted in the reviews for McLane House on almost all booking sites.

Kristi walked around checking on little things, but when Jonah mentioned to her that she really didn't need to micromanage, she flushed and apologized.

"Why don't you quit looking for dust and go smile at the guests?" he suggested.

She found her visitors—all six, other than Dallas Wicker—out in the courtyard. The sun was low, the day was balmy and beautiful and it was just such a time when the courtyard should be enjoyed.

"Miss Stewart!" Carl Brentwood said, apparently delighted that she had appeared. "Will you join us?"

"Of course," she murmured. "Thank you." He had drawn out a chair.

She noted that Shelley's séance must have been a bonding experience for all of them—Granger Knox was relaxed, a beer in hand, one leg crossed over the other. His daughter, Lacey— beneath his watchful eye—was seated next to Carl, with his wife on the actor's other side. Janet Knox seemed pleased they were all so chummy-chummy with the young up-and-coming actor. Young Lacey was staring adoringly at Carl, while Murray Meyer rolled his eyes. Clare Danson seemed obsessed with her smartphone, barely glancing up.

"Everyone is excited to start filming," Carl told Kristi.

"This is awesome! I can put that I was in a video with *Carl Brentwood* on my résumé!" Lacey told Kristi. She was a pretty girl, and so enthusiastic. Kristi realized she should just be happy for this group—they all wanted to do the same thing.

And it wasn't as if plenty of people didn't come to Savannah looking for ghosts.

She'd taken it all with a grain of salt—until she'd come across her own ghosts, she realized.

"Well, then, it's set," Kristi said.

"We really can't thank you enough," Clare told her, finally tearing her eyes away from the small screen in front of her. "I mean, I know you set up séances all the time, but to allow Carl to film, well, we're truly appreciative. We have paperwork for you. For the house, and for you. We're hoping you'll be available for an interview. If you're willing."

Kristi smiled—not ready to commit until she'd figured out what she might say.

"Well, there's great history to the house," she said. "And I do know the history."

"I haven't seen Mr. Wicker again," Carl told her. "But I swear, we'll convince him, we'll make it worth his while…we'll handle it…however he wishes."

"It's fine. I spoke with him," Kristi said. "I don't think he wants to be part of the séance, but he's okay with your camera crew."

"Whatever he wants," Claire Danson said, obviously delighted. "I guess you don't really understand what we're doing… Carl has a huge online presence. He does videos all over the country, kind of hip history, or hidden hot spots, and we've been working on a piece about Savannah, but when we booked here and found out about the ghost stories…well, the hits on this are going to be amazing. We'll draw in all kinds of new sponsors."

"Claire found the booking here," Carl said. "She knows Georgia."

"I had family here at one time," Claire said. "There are so many great and historic places! I love the 17Hundred90 Inn and Restaurant, the Olde Pink House Restaurant…the Ballastone, the Mercer House…made famous by *Midnight in the Garden of Good and Evil*! But for history and intimacy—and a place with a fabulous reputation, there's just nothing like McLane House," she finished, inclining her head with compliment.

"Well, thank you. Thank you very much," Kristi murmured.

Darkness was falling for the night. There were massive streetlights all around Johnson Square, stretching out to cover most of her yard. But while the courtyard itself was well illuminated, beyond that, past the old stables and smokehouse, shadows reigned.

Kristi squinted. She thought that she'd seen a shadow move within the darkness.

"Excuse me," she said, rising.

She left them and hurried along the path that led to the monuments, now shrouded in the edges of the night.

While they were due for a full moon that weekend, cloud cover now was heavy. At first, Kristi didn't see him. And then her eyes adjusted—Dallas Wicker was standing with his hands on his hips, staring around the far rear of the property.

"You know, you're also a guest here, and the courtyard is open with all kinds of people who would be delighted to see you," she told him. She frowned. A patch of earth near the monument looked like it had been dug up, or at least disturbed, and he was suspiciously close. "Have you been digging in my yard?" she asked.

"I have not," he assured her.

"You know, we really, really, really frown on people digging in the yard."

She realized suddenly that she wasn't alone; the ghost of Justin McLane was by her left side. Monty was to her right.

"They've been digging since the revolution," Justin said wearily. "Always looking for old bones, or artifacts, treasure… Lord knows what!"

"I wasn't digging in your yard," Dallas informed her, his expression amused. "Evidently, however, someone was. Maybe they weren't looking for *old* bones."

Kristi gasped when she caught his strange emphasis. "You're insinuating that…that someone might be digging for new bones? Fresh…bones?" she demanded.

"Such indignation," Monty said, laughing softly.

She wished that she could kick a ghost—and make it hurt. She tried not to blink; tried not to look at him.

"Two people have disappeared from this area recently," Dallas said.

"And…you think that there might be bodies in my yard?" She was nearly sputtering at the ridiculousness. "What exactly are you suggesting?" she demanded.

"That someone somehow associated with the house just might be involved in the disappearances," Monty said.

"Exactly," Dallas said.

Kristi froze.

Dallas Wicker had replied to the ghost.

She blinked; she must have imagined it. Maybe he had misheard her?

"I would really appreciate it if you weren't out back here this late at night. We don't like people interfering with the monuments and the garden area."

Monty made a snorting sound. "Someone should be watching out," he said.

"Yes, they should be," Dallas agreed.

"Should be—what?" Kristi asked.

"Oh, for the love of God!" Justin exclaimed, "Mr. Wicker, will you please tell her that you see us quite clearly, and that your hearing is excellent. It will make the next few days far more pleasant if you both stop running around pretending that you don't commune with the dead."

Dallas Wicker shrugged, looking at her. "I see Lieutenant Justin McLane and Captain Monty McLane as well, Kristi."

She stared at him.

Then she simply turned and walked away.

Her other guests had left the courtyard. They were tidy guests; they had taken their cups, glasses and pastry plates from the tables back into the house. Nice, no mess.

At the moment, she wouldn't have cared. She would have gone striding right past any mess.

She hurried through the parlor and up the stairs to her room. She closed the door, twisted the old key in the lock and threw herself on her bed.

She wished she could go back two weeks. She wished desperately that she had known Lachlan Plant would be heading somewhere at a ridiculous hour, passing by the Johnson Square area. She could have run out, grabbed him, dragged him into the house, and the sweet and optimistic man might still be alive and...

Ghosts wouldn't be haunting her.

Deep in her thoughts, she was startled to hear something at her door.

The ghosts themselves again?

She dragged herself up and went over to her door. No one had knocked; she'd heard the doorknob rattling—as if someone wanted to gain entrance without knocking.

Her ghosts had just promised to knock...to be polite!

A guest? What guest in her house wouldn't knock?

She hesitated. The doorknob wasn't moving. She gripped and turned it, throwing the door open.

The hallway was empty.

She stood there, staring down the length of hall. Foolish. The sound had been her imagination. Or had it? If she'd jumped right up and immediately opened the door, would she have seen someone there?

The door next to hers opened; Dallas Wicker stepped out, looking at her.

"Is something wrong?" he asked her.

Was something wrong? She was being plagued by the ghosts of her ancestors, and, apparently, this man saw them, as well.

"No, nothing. I thought I heard someone in the hall."

"Yeah, I thought I heard someone out here, too."

She swallowed hard. "Ghosts?" she asked quietly.

He shook his head. "Not that I know about. You know, I've had some good conversations with Captain and Lieutenant McLane. They're outside tonight—watching."

"For whoever was digging in the garden?"

"Yes."

She just stood there, staring at him. "And you really see them?"

"I really do."

"And you see—others?"

He nodded gravely. "I do."

"Why are you really here?"

"Because people have died and gone missing."

"You're not a private investigator."

"Yes, I seriously am."

"But you're more."

He didn't answer immediately.

"You want me to trust you," she said. "How can I, if you won't trust me? I don't understand any of this. Sad things happen, bad things happen, but..."

She wanted to protest again that McLane House could have nothing to do with anything that was going on. She wanted to point out the ridiculousness of linking the strange events taking place in the city together. Then again, she'd never been plagued by ghosts before, and they'd appeared to warn her of danger.

"What are you? A ghost hunter of some kind?"

He smiled at that. "No."

"You don't have to hunt them—they just walk right up to you, right?"

"Sometimes," he said.

"Then why don't you just find some ghosts and ask them what happened?"

"I wish it worked that way."

"Then what way does it work?"

He turned and glanced down the hallway. They were alone.

Or so it seemed. But she was suddenly certain that he didn't trust any kind of a hallway—in fact, he'd be very careful about what he trusted, period.

She stepped back into her room. "Please," she said softly.

He nodded and joined her. She backed into her room, finding the chair where she had sat when her great-uncle had still been alive, and she had spent her days reading to him, holding his hand, just laughing because to him, life was funny, life had been good, and if his end was coming, well, yes, it had been a really good run. She found the familiarity of the cushions comforting.

"You're new to...the dead?" Dallas asked her.

"New to the dead..." she repeated, watching him.

"You've just started seeing the dead?" he asked. He knelt down by her chair, smiling oddly and gently. "It's new to you.

In fact, I'm thinking maybe you just saw them for the first time before you plowed into me on the front porch?"

Hands gripping the arms of the chair, she nodded. "But—but I guess, they're…my ghosts? They are my ancestors. But I saw…"

"You've seen others now?" he asked.

"Just one. A Revolutionary soldier. At the cemetery."

"Once you realize the ability, it opens you up to others."

"You're *not* new to ghosts," she said drily.

"No, I'm not." He hesitated a minute. "I had an experience when I was very young. A ghost helped me out, and since then… well, anyway, here's the thing you must remember. Ghosts are— people, essentially. They don't become omniscient. Some barely gain any more wisdom than they had while they were living. Some are better than others at being seen. Some talk easily, many don't. There are certainly many about who never learn to materialize for anyone. Most people do not see the dead— they may sense them, but they don't see them, and they cer- tainly don't get to carry on conversations with them. You have to remember…people are people, and there are things that do not change with death."

Kristi shook her head. "Why do some stay around—and some go? Monty said Trinity wasn't here anymore."

He hesitated, and then said, "I don't know. I don't have the answers to the universe, or God, or the hereafter. I just know that for some, there is a reason to stay. They need to help solve their deaths…they've left someone behind they feel they can help. Maybe they even stay because history may not tell all the truth, or because they don't want history to be forgotten. I'm not sure. Some stay only so long, and then move on. Some seem pleased to be here, to do what needs to be done, to watch over the living."

She began to smile slowly.

"What?" he asked.

"It's all too unbelievable," she whispered.

"Except that it's not," he told her.

She shook her head. "Okay. But the ghosts are worried. I just don't understand. How could these local deaths be related, and how could they be linked to this house?" she whispered.

"I don't know. But that is why I'm here."

"But you're not ghost hunter."

"No. I came to find out what is happening."

"Are you really friends with Lachlan Plant's family?"

"I am associated with someone who cares about him, someone who plans on being responsible for the burial. He's put in all the extra money that's needed for Lachlan to be buried here, where he found his last friends, in Savannah."

"And who is that?"

He hesitated again.

"Who are you?" she demanded.

He sighed deeply, looking away for a moment. "Kristi, I am here just in the capacity of a private investigator."

"But what are you really?"

"FBI. Part of a special unit."

She shook her head, frowning. "FBI... I thought that they only got involved in serial killing, kidnapping... I don't know, cybercrimes, things that cross state lines."

"Yes. That's just it—we haven't been asked in officially. So, I'm here as a private investigator—until things change."

"You're sure they're going to change?"

"Sadly, yes."

"Because?"

"We're going to find a body," he told her.

CHAPTER FIVE

The household started early; Dallas had barely come downstairs when he heard Jonah's footsteps behind him. The older man beamed. "You are an early bird—I think I just hear Genie and Sydney arriving now."

Dallas shrugged. "I like mornings," he said.

"And nights, too, huh? Saw you down in the parlor, late last night."

"Guess I'm not much of a sleeper," Dallas said.

Jonah paused. "Your room is all right?"

"The room is just great," Dallas assured him. He hesitated, because Jonah was looking at him. "I was just heading outside. I love mornings alone."

"Well, you should have some time. Our famous breakfast will be in just a bit," Jonah said.

"Thanks. Looking forward to it."

Jonah went through to the kitchen; Dallas headed out back to the courtyard. He found a seat at one of the tables some distance from the house and pulled out his phone—he thanked God for cell phones. They made it possible to talk away without anyone thinking you were crazy when they saw you sitting alone.

He had barely taken a seat—setting the phone on the white-painted wrought iron table—when the seats next to him became occupied.

"How is she doing?" Monty asked.

"You're referring to Kristi?" Dallas asked.

Monty gave him a look that indicated he might well be an imbecile.

"She seems to be doing all right. In all this time…you never showed yourselves to her?" Dallas asked.

"Kristi didn't live here before—she didn't grow up here," Justin explained. "Of course, we've watched over her through the years—"

"To the best of our ability," Monty added.

"But now…" Justin said.

"It's like a disturbance in the Force," Monty said.

"The Force?" Dallas queried.

Justin sighed. "Jedidiah McLane—our great-great-whatever who just passed away—was a huge fan of the Star Wars movies," Justin explained.

"TV—fabulous invention!" Monty said. He smiled, but then his smile faded. "The point is this—there is just a sense…a stirring, if you will. We see what goes on—overhear people talking. And it feels wrong, as if something going on does have to do with the house."

"We would sometimes walk across the square with Jedidiah, over to Ian Murphy's house," Justin said. "He was a fascinating man. He had all kinds of artifacts—left them to the historical society. He has a grandson going to school out in California—the kid came back for the funeral and all, and the house is his, but he made sure that things that should be preserved go to a museum. He's a nice kid—has a caretaker watching after the house until this summer, when he's graduating and coming home."

"Murphy was a good man?" Dallas asked.

"Ian was great." The answer came from the doorway; Kristi

had apparently opened the door just in time to hear the question. "He was kind, giving—and he loved stories. He and Jedidiah could talk for hours."

Dallas quickly stood—as did the ghosts. As Kristi approached, Dallas pulled out the chair across the table for her.

"We can't quite manage chairs," Monty said apologetically.

"They're quite heavy, I'm afraid," Justin said.

"It's quite all right, thank you," Kristi said, taking a seat. She looked at Dallas, and then apologetically at Monty. "Ian and Jedidiah argued the Civil War over and over. Ian didn't believe that you'd have killed your wife, Monty, but he would often be the devil's advocate on the subject. What happened here occurred with only the family present—and a small company of Union soldiers. Ian used to argue that it was possible that Monty meant to kill one of the Union soldiers, that he drew, and maybe Trinity tried to stop him, and when the first bullet flew—suddenly everyone was dead."

"I would have never harmed her, never in a thousand years," Monty said passionately.

"You were on the wrong side, son, the wrong side," Justin said.

"Well," Kristi told him, "if it makes you feel any better, no one in your family ever believed that you were guilty of having killed her."

He smiled at her. "I was grateful. I heard you defending me the other day."

"The wrong side," Justin said again, shaking his head.

Monty let out a long sigh and leaned forward, speaking passionately to Justin. "You—of all people—should understand where we were at the time! You were there at the beginning. Have you forgotten—there were thirteen independent colonies? The first movement was the Lee Resolution, crafted during the Second Continental Congress. I repeat—thirteen independent colonies, and the citizens of those colonies deeply resenting the fact that they had no representation in the British parliament. When Jefferson was asked to write the Declaration of Independence, his greatest difficulty was in creating a document that would please thirteen *separate* and distinct colonies." He looked at them, frustrated.

"Yes, and they were fighting for states' rights, but the right that meant the most was slavery," Justin said.

"Yes, I know!" Monty said. "And, yes, we can all see so clearly. Slavery was a total abomination. Today, any sane man looks back and wonders what the hell we were thinking. No human being has the right to own another. I absolutely condemn it. But remember, back then—we were barely beyond being separate and distinct colonies. Lee was a Virginian—he was as loyal to Virginia as you were, Justin, to a patriotic cause, and just as I was loyal to Georgia. I wasn't a horrible human being." He paused, letting out a long sigh. "I did not kill my wife, I did not kill my father. I loved my wife, and I..."

He paused again, seeming to take a deep breath, and he looked at them all. "I'm not helping any here, am I? But I swear we want to help."

"We kept guard on the yard last night," Justin explained. "But no one came here—no one at all."

"Tell me, Kristi, you knew Ian Murphy. And Lieutenant, Captain—you certainly saw the man, and watched many of his interactions with Jedidiah. Would he have jumped from his balcony?" Dallas asked.

"I don't believe so," Monty said. "He declared he'd go out on his own terms, but...he wasn't that badly off yet. I mean, sure, he hated chemotherapy, but he was through with a bout of it, and he was doing well enough."

"Not that either of us would know what it is to suffer through disease," Justin said.

"Kristi?" Dallas asked.

She wasn't looking his way; she was staring at Monty. Dallas seemed to have startled her, and when she turned to look at him again, he was startled anew by the very simple and pure beauty of her face, the kind that took his breath away. It wasn't so much an innocence in her eyes, but rather an honesty. Something leaped in his chest, and he realized that though he might be working, he was feeling far from professional.

She shook her head. "I just don't know. They were both ill. Ian died before Uncle Jed, but the last time I saw Ian..." She lifted her hands. "The last time I was there with Jed, Ian was especially cheerful and seemed to be doing fine. He did tell us that day that when it came down to it, he wasn't going to live in miserable pain. He also told us that his affairs were in order—his son and daughter-in-law died young in a boating accident—and he'd arranged everything for his grandson. I've met Jamie Murphy, and he's a bright and giving young man. He had been home, and he'd gone through many of Ian's collectibles with him so that they could be given to the proper museums. Jamie promised that no matter what, he'd finish up at school, and that's what he's doing. He was here for the funeral." She hesitated, looking at Dallas. "I can call Jamie, if you wish to speak with him."

Dallas was thoughtful a minute. "You and Jamie are friends?"

"He's about six years younger than I am, but yes, we're friendly. We bonded over the fact that we both grew up with slightly obsessed grandparents. Though I didn't actually grow up here, you know. But I was a lucky kid. I spent a lot of time with Jedidiah."

Dallas knew that her parents were still alive, because of the extensive files Adam Harrison had given him.

"I'm curious on your front—didn't your parents want this house?" he asked her.

She laughed. "Lord, no! My dad can't stand old houses. He and my mom live in San Diego now, near my older sister, who is a makeup artist and has three little kids. They wouldn't leave her and those babies for a gold-plated mansion. My parents are also doing just fine, financially—they invested well." Something in her face suddenly hardened as she glared at him. "Dad loved his uncle Jed, and we all spent plenty of time here growing up, but it made sense—felt right—that McLane House come to me. There's no bad blood in my family over this inheritance."

"I wasn't suggesting that!" he assured her. She had a temper on her as well—and she was fiercely loyal. "I was hoping you could get Jamie Murphy to allow us entry to that house."

"Oh! Well, of course. All I have to do is call Jamie. He'll be more than willing to help. I'll go ahead and text him—just tell him I'm looking for some notes Jedidiah had told me about that referred to the history of both houses. I know he won't mind."

"That would be great," Dallas told her.

Sydney came out of the house, bearing two mugs of coffee. "Good morning, you two! Early risers, huh?"

She was oblivious to the ghost she leaned past to set the coffee mugs on the table, but she shivered as she moved back. "A little bit of chill in the air this morning, eh?"

"A bit of a chill," Dallas agreed. "And thank you! We could have come in for coffee. You didn't have to come out here."

"I don't mind," Sydney said. She grinned. "I'm a hospitality major—I'm going to own half the city one day, I swear it! And I'm learning from Kristi. She always looks for the little things to do that make a guest more comfortable."

"Thanks," Kristi said lightly.

"Besides, I want to talk to you, if I may, please—if I'm not interrupting anything important," Sydney said.

She was waiting for Kristi to say okay, take a seat; the ghosts of Monty McLane and Justin McLane quickly stood.

"Uh—sure," Kristi said.

Sydney slid into a seat. "May I be here for the séance?" she asked.

Kristi frowned, looking at her. "Sydney, you know that I…"

"You think that Shelley is a crock, right?" Sydney said flatly. "I do, too. She changes her story for whoever is in the house— you know, if they want Monty McLane to have been guilty, she hears Trinity crying, and the indignation of the Union troops. And if they want Monty to be innocent, she tells the story that way—that Monty is haunting the house to reach his Trinity. She is absolutely full of it."

"Okay, but…"

"Carl Brentwood!" Sydney said, her eyes wide. "I want to be in a video with Carl Brentwood."

Kristi grinned. "Sydney, if you—and Genie—want to be in the video, of course you can be. You know this house like few other people, and if anyone deserves to be in a video they want to be in, it's the two of you."

"The director and cameraman—same person—is supposedly going to show up for breakfast. I just wanted to ask you if you were okay with me before the dude got here."

"It's just fine with me," Kristi assured her.

Sydney leaped back up. "Super! I'll tell Genie. She never really saw anything that Carl Brentwood was in, but hey—he really is a nice guy. She likes him. A séance and a video—they kind of break up the day-to-day, you know? Thanks!" She started back, and then turned around, grinning.

"I'd have brought you both coffee anyway," she said.

"I know," Kristi told her.

Sydney ran off and Kristi stood. "I'll text Jamie Murphy right away," she promised him. "I've got to go meet up with this cameraman-slash-director. I'll let you know as soon as I hear anything."

Monty was standing in front of her when she turned. He smiled. "This is one séance I'm looking forward to."

Kristi paused, frowning at him. "Can she… I mean Shelley. Can she…summon you?"

Monty laughed. "No. Shelley has no gift for the dead—she

reads people. But trust me, she can't make anything happen at this séance. Nothing at all."

Kristi nodded. "Thanks," she told him softly. She glanced back at Dallas, and then hurried into the house.

Dallas stood slowly. He was very interested in seeing what was going to happen at the séance.

"The house is awesome," Matthew Guyer said. "Absolutely fantastic. Miss Stewart, if it's all right with you, we'll do our interviews in the front parlor and the courtyard. Maybe, if you don't mind, you could even tell us about your Revolutionary War ancestor out by the monuments." He was a man of about forty, sun-bronzed, with a crinkled face and cheerful smile. "Let's face it, the house is known to be haunted. I think it's cool that one of your ancestors was hanged as a spy—he gave the ultimate full measure for the birth of this country."

"I'll be happy to talk about Justin," Kristi told him.

She sat with Matthew, the main videographer and director for the project—"Call me Matt," he'd said—and Carl Brentwood, Murray Meyer and Claire Danson in the front parlor; although the séance wouldn't be until the following night, two leaves had been added to the big round mahogany table there, enough to allow for all those who would participate in the séance, along with Shelley.

"And you're going to be here for the séance? I mean, if the ghosts were going to show up for anyone, they'd show up for you, right?" Matt asked.

"I'll be here. I won't be at the table."

"Ah, that's too bad," Matt said, looking at Carl.

"Two of the people closest to the house will be at the table," Carl told him. "Genie and Sydney, chef and housekeeper. Kristi is kind enough to let us do this—I think we'll let her stay off camera if she wants."

"Seriously, you're better off without me," Kristi said.

"You live here, and in Savannah—and you doubt the existence of ghosts?" Matthew asked, and she wasn't sure if he was teasing or not.

"Oh, I think we're all haunted by ghosts in one way or another, Matt," Kristi said. "But here, in my house, I'd like to be part of the control, I guess."

"That's fine, of course," Matthew said. "So, at the table, we'll have Carl—center, right across from the medium, Shelley. Then the Knox family—Granger, Janet and Lacey—to Carl's right. And to his left, of course, your people—"

"Genie Turner and Sydney Gary," Kristi provided. "Genie created that delicious tart you just ate, and Sydney is the lovely young woman who served it to you."

"Great. So they can be to Carl's right with Claire and Murray. Except..."

He paused, frowning.

"What's the matter?" Carl asked.

"We need the sides to be even—I want you exactly across from the medium, and that will put four other people on one side of you and only three on the other."

"There's a gentleman who manages the house," Kristi said. "Jonah—"

"Kristi..."

She looked up and saw that Genie, Sydney and Jonah were watching the meeting, and it was Jonah who had spoken. He walked over to her. "Forgive me. Kristi Stewart, I swear I would crawl buck naked through crushed glass to help you on most things, but... I just can't. I just can't be part of any séance."

Kristi laughed softly. "Jonah, you don't have to crawl naked through crushed glass for me—nor do you have to be part of the séance. Carl, if you want another person, we'll find one easily, I'm sure."

"We don't want just anyone," Carl said with dismay. He

brightened. "Maybe Mr. Wicker will change his mind, and he'll be willing to be a part of it."

"I think it may seem silly to him," Kristi said.

The man walked down the street and chatted with the dead as if they were old friends—he really would find a séance ridiculous. She had thought them silly, and now...

Now she wished she'd never heard the word *séance*.

"I have friends in the city," Kristi suggested.

"Let me at least ask him, Kristi, please," Carl begged.

"A stranger could be good—they won't be biased. I mean, I don't think that Mr. or Mrs. Knox or their daughter are biased in any way, but..." Claire said, and then paused, smiling gently as she looked at Kristi. "We're going to ask about Trinity and Captain Monty McLane. I mean...well, she and he are the ghosts who haunt the house. You even have a mannequin of Monty up in the window, so you must have an opinion on what happened."

"The mannequin has been there for years," Kristi said.

"Years!" Jonah agreed.

"Well, still," Murray Meyer said, breaking in after a long silence and listening to the others, "the history books swear that Monty shot down his beloved Trinity. I mean, I know you object to that version of history, Kristi, but it is the one written down. Sad, and yet...well, your ancestor might have been a fine fellow just caught up in pain and agony. And I sure hope he comes out and tells us."

"History was written by Albert Huntington—the Union colonel who took over the house after the official surrender of the city," Kristi said, irritated. She shook her head. "He might well have written anything."

Claire laughed softly. "Still singing 'Dixie' and hating Yankees, huh?"

"No. Not at all. We're one great country. We strive toward equality these days, and I am passionate that we do, Claire. I'm just saying there was no one else here at the time—except for Albert Huntington and his men. Josiah McLane was a boy at the time, and not in the house when his family was slaughtered. People have always been people, Claire. And being on the winning side doesn't automatically make a man good."

She realized they were all looking at her uncomfortably—of course she would be defensive; it was her family.

"Good Lord, people, the Civil War ended in 1865. I'm sure as hell not still fighting it—like I said," Kristi reminded them, "no one knows what really happened here! Don't feel sorry for me, and please, think whatever you want to think." She was too aggravated to sit any longer. With a smile she rose. "Matthew, please feel free to stay at the house as long as you like for your camera angles and whatever. I'm sorry we don't have another room, but I'm in love with the 17Hundred90 House myself, and I know you'll be comfortable there. I have some work, so, if you don't mind, I have to go, but... I'll see all of you later!"

She managed a gracious smile, grabbed up her handbag and headed out.

She realized she had gotten angry and walked out of her own house—with nowhere really to go. She didn't know where Dallas Wicker had got to, but she did know she needed to leave— or else she'd turn into a truly horrible hostess.

She dug out her phone; Jamie Murphy had gotten back to her. Kristi was more than welcome to spend all the time she needed at the house. He hoped all was well with her and if she made any "cool" discoveries, she was to let him know.

She texted back a thank-you.

He texted in return.

Keith Hollis the yard guy has key, but I think there's one at your house, too, in a drawer in the kitchen. Gramps always told me that if I was locked out, there was a key at McLane House. Let me know if you find it—on some kind of cartoon character keychain.

She was happy to go to Ian Murphy's house—if he was haunting the place, he'd be one nice ghost. And he'd make life easy—she'd just ask him if he'd been pushed off the balcony!

She didn't want to go back inside—she'd just escaped. Sad, to think that she wanted to escape her own house—a place she loved.

But if she wanted to see if she had a key, she had to go back. She hadn't walked that far, just over to the obelisk in the square, the one that honored Nathanael Greene.

She turned and headed back, but didn't go to the front. She walked around to the side entrance and fumbled with her own keychain to find the key to the side door. When she entered, Genie was in the kitchen rinsing the morning dishes and setting them into the dishwasher.

"Sneaking in, eh?" Genie asked her.

"Yes."

Genie sniffed, "Frankly, you want my opinion? You shouldn't sit that séance out."

"Genie—what if I freak out and tell everyone that Shelley is moving the table with her knee?"

"You're not going to freak out—you never freak out. But if you don't become involved, God knows where those people will lead Shelley. Before you know it, they'll have every McLane who ever lived doing something wicked. Or worse—they'll create some kind of evil ghost or do something awful. I mean, Sydney and I can try to lead things in the right direction, but we're not you." She studied a plate, decided it was rinsed well enough and set in it in the dishwasher.

"Haven't you realized yet that people believe what they want to believe?" Kristi asked her.

"I believe Sydney has a crush on our young actor. Oh, and

a crush on the PI guy, too. Not in a bad way—you know Sydney. But if the actor wants her to see a ghost, she's going to see a ghost. It will just be better if you're part of it."

"Have you worked on Jonah yet?"

"You heard Jonah—crushed glass. He'd crawl through it buck naked. But no séance. I think he means it. When Jedidiah was so sick and Jonah was answering for him, Jonah allowed the séances, but he always hated them."

"Um, maybe. I don't know. I'll think about it," Kristi said, moving over toward the counter and rummaging through the drawers.

"Kristi, what are you doing? Can I help you any?"

"I'm looking for the spare key to the Murphy place."

"Oh—here," Genie said, walking over to the drawer next to the refrigerator. "It's on some kind of a cartoon keychain." Genie paused and stared at her, frowning. "You going over to the Murphy place?"

"I am."

Genie opened the drawer and produced the keychain, handing it to Kristi. She shivered. "You think you should go over there alone?"

"Why not? Ian Murphy and Jedidiah were best friends."

"Bad juju," Genie said.

"Bad juju—from a nice man? And since when did you believe in juju?"

"I don't know," Genie said. "Lately, I guess. Anyway—"

"Not to worry. I'll be fine."

"Okay. Why are you going over there?"

"There's just been a lot of speculation lately…about this house."

"And you think you're going to find answers—when Ian and Jedidiah looked for them over and over again throughout the years, and came up blank?"

"Who knows?" Kristi said. She gave Genie a quick hug.

"That was nice—but what was it for?" Genie asked her.

Kristi laughed. "Caring!" she told her.

Key in hand, she hurried out of the house and toward the square. A tour guide was talking about Oglethorpe and the founding of Savannah.

Oglethorpe had been quite a man, Kristi thought. He'd founded the colony with a tremendous generosity of spirit, lived in a tent for a very long time, and made friends with the Yamacraw, the local Native American tribe, and meant it and stayed friends. He'd outlawed slavery; he'd planned the city as the old town still stood, with the beautiful squares and symmetrical design.

The Murphy house was on the other side of the square and technically—like McLane House—on a side street.

Kristi paused in front of it; the yard had been kept up. It could use new paint, but it wasn't peeling badly in any way. It still looked forlorn. As if the house itself knew the master was gone and would not come home again.

Kristi thought of Genie's words as she headed up the walk and the few steps that led to a porch very much like her own. *Bad juju.*

There was plenty of voodoo in the city, and Kristi knew a number of people who practiced voodoo as their religion—using it just as lovingly and respectfully as any other religion or sect. No one practiced *bad juju*—at least, not in her circles.

She slipped the key into the door and then stepped into the front hallway.

She'd been in the house so very many times. As a child, as a teen—babysitting Jamie Murphy. As an adult, sitting with Jedidiah and Ian as they argued. They were both well-educated; they agreed on so much, and yet, they were quick to take on arguments for the sake of debate, but always ending their conversations as friends.

Ian's bedroom and office were both upstairs.

Kristi was surprised to discover she didn't really want to go to the second floor—and she was more surprised when she spoke aloud to herself. "Dallas Wicker is the one who wants to be here—and he disappeared on me!"

The house remained silent.

Because of her recent discovery of the McLane ghosts, she still hesitated in the entry. Feeling ridiculous, she called out. "Ian... Ian Murphy, are you...here?"

And still, the house was silent.

Shaking off her caution, she ran up the stairs. She burst into Ian's office, where little had changed since he died. His desk was massive, and the entire office was lined with bookshelves. Ian had history books that ranged from ancient China to Africa, Europe and the New World. He'd collected reference books on subjects from anatomy, biology and chemistry to zoology. He'd visited museums all over the world, and from every single one, he'd brought back the catalog. One of her tasks, for an allowance Ian had insisted on giving her when she had been young, had been to organize some of his bookshelves. It had been an easy task—she'd been enamored with his library.

Despite the range of his interests, Ian Murphy had always kept an entire wall dedicated to the United States—and to the wars that his country had fought, from the revolution to the present. Several shelves were dedicated to the Civil War.

"Where to begin?" she murmured. It was dim in the office, faint daylight sneaking in through half-shuttered blinds. A little dust had started to coat the room.

While she stood there contemplating, she heard a strange skittering sound; it seemed to come from downstairs, directly beneath her.

The kitchen was right below.

She froze, wondering if someone could be in the house. There could easily be someone in the house, she told herself. Jamie had told her a caretaker was looking after the place—Keith Hollis.

She should have called him to begin with, so she didn't scare or startle anyone.

She turned to head back down the stairs and then froze; she thought she heard the back door open and close. Again, she tried to assure herself it was perfectly natural.

But why would the yard guy slip out quietly—especially if he had heard her? Or had someone just slipped in?

Suddenly frightened, she went flying back down the stairs. Throwing the door open, she launched herself outside—and nearly plowed right into Dallas Wicker.

He caught her by the shoulders, half-smiling as he looked into her eyes.

"More ghosts?"

She shook her head. "I—I tried to find a ghost."

"Really?" He seemed surprised. And then immediately worried. "What happened—why are you running out?"

Sunlight was streaming down. It was a beautiful day. There was no darkness, and no shadows whatsoever surrounding them.

She felt silly.

"I don't know," she said honestly. "It's an old house, and it creaks and... I scared myself."

"I don't think of you as being a nervous person," he told her.

"Even after I nearly knocked you over?"

He was quiet for a minute, then indicated the door. "Want to go in?"

"Okay. How did you know I was here?"

"Genie—I asked her at the house."

They entered; he closed and locked the door and looked around the entry, the stairs that led up and the hallway that led off to the kitchen and dining rooms.

"No one should be in here, right?"

"No, not unless the guy watching over the place had to come in for some reason. The yard guy—his name is Keith Hollis. As

far as I know, he's the only one. But then again, until I texted
Jamie Murphy today, I didn't know I had a key."

"Your uncle had a spare?"

"Right. Ian had told Jamie if he ever locked himself out, he
could come over and get a key from Jedidiah."

"Okay, two things—call or text Jamie Murphy, and then
ask if it's all right to call the yard guy and find out if he's been
in here. Then you can let him know you're going to be going
through some of Ian's notes and papers."

Kristi wished she didn't feel quite so much like leaning against
Dallas. Wished she wasn't so aware of the weight of his hands
on her shoulders, or even the feeling created by his small smile
as he reacted to her, looked at her. He was a guest; she barely
knew him. No, he was worse than a guest. He'd admitted to
her that he was FBI. That meant he was looking for...for very
bad things.

She shouldn't be feeling so powerfully attracted to him.

She moved away quickly, pulling out her phone. Jamie re-
sponded to her right away, telling her he was in class, but if she
needed to talk, he'd be free later. She texted she just wanted to
let Hollis know she was in the house, and Jamie texted her a
phone number.

She'd met Hollis before—he did some of the yards in the area.
While Jonah had done most of the work at McLane House—
along with boys hired now and then to give him a hand—she'd
considered hiring Hollis. Jonah was getting too old for a lot of
the heavier labor.

She just hadn't managed to tell that to Jonah yet.

As she made her call to Hollis, Dallas moved off, looking
into the kitchen and dining room. She was surprised to feel an
uneasy tingle of fear as he disappeared from view through the
archway to the dining room.

Hollis answered; Kristi identified herself and he seemed glad to hear from her, and he thanked her for letting him know Jamie had said it was all right for her to go through Ian's papers.

"Great to hear from you, Kristi. You doing okay? I always knew what store both Ian and old Jedidiah had in you—they'd be happy to hear you were going through all the books. I helped Jamie—saw to it that an old Enfield, a cache of buttons and all kinds of other stuff went to the museum, but...well, you know. Jamie wanted time to go through the books and notes and all. I'm sure he's happy you're there."

"Thanks, Keith," she said. Dallas was still in another room. "Hey, has anyone been in here?"

"Just me. I come in once a week and check the doors and windows. I was thinking to call Jamie about bringing someone in to dust, but haven't gotten to it yet. You use the key Jedidiah had?" Hollis asked.

She actually pulled the phone away from her ear and looked at it for a second. Apparently, everyone but her seemed to have known she had a key to the Murphy house.

"Yes, that's right," she said. "I talked to Jamie before I came in, of course."

"Of course," he said easily.

"Keith, does anyone else have a key?" she asked.

"Not that I know about," he told her. "Why?" he asked worriedly. "Does it look like somebody broke in there?"

"No, no, everything is fine," she assured him.

"Well, good luck with those books and papers, Kristi," he said. "And thanks for letting me know what's going on." She hung up and hesitated, looking at the archway off the hall.

She headed into the dining room. The drapes were closed, and while little pieces of sunlight made their way through, the room was in shadow. Lace covered the table, which held a candelabra centerpiece, candles long put out. The old cabinets held dishes, just waiting to be set upon the table for a dinner party. All looked as it had when Ian had been alive. Except there seemed to be an aura of death, of lives lived and lost, of something just a shade eerie, and just a shade sad, about the whole place.

"Ian?" she said softly, but there was no reply. And yet, she had a feeling someone had been there, someone moving through the closed and lost world who didn't belong there.

Kristi walked into the kitchen; the coffeemaker stood on the counter, the butcher-block table was clean.

There was a sudden rustling sound, as if the wind had picked up beyond the house, and as if it hid a multitude of other sounds, whispers within the house...

There was someone near.

She bolted toward the back door just as it opened, and Dallas Wicker stepped back into the house.

He looked at her, frowning.

"Someone is in here!" she whispered.

CHAPTER SIX

"Now?" he asked softly.

"I—I don't know. I was just standing here and…well, frankly, if I hadn't met my own ancestors recently I'd have thought that… I'd have thought that the place was haunted. But… I don't think that Ian is here, I think he went on… I don't really know what I'm talking about," she whispered frantically. "But I had a feeling…"

"Feelings should never be ignored," he told her. "Stay behind me, and let's take a look around."

He went cautiously room by room, downstairs first, and then the upstairs. She stuck so close behind him she could feel the warmth radiating from his back.

"Attic?" he asked.

"There's a ladder. It pulls down from the ceiling at the end of the hall," she told him.

She showed him; he dragged a chair over from Jamie's room, stood on it and pulled on the rung that brought the ladder down. He crawled up. She waited just a moment in the silent hallway, then she quickly followed him.

The attic was as neat as the rest of the house: old trunks shoved to the side in neat rows; a dressmaker's Judy by the window, a few cupboards that held more dishes and other pieces of life lived long ago.

One trunk was labeled Photos. She remembered sitting by the trunk with Jamie after Ian had died, going through the pictures. She knelt down and opened it. The old photos had been carefully stacked; Ian had seen to it that precious photographs—taken in the time near the birth of the art of photography—had carefully been preserved in special glass frames. She dug through them as Dallas Wicker knelt down by her side. Finding the old photograph she wanted to show Dallas, she slipped it carefully from the pile.

"That was before the war—the Civil War," she said.

He smiled. "I figured that," he told her.

"That's the McLane family—Monty, Trinity and Josiah. Josiah wasn't in the house when his parents and grandfather were gunned down. Thank God. He might have died, too, and then… well, none of us after would have existed. I always loved this photo. Jedidiah never claimed to know the truth—he liked to believe that Monty wouldn't have killed his family, but he always told me he just didn't know the truth. I only know now because…" She sat back on her haunches. "This is real. I'm really talking to ghosts—and you really see them, too."

"Yes, it's real," he said.

"Why now?" she whispered. "Why—right when you arrived, and I crashed into you on my front porch?"

"We have no answers beyond the fact that sometimes, just sometimes, the essence or soul of a man or woman stays behind. For some of us, we see ghosts from a very early age, and with others, we see them when it suddenly becomes important in our lives to see them. I wish I could tell you more."

"So—there are a lot of people who see the dead?"

"I don't know about a lot. Maybe it's one percent of the population—it's not the kind of thing you can ask in census surveys," he said, smiling.

"But you know others."

"I work with forty or so people who all…are gifted. Sometimes, different ghosts appear to different people and…hey! I think you're extraordinary, you know. You only freaked out a little when ghosts started talking to you."

She set the picture back down and carefully closed the trunk. "I love that picture. I know Jamie wouldn't care if I took it, but it's there because—way back—the Murphy family and the McLane family were friends, and that Murphy ancestor was in love with what was new technology back then, and, well, Jamie wanted to hang on to the pictures. And I'm staring at this, and we were supposed to be searching the house."

"It was a good idea, searching the house," he said.

"But now we're both up in the attic, and we haven't found anything. And—"

"Let's try the basement," he said.

He headed back to the ladder; she quickly followed.

They crawled back down the ladder and Kristi pointed out the back stairs that led directly to the kitchen. From there, they made their way down to the basement.

It was very much like the rest of the house; clean and neat and yet cast in that aura of something left behind, something loved but abandoned, haunted by the years gone by. Old furniture sat in the center of the large space—the basement was the entire foundation of the house. Off to one side were the boiler and the furnace, all upgraded through the years. And beyond some supporting columns, there was a Ping-Pong table. There was a sink and paraphernalia for canning and jarring—Ian had still kept a garden with vegetables and herbs, and Jamie had dabbled with canning now and then himself. Mason jars filled simple shelves above the heavy iron sink.

There was no one in the basement, and no sign that anyone had been there.

Not to Kristi, at any rate.

But Dallas Wicker hunkered down and ran his fingers over a section of the floor.

"What is it?" she asked.

"Looks like something might have been dragged through here," he said.

"Some of the yard tools are kept down here," Kristi said pointing.

"Right," he agreed, and stood.

"So…do you think someone has been in here?" she asked.

"Yes—but whether it was just the yard guy or not, I don't know. I don't know the house. I didn't know Ian Murphy," he murmured. "So, now. The back is locked—two key bolts. Do you know if one key works on all the locks?"

"I, uh, no—I didn't even know I had a key until an hour or so ago. I've never let myself in here before. Apparently, we had a key just in case Jamie got locked out."

"But wasn't Ian always here?"

"Pretty much. But Jamie is a young adult. And he went out at night, and Ian was on sleeping pills. Jamie might be out at night with his friends, so…"

"So, that key has been in a drawer in your house for a long time—years, right?" he asked.

"I… I guess."

"Anyone could have copied the key."

"Hey!" she protested. "What—are you trying to add to my paranoia?"

"Paranoia isn't always a bad thing," he told her. "Anyway, I'm here now. And, if someone was here, they're not here now. Want to show me where all the debating and reading and whatever went on?"

"Sure. This way."

She led him up the stairs to the office that connected to Ian's bedroom. They'd scanned the room already, but now Dallas Wicker surveyed the extensive library.

"There could definitely be something here," he said softly.

"Like what?"

"I don't know," he told her, hands on his hips as he looked at her. "If I knew…"

"We're in the Murphy place now, but you're back to thinking that McLane House somehow is involved in two deaths and two disappearances," Kristi said. "I have to tell you, I am feeling very uneasy about all this. Seriously, just what evidence do we even have?"

"That's what we're going to look for," he told her.

She stared back at him, thinking of how he had arrived—on her doorstep. And how, suddenly, now, when she'd known the house all her life, the ghosts of Justin and Monty McLane had appeared before her, worried, certain something was wrong.

Still, maybe she was truly having a psychotic break, believing this man—an agent for real?—saw ghosts just the same. Maybe she'd invented Dallas Wicker. He was unbelievably good-looking. Other people had seen him, right? Suddenly she was struggling to recall Dallas talking to other people at the house. No. He was real.

"Okay," she said. "I'm wondering."

"Wondering what?" he asked her.

"Well, I knew Lachlan Plant, and he was a super guy, so nice, enthusiastic. I knew Ian Murphy well, of course, and…"

"What?"

"Maybe they did know each other. Ian's energy was down, but you know, people are supposed to keep up with exercise while they're sick, both to keep the body strong, and for psychological reasons. And, like I said, Lachlan was just a good guy. Maybe Ian went to the gym—and maybe Lachlan was going to work with Ian. Maybe Ian told Lachlan about whatever he was work-

ing on, about something he might have discovered, about…"
Kristi said, and then broke off. "About what—that's what we
don't know. But if we find out they did know one another, we
at least have a connection."

"My dear Miss Stewart, I believe you could be on to something," he told her, and he pulled out his phone. He typed out
a quick text, and when he looked up, he was smiling.

"We'll know soon enough," he told her.

"Oh?"

"I'm working with a guy here—a police detective. Joe Dunhill. This is a start. We can also go to the gym and maybe verify
the fact that Ian Murphy saw Lachlan Plant at some time. But
maybe he just called him. Maybe Lachlan was even on his way
over here when he died."

The house suddenly seemed to be closing in on Kristi. She
wasn't sure why; she'd loved Ian, Jamie was her friend and she'd
always felt at home and welcome there. Maybe it was her prox-
imity to Dallas, the feeling she had when he was close to her.

She was so very attracted to him. And she needed to concentrate on the task at hand, and not be distracted by these new
feelings.

Maybe she was feeling too much.

"Why don't you look through these things—and I'll run over
to the gym?" Kristi suggested.

He hesitated. "That would be logical."

"Great." She turned to hurry out, but then paused, walking
back over to the desk to retrieve her purse and hand him the
key so he could lock up. "I'll meet you back at my house!" she
told him.

And she fled.

She didn't understand it; she liked Dallas, really liked him.

But her world, her peaceful little world she had just been creating and coming to know and love, had been shattered. First
by the frightening realization that she could speak to the dead,

and now by the notion that she maybe wanted someone else in her life.

She hoped Dallas understood she was afraid, and she needed some space.

To run.

Run...or throw herself in his arms, bury herself in all the longing and attraction and beg him never to leave her.

That thought startled her. That wasn't going to happen.

She ran across the square, and then she slowed her gait, and finally managed a brisk walk. At least, by going to the gym, she was doing something. Moving forward.

Moving forward to get where?

The gym was almost on the water; she walked quickly, and before another few minutes had gone by, she reached it.

She saw the large sign above the door that advertised "World of the Body in Motion."

The gym was open from seven in the morning until eleven at night, continually brightly lit and offering machines and trainers for every age and body type. Therapists were also on call, and in the rear, there was a spa that offered massages and all kinds of body treatments.

For a moment, Kristi stood just inside the doorway. She had a membership; she just hadn't been in a very long time, between the house and work and now...

"Kristi! Hey!"

She looked toward the reception desk. A woman named Amy Simmons was working the desk; she was a very pretty—perfectly fit—young blonde. She and Kristi had gone to high school together, and while they didn't do lunch every week, they were still friends.

"Hey, Amy."

"Have you come to work out?" Amy asked her. Kristi was dressed in a tailored cotton shirt and jeans—not exactly workout

clothing. And she only had her small shoulder bag with her—
she was obviously not carrying her clothing.

"Uh, no, I—"

"You should join one of my classes!" Amy said. "You're young,
and you're agile, and you run around that house of yours and
back and forth with your work. But there's more to keeping in
shape, you know, and longevity can be related to us all really
respecting our bodies, you know?"

"Yes, I really do have to get back into working out," Kristi
said. "But—"

"I know, I know, so many people have been bummed out by
what happened to Lachlan Plant. Such a great guy. And he was
in such amazing shape—go figure that such an accident could
happen to such a man," Amy said. "So, so, sad. We all loved
him here. Oh, and guess what? You know how we were doing
a collection to get him buried? Somebody put in several thousand dollars—enough to get us up to goal, get him into a good
funeral home, and into a plot in Bonaventure. He loved that
cemetery—I know it would make him happy."

Kristi smiled; she and McLane House had put money into the
fund, but she hadn't had "thousands" to offer anyone.

"Amy, did Lachlan work with older customers?"

"Older, younger—you name it. He was a licensed physical
therapist as well, you know."

She wasn't sure she had known.

"Did Mr. Murphy ever come in here?"

"Mr. Murphy—you mean, Jamie Murphy's grandfather?"

"Yes."

"When he's home, Jamie comes here. I don't think I ever
saw his grandfather. Sad, so sad, about him, too, huh? But of
course, he lived a full life—he was in his eighties, right? I mean,
we can live to a hundred or more, and the value of a life can't
be judged on age, but at least he got to live, you know what I
mean?" Amy asked.

"Yes, at least he got to live," Kristi murmured.

"Well, who knows?" Amy asked. "Maybe Jamie did ask Lachlan about working with his grandfather, or maybe he was even in at some time. He's not in our records—just Jamie. But if he just came in and talked to Lachlan, I might not know. I work days from six in the morning to two—he might have stopped by at some other time. Hey, come back in and work out and ask around, if you want to know. Hey, why do you want to know?"

"I was just thinking about him, I guess," Kristi said. "He and Jedidiah were really good friends. Anyway, thanks."

"We're going to have a service for Lachlan on Saturday, and then burial out at Bonaventure. It's going to be in the paper and all, but I'm guessing you're going to want to come," Amy said.

"Of course," Kristi said.

Séance on Friday, funeral on Saturday. What could be better?

She smiled and turned to leave, but before she could do so, another of the gym's trainers came hurrying toward her. Boyd Morris, an old friend—and a friend to Lachlan, as well.

"Kristi, hey, you coming back in?" Boyd asked.

"Yes, soon," she assured him.

He glanced at Amy. "She told you about us being ready to bury Lachlan, right?"

"Yes, and I'll be there. Hey, Boyd, do you know what he was doing around Johnson Square on the night that he died? Oh, and I know what I wanted to ask you—did he know Ian Murphy?"

"Did Lachlan know Ian Murphy?" Boyd pondered, and then he shrugged. "Sure, he must have known him. Lachlan worked with Jamie sometimes. Jamie surely talked about his grandfather. Ian was a cool dude—well, didn't expect what he did."

"Yep, it was shocking," Kristi said. "He was a great guy."

"Well, who knows. I'm sure Lachlan must have met old Ian somewhere along the line. I mean, Jamie has been out in California for years now, but he always came home to be with the old man for Christmas and all that. I'm sure Lachlan would have met him somewhere in there. I mean, this is Savannah! We're still kind of like host city for Southern charm, right? Locals know locals and all that."

"Yes, we do," Kristi agreed. "Anyway, thank you. Amy, Boyd, I'll see you at the funeral. Thanks for letting me know."

She smiled, waved and left the gym, and started on the short walk back to Johnson Square.

Looking up at McLane House, she was surprised—for the first time in her life—not to want to go in.

It was her home now; her family heritage. She walked up the path, the steps to the porch and into the house.

Murray Meyer was there, in the front parlor, with Carl Brentwood and the videographer, Matthew Guyer. Guyer was enthusiastically pointing to all the wonders of the house he meant to capture in his video.

"Kristi!" Carl greeted her with enthusiasm. "We're just about all set here for now. I was going to take Matthew to the Olde Pink House for a drink and to see the place. Want to come along with us?"

"Oh, thank you, that's sweet of you. I'm sorry—I have to get some work done. But…"

She spoke and then hesitated.

"But?" Carl asked her, smiling broadly.

"I'll be the extra person you need at the table for the séance."

She spoke quickly, before she could change her mind.

He thanked her profusely.

She excused herself rushing up to her own room. She leaned against the door when she closed it, praying no ghosts would come to haunt her then.

They did not.

She wanted to bury her head beneath her pillow and pretend none of it was happening.

Somehow, she managed not to do so. She glanced at her phone, and then quickly texted Jamie Murphy: Can you talk?

He answered her quickly.

Give me about ten minutes; I'll call you.

Kristi sat down on her bed to wait.

Dallas was completely absorbed in Ian Murphy's office; his volumes seemed endless, and he wrote notes detailing new information in the margins, or just notations on what he had concluded from what he had read. Ian Murphy had been a true lifelong scholar.

He had maps of Revolutionary battles, battles during the War of 1812 and more. There was volume upon volume on James Oglethorpe, the general, peer and philanthropist who had founded Savannah in 1733, and immediately became friends with Tomochichi, the Native chief who would be his lifelong friend. The man had been an idealist and a dreamer, taking part in the planning of the squares in the city that had lasted through time, making downtown Savannah one of the largest areas on the National Register of Historic Places.

He had volumes on Justin McLane, the Patriot who had died while trying to smuggle British plans out of Savannah, but not before he had served with Francis Marion, the South Carolina "Swamp Fox," who had so harried the British up in South Carolina.

"Justin, you were a good man," Dallas said aloud.

Dallas sat at the desk, and mused on why Justin had stayed— he never did know exactly why some people stuck around as ghosts and some did not.

Justin had been honored by his countrymen. He had nothing to prove.

While Monty...

Had Monty stayed on to prove his innocence?

Or perhaps he was still searching the earth for his beloved Trinity.

He gave his head a shake. He had to try to figure out why someone would have killed Ian Murphy and Lachlan Plant. And why a businesswoman would have disappeared, and why someone had recently taken Simon Drake.

How did it all come together?

He looked at his phone, willing it to ring. He stood and slid the books he had taken down back on the shelves where they belonged, using a bookmark from the desk between the volumes, allowing him to see where he had left off.

He looked at his phone again.

The hell with it.

He dialed Kristi Stewart's cell phone number.

She answered it, a wary note in her voice. "Kristi Stewart, may I help you?"

"It's me. Dallas."

"I didn't know you had my cell."

"Jonah gave me this number and his number," Dallas explained. "I...uh...did you find anything?"

"I don't know. I found out they're going to bury Lachlan this Saturday." She was quiet. "You know how it all came to be paid for, right?"

"I do. I'd like to attend."

"Of course," she murmured. "Did you find anything?"

"I'm still here, looking. Lots of things, but not what we're looking for, I don't think." As he spoke, he idly opened the drawers of Ian Murphy's desk, even though they'd been through them earlier. "Are you still at the gym?"

"No, I'm back... Did you talk to Detective Dunhill?"

"Yes, they're going to pull phone records, looking specifically for any communication between Plant and Murphy. Poor Joe—they're letting him run with this, but I don't think they're giving him a great deal of credence. How about you? Any confirmation from the gym?"

"Maybe. One of the trainers thinks that it's likely Ian and Lachlan knew one another. Jamie did use the gym, and when he was here, he often worked out with Lachlan. Jamie would have talked about his grandfather. I'm going to have a call with him soon."

"Good," Dallas said. He wanted to say more. He wished she was back there with him.

"Dinner?" he heard himself say; he winced, certain she would turn him down.

There was a slightly too-long silence on the other end.

He went on, "It's a meal one eats at night. We skipped lunch—but then, of course, the breakfasts at McLane House are certainly a meal, so…"

She was still silent. Yes, she would refuse him.

"All right," she said. "But I'll help out here for our afternoon tea service first. So, about seven? I mean, you're obviously welcome to be back here for tea, but…if you're not…"

"I'll be back," he told her. "See you soon." He hung up.

In one of the drawers, there was an old book—another Civil War story by the look of it. Dallas took it out and set it on the desk. He'd start with it next time, and re-shelf it properly after.

He left Ian Murphy's room and headed down, pausing in the parlor by the entry.

There was *something about the house…*

"Mr. Murphy?" he spoke softly aloud.

Kristi had tried, too, he was certain. Kristi had known and loved Murphy; Murphy had known and loved her. If anyone, he'd appear to her.

And still…

There was something.

It was almost as if a dark, shadowy mist had permeated the house. It wasn't a sense of evil. Just something that lurked in the

shadows, and couldn't quite be seen, couldn't quite be touched...
And, yet, it was there.

Tomorrow, he'd start reading again. The answer had to be up
there somewhere, somewhere in Ian Murphy's extensive library.

"Is someone here?" he asked aloud, a little desperately.

There was no answer.

And yet that dark gray mist still seemed to hover, a strange
miasma, and it was as if the house itself was...

Breathing.

Dinner. A date? Were they just going to find some food—
easy enough in Savannah—and chat about their horoscope signs,
or...what?

No. Dallas probably wanted her away from the house again,
attention undivided, certain if he quizzed her long enough, she'd
know why a trainer and an old man were dead and businesswoman and a politician were missing.

Kristi still decided to shower, and to find one of her favorite
little black dresses.

She brought the phone with her into the bathroom—just in
case. She dressed with it on the bed in front of her.

Jamie Murphy still hadn't called her.

When she was dressed, she called him.

He answered right away. "Sorry, sorry, Kristi. Professor got
a little long-winded. Is everything all right? Is there a problem
with the house?"

"No, no problem—the house is just fine. And I won't mess
anything up. You know that."

"You're welcome to anything there. You know that. So what's
up?"

"There's a man staying here who is a private eye, working
for an old friend of Lachlan Plant, just wants to try to understand what happened."

"Lachlan didn't have family."

"I know. This is just an old friend. But I think he provided the rest of the burial money—Lachlan is going to have a funeral and be buried on Saturday."

"That's great. I wish I could make it home for the funeral, but there was my grandfather and Jedidiah and I'm afraid I'll be kicked out if I leave again."

"No, no, I wasn't suggesting you should come home—you need to make it through school, Jamie. I just wanted to ask you. Did Ian ever...did he and Lachlan know each other?"

"Of course."

"Of course?"

"Kristi, it's Savannah—I mean, the city is kind of a small town where everyone knows everyone's business. Locals all know each other."

"Lachlan wasn't a local."

"He worked for the local gym. Hey, Ian walked over and met me sometimes for dinner or something—when he was feeling well."

"Did you ever suggest they work out together?"

"Sure. I talked about my grandfather to Lachlan. I talked to Gramps about working with a trainer—it would have been good for him."

"Did they ever meet?"

"Maybe? I don't know. But Lachlan had told me he'd be willing to go to Gramps' place to help him, so, sure, maybe. He thought he was cool as could be, you know."

"Who thought who was cool?" Kristi asked.

Jamie laughed. "Lachlan thought Gramps was amazing—the amount he seemed to know about everything. In fact, he said once, if we ever got a game of Trivial Pursuit going, he definitely wanted to be on my grandfather's team." He paused. "You know, they definitely had to have met. Lachlan couldn't have said some of the things he said—felt the way that he did—if he hadn't known Gramps."

"So," Kristi said, and she felt as if she was far, far away, watching herself rather than doing the actual talking. "It's likely they did know one another and they might have shared information."

"Sure. Hey, really—is everything all right? There is no problem with the house?"

"Everything is fine, Jamie, I promise."

"Okay, cool. Call me, text me, whatever, if you need anything else."

"Thank you. Um, study hard, huh?"

"Will do."

She hung up on Jamie and almost called Dallas right away, but a glance at her phone clock told her that if she meant to help with their tea service, she needed to get downstairs.

Dallas would be there soon enough.

Matthew Guyer was back with Carl Brentwood and his crew. They always had plenty extra for their tea. Kristi smiled at him and hurried through to the kitchen; Genie was slicing cheese and Sydney was pouring hot water into a pot.

"Tea drinkers, this crowd," Sydney said. "One pot of coffee, but this is the third big pot of tea I brewed. No drinkers among the crew—not even Granger Knox tonight. Maybe he watches out because he has a young and susceptible daughter."

"Maybe. What can I do?" Kristi asked.

"Want to put out a few of my famous biscuits?" Genie asked. "I do believe I outdid myself today, I've got plain, and I did up a batch of blueberry—and you can put out some of those preserves, too, if you will."

"Yes, ma'am," Kristi said, stepping in for a tray and arranging biscuits.

"Haven't seen the PI guy around all day," Genie told Kristi. "Told him you were at the Murphy place—he found you okay?"

"Yes, thanks," she murmured. "Anyway..." She needed to get her tray done and get out of the kitchen; she was blushing, and she definitely wasn't hiding her own interest in the "PI guy" very well.

But she was saved by a tapping on the back door; it wasn't locked, because it opened, and Shelley—in a black dress with a colorful silk cape around her shoulders—came hurrying in.

She stopped, looking at them, a broad smile on her face. "I am so excited. So, so excited! I can't wait. I'm going to star in a video—now I will be *the* Savannah medium!"

"Yes, and that's great," Kristi agreed softly, sweeping up her tray. "Are you supposed to be meeting with Carl Brentwood and his people? They're all out there, talking about the séance, I'm sure."

"Cool, and thank you—thank you for this opportunity, Kristi!"

"Sure." Kristi headed out the door; Shelley was right behind her.

"I heard you're going to fill in. It's going to be a really big table, not all that conducive to raising the spirits, but this house is very haunted, I'm sure it will be fine, whatever we do. And, Kristi, I'm glad you're going to sit with us. You just don't know. I have a feeling about you—the ghosts are just going to show up like popcorn out of a cooker, I'm sure of it!"

"Shelley," Kristi moaned, setting her tray down on the table. She turned and stared at the medium. "Everything will be on camera, so be careful, huh?"

Don't go shaking the table with your knee.

Shelley waved a hand in the air. "Not to worry—it's going to be great. Just great. Chock-full of the undead, all anxious and with something to say!"

"Shelley!" Carl Brentwood had seen the medium arrive.

Kristi smiled at them both and excused herself back to the kitchen, where she grabbed her bag and told Genie, "You guys are on your own—I'm out of here!"

For the second time that day, she fled.

And, for the third time, she ran right into Dallas Wicker.

"Hey! I...guess we're going now," he said.

"Yep."

"Where?"

"Anywhere!"

He looked back up at the house, seemed thoughtful for a moment.

"It's the same..." he murmured.

"The same what?"

"The gray, the..." He stopped speaking and then turned his eyes deliberately to her and smiled. "Never mind. The city, my lady, is filled with exceptionally fine restaurants. What's your pleasure?"

"Whatever—that way! Let's just go."

He nodded, studying her.

"As you wish."

CHAPTER SEVEN

"As long as I can remember," Kristi said, as they walked and neared the restaurant of her choice, "I've loved the 17Hundred90 Inn and Restaurant."

"Sounds good," Dallas said.

"It's haunted, of course. It was actually built in 1820, but that was a bad year. So many died in a yellow fever epidemic. Room 204 is the most haunted—Anna was a young girl, in love with a sailor. He loved her, too, but the owner of the inn back then wouldn't let her go to him—the sailor thought she didn't love him, and he sailed away. She then plunged to her death—there's a mannequin of Anna in the window for all those on the ghost tours to see. We seem to like mannequins," Kristi said.

"Yes, you have a mannequin of Monty McLane," Dallas noted.

"Always looking out, protecting his home—looking for Trinity. Anyway, seriously, this place is fantastic for dinner. And I guess our stories and our mannequins work because people, including all manner of celebrities, call way ahead to book Anna's room."

"What about McLane House?" he asked.

"Ah, well, we're different—the murders took place out front, and no one knows exactly where Justin McLane was hanged, if it was even on the property—and if they were really buried on the property."

"You haven't asked him yet?" Dallas asked her.

She flushed. "No! Anyway, I just wanted out of the house. So, it's basically confirmed that Ian Murphy and Lachlan knew one another. They seemed to be building a friendship based on mutual respect of trivia and learning, so if Ian Murphy did know something, he might well have told Lachlan. But the more I think about it, the more I think we're stretching to believe anyone would have killed both of them for anything that Ian Murphy knew. First off, Jamie is doing just fine out in California—wouldn't he have also known whatever his grandfather knew?"

"Not if it was something Ian Murphy just learned. They died a little over two weeks ago now, right? Just a day or two apart."

Kristi nodded, looking downward. "Ian...and then a few days later, Lachlan."

They'd reached the restaurant; Dallas opened the door. The hostess greeted Kristi.

When they were seated, she gestured around. "Isn't it nice?"

"It's great," he said. "Charming old brick, cozy seating, bar... mantelpiece. I love it, too."

"You've been here before?" she asked him.

He lowered his head. "Yeah, I've been here before." He looked up at her. "Kristi, I lived the first ten years of my life near here, just on the outskirts of the old town, toward I-95."

"You—you're from Savannah? Oh, my God, I feel like a fool. I must be telling you so many things that you already know!" she said, eyes wide—looking betrayed.

He shook his head, suddenly determined for her to understand. "I was young when I left. Ten. I'd been staying with my mom and her family—waiting for my dad to finish his stint in

the military." He hesitated. "I really grew up in Fredericksburg, Virginia."

They were briefly interrupted by the waitress, who brought
them water and took their orders.

"So… Savannah was your home," Kristi prompted him once
they were on their own again.

"For a short time—then, as I said, Fredericksburg."

"But—"

"I never considered Savannah my home." He paused again
and then figured at this point, he really needed to just lay it out.
"My mother was attacked one day, leaving the bus on her way
home from work. She was left for dead, and her injuries were
such that—she did die. Because of that, I can't really embrace
Savannah as home, though it's a wonderful city. And I always
knew what I wanted to do with my life because…because nothing really changes emotion, but knowing you've done something
to put someone heinous away is…it's something that matters,"
he told her.

"Oh, my God. I'm so sorry."

He winced. "I didn't tell you that to gain your sympathy. It
was a very long time ago." He leaned forward, so he could speak
quietly. "And I came to know ghosts because a ghost helped
me. I was a kid, acting out. I'd run over to the local cemetery
one day, and a man started talking to me. It was a war hero—
Revolutionary fellow—and he led me to a man who had been
attacked and severely beaten. Just as my mother had been. I got
help, and the man lived—and he testified against the three drifters who had attacked him—and my mother—and my mother's
killers were put away," he finished.

She was staring at him in pure horror and he tensed up; he
didn't want her feeling sorry for him.

"The thing is… I was helped, and at the very least, I got justice for my mother. I knew not to try to tell anyone a dead man
had helped me. I kept my talent to myself. But then I knew I

wanted to be in law enforcement. It's hard to watch what crime, cruelty, greed and brutality do to others, but when you can bring someone to justice—and perhaps stop killers from moving on to the next person—it's a pretty amazing thing."

"I'm so sorry," she said, still looking at him. Their crab cakes had arrived a little while ago; she hadn't touched them.

"It's in the past," he said. "And, thanks to my ghost and the injured man, her killers were stopped and put away, and I get to believe maybe someone else didn't suffer the same fate."

"You were ten—and you weren't terrified?" she asked.

He smiled at that. "Hell—yeah, I was absolutely terrified."

"But you…you managed."

"I think we accept things more easily when we're younger."

She finally moved a piece of crab cake around on her plate, and then she looked at him again.

"So, you're really FBI."

"I really am."

"Then you must…you must deal with terrible things all the time." She inhaled a very deep breath and looked at him. "Did you—did you ever see your mother again?"

He smiled at her. "No. But I did become pretty good friends with my old friend who terrified me—and then helped me out that day. Major Louis Falmouth—he was one of the first people to arrive in Savannah after Oglethorpe had established the city, and he was a man far ahead of his time. He was killed during the war, but… Louis has saved a lot of lives. My aunt's place is on the outskirts of the city near a forgotten—but really beautiful—old cemetery. It's used for a lot of drug deals, and—" he paused, shrugging "—Louis has managed to trip a lot of dealers up for the cops to get and scare a lot of people straight."

"You go back and see him?" she asked.

"I do. He's a big believer in bad things happening when good men do nothing to stop them."

"I'm still so sorry."

"Well, here's the good. My mom used to bring flowers to the cemetery—to honor those who weren't in a well-known place, such as Colonial Park Cemetery, or somewhere as beautiful as Bonaventure. He told me he saw my mother...leave. She was smiling and looking up to the light. He said it was as though she was already an angel. I like to believe that."

Kristi nodded. Then she shook her head. "Why do some stay—and some go?" she wondered.

"I don't know. Maybe some stay because we just aren't supposed to forget. We do, you know. As time goes by, we forget the wrongs done to people. We like to forget that some of our founding fathers came for religious freedom—and then condemned those who didn't worship as they saw fit. We forget the horrors done to Native Americans, and that slavery was an abomination—just as any type of prejudice remains an abomination today. Anyway..."

"All the horrible things you've seen—and you're looking into a death that might have been accidental, and the death of a very old man."

"Because, life, while we live it, is a gift—and no man has the right to take that gift away from another man."

She leaned forward. "Okay, say that Ian did discover something that might shake up history, or point a finger somewhere someone doesn't want a finger pointed. What about Eliza Malone and Simon Drake?"

"We're back to Eliza's determination that businesses become involved in fighting crime. And Simon's platform—every crime, no matter how cold, deserves to be solved. They both were trying to clean up the city," Dallas said.

"Okay, so, we go back to Ian's house. We delve through his papers until we find...something that connects them all. Or, we don't."

He nodded. "I've really just begun. There are many people I need to speak with—I've started on Simon Drake, and I know he was hurrying to meet someone. That someone might have been Ian Murphy."

"But Eliza disappeared two years ago. If Ian had known something, I think he would have said so after she disappeared. He certainly would have read about all her efforts against crime."

"That is a puzzling problem," he agreed.

"So, tomorrow…the séance," she murmured. "I—I agreed to participate."

"Did you?"

"The number of people at the table is important to the aesthetic of filming," Kristi told him. "It's apparently important that Carl Brentwood be exactly opposite Shelley. Shelley, of course, is in seventh heaven, thinking this will make her the most important medium in the city."

Dallas smiled.

"Are you all right with being at the table?"

"I might as well be," she said. "It's my house, and now…now I know for sure it's got ghosts. I'm fond of them, too. It's amazing to see that even though they died so long ago, they watch, and they learn, and they seem to become very wise and wonderful human beings. I'm kind of sad—Jedidiah would have loved to have known them."

They'd finished eating, and were lingering over coffee.

"I guess it's time to go back," Kristi said.

"I have to walk you home," he teased her.

Dallas enjoyed the walk; he liked hearing Kristi talk about how she thought Savannah was especially beautiful by night. "There's a mist over the city, or so it seems. By day, even the really old parts are bustling and alive, and by night…it's grown quiet. There are areas of the city where you could close your eyes and go back hundreds of years, and almost see it as it all began," she commented.

"Seriously," she said, and in her enthusiasm, she set her hands on his shoulders. "Close your eyes for a minute. Think back, way back…and when you open your eyes again, ignore the cars and electric lights…"

Her words came to his ears, and against his face and lips in a soft breeze. When she trailed off, he opened his eyes and hers were still closed. Yet it seemed that she had stopped speaking just because they were so close.

And she had suddenly realized it, the same way he had.

"You're right," he said quietly, aware of her on an almost painful physical level. "You can feel the energy here."

"Yes," she said softly. Then she gave him a quick, tight smile, removed her hands suddenly from his shoulders and added, "Okay. I guess we'd best move on."

They came to her house. The front of the house was off of the square, and by night, at that moment, the street was empty.

Looking up, Dallas could see the mannequin of Monty McLane in the window. It had one hand on its hip and stood in a jaunty manner, hat pulled low, dark locks curling down by the collar.

"Which room is he in?" Dallas asked Kristi.

"Oh, he's not in a guest room at all," she told him. "There's a little room off the hall—very small. I think it was once a dressing room for the bedroom in the center, but now it's just got a little love seat, a lamp and some of Genie's and Sydney's favorite magazines, and some *GQ* for Jonah. It's a little escape for them during the day. Monty stands at that window." She hesitated, smiling. "He used to be in Jedidiah's room—my room. We think it was created sometime in the 1800s—right when wax museums became a rage. But Jonah never wanted him in a guest room. He had a friend who had stayed at the 17Hundred90 Inn and Restaurant, and she'd been freaked out every time she had to pass the mannequin to get to her room. Ghosts didn't scare her—the mannequin did."

"Like clowns and dolls," Dallas said. As he spoke, he saw

the real thing—or the real specter—of Monty McLane coming around the side of the house.

"Evening. All is well," Monty told him. He inclined his head politely to Kristi, but addressed Dallas. "We are keeping guard, Justin and I. Guests are all in, as well. You are the last to return," Monty said, and he saluted.

Dallas saluted in return.

Monty walked around the side of the house again as Kristi and Dallas headed up the steps to the front; she used her key to open the door, and he made certain to lock it when they were in.

"Why would people be digging in the yard?" Kristi wondered.

"I think the answers lie across the square, at the Murphy place," he said.

Upstairs, they lingered awkwardly for a moment in front of his room.

He reached out and took one of her hands in both of his. "Thank you," he said softly, "for showing me the city through your eyes."

She didn't pull her hand away. They stood for a moment. Her gaze dropped to where their hands touched.

"I… um…" she said, and then he wasn't sure if he released his hold, or if she did pull away.

"Good night," she told him.

Dallas watched as Kristi locked herself into her room, and then he went to his own. He slipped off his jacket, and put his Glock and holster onto the bedside table. He pulled out his computer. With a heavy sigh, he booted it up and started going through files. He had barely begun before there was a tap at his door.

It was Kristi. She had changed into a flowing silky black robe.

"Hey," he said, when he could find his voice.

She slipped in. "I was just wondering…"

"What's that?" he asked.

She looked exceptionally beautiful in the dim light of the

room, almost as mystical as the ghosts of McLane House, golden hair tumbling around her shoulders, shimmering against the black silk of her robe, eyes wide and luminous.

"I… I don't understand what's happening. I can't believe that anyone in my staff could have had anything to do with anything heinous—whatsoever. But maybe I'm too lax around here. Maybe people—strangers—can get in too easily. What if we're somehow locking ourselves in with a killer?" she asked.

"I—I would never let anything happen to you," he said softly, moving closer.

She stepped suddenly into his arms, hands slipping to his neck, body pressed to his. Her lips touched his, and he instinctively pulled her in—it would take a better man than him to resist. Her mouth was sweet and provocative at first, seductive, and then he—or she—deepened the kiss until it was something passionate, something that took them both unaware, perhaps, and he drew her closer and closer. His mouth traveled from her lips to her throat, and their embrace grew more frantic and urgent until she stumbled forward, and her movement brought him with her so that they tumbled back onto the bed. And it was there she suddenly drew back, rising above him—apologetic.

"I am so sorry… I mean, oh, Lord, are you… Is there someone, will I get you into any kind of trouble? I am so sorry…"

He didn't let her draw away. He held her there, promising her, "I am not married, I have never been married and I am not in a relationship. You?"

"No, not in…forever. Two years ago, before I started spending so much time with work and Jedidiah… He was an ad exec, and he was transferred to Chicago, and I knew I wouldn't go, and…too much information, right?" she whispered.

He rolled, rising above her, smiling. "Marina Hall, couldn't take the life I was living… And I couldn't ever let her know how I knew some things. We were destined to fail. A two-or three-night stand with a cop in Vegas that we both knew wasn't going anywhere…" He paused. "In a very strange and probably almost unbelievable way, I have been captivated by you since you plowed into me out on your front porch, and nothing that's happened since then has done anything but convince me I absolutely have to be with you."

She reached out and drew him down to her, and they locked in a kiss again. They struggled together to remove his shirt quickly; her robe seemed to melt away in a pile of black silk.

She was everything he'd imagined, skin so soft as he caressed the length of her back. Her fingertips moved from his shoulders and down his back while his kisses streamed lower, over her throat and breasts and down to the lean, smooth plane of her belly. They adjusted again, dealing with the annoyance of his belt buckle and jeans, and he rose to toss the offending clothing to the floor and came down to her again.

They tangled into a deep, passionate kiss, and then she pulled away and looked at him again. "But…it's all right?" she questioned.

"All right?" he queried, grinning. "I was thinking it was fantastic…"

He didn't finish; her lips were on his again, and then she was showering his shoulders with kisses, shimmying down his body in the most provocative way. Searing flashes of heat tore through him.

"Definitely fantastic," she murmured. "I just meant—"

This time, he didn't let her finish. He pulled her back up to him and caught her words with his mouth, indulging in another long kiss, deep, wet, like a bond that drew them together, that made them one. Then they both writhed against one another, planting touches and kisses here and there on their flesh, until the play and caressing became all but unbearable; they paused just briefly, and he stared into her eyes.

"I think you make me halfway insane," he whispered to her.

"That's all right," she whispered. "I might be entirely insane."

He captured her mouth again as he lowered himself into her, slowly, and then completely. She sighed, and then gasped as he began to move.

They made love slowly and excruciatingly, then urgently.

Night and shadows seemed to dance around him; it was sex but more. He rose to heights he didn't even remember, and he realized there was nothing else like this because she knew him, knew so much about him, knew a part of him that few else did...

Climax with her was incredible, and the feeling remained as she lay against him, as they felt the urgency drift into mist, and the beauty of just lying there, touching, not talking...

And then, as suddenly as she had come to him, she rose.

"Oh, wow. I really had no right. I mean, you're a guest here."

"You're the most welcoming hostess I've ever known."

"Oh!" she exclaimed, on her knees, staring down at him in horror. "You don't think that I... Oh, my God, I've never, never—"

He rose and caught her to him. "I know! I was teasing."

"How do you know?" she whispered, falling to his side again. "You don't know me, you don't really—"

"I know everything I need to know," he whispered, pulling her to him so that her head rested on his chest, so he could draw his fingers through the gold tangle of her hair. "How do we know people? Sometimes, we just do."

She managed a weak smile, and then she whispered, "I should go back to my own room."

"Why? You know you're safe here."

"I really didn't... I mean..."

"It's all right. Don't go. Stay here with me."

"Okay," she whispered after a moment. "But you have to know, I'm not that terrible a coward, I will be all right and when it's time you have to leave..."

"Not tonight!" he whispered passionately.

Maybe never, he thought, and he wondered if he wasn't caught up in the moment, in Kristi…

No. There had been something. From that first moment she had crashed into him, when he had held her, seen her eyes.

"Not tonight," he said again, wrapping her into his arms and holding her to him. "Not tonight."

"You're asking about Eliza? Again—now?"

The man staring at Dallas from behind his desk—Eli Harrington—was in his early fifties, perfectly dressed in a blue designer suit and very bitter. He'd barely risen to shake Dallas's hand, and now he was having trouble being courteous in the least.

"The case remains open. Joe Dunhill has never forgotten. Sir, you have to understand that leads dry up. The police never had anything except that Ms. Malone was heading to a meeting she didn't explain to anyone—and she was last seen in the Johnson Square area."

"How do you disappear from Johnson Square?" Harrington asked, his tone still filled with anger and pain. "And it was two years ago now. I guess they are finally looking at Eliza's disappearance again because of that politician who went missing. I mean, twice. People just vanished."

"I'm hoping if I can find out more about Eliza, I can understand better where she might have been headed—and if we could figure out where she was going, we just might figure out why someone was trying to stop her," Dallas said.

Eli Harrington stared at him. He sighed, and it was as if he breathed out all his anger. "First off—we weren't having an affair. We were business partners. We couldn't have been having an affair."

"Because Eliza was gay—I know that," Dallas said.

"Do you think she was killed because…because she was gay?" Eli asked.

"I don't think what happened to her had anything to do with sexuality," Dallas said.

"But you do think she's dead. That wasn't a question. I know she's dead. She didn't just disappear on purpose. She loved what we did, and our company worked very hard to put the right people in the right places—residential real estate, and commercial. If you couldn't care less about being in the historic section, it's more economical—most of the time—to be outside of the designated area. Eliza had a way with people, and she could charm them and find out what was more important to them…which was why crime was a big issue to her. When she told someone that an area was safe, she wanted it to be the truth. It hasn't been the same since she's been gone," Harrington said. He shook his head. "Sometimes it's the best people, huh?"

"Yes, sometimes it's the best people," Dallas agreed. "Was she friends with a man named Ian Murphy?"

"The old guy who took a header a few weeks back?" Harrington asked.

"Yes. Mr. Murphy had a house off of Johnson Square."

Harrington sighed again. "The police know all this, but the last time I saw her, she kissed me on the cheek and winked and said she was drawing the whole neighborhood in—it was going to be great. We would have a citizen's crime watch to rival anything anywhere in the country. So, heading toward Johnson Square…she was seen there. A bit of her walking by was caught on a bank security camera. But you know that, right?"

"I have the files," Dallas said. "Do you think it's possible she was going to see Mr. Murphy that night?"

"Anything is possible. Like I said, she was talking to just about everyone—especially people with homes or businesses in the historic district." Harrington hesitated. "Now Simon Drake is gone, too. It's like there's a black hole out there somewhere—the two of them just stepped through it, and that was it!"

Dallas stood. "There are no black holes. The two of them

are somewhere. I do intend to find out where, Mr. Harrington. Thank you sincerely for your time. I know this is painful."

"Dunhill called you in, huh?" Harrington asked him.

"Yes."

"He's a good man. He never wanted to give up. He just walked that square night after night after Eliza disappeared. He went door to door. He searched and searched for her." He took a deep breath. "The law says an adult who wants to disappear has the right to do so—and at a point, I guess, the law has to give up. Joe never gave up, though. I'm grateful for that. Like I said, I know Eliza didn't suddenly choose to disappear. She loved her life, loved her work—loved me and my family. She'd have never done this to the people who cared about her. I know she's—dead. Thing is, whoever the hell killed her has to pay. They took her life—and they took a great woman from the city, and a great friend from people who loved her. I'm going to go out on a limb and say that Simon Drake is dead, too. Find who did this. Make them pay, Mr. Wicker. Can't bring back the dead, but hey—I'm human. I want them to hurt."

"I understand," Dallas said quietly. He thanked the man again for his time, and left the handsome offices on Bull Street that Eliza Malone had shared with Eli Harrington.

He believed Eliza and Simon were dead, as well.

Dallas began the walk back to McLane House; when he'd gone out that morning, Kristi had already been in the kitchen with Genie and Sydney—breakfast was being served. Kristi had given him a smile, and a kiss on the lips—in full view of her staff—before he'd headed out for the day.

He'd heard the titter of delighted laughter that had passed between Genie and Sydney, and he was sure Kristi had been quizzed mercilessly as soon as he had walked out of the kitchen.

He was glad; it made him smile just to think about her. It quickened his step to remember the details of the night they had shared.

When he'd passed through the parlor, Carl Brentwood had stopped him excitedly, and while he'd assured Carl he didn't want to be at the table for the séance, he was more than happy to be in the house and observe while it was going on.

The cameraman-slash-director, Matthew Guyer, arrived just as Dallas was leaving; Guyer wanted to do a number of interviews with people who worked for, or—in Shelley's case—were associated with McLane House.

Dallas had been tempted to stay and observe the interviews, but he'd also considered it important to speak with Eli Harrington as soon as possible. Dallas hadn't been in Savannah long, and cases could take a very long time to solve, but he couldn't help but feel a sense of urgency.

He wondered if it was a growing fear for Kristi's safety—something that went along with his growing desire. He tried to separate his feelings, but he knew, in this case, *feelings* were important—even those, or especially those, he had for Kristi.

She'd known Lachlan Plant, she'd been close to Ian Murphy...

At least, to the best of his knowledge, she'd had nothing to do with Eliza Malone or Simon Drake.

Everything seemed to be gelling on the one concept—each of those missing or dead had been involved with the city on some level—and the history of the neighborhood. Somehow, it tied into the Murphy place, or Ian Murphy...possibly the McLane house, and, perhaps, Jedidiah McLane as well.

They really needed to get into Ian Murphy's house again—and methodically go through every single book in his library. His books often were his notes—and his ideas, and his discoveries.

But first, he wanted to get back to McLane House.

And Kristi.

"This is wonderful, Kristi. Thank you so much!"

Kristi smiled broadly at Carl Brentwood. She was amazed

what her night with Dallas had done for her mood... Yes, her mind strayed now and again to his hands, the way they felt upon her flesh...

And today she felt she was looking at the world with new strength and optimism.

"I'm happy to do this," she assured Carl.

"I'm going to get the whole interview with you right in front of the monument, between the cherubs in the ground there," Matthew Guyer told her. He had his camera set on a tripod in the back of the courtyard. "I'm thinking you two just talk. Conversational. Tell Carl what you think he needs to know about McLane House. And don't worry about mistakes, do-overs or hesitations. I'm an excellent editor."

"Okay. Tell me when you're ready."

Matthew did a countdown and cued her. "We're rolling. Whenever you're ready."

Kristi began, "Savannah was captured by the British in early 1778. But all the powers that be knew it was important to hold the South, and especially the port of Savannah. Major General Benjamin Lincoln had just been appointed the Southern commander of the Continental Army. He needed people, first, and he needed more, and he asked for help from the French—and the Battle of Savannah was planned. During the war, Washington employed all manner of spies—and Justin McLane was one of those spies. While Lincoln planned his assault, Justin made his way into the city, pretending to be a merchant sympathetic to the loyalist cause. He gathered information to be brought to the troops outside the city—Savannah was surrounded by marshes, making it easier for men like Justin to navigate, and not so easy for those who did not know the terrain. Justin was able to come and go several times, and was aware of the plans being made in 1779. Meanwhile, sadly, mistakes were being made. General Casimir Pulaski came down with his Polish troops, and Admiral d'Estaing was enlisted to bring in his French naval fleet. Things might have gone well, but there was too much hesitation on the part of the Patriot forces, one section waiting for another when, if they'd attacked swiftly, they might have prevailed."

"That's history, isn't it?" Carl said. "We can always see clearly with hindsight."

"That's the way it is," Kristi agreed.

"Go on, please—what happened?"

"The Siege and Battle of Savannah turned into one of the bloodiest events of the revolution, and, in the end, many heroes were killed, and the British did not leave Savannah until 1782. The renowned Pulaski was killed in the engagement, as well as hero Lieutenant Justin—my ancestor. On his last trip out of the city, he was captured while leaving a tavern. Furious, his captors found out he was a loyal Patriot, and he owned property in the city. Legend has it he was dragged here on a cart, and hanged from one of the old oaks on the property. Luckily, his wife and son were in Charleston, and they survived, and when the war was over, this property came back to the McLane family. But Justin's body was never found, and it's presumed he was buried here in an unmarked grave. And, thus, you see, we have a lovely monument erected to him, honoring him, no matter where he may lie."

"And...cut! Perfect!" Matthew Guyer cried. "Just what we wanted—short and sweet and beautifully to the point. And the light was perfect. Oh, did you sign the waiver Claire had for you?"

"Yes, I signed a waiver," Kristi assured him.

Carl walked over to review the footage, and Kristi asked if they were finished with her.

They effusively thanked her again, and she headed into the house through the side doorway.

Genie and Sydney were busy setting out trays—food wouldn't go on them for a long time, but they were ready to roll things out when the time came.

"Tell me, isn't this going to be a little bit weird? Shelley is a psychic, right? But we're having our little tea and cocktail party before the séance—doesn't that mean she'll talk to people and figure them all out before we get to the séance?"

"Yes, I'm sure she plans on that," Kristi said, opening the refrigerator door and finding a bottle of water.

"Does it matter?" Sydney asked, hugging her arms to her chest rapturously. "We're going to be in a video with Carl Brentwood. Oh, Kristi, you'd see it, if you weren't so enamored of Mr. Wicker. Okay, okay, I get that, too, he's tall, blond and übermasculine! But hey—I'm younger. And Carl Brentwood is so hot!"

"Still, you two have to keep an eye on Shelley for me, huh?"

"We'll be there, the three of us," Genie assured her.

Kristi smiled and started into the back parlor. She hesitated; the room was empty. Walking to the back windows, she looked out.

Back out by the monuments, Carl and Matthew were chatting with Granger and Janet Knox's pretty young teen daughter, Lacey. Lacey was going to be interviewed about her stay at McLane House.

Shelley was also out in the yard, deep in conversation with Claire Danson. Carl's agent, Murray Meyer, went hurrying over to them; he seemed concerned.

The women glanced at one another as he approached, seeming cautious. Then they beamed broadly at him, laughing at something, and the moment was gone.

And, yet, walking through the house, and then back to the kitchen, Kristi couldn't help but wonder if Shelley had been planning something with Claire, something very sensational for the night to come.

CHAPTER EIGHT

Coming around the corner from Johnson Square and into the McLane house yard, Dallas saw Jonah, carefully pruning one of the magnolias in the front yard.

"Hey, there, son, heading back into the house?" Jonah called to him. And, as Dallas neared him, he added, "Be afraid. Be very afraid!"

Dallas stopped by the tree and Jonah. "Why's that?" he asked.

Jonah shook his head. "They've got ghosts coming out of the woodwork—and the séance hasn't even started yet," he said.

"Well, I guess Carl Brentwood will make the house famous," Dallas said.

Jonah scrunched his face as he looked up at his work. "The house is famous enough, the way I see it. Hell, whatever happened here…well, it was in the past, and a man was just doing what a man had to do, one way or the other." He shook his head.

"As far as bed-and-breakfast establishments go, yours is pretty small—seven rentable rooms. With this exposure, you know you'll get the attention you need to stay booked all the time," Dallas offered.

"She's a flimflam artist," Jonah said.

"You mean Shelley?" Dallas asked.

Jonah nodded. "She'll say whatever those people want to hear. You mark my words—she'll say anything at all."

"Well, Kristi will be at the séance—she'll watch what's going on."

"She will. That Kristi, she's a strong one. Stronger than she lets on." He grinned suddenly. "But then, you know that."

Dallas studied Jonah. The man obviously knew something was going on between Dallas and Kristi. He almost felt as if he needed to ask Jonah's permission to see Kristi, as if they had slipped back a hundred years and he needed someone's blessing.

"And thank the Good Lord!" Jonah said. "That girl, she gave up just about everything to make sure Jedidiah was okay, that he got out, that he did things. She looked after old man Murphy, too. She needs some fun, she needs someone…well, I guess you'll move on soon enough, but it's a fine thing to see her spending some time with you."

Dallas lowered his eyes for a moment, and then raised them to Jonah. "Jonah, I know she appreciates you—everything you do. Thanks to you, Genie and Sydney, she does have the help here to keep her being able to…have a life."

"She's a beautiful girl—and a fine one. Don't you forget that," Jonah said.

"I won't," Dallas said. He offered Jonah a smile. As he looked up, he saw the mannequin of Monty McLane, standing in the central second-floor window. "Guess I'll go on in and see what's going on. What time is the séance?" he asked.

Jonah laughed. "Not until darkness falls, of course. You and me—we're going to watch out for all those candles they'll have burning. Shelley is bringing in her crystal ball, and they're getting the table all set up. You ask me? That Carl Brentwood should be filming something at the Sorrel-Weed House. It's a museum—and it's got a legend, too. Mathilda Sorrel was supposed to have suffered fits of depression and then threw herself off the balcony to the courtyard. But there's also the story that Francis Sorrel was seducing a beautiful young slave. Those would be some interesting ghosts, right?"

"Right," Dallas agreed. He waved to Jonah and went up to the house. He didn't see Kristi in the parlor; he did run right into Shelley, Carl and the videographer, Matthew Guyer. Guyer introduced him to another three men: one who would be on the second camera after setting up some inconspicuous extra lighting around the room, and two soundmen.

"Will you be here?" Carl asked him.

"Oh, wouldn't miss it," Dallas said.

"Perfect—if you don't mind, we'll have you stand here—next to the mantelpiece. The main light switch is there—if anything goes terribly wrong or someone winds up too scared, we'll have you hit the lights right away," Carl said.

"Sure," he told Carl. "I'll be ready." And then he fled up the stairs. He tapped on Kristi's door, but she wasn't in her room. He started for his own room; he needed to call in to Krewe headquarters and report in—and find out if they had any new information for him.

But instead he walked down the hall, hesitated and then pushed open the door to the little room that had been set up something like an employee lounge—the little room that held the mannequin of Monty McLane.

He closed the door—he was looking at the back of the mannequin. But as he watched, it seemed that the mannequin turned, and approached. It was the ghost of Monty McLane.

"I like to invade my likeness at times—and watch the streets below. Sometimes I move a little and there's someone on the hearse tour or a walking tour who has a bit of a sense of something, and they see me—I give them a thrill," Monty told him.

"I'm sure the ghost tour operators are appreciative," Dallas said.

Monty shrugged and sat haphazardly down on the employee sofa, dangling a leg over the far-right arm of it.

"They're going to make a mockery of me tonight!" he said softly.

"Kristi won't allow it."

"And what shall she say? That her dead great-great whatever assured her he didn't kill his wife, that he loved Trinity with all his heart? They'll all just say, well, of course, that's the way you want to see it." The ghost let out a sound like a sigh. "There is no way to prove the truth—it all died all those years ago in 1864."

"Monty," Dallas asked, "who else is here? Am I missing anyone?"

Monty shook his head. "Justin is here...and I am here."

"You're sure?" Dallas asked.

"I have spent time eternal praying my Trinity was with us as well, that I could see her again, tell her how sorry I am...she died because of me." He looked sadly at Dallas. "Trust me...if she was here... I would have found her by now."

"Dallas?"

Kristi was calling him.

"Excuse me," he told the ghost of Monty McLane, and he stepped back out in the hallway.

"I heard you were back," she said. "I thought you might want to come with me...over to Ian's house. I just did a little bit about Justin McLane in the back. I'm getting aggravated, staying around here while they set up. Shelley is holding court, going on and on about the way she 'knows' the ghosts of McLane House, and I..."

He pulled her into his arms. They were alone in the hallway.

"Kristi, you can stop all this," he told her softly. "If it's bothering you, if you think Shelley is going to come out with all kinds of outlandish things..."

She shook her head. "No. I'm going to sit at that table—and if I see her moving the damn thing with her knee again, I'm going to call her out!"

"All right," he told her. "I'll be nearby. Watching out for...

well, I'm not sure what I'll be watching out for her. Shelley can only do so much damage," he said, and tried to assure her. "And, if you're worried, I'll be right there."

She nodded.

"So, shall we head to Ian's house?" he asked her, letting her out of his embrace.

"Of course, yes, yes, but—did you learn anything this morning?" she asked anxiously.

"Yes, I learned that Eliza Malone did know Ian—and she might well have been on the way to see him when she disappeared."

Kristi shook her head. "Eliza has been gone for two years—it doesn't make any sense that Ian might have some interesting information all the way back then that cost her…well, caused what happened."

"Let's see what we can find," he told her.

Kristi looked at the title of the book she was reading. It was not an imaginative title, but she noted the copyright on the book was 1908, and it had been written by a man who had been a Confederate soldier during the conflict. She'd known and read bits and pieces of several of Ian Murphy's books on the Civil War, and each time she did, she marveled that he had such an extensive library of collector's quality books.

This one had been written by a young enlistee named Anthony Jenkins who had joined the army at the tender age of eighteen, right after Georgia had become one of the first Southern slave states to form the Confederacy in 1861.

His parents had worked for a newspaper; he'd never owned a slave. In his preface, he talked about looking back over the years—while the years of Reconstruction had been brutal on many, he was glad the war had ended with the Union intact. The Great Conflict had brought together one of the greatest nations on earth. He was not trying to whitewash the South, just set the record straight. Many men in the Confederate government and army had been abolitionists—their loyalty to their native states had caused their involvement in what had been proved to be the wrong side of the war.

"Anything?" Dallas asked her.

She glanced up quickly, amazed to realize the tome she was reading had drawn her attention to the point where she'd lost herself.

And, she'd been drawn from the point as well that Ian's house now somehow disturbed her; it seemed at all times it was enshrouded in a strange mist, something that weighed heavy on the house, or on her.

Imagination… She expected a ghost to jump out of the woodwork at any minute.

Or worse…a killer.

Besides the fact that in a matter of days, she had become way too enamored of Dallas Wicker, she was very grateful he was there.

He carried a big gun.

"Regretfully, I've become totally engrossed by this man's writing—and it has nothing at all to give us. Ian has such an amazing library here, Dallas. This book—it's in excellent condition and it was published in 1908 by a young Confederate who survived the fighting, returned to Savannah and wrote his own impressions of the war."

"I hope Jamie Murphy appreciates this library," Dallas said.

"Oh, not to worry there. Jamie is a good kid. He'd never be careless with this treasure trove."

"Good to hear," Dallas murmured. He lifted the book he was reading. "This one is similar. It was actually in Ian's desk drawer, so I thought I'd read it next. It was written by a Union soldier who survived the war—he was with the troops who were billeted in what's now the Colonial Park Cemetery. He regrets the vandalism he and his fellows practiced in the cemetery—moving stones around and changing dates on them. Thing is, these books are so personal. This man, a career soldier named Emory Huntly, writes about the bitterness everyone was feeling by the end of the war. And, in his book, he admits that in hand-to-hand combat in the woods of Virginia, he and a Confederate came face-to-face—almost shot each other, and then walked away, as if they both knew they were family men, they had children, that, by then, they just wanted to survive."

"Would someone have killed over any of these stories?" Kristi asked. "The Civil War ended in 1865."

"And now, over a hundred and fifty years later, we're still trying to get past it. I don't know, Kristi. I don't get it either—but it does seem everyone who died or disappeared had something to do with Ian or Ian's house."

"Makes no sense," Kristi murmured.

Kristi sighed and walked over to where he had taken a seat on the floor in the midst of a pile of books. "I think it's fun and enlightening to read them," she said. "But history is known. There was a lot of ugliness. We all know that. History does not paint us as a very pretty people at times," Kristi added.

She hunkered down by him, but she didn't touch him. Something about Ian's house was making her feel uncomfortable. It was that miasma, as if something was just…maybe not evil, but horribly sad. And it shouldn't have been; Ian had led a great life. Jamie was a good man…the house should have had a feeling that was…good.

He looked at her curiously. "What is it?"

"I don't know…just a feeling. Like the air is somehow…wrong here. And I don't want to touch you here because I…don't want us tainted by it. That makes no sense, I know, but…"

He stood, drawing her to her feet. "We have to get back for the séance. But do you think it's okay if I take this book with me? I'd like to keep reading it."

"As long as you return it, I don't think Jamie will care in the least."

"Then let's get going," Dallas said.

Kristi hurried down the stairs; Dallas followed. She paused at the entry and turned back, thinking the miasma that haunted the place seemed to rise from the floor.

"What is it?" Dallas asked.

"I don't know. Crazy, huh?"

"Nothing is crazy," he assured her. "Well, a great deal in the world is crazy, but whatever you're feeling...no."

"You don't feel it?" she asked.

He shook his head. "Not as strongly as you clearly do. But that doesn't mean it doesn't exist," he said. "There are those who remain who want to be seen by everyone; there are those who remain who don't know how to be seen, and they have to try very hard, and perhaps reach out to someone they feel just might be the right one to accept them."

Kristi drew a breath and threw open the front door. Out in the sunshine, she turned back to him.

"I think I'd have had myself committed to a padded cell, if it hadn't been for you."

His eyebrows knotted together. "Kristi... I'm here for you, no matter what. You don't have to come to me...because..."

She laughed. "Oh, please, Agent Wicker... I can't believe you're not aware of your many assets!"

He laughed. "Well, thank you, Miss Stewart. Since, as I said, I've been absolutely infatuated since meeting you in my arms..."

She laughed and hurried ahead of him. He followed, and then paused, looking back at the house.

"What?" she asked him, and stopped. They were on the square now, but looking back, they could still see the Murphy house, historic and beautiful by day, and still...

A haunting edifice to the past.

He looked at her. "I feel like we're being watched."

"I told you—there's something there."

He was thoughtful, and shook his head. "I don't think we were being watched by any of the...dead. This is more real."

"But we were in there—we didn't see anyone. We didn't hear anything."

"Someone could have a key," he said.

"I guess, but I didn't even know that key was in my house—not until Jamie told me," Kristi said.

"Still, you run a bed-and-breakfast. People are free to enjoy the house—you've made it very open. They're welcome to get water or make coffee at any time, right?"

"Well, yes, but someone is usually always around. Genie and Sydney... Jonah. Someone is always around."

"Easy to slip into the kitchen, find the key, chat with someone and slip out—and then return the key once it's been copied."

"I guess—but why?"

"Have you had any strange or unusual guests or visitors?"

She gave him a perplexed and even slightly aggravated look. "Sometimes it's quite difficult to define strange or unusual. But I don't think so—why?"

"Because there is something in the Murphy house," he said softly. "We just have to figure out what the hell it is."

Ghosts were big business.

One of the major networks took a poll a few years back, and they'd learned that at least 50 percent of the population believed in ghosts, and thought they had seen a ghost or been touched by a ghost in some way.

That made it natural that Shelley Blake's séances should be a very popular occasion, and natural that a rising young star like Carl Brentwood—with his amazing social media platform—might well want to record a séance in a city like Savannah.

Kristi and Dallas arrived back in plenty of time for the pre-séance tea and cocktail hour. Carl Brentwood was somewhere right around twenty-one, but he had opted for tea. Of course, this was his business, and that he took it so seriously, Dallas thought, was admirable. But he'd liked the young man in general; he was boyish and upbeat, and always courteous and careful of the people around him.

Murray Meyer didn't seem particularly enthusiastic about what they were doing; while he was polite and respectful, he had a weary attitude about him most of the time, as if the business had done it's work on him, making him jaded—a "show me the money" man.

Claire Danson, on the other hand, seemed almost as excited at Carl.

"You can't imagine the power of social media these days," she told Dallas, helping herself to one of Genie's delectable little puff pastries.

Granger Knox told Dallas he was going along with the whole thing because of his daughter. "She's so excited. I just wish... I kind of wish the kid wasn't so nice. She's getting a bigger crush on him daily, and there's no future there. He'll go back to Hollywood, and we'll go home, too."

Janet walked up while they were talking. She had heard her husband's words. "But, Granger, my love, she'll always have this! She'll always be able to say she was in a video with Carl Brentwood. And how do we know? Maybe one day our little girl will be just as popular as Mr. Brentwood. She's very serious about pursuing her acting career. And," she added, smiling at Dallas, "she's been accepted into the program at NYU."

"Congratulations," Dallas said. He'd noted that, as expected, Shelley had been talking with everyone during the cocktail party—which would, of course, make it easy for her to hone in on what her séance attendees wanted to hear.

Shelley suddenly spread her arms toward the heavens and spoke loudly.

"A full moon tonight, my friends—a beautiful full moon. The moon, of course, has powers, you know."

"One of them is called gravity," Granger commented.

Shelley paused in her dramatics to look at him and smile indulgently. "Yes, the moon has gravitational influence, that is true, controlling the tides, and perhaps a great deal more. A full moon has been known throughout history and culture for its powers. I find it quite fitting that tonight, we will have the full moon with us. We will begin shortly."

"I'm going to go take my seat," Janet said. "Granger, dear, come along. We'll put Lacey next to Mr. Brentwood—that will give her the most exposure."

Granger made a face and followed his wife.

Dallas heard footsteps on the stairs and looked up. Kristi was coming down, followed by the ghosts of the house, Monty and Justin. She shrugged, smiling as she met up with him and whispered, "They've promised to observe—and to behave."

Dallas nodded gravely to the two of them.

"Kristi is going to protect us," Justin assured him.

"Protect me—no one disputes the fact you were a hero," Monty told Justin gravely. "Thank goodness for that, at least."

The sound guys had wired everyone with small microphones, and the cameramen had taken their positions; Genie and Sydney and Jonah had done a quick runaround, picking up plates and glasses.

"Take your seats. I'll fix the room," Shelley said. "Now, I know we're filming, but we can't have the house alive, blazing with lights."

"It's all right, Shelley," Carl assured her. "They're working with the right equipment. They'll pick up what's going on, even in low light."

"All right, then!" Shelley said, beaming. She'd dressed the part again, with a silk scarf tied around her head and a flowing caftan over her simple, floor-length dress. She'd brought her crystal ball, and it sat dead center in the table.

Dallas leaned against the wall, by the side of the fireplace. Jonah was standing guard at the archway to the kitchen.

"Miss Stewart, it's your house. I'd be honored if you'd sit next to me," Carl Brentwood told Kristi.

Kristi smiled, and took the seat he offered. Next to her were Claire, Murray and Genie—and then Shelley.

On Carl's other side were Lacey, Janet, Granger and Sydney.

Sydney was clearly excited; Genie looked a little bit wary.

"We're rolling," said Matthew Guyer quietly. "Go ahead whenever you're ready."

"All hold hands, please," Shelley asked. "We've gathered here tonight to speak with the ghosts of McLane House. This home has witnessed approximately two hundred years of history, and been here through what has been good, heroic and magnificent, and through what has been ugly and painful, as well. The crystal on the table will help harness energy, and yet, we must all understand that spirits will appear when they wish, and so, we must hold our own bond. We believe the spirit of Trinity McLane, shot down and thrown into the earth, restlessly roams the house. We believe, too, that Justin McLane might well be here, and perhaps Jedidiah, who has not been gone so very long."

Dallas heard a sniff near him—it was Monty. He looked very offended.

"Hold hands, my friends, do not break the chain. Feel the warmth and life of one another, and look into the crystal ball." She paused for a long moment, then raised her voice slightly. "Spirits of McLane House. We seek to commune with you. None comes to offer harm. If anything, we wish to help you. If you wish to move on, we would help you move on. If you wish to speak, please speak." She suddenly began to weave, a keening sound coming from her lips. "I feel them," she whispered. "They are among us."

Dallas looked over at Kristi. To his surprise, she was staring hard at the crystal ball, and she looked as if she was deeply disturbed.

"What's going on?" Dallas murmured softly.

"We're right here," Justin told him. "We're not doing a thing."

"Give us a sign, of spirits, we beg of you!" Shelley said.

Lacey Knox gasped suddenly, eyes wide. "I feel... I feel a presence."

"I feel it, too," Granger said, as if totally confused by whatever it was that he was feeling.

"Who is it who is with us?" Shelley asked. "Trinity...are you here? Are you hoping to move on? We know how brutally your life ended, shot down by love... Are you with us? Let us know, give us a sign."

Nothing. Shelley didn't even try to jostle the table.

"I feel it, too... Maybe it's Justin...or Monty!" Lacey said.

"I really feel something," Claire Danson said, the look on her face amazed.

Then, the table did jostle. That brought about a series of gasps—from everyone but Kristi.

She was still just staring at the crystal ball. She seemed transfixed, and unaware of everyone around her.

And then even Dallas felt it—something.

It was as if a strange mist had settled over the house, concentrated on the table. It gave the impression of something painful, hurt and remembering...and still hurting.

"Kristi," Carl Brentwood whispered.

Kristi didn't seem to hear him.

"I do believe it is Monty McLane, forced to wander these rooms for all eternity, for the terrible wrong he did," Shelley announced.

"Damn that fake of a woman!" Monty's ghost declared. "I am tempted to knock the table over—right on top of her."

"That would just confirm for certain that she had summoned you," Justin said. "And that she was right about you."

Kristi spoke up, sounding almost as if she was the medium—and had gone into a trance. "It's not Monty, and I do not believe he gunned down the woman he loved. It's not Monty, and it's not Justin…and it's…not a spirit of this house!"

Now Shelley looked shocked; she knew Kristi didn't set much store in any séance, and so she was the least likely of the group to say a ghost was among them.

All eyes were on Kristi—in Shelley's view, it must seem she was stealing the spotlight.

But Shelley was a show-woman, and she quickly rallied. "Sometimes…sometimes a spirit is known more to one than to others. Kristi, can you tell us what happened to this ghost? Who—is it, then?"

"It is a woman," Kristi said, seemingly mesmerized by the crystal ball. "She is crying out for help. She lost her life near here, and…"

Kristi stopped speaking.

"A woman—who lost her life near here?" Granger asked, his voice harsh. "No, there is no woman… I feel it. It—wouldn't be a spirit who doesn't belong here. Kristi, concentrate. It is Monty, and he is tricking you!"

"He knows how you feel, Kristi," Shelley said. "He is pretending he is someone else, because he does not like to be blamed for what happened."

"Monty did not kill his wife and father," Kristi said.

"Perhaps it is Trinity, to tell us all the…truth…" Lacey Knox said, as if she had to speak—lest she go unnoticed in the video.

"It is not Trinity," Kristi said.

She hadn't stopped looking at the crystal ball; Dallas didn't think she had even blinked.

And, while he didn't know if others saw it or felt, he was convinced there was a mist in the room, that something was happening…that someone, other than Monty and Justin, was really there.

Something, *someone*, felt by the others, but only seen by Kristi.

"I'm so cold!" Claire said, shivering.

"Of course, because a presence is among us!" Shelley said.

"She is here, and she is determined, she needs help, but she will stay until the truth is known," Kristi said.

She even *looked* as if she was in a trance.

"Who? Who is she?" Murray Meyer demanded.

Shelley was no longer the star of the little charade; all eyes were on Kristi. "She knew—she knew secrets," Kristi whispered.

"You mustn't let the spirits fool you," Shelley said. "Monty!" she cried out. "Please, Monty, I know you are here, and you must behave. What you did, you did for love. It was not right, but we can understand. You fought so hard. You were stationed at the fort, but the Yankees had the fort. And the city fathers surrendered. You just wanted to see your beautiful wife again, talk to her, touch her. Perhaps you'd even heard rumors that Colonel Albert Huntington meant to take your home—*your home*—as his headquarters. Perhaps you'd even heard that Trinity had approached him, maybe begging for mercy for herself and your father and the house, and that…mercy had a price. You are not condemned, sir. What you did, you did in a fit of rage, and today, you would be understood in our courts, and…"

"Shelley," Kristi said flatly, her eyes off of the crystal at last and onto the medium, "that's not what happened. The only account of what happened was in records written by Colonel Huntington—and what do you think he would say? He would have been called upon to answer for the cold-blooded murder of a civilian woman and two others!"

"Blaming the Yankees," Shelley murmured.

"I am not blaming the Yankees—it was a war, and both sides believed they were right, and that God was on their side. I'm speaking about one man."

Dallas had to wonder just why she had ever agreed to sit at the table. But if she hadn't been there, Shelley might have had them all convinced Monty McLane had been a monster—and not only was Trinity there with them, but she was trying to serve them all tea.

Dallas was tempted to stride over and assure Shelley she didn't know what the hell she was talking about.

He held on to his temper, watching Kristi again, trying to ascertain what she had seen.

"Kristi, Kristi, you are making the spirits afraid, they are backing away!" Shelley said.

"No, no, not at all," Carl Brentwood said. "This is really happening. It's settled over Kristi, I can feel it coming for her. The cold wafting over me, I just can't see…but I can feel, and there is someone here!" He was staring at Kristi with amazement.

"Who is she, Kristi, who is she?" Claire Danson demanded softly.

"I—I don't know. She's gone," Kristi said.

She was lying; Dallas was sure. Kristi was seeing something… someone. And he couldn't see them, and apparently, neither could Justin or Monty.

"What the hell?" Justin muttered, walking over to the table.

"There's still someone here," Murray said, frowning.

"I believe it's Justin now," Kristi said softly, turning her attention back to the ball.

"She knows damned well it isn't me," Justin murmured, taking a few steps towards the table. "She knows that…she knows that I'm over here."

"She has a reason," Dallas said as softly as he could, eyeing the cameraman—Matthew—nearest him. But Matthew didn't hear him. He, too, was focused on Kristi.

Shelley tried to seize hold of the séance once again. "Justin, yes, it is you! And we're so sorry you died so young! We honor you, sir, as the great hero you are. Thank you, thank you so much…"

Justin stepped away from the table, looking back at Dallas.

"That woman is so full of…of horse dung!"

"It's gone," Carl Brentwood said. "Gone…it's warm again, the feeling is gone, the sensation was gone, but…it was here!"

Shelley moaned and closed her eyes. "They have left us…"

She allowed her head to crash dramatically to the table.

Jonah flicked on the lights by the archway door. Shelley lifted her head.

"That is all for tonight, my friends. We have contacted the spirits of the house, and they have given of themselves, and now…they are gone. Thank you all, thank you for your steadfast and giving participation. And I thank the moon as well, for, as I said, that moon has power, and that beautiful power came through for us tonight."

She rose; Carl Brentwood did the same, turning to his cameraman. "It was real!" he said excitedly. "Real—oh, my God, I felt it! It's true—McLane House is totally haunted!"

"Cut!" Matthew called. "Shelley, that was great—absolutely great! And Kristi, you were magnificent. We're going to set up for post-séance interviews. Kristi, I'm hoping you'll talk to me, and maybe—"

"I don't know who she was," Kristi said. "I just don't know. Excuse me."

Kristi stood, and raced up the stairs.

CHAPTER NINE

Kristi had fled to her room quickly—but not fast enough to outrun the real haunts of McLane House.

"I felt her, too—I mean, I know someone was there, a woman, if you say so—but I didn't see what you saw," the ghost of Justin McLane told Kristi, frustrated. "I mean, well, you're saying it was a 'her,' and I'm assuming you're correct. Many generations' granddaughter, you are truly gifted. We could see that you were experiencing something, but we couldn't see what you were seeing—even I, a ghost, must admit it was quite a spectacle." He paused and looked over at Monty. "Do you think it was Trinity?" he asked softly.

"No," Monty said. "Don't you think I'd know if it was my wife? I pray daily I might somehow see her, feel her, touch her again!"

"It wasn't Trinity," Kristi said.

Then the knock she was expecting came at her door, and she hurriedly opened it, allowing Dallas to come in.

The first thing he did was take her anxiously by the shoulders.

"Are you all right?" he asked. "I came as soon as I could get away."

She loved the worried look in his eyes, and his touch on her, as if he would battle the world or anyone in it—for her.

"I'm all right. I think I handled it all okay."

"Yes, you did," Dallas said. "And you thrilled everyone down there. But, Kristi, what did you see?"

She closed her eyes. She still couldn't believe it had happened; she just simply hadn't believed Shelley could summon any real spirits.

And she certainly hadn't called anyone she'd intended to!

But looking into the crystal ball, Kristi had seen a face. She'd thought it a trick at first—a projection somehow orchestrated by Shelley or the cameraman or someone who wanted a spirit to appear—one way or another—in the video.

But there was nothing artificial about the face; it had been that of an older woman, terribly distressed. She had looked straight at Kristi, and she had said, "Help me, please, dear God, help me!"

"I saw a woman's face, in the crystal," Kristi explained quickly. "And..." She paused, remembering the way the woman had looked at her, and how she had looked around nervously when the others had been saying they felt something, too...

"Oh!" she whispered suddenly.

"What is it?" Dallas asked.

"She was afraid... I think she was afraid of someone in the room!"

Dallas looked at her, frowning. "Did you recognize her? Was she someone you had seen before?"

Kristi thought about that for a moment and then said slowly, "Maybe. She wasn't someone familiar, or even someone I knew as a casual friend. But you may be right... I may have seen her at some time. Passed her on the street, in a store, something like that."

Dallas stared at her one more moment and then strode over to her computer. He keyed in something and then called over to her.

He'd pulled up the picture of a woman, perhaps in her fifties, attractive and with a beautiful smile.

It was the face she had seen.

She gasped. "It was Eliza Malone! Oh, I should have known right away. I remember when she went missing, the police and everyone tried so hard to find her. I should have seen it immediately. I should have let her know that I… I'd help her!"

"So…she is dead," Dallas murmured.

"Maybe not!" Kristi said. "Maybe she's imprisoned somewhere, and she managed to astral project herself to me. She was asking for help. Because she wants to be found."

Dallas was silent. Monty McLane placed a ghostly hand on her shoulder.

"Kristi, she was asking for help because she wants her body to be found—and for whoever took her…killed her, to be brought to justice."

Kristi sank down on her bed, still shaken. "I should have told her somehow that we'd help her," she muttered. "Except, how do we? People have been searching for her over the last two years…"

"She disappeared, and she was murdered," Dallas said. "And what we have to do is find the body. Kristi, she appeared before you because you can help."

"How?"

"Because she's here."

"In this house?" Kristi demanded.

He shook his head and said gently, "Not necessarily in this house, but somewhere near."

"So…we start digging up the streets?" Kristi asked. "It looked like someone was already digging in the yard."

"Yes…and no, of course not, in regards to the streets," Dallas told her. "We try to make contact again," he said softly.

Kristi sank down on her bed.

"We can take to the streets," Monty said, "get out there, wander around—see if somehow we can find her. The thing is…"

"Thing is," Justin said, "it's not easy to learn how to make contact—when you're dead. Monty and I have been around a very long time. For years, I could see people...and they couldn't see me. Well, only certain people ever really have that kind of sight anyway, but it takes time and trying and learning to materialize."

"But she's desperate. She wants justice," Kristi said.

Justin added, "There are times when the dead are just excellent—fast learners. With a natural talent. Just as some people are born artists or musicians, some of the dead just...hit the streets running, so to say."

"But not all that often. She may be very hard to find," Monty said.

Dallas had been listening to the ghosts; he'd also been thoughtful.

"You said you thought she was afraid of someone at the table?" he asked Kristi.

"When she first appeared, she was looking right at me. Then she looked around, and something changed, and she was gone," Kristi said softly. "But the Knox family isn't from around here—neither are Carl, Claire or Murray. The only people who might have been here two years ago are Jonah, Genie and Sydney."

Dallas had pulled out his phone and was going to call someone.

"No, oh, no! I have known them all forever," Kristi said. "They aren't murdering people. It's impossible."

Dallas ignored her; she didn't know who he was talking to, but whoever it was, he didn't have to exchange a lot of niceties—he was giving whoever it was the names of everyone in the house: the help and the guests.

"I'm telling you—it's impossible," she whispered. "I shouldn't have told you anything, I should have just...just waited, or..."

"Kristi, stop it!" Dallas said. "I'm not accusing your people of anything. I'm having the best people in the world find out everything they can about everyone who is in this house."

She fell silent, knowing he was right—and resenting it anyway.

"Jonah was with me when Jedidiah died. Genie and Sydney were wonderful. They cared for him in a way you could never imagine," she said after a moment.

"I told you—I'm not accusing them," Dallas said quietly.

She didn't answer. There was a knock at her bedroom door and she hurried over to swing the door open.

Carl Brentwood was standing there, hand raised ready to knock again.

"Kristi!" he said.

"Carl, what can I do for you?" she asked, trying to smile as normally as possible.

"First, I want to thank you—you did amazing, Kristi! And then, I'd love to interview you again. Would you please…"

He broke off, seeing that Dallas had come up behind her.

"I'm so sorry—I didn't mean to interrupt."

"It's all right. We were just talking."

"About the séance?" he asked eagerly, excited.

"Not exactly," she murmured.

He looked awkward.

"It's fine, really," she said.

"Well…then, I…uh… Could I talk to you again?" Carl asked.

"Talk to me?" she repeated.

"About the séance, I mean. It was… Wow. I know you weren't sure about doing the video, but it's going to be amazing, and I'm promising to do good things with it."

"Carl, I'll do an interview, but you don't know what I will say," she told him. "I don't know myself."

"It's all right—you say what you think and what you feel."

She could feel Dallas was behind her, ready to protest on her behalf.

"Sure, I'll come right now," she said, heading out of her room. She turned back and looked at Dallas. He could follow—or not.

She shouldn't be upset with him; Dallas played it logically, by the book. He was an investigator... He was FBI, after all. And people had died.

It was just that everything around her suddenly seemed to be different from what she had known and loved all her life.

They had to be wrong. Just because Eliza Malone's face had appeared in a crystal ball, the woman didn't have to be dead. It didn't mean McLane House was involved.

But Kristi was afraid. And she had never felt fear like this before.

She hurried down the stairs. Both parlors were still a bevy of activity.

Genie was excited, running up to Kristi as she came down the stairs. "Oh, Kristi, that was incredible. I've been in this house for years and...when I think about it, now and then, I'd get a feeling of the temperature changing, or maybe even of someone nearby, watching, but, well, I'd brush it off. But after tonight... I believe there are ghosts in this house," she said.

"Genie, I'm so glad you had a good time," Kristi said.

Genie looked behind Kristi, where Dallas had followed her. "Mr. Wicker, you should have been at that table. Or, maybe you didn't have to be. Did you feel it, too? It was like the air changed, as if, as if you could *feel* that someone else was there. Kristi—you're a catalyst! Oh, my God, being there with you was amazing—scary as all get-out, but so amazing. Mr. Wicker, from where you were, did you...get that?"

"Ah, Genie, I was just an observer, you know."

"Good for an investigator to be an observer," Genie said.

"Always," Dallas said, his tone pleasant.

Carl came through from the other parlor and said to Kristi, "I think Matthew is ready—if you will?"

"Sure, why not?" she said softly, trying to sound pleasant.

Matthew was set up right by the stairs; she realized he could easily get shots of his interviewee—and of the portraits that lined the stairway walls. Of course—she doubted Carl would work with anyone who wasn't good at what they did.

"Kristi, I'll put you right here," Matthew told her. "And Carl right beside."

"Perfect," Kristi murmured. She was aware Genie and Dallas had gone to stand behind him and that the others were coming in from the front parlor. Jonah leaned against the kitchen archway, much as he had done during the séance itself. Sydney was near him, grinning and rolling her eyes, as if in disbelief Jonah might still think it was all a sham.

Kristi didn't see Shelley, which surprised her.

She'd have thought Shelley would have dramatically worked her moment as long as she possibly could.

Maybe she'd gone to the kitchen, or elsewhere. Perhaps even outside—to commune with the beautiful and giving full moon.

"Where are the rest of your crew?" Kristi asked Matthew.

"Had to film another excursion tonight—at another house," Matthew explained briefly.

"And where's Shelley?"

"Oh, we interviewed her first. She was on such a high—but said she had to leave, too—had something else to do," Carl said.

"I see," Kristi murmured, looking around at the others.

Murray, the staid and gentlemanly agent, still looked a little thunderstruck—as if he had felt something himself, but didn't trust his own senses.

"Quiet, people, please!" Matthew called out. "You're all welcome to be here, but the little microphones are sensitive. You can be here, just…you need to keep quiet."

"Yes, of course," Claire demurred, and then a hush fell over the room.

Everyone was watching.

Everyone.

Justin and Monty had made an appearance as well; they were standing near Dallas, as if they were a band of close friends.

"Kristi," Matthew said. "Just answer any way you like. We're trying to be real—not sensationalist."

"Sure," she muttered.

Matthew raised his fingers, starting a countdown, out loud at first, and then in silence as he got to three, two, one.

"Kristi Stewart—owner of the McLane house, descendent of the family—we want to thank you again for allowing us to have this séance, and to film it for those who might want to come to beautiful Savannah, and McLane House."

Kristi smiled. "It can be very beautiful, yes."

"McLane House," Carl said. "Your house—with a twisted and sad history."

"I've already spoken about Justin McLane," she said pleasantly.

"You have. And Shelley believes he was here with us tonight, but, Kristi—you had me shaking! Through you, I felt cold, and a strange swirling darkness, and a—a presence."

"Old houses can be drafty," Kristi said.

Carl smiled. "You said...she's here. But it was not Trinity McLane. Who was it?"

"Who knows?" Kristi asked. "It was a séance. And we're all very susceptible to suggestion. I thought I saw a face, but..."

"Trinity."

"Definitely not Trinity." Kristi offered him as sweet and giving a look as she could manage. "I would know if it was her—I grew up with the legend of this house."

"Ah, yes, but—that's just it! What everyone finds so fascinating is the story about Trinity and Monty McLane."

"All we know for sure is a story," Kristi said. "We have no facts surrounding any of it."

"But it's Trinity, they say, who haunts the house. And there was speculation of an affair between her and Colonel Huntington, wasn't there?" Carl said.

"There's absolutely nothing in history to indicate that. And the only report of the action at the house came from Albert Huntington himself. Many people believe Huntington wound up shooting and killing Trinity by accident—when she jumped in front of her husband, probably not believing that Huntington would shoot her. You have to remember, by the time Savannah surrendered, bitterness was running really high. We Americans today are grateful to be the country we are—always imperfect, but ever striving for unity, for equality, and all good things. But back then..."

"Kristi, tonight, we all really felt something. It was amazing. I've been at a séance here before, and it was great, but tonight— tonight was the next level. I can't help but feel it's because you were there, with us, that perhaps the ghosts of the house long to talk to you."

She forced a smile. "Oh, I think if the ghosts of the house wanted to have a conversation with me, they would just come right out and do so."

"But everything seemed to center on you, Kristi. We all know you saw something, someone—the 'her' you were saying you saw. We felt the presence. I still get shivers—I was so glad to be next to you!"

"Hard to tell after a séance, isn't it?" she asked sweetly. "We were all holding hands, the lights were low and, beyond a doubt, we felt the past, we felt history sweeping through us."

"Kristi, please, be honest. Did the ghost of Trinity touch you tonight?" he asked very softly and very seriously.

"I, like you, can't explain exactly what I saw or felt. But there is one thing of which I'm certain—the ghost of Trinity McLane was not here tonight, and I'm equally certain we don't know the true story of what happened. But my strong feeling is that Monty McLane did not kill his wife."

She could see Dallas was smiling—as were the two ghosts by his side.

She was doing all right; holding her own.

"But, Kristi, you *saw* a woman. You were looking into the crystal ball, and you said, 'She's here,' or something close to that. And the whole room was chilled, and we all felt it."

"Honestly, who knows what I really saw. In my mind, yes, there was a face in the crystal ball. Now the lights are on, the mystery is gone..."

"But it wasn't Trinity."

"No, I can assure you emphatically, it was not Trinity."

"Do you think Justin looks out for his heirs on this property? He never did live in the house—it was built after he was killed."

"He never lived in this house, no. I guess we've been pretty pragmatic about keeping the property and now the house in the family. Who knows? Don't we all want to believe those who have gone before us look out for us?" she asked.

"Of course."

"So." She shrugged. "Maybe he is a kind and benevolent ghost, looking out for us."

"Ah, well, maybe one day, the truth will come to light!" Carl said. "However, whatever, you were incredibly special tonight, and I am honored to have been by your side. You have something—something very special."

"Thank you," she told him.

"McLane House is haunted," Carl said. "You'll never convince me otherwise."

Kristi smiled directly at the camera. "Perhaps, but if so— they are the warmest and most welcoming ghosts you'll ever want to meet!"

"And I can attest to that—everyone at McLane House is warm and welcoming. Kristi, thank you!"

"Carl, thank you!"

Matthew lifted a hand in the air, indicating a wrap; they both smiled at the camera.

"Cut! Perfect!" Matthew said. "Well, almost perfect. I mean,

it would have been perfect if you had seen Trinity tonight, but...
hey, we said we wanted the truth."

Kristi rose, removing her microphone to hand back to Matthew.

"I didn't see Trinity," Kristi said.

"Oh, wouldn't it be cool if we could just see her," Sydney
said. "I look at her portrait on the stairway often enough, and I
even talk to her when I'm working sometimes."

"How scary!" Lacey Knox said, shivering. Janet protectively
set an arm around her shoulders.

"Not scary at all," Sydney assured her. "I love to believe she's
here, that she wanders the halls, and maybe...maybe cares for
people. If she's here, she's not mean—she's just lonely."

"You know," Murray announced, looking at Carl and shaking his head, "maybe it's a good thing Trinity isn't here—as
Kristi says. I mean, the past was ugly. Slavery was ugly. What
the North often did to the South in retribution was ugly. The
past should be the past—and we should look to the way we behave in the future."

"And think!" Granger said. "People have to learn to think
differently—and behave like a group of human beings, and that
as humans, we're all the same, no matter where we came from,
what country."

"That was beautiful, Granger!" his wife said.

Kristi smiled. "And a worthy notion. You should be in politics."

"I've thought about it. We have to quit putting bandages on
situations—and get to the root of the disease," Granger said,
nodding appreciatively to Kristi. "I've even looked into running, starting small, you know—and maybe moving on up."

"Dad, you're actually too good a man to be a politician,"
Lacey told him.

"There is that!" Carl said, laughing.

Genie, who had been quiet and in the background, spoke up then.

"The man who just went missing... Simon Drake. I'd watched him speak. I'd read up on him, and knew a lot about his beliefs—and his private life. He was a good man. A really good man," she said somberly.

The others, Kristi noted, were uncomfortably silent. They'd been casually chatting—and Genie had brought up a bad situation.

"Maybe the police will find him, Genie," Sydney said.

Kristi didn't think she could just stand there any longer. The distance of time from the séance really was making her wonder exactly what she had seen, and being in the group was making her uneasy—she needed to get away.

"Well, excuse me, will you," Kristi said. She looked across the room at Jonah—who still seemed to be shaking his head over the entire event. "We need to finish tidying up, and I, at least, have to get some sleep. I'm too old for a really late night."

Sydney laughed softly. "Kristi! You're not that old—though, Genie, Jonah, I don't know about the two of you."

"Hey!" Jonah protested.

Sydney laughed softly. "I'm meeting some friends down on the riverfront. Lacey, I was thinking, you want to come with me?" She turned quickly to Lacey's parents. "We won't be drinking—there's just a good band playing, and it's a brewery that makes its own root beer and ginger beer, too. I promise, we won't contribute in any way to her delinquency. Oh!" She turned, suddenly hesitant, to Carl. "You're invited, too, of course, Carl—I can't tell you how I'd impress my friends, bringing you along. Oh, okay—everyone is invited. It's a great rock band that's playing—they do their own things, and they cover old dudes, too, great dudes we've lost, like Tom Petty, George Harrison and even Johnny Cash, Elvis, Freddie Mercury and Roy Orbison!"

"I've seen them—the Savannah Six," Kristi said, turning to

Granger and Janet Knox. "They're an excellent band. And the brewery is family oriented, and they craft the best root beer I've ever tasted."

She didn't care what they did; she just wanted to escape herself. But she forced herself to behave normally.

"Mr. Wicker—you would love it," Sydney said.

Dallas smiled. "I'd love to some time. I have work tonight. Give me a rain check, will you?"

"You're just going to go on now? It's ten o'clock," Granger said.

"Um, not that late," Sydney said sweetly. She cleared her throat. "For a lot of people, the night is just beginning."

"We're not a lot of people," Granger said.

"Certainly not, sir," Sydney murmured, looking at Kristi.

"The bands don't even start playing until nine or ten most of the time," Kristi said. "Like I said, I'm heading up to bed for the night, and you all can get some sleep—or go be tourists and have a nice night out!"

She turned, heading into the front parlor and gathering up the last cups and saucers and a wineglass. Sydney followed her. "Hey, I didn't mean to be rude to a guest."

"You weren't. Lacey Knox is eighteen. Nice that she respects her parents, but if she wants to go with you...never mind. It isn't my business."

Sydney walked across the room, finding a leftover pastry plate. "I think we've got it all—oh, and I won't be late in the morning. I promise."

"I'm not worried," Kristi assured her.

As she spoke, Janet Knox came hurrying into the room, smiling broadly. "We're going—we're all going. I mean, Granger and I—and that amazing Carl Brentwood. Would you believe that? He's going to come out with us common folk! What a fine, nice man," she said.

"He is a very fine, nice man," Kristi agreed, softly beneath her breath, "but a human being, and not a saint!"

Sydney heard her; Janet didn't. Janet's hands were clasped rapturously.

Kristi didn't care; she was just eager for them all to leave.

They took too long for Kristi's state of mind. She smiled and hurried into the next room and asked Jonah if he minded making sure they were all set, and when he assured her he was just fine watching their part of the evening wind down, she flew back upstairs—aware that Dallas saw her go, but he was politely listening to Carl, Claire and Murray as they explained the importance of Carl's online presence.

When the group was all out, he would head up, she knew.

Up in her room, she sat down at her work desk, remembering she had deadlines.

But she couldn't concentrate. All she could do was sit there and see, in her mind's eye, the face in the crystal ball, and the way the woman knew her, and how she asked for help.

The house was quiet—the ghosts had made themselves scarce.

Maybe they, too, were headed for a night out on the town.

Eventually, she turned away from her computer, having written one line. She headed back downstairs, and found Jonah watching sports in the back parlor.

"Hey—everyone left?" she asked.

"They all went to the riverfront, except for Genie, and Mr. Wicker told Genie he'd give her a ride home. He should be back soon. And me... I am just enjoying the peace and quiet." He shook his head. "That whole group of our guests...excepting, of course, Mr. Wicker, all decided they must enjoy that fine moon and walk to the river—a few blocks. With or without the moon, it would be foolish not to walk, but they were all going on and on about it. Hey. Fine performance tonight, Kristi."

"Pardon?"

He laughed. "I know you don't set any more store in ghosts

than I do—but the way you were staring at that crystal ball and going on? Bravo!"

She smiled weakly. "Glad you enjoyed it."

"Honestly, I enjoyed my chats with Jedidiah—and with old man Murphy. Jedidiah and I... When we were younger, we used to love all that reenactment jazz. Him and me, we fought tons of battles over and over again. We listened to some of the best historians in the world, and you know what I learned?"

"What's that?"

"That everything in life—and probably death—is perspective. We all sat in this same room tonight—and saw something different. Hell, if we all went to the same movie, we'd see something different. Even the weather—to some, it's too hot. To some it's too cool." He shrugged. "And as far as war goes, well, hell, the truth is always in the winning, right?"

She smiled.

"Perspective—you're right. It all has to do with who is looking at what." She paused and said, "Thank you, Jonah. Thanks for your help—and your logic and perspective!"

"Night, Kristi. You get some rest, huh?"

"Yes, sir!"

She left him and hurried upstairs and got ready for bed. A hot shower was delicious. She thought about trying to work again, but she was far too restless.

Maybe she should have gone to the riverfront herself.

She turned on the television.

The news was on. The national news was usually wild enough to engross anyone these days, no matter what one's political thinking. But it was a local broadcast; the police were speaking with a reporter, once again asking for help in the disappearance of Simon Drake.

And they compared it to the still-unsolved disappearance of Eliza Malone just two years earlier.

They showed a smiling Eliza, speaking at a high school.

And it seemed to Kristi that, even in the TV footage, the woman was looking at her, heartsick and earnest.

"Why won't you help me?" she whispered, staring hard at Kristi. "Please help me."

CHAPTER TEN

"They're all such nice people," Genie told Dallas as he drove. "When Jonah told me we were having a young actor, I was not pleased—especially when he was booking three rooms for himself, his media person or whatever and his agent. I mean, I watch TV. Actors can be all worried about people getting in their space, but from the shows I've seen, the managers and agents and all are worse. Demanding. But I was wrong. Carl is just as nice as can be—he stops on the streets and signs autographs when people ask him. He's just kind and good with people all the time, and while I'd never heard of him, Sydney assures me he's really famous. And Claire actually picks up after herself, and Murray is quieter, but he's fine, too."

"So, you've enjoyed having them there," Dallas said.

"Oh, yes."

"And what about the Knox family?"

"Oh, they're nice. Granger is always worried about his daughter, his daughter is always trying to do something on her own and Janet is just fine. They're fine—they're just like the usual guests, you know." She paused and turned and grinned at him. "And you're really okay, too, by the way."

"Thanks." He drove in silence for a minute and then asked, "What about Shelley? How do you like having her out?"

"Shelley... Well, she's... Shelley. She's been coming around as long as I can remember. Jedidiah used to just sigh when she came out with things like, 'Oh, Trinity, you poor sweetie, I feel you... oh, yes, I feel you and your pain!' She's very dramatic and likes to play the part. But hey, it's her living. She's just a little over-the-top for me. I think she irritates Kristi though. I mean, Kristi is Kristi—she's just nice to everyone and didn't want to upset the cart after Jedidiah died. I mean, we all kind of waited—Sydney, Jonah and me. We didn't know if she'd want to clean house and start over, but she was so sweet, said she needed all of us. She wanted to keep working on her own business... With us still at the house, she could. But she pitches in, and once she told me she never understood why anyone would fix what wasn't broken. And the thing is with Shelley, well, I don't think Kristi would hurt her by bringing in someone else after all these years, but she is absolutely convinced that the story that was told by the Union colonel is true—and that Monty was a murderer. That bothers Kristi—always has."

"Does Kristi say something every time?"

"Oh, yeah. But it doesn't stop Shelley, she just sighs and tries to be comforting, you know? Man, but tonight was something different!" Genie shivered. "Now I will be looking over my shoulder—afraid of faces in the window! Oh, that's my place—right there."

Dallas pulled the car over to the curb and went around to open Genie's door. He walked her up the path to her house and waited for her to open her door.

"My, my, son, you are a gentleman," Genie said.

"Do my best," he said. And then he added, "You make sure you lock your door, and be careful, okay?"

"Sure, but I'll be okay. I don't hang around Johnson Square, and I've never been over to the Murphy place!" She shivered. "Creepy place."

"You don't like the Murphy house?"

Genie was thoughtful for a minute. "Strange. I used to love it. But...a while back. I mean, before Ian even died...there was something. Seemed like it was suddenly a dark place, a scary place. I enjoyed when Ian came over to our place. He was a cool guy, friendly, sweet, picked up, helped out...such a shame about him. He and Jedidiah—they were such good friends."

"So—just one day, his house started to bother you?"

"Like night coming," she said. "You know, it goes from bright, to soft colors in the sky, to dusty colors, and darker bit by bit. It was like that." She sighed. "Guess he found out about the cancer maybe about two years ago. Maybe that was it. Or, maybe, just the bad stuff happening around it." She shrugged. "That's an interesting thought, isn't it?"

"Yes, it is."

She paused, looking up at the sky. "The moon really is so beautiful tonight. But I'll bet you it isn't bringing that glorious light all the way down to the Murphy place. You mark my words—that house will still look like it's all covered in darkness."

"Maybe, but...if Murphy was such a good guy, his house can't have...well, I guess, after tonight, I'd say it couldn't have any kind of an evil spirit attached to it."

"Doesn't have to be Murphy, and may not be evil, just...well, it scares me. And I'm real glad I wasn't having to wait for the bus tonight, so thank you again for the ride!"

"Not a problem."

She was closing the door and he'd started to turn away, but she suddenly opened the door again and called him back. "Mr. Wicker?"

"Please, just call me Dallas."

"Dallas... I, well, I know you and Kristi... I mean, it's fine. Better than fine...it's great. But... I'm worried about her, so tonight…especially tonight…watch out for her, will you? I mean, being at that séance… It was creepy! And I'm scared for what she saw. And kind of scared 'cause of the moon. Silly, huh?"

"Not much is silly—not in my mind. I will watch out for her," he promised.

She smiled, and then closed and locked her door. "All in!" she called to him, waving through the door's small window.

"Thanks. Good night."

In his car, he put a call through to Detective Joe Dunhill, and put him on speaker so that he could get going back to McLane House.

Dunhill answered, sounding anxious, as if hoping Dallas had something solid.

"I think Eliza Malone is dead—and her body is either hidden somewhere in or around the Murphy house, or the McLane place."

"What makes you think that?"

Dallas hesitated. "Gut feeling—and I'm here because of your gut feeling, so don't go knocking it."

"Okay…you want me to start digging around the Murphy house? Come on, you know that isn't legal, and we can't just go blindly poking around. We can't even get a search warrant for 'somewhere around one of these places.' Oh!" he said suddenly, groaning. "Your séance!"

"You know all about the séance already?"

"Oh, yeah, it's all over the internet already—Carl Brentwood or one of his people posted a teaser for it, and there's a backup to the teaser—Carl talking for just a minute directly to the camera as they're setting up the room, with a promise more will be coming by midnight—witching hour, as he said."

"That's just great. The area will be thronging with his fans, people trying to get close to him. And fans can be crazy."

"Everyone already knows he's in town."

"So now they know where he's staying. They could swarm the area—which will make it hard to figure out who is doing what."

"You think that—you think that more is going to happen?" Dunhill asked.

Dallas was silent, and then said, "Theory. Ian Murphy was connected to all of this, and I think it's because of something he knew. Maybe he didn't even know what he had could be dangerous, and he was quick to share it with others. Eliza Malone was the first. Then, for some reason, it all stopped for two years. Then started up again—Ian and Lachlan Plant died just two days apart, right?"

"Right—and Simon Drake disappeared two weeks later. But Ian was dead by the time Simon Drake disappeared."

"That suggests Ian Murphy had no idea of what he had or knew. The killer—or killers—could feel that the information might be coming to light again. Wait, actually, all this may help. With all the excitement over Brentwood's video, you can get police protection of some kind, at least, over to the McLane house."

"Sure, I can have a patrol car go by. Listen, we've had good police work in the Historic District from the get-go."

"I'm not saying you don't have good cops—I'm saying this killer is good."

"All right. I'll get someone watching the house."

Dallas wondered for a moment if that would help—Monty and Justin were watching over the house. Then again, no one else saw them, and they wouldn't be a deterrent if someone came around feeling homicidal.

The thought suddenly made him anxious to get back—Kristi and Jonah were alone at the house. He didn't suspect Jonah of being a killer, but then, who in the house might be? He'd been driving in that direction and he was almost in front of the house—but he wanted to get in.

"Get me some cops to watch over things. I'll get back to you in the morning. I have my people checking backgrounds on the employees and guests at McLane House. Maybe I'll have something by then—at least, a direction."

"All right," Dunhill told him. After a moment, he added, "And thanks. For, uh, being here."

"You really have to thank Adam Harrison."

"I do. And on that 'gut' thing—trust me. I get it."

"Talk to you in the morning."

Dallas hung up; he was almost at the house.

He parked the car. Anxious as he was to get to Kristi, he paused, and looked far across the square.

The moon that night was a majestic, glowing silver orb.

But maybe Genie had a point.

Maybe it was just the direction the moon shone, maybe it was geography, the size of Johnson Square, the shadows created by such a fantastic glowing orb in the sky.

But he couldn't help but feel it; Genie had been right. Not even the glow in the sky seemed to touch the strange darkness that lurked around the distant corner and seeped onto the street, settling right around the Murphy house.

Being in the room was becoming torture. Kristi just kept seeing the face.

And then she heard the sound. As if someone was in the hallway.

As if they stood outside her door.

She could almost feel breathing…

Silly—it was probably Dallas. He'd come back, but now was afraid to wake her if she'd finally gone to sleep.

She waited a few minutes, and then gave up, flying to her door and out into the hallway and over to Dallas's door. She knocked and whispered his name.

"Dallas?"

There was no answer.

She knocked harder and tried the door, but it was locked. She had a skeleton key, of course, but it was downstairs. And she didn't need the key—if he was there, he would have answered.

She didn't want to go back to her room—at first, she'd wanted nothing except to escape. But now, she was very weary of her own company. And all that raced through her mind.

Maybe Jonah would still be awake, watching sports, or reading, or even puttering around the house.

She had no idea where Monty and Justin had gotten to, and assumed they had gone back to the courtyard, watching, as they had been doing the past few nights. If nothing else, she could go outside and wait with them.

She smiled to herself. She now needed human contact— whether the person was alive or dead.

The hallway felt exceptionally empty; her steps seemed loud as she hurried down the stairs.

The back parlor was empty; Jonah had apparently gone to bed.

She looked in the front, but there was no one there, and when she checked the kitchen, she saw they had cleaned up well—it was sparkling and ready for the next morning. She headed back out to the rear parlor, and then to the back door, looking out through the window.

Moonlight showed the trees and the tables, more brightly than usual, and yet, by that new light, enhanced shadows seemed to be everywhere, and nothing was clear.

For a moment, her limbs seemed to freeze.

There *was* someone out there.

A large man was at one of the courtyard tables; he seemed engrossed in something he was reading on his phone. She could see nothing of his features.

But he saw her, and he stood, pocketing his phone, and stared at her.

Then, he started walking toward her. Engulfed in the darkness, he seemed to be something incredibly evil, made of shadow.

She started to back away, and then a gasped scream escaped

her, for she backed into someone warm and very solid, and hands came down upon her shoulders.

Before she could really scream, she heard Jonah's voice at her ear, which immediately made her feel as if she had truly become a paranoid idiot.

"Granger Knox…sitting out in the courtyard all by himself. Couldn't spend one evening listening to music with his wife and daughter."

"Shush," she warned. "He's coming this way."

"And I'm out of here!" Jonah said, turning away. She heard his footsteps on the stairs; he was hurrying on up to his own room.

Kristi opened the door and went out. "Hey," she said to him. "I didn't mean to bother you. You're fine out here in the court-yard."

"Ah, Kristi, it's you!" He waved.

Outside, with her eyes adjusted to the moonlight, she could see him far more clearly. He pulled out a chair for her.

She wondered if she would have been less unnerved by him or more so if she had seen his face clearly in the moonlight at first—he had the look of an old pit bull, face wrinkled and worn with the years, jowls long and hanging.

"Miss Stewart—thought you were headed up for some sleep," he said. "But, well, it's lovely out here. Quiet. Join me?"

She smiled and accepted the chair.

"I couldn't sleep. But I thought you had headed down to the riverfront."

"Just not in the mood, I guess. I almost went," he said. "Wait, I did get to the riverfront, but didn't feel like going to a club." He grimaced. "My poor daughter and sweet little Sydney were both a bit brokenhearted, I think. People recognized Carl Brent-wood on the street, and he wound up being charming for some time with his fans—and then he slipped away in a car that Claire Danson somehow conjured. He didn't make it to the bar. Still, the rest went on! I told them not to worry about me—I was just going to walk back here."

"Ah, I see."

"Saw someone behind you in the house—it gave me a fright. I was going to run in and come to your rescue—and then I saw it was just Jonah."

"Yes, it was Jonah. But thank you—for intending to come to my rescue!"

"Of course!"

"So, you were just sitting out here."

He smiled at her and patted his pocket. "Books on a phone— imagine that, huh? I download stuff and I can read anywhere, anytime. Pretty cool, huh?"

"I agree. What are you reading?"

He grinned. "Savannah history, of course."

"Anything good?"

He shrugged. "I was reading about the surrender of Savannah… Well, I can't tell you anything—you're the expert."

"I'm not a historian," she said. "I just grew up here. And I really do love the city, so I take an interest. I mean, things aren't all just perfect or anything—we have ugly bits of history, too."

"Like here—at McLane House."

She was silent.

"Ah, Kristi, naturally, you have to believe the best of your ancestor. I was trying to see if there was some way to help you out with your theory, but…didn't find anything, other than the fact Monty McLane definitely had the opportunity to get home, and that… Look, a lot of men would kill their wives before accepting they might have an affair with another man. And that is the way the story goes—unless you have tangible historical proof?"

"I'm afraid I do not."

"Well, there you go, there you have it—and it makes for such a great story, huh? Heck, I'm in construction—don't really know anything about this kind of thing, and I was completely wowed tonight!"

She smiled weakly.

"I'm surprised you hire Shelley as your medium," he told her.

"Oh? Why?"

He hesitated, looking out back, toward the monuments. "Well, she says it's just sad—she never wants to argue with you, because she understands. But she's convinced Monty is a murderer. Oh, she's also convinced Trinity is here—she just has to do the right thing to find her, hit the right night, touch the spirits correctly or some other kind of mumbo jumbo."

Kristi kept her smile plastered in place. "Well, Shelley just believes and feels what she...what she believes and feels!"

She didn't have to hold her false smile for long; the back door opened. In her present mood, she jumped.

"It's just Mr. Wicker," Granger told her. "You're nervous?" he asked.

"I guess I am. Dallas, thank you for taking Genie home."

"Pleasure," he told her. To Granger he said, "Out enjoying the nice night, are you? You didn't enjoy the band?"

"Too many people for me," Granger said with a shrug.

Kristi yawned. "Well, lovely as this may be... I think that I will turn in for the night!"

She turned, touching Dallas's arm as she slipped by him.

In the house, she all but ran up the stairs, refusing to even glance at the portraits.

In her room, she paced nervously.

It seemed like forever...

It was a matter of minutes before she heard a soft tap at the door.

She hurried to the door, and then thought to ask softly first, "Dallas?"

"It's me." She threw open the door, ready to throw herself into his arms. She managed to hold herself back, and also tried to appear as if she hadn't been crawling out of her own skin since he had left her.

She stepped back, allowing him to come in.

"Did anything…happen?" she asked him. "Did you learn anything?" she added anxiously.

"Kristi, I just gave Genie a ride home."

"Right."

He stepped forward, slipping his arms around her and pulling her tightly to him.

He kissed her lips. Gently. Then he looked into her eyes.

"I spoke with Joe Dunhill, and there will be extra police presence around the area tonight."

She frowned. "Now? But I'm telling you, Eliza Malone is already dead. And, if the same person or people took Simon Drake, then…"

"And if someone else stumbles upon whatever caused disappearances and deaths, that person could be in danger, too."

"But we have to find Eliza."

"Kristi, it's illegal—even for the FBI—to blindly dig up property."

"But I own this property—we can dig it up all we want."

He smiled. "We can get some equipment out here. Geophysical tools, like ground-penetrating radar, that kind of thing."

"Well…can we start?"

"Now?"

"Yeah."

"Kristi, I have to get the equipment out here. I can get that tomorrow. I've talked with my tech and research people, and we'll have a better picture of the people involved. And, as you've said—we can start here. In the morning."

He pulled her close again, smoothing down her hair.

"But how do you stand it?" she whispered. "We—we know she's out there."

"We stand it," he said softly, "because we all do this pretty much every day, and we learn that you have to sleep and live and eat and..." He lifted her chin and smiled at her. "Make love."

She smiled back. "I'm just so on edge, so nervous."

"I can try very hard to help you relax," he said sincerely.

She had to smile in return, and when his mouth touched hers again, she matched him with some very hot, deep and wet kisses in return. His lips traveled down her throat, and she stepped back, sliding her fingers beneath his jacket to ease it from his body. He caught it, and then stepped back to slide his holster and gun from the small of his back, then set them down with the jacket. He looked at her again with a broad smile. He kicked off one shoe and then the other and she laughed, and she was back in his arms, struggling to kiss and touch and remove clothing all at once.

The clothing quickly wound up strewn about the room; she realized the drapes were open because the moonlight, silver and glowing, fell upon them as they stood there, and she paused to run her hands over the sleekness of his body before moving to close the drapes. Her window looked over the courtyard, not the street—thankfully!—but they had left Granger Knox out there, and her ghosts were, in a way, parental, and she certainly had no intention of entertaining anyone with a show. She glanced out, and saw nothing but that glorious moon glow, and then quickly pulled the drapes across the window. She started to turn back to him, but he was already behind her, the fullness of his body flush against hers, and he pulled her back to him before spinning her around and finding her mouth again. They stumbled to the bed, fell upon it, and the breathless kissing all over each other's bodies continued, and Kristi marveled that the man could make such a tender caress out of his movement one moment and such an urgent and intimate touch out of the next. She thought that she'd never imagined anyone so amazing, in bed and out, and then she wasn't thinking at all anymore because his lips were moving over her body, moving downward, and sensation was ripping through her at a frantic pace.

Little shivers of ecstasy spilled through her as he drew up over her again, whispering, "How am I doing?"

"What?"

"As a distraction…how am I doing?"

She caught his face between her hands and pulled her to him, and she knew he was quite certain she would whisper something tender or sensual or…

"Do shut up, Mr. Wicker," she murmured, and kissed him. Then they were entwined together, he was within her, and she could whisper breathlessly that he was doing quite well.

The whole world was receding, and, wait, he had actually become the world.

Later, when they lay together, still entwined, she wasn't anxious anymore.

Morning would come.

It would, in fact, she thought, come way too soon.

CHAPTER ELEVEN

Dallas thought he could have stayed in bed all day; it felt so good to be there, to open his eyes and watch Kristi sleep, blond hair splayed in wild abandon over her naked back.

But he forced himself to rise just as the sun began to peek over the roofs of the houses across the square. Gathering his clothing, jacket, gun and holster, he quickly slipped back into his own room. He'd showered and made it downstairs before anyone else was up.

It wasn't even six; he could call in to headquarters soon— even if Angela Hawkins was still home, she'd be ready with information for him. But he'd give his fellow Krewe of Hunters agent the courtesy of another hour of sleep, at least.

No one was up, per se, but that didn't mean the courtyard was empty.

Monty and Justin—were they only flesh and blood and alive—might have been any guests at the B and B. They were seated at one of the courtyard tables, Justin with his legs casually crossed, and Monty with his elbows on the table.

Both looked up as Dallas arrived; neither bothered to stand, but smiled.

"Take a seat—preferably not on either of us," Justin said.

"Like that oaf last night," Monty said, shaking his head.

"Not that I think of Granger Knox as the greatest gentleman," Dallas said, "but to be fair, he doesn't see you."

"You'd think he'd have some sense of something," Monty said.

Dallas shrugged. "Some people do. Many people don't. Was anyone back here last night other than Granger Knox?"

"No, just Mr. Knox, and he is quite the odd duck," Justin said.

"How so?" Dallas asked.

"I saw him come back from the riverfront, fumble around for his key—pause, and look up at the house and study it. He raised a fist to the mannequin of me, and then opened the door to the house."

"He was inside for a while," Justin said, "because Monty had walked around to the back several minutes before he opened up the back door and came out here to the courtyard."

"Maybe he went to his room."

"I don't think so. Jonah had been downstairs in the back— then I think he was in the kitchen when Knox came back here. Knox kept fiddling with his phone. He told Kristi he'd been reading a book, but I don't think he was reading anything. He kept poking at the phone and muttering to himself. He was annoyed with something."

"Maybe he's just a jerk," Dallas suggested.

"And you're an investigator!" Justin said.

"Yes, and I have people checking on Granger Knox and his family, and everyone staying here. I'm investigating, I promise. Information on everyone is coming."

The two of them nodded at him solemnly. Dallas's phone rang, and he reached into his jacket pocket, and smiled as he saw the caller ID.

It was Angela, Jackson Crow's wife, and with Crow, one of

the original six from the first case investigated by the Krewe of Hunters.

She was brilliant with research, able to find information that might have been impossible for anyone else to acquire. At headquarters, they now had several dozen agents—and two floors of forensics and tech and anything else that might be needed. They were almost self-contained, and their offices were separate from the main DC offices, and from Quantico, as well. They had all trained at the academy there, and many of them had worked there for years before joining the Krewe. But once a man or woman had joined the Krewe, they were at a separate and distinct facility.

Jackson might be the official field leader, but Angela might well be described as their queen—a beloved queen at that!

"Good morning," he told her, glancing at the two ghosts to let them know it was business.

They knew; they were going to watch him eagerly anyway.

"Good morning, Dallas. Everyone all right?"

He glanced at the ghosts.

Was *dead* all right?

"So far—we had a séance last night, and—"

"I saw the séance."

"What?"

"It's online. I've watched it a few times," Angela told him. "Who or what did Kristi Stewart see? Watching her, I'm sure she must be...talented, gifted, a seer—whichever you choose."

He glanced around to assure himself only the ghosts could hear. "Kristi is new to this—she just came into it, as a matter of fact, the morning I arrived in Savannah."

"And she's doing okay?" Angela asked.

"She's remarkable. But the séance was different. She believes she saw one of the missing people—Eliza Malone, the businesswoman who disappeared two years ago. She saw Eliza's face in the crystal ball."

"What about the medium? I mean, I'm about to tell you what I have on everyone, but I'm asking about her abilities."

"A performer, no more, in my opinion," Dallas told her.

"You're alone now? You can talk—or rather listen?"

Dallas looked at the two ghosts—both were watching him.

"Well, I'm not exactly alone."

"Oh?"

"I'm in the presence of two very fine gentlemen of the dearly departed variety, but they're doing their best to help us in every way they can," he said, nodding appreciatively to the two. "I'm ready and set to go—or rather listen," he said, and he leaned back.

He had a feeling Angela had a lot to tell him.

Kristi awoke smiling, instinctively reaching a hand out to touch Dallas.

But she touched nothing.

She opened her eyes; his side of the bed was empty. He must be up early, showering, changing, getting ready for the day.

She was anxious to find out what he was talking about—*geophysical equipment.*

She wanted to get started. It would probably take a little time—even for Dallas—to acquire the tools.

She reminded herself, cringing a little, that she wasn't free that day—she had a funeral to go to.

She closed her eyes and yawned and rolled to her back, and then opened her eyes.

She nearly screamed, but managed to swallow it.

She was actually getting better at this!

There was a woman standing at the foot of her bed.

No...

Not quite a woman.

Kristi could see right through the apparition who was there, barely appearing, her arms outstretched. Her face was the same face Kristi had seen in the crystal ball.

And she knew now, of course. It was Eliza Malone.

And no matter how she hoped otherwise, she knew in her heart that the woman was dead. And her body must be somewhere near.

Eliza's eyes were so sad; her lips moved, and the barest breath of sound seemed to escape from them.

"Please, you must find me…must…help. I try so hard… I think you see me, I think you can help me…"

Her voice drifted into nothing but air.

And the pale, transparent apparition disappeared just as cleanly into nothing but air, as well.

"Well," Angela said, beginning with her summaries on the people in the house, "I hope you'll be pleased to hear that the young actor—Carl Brentwood—comes across as everything he appears to be. He was in a magnet theater school out in California, and he was picked up at the age of twelve to be on a cable show. He started becoming very popular in a sitcom, but even while filming, finished high school and went on to UCLA. He has an excellent work reputation, and he's huge with the young crowd, online, and in person. I can't find where he ever even got a parking ticket—never had any scandal involving drugs or alcohol."

"He's a nice kid," Dallas said. "I don't think Kristi Stewart would have let him video here if he wasn't."

"He seems to be a fine enough fellow," Monty said.

Dallas realized the two ghosts could hear Angela's voice.

"I don't think he's involved with anything," Angela said. "He's never been to Savannah before. His dad is a soundman with one of the major studios, and his mother is an artist. Her parents were immigrants as young children from the Ukraine. On his father's side, the parents were also immigrants—English."

"So, he comes off as squeaky clean?"

"Squeaky clean and polished."

"Sometimes that can be scary."

"True. All right, we'll move on to his people—Claire Danson and Murray Meyer. The agent, Murray Meyer—interesting fellow. He's been a theatrical and film agent for nearly forty years, and his roster has included many A-listers, and he's often specialized in the young and up-and-coming. His wife of thirty-plus years died just four years ago. He could easily retire if he wished, or rest on his laurels and let his associates do the legwork. He picked Carl out of a school play, so he's been with him now over a decade, and I guess he takes a special interest in him, traveling with him to film sites and so on. He has been in Savannah several times—he represented a number of actors in a major flick filmed in Savannah about ten years ago, and he's traveled to Georgia three times in the last five years—a major television series has been filming there for the last several years. He's originally from Massachusetts, and his parents before him were from Massachusetts. The only legal difficulties he's had have to do with championing his actors during various negotiations—he's a stand-up kind of guy for them. No children—his passion seems to be his work."

Justin sighed. "Not a bad man, a Hollywood type, wrapped up in his own concerns, with little care for others."

"What about Claire?" Dallas asked.

"Claire Danson, divorced eight years, no children, born in New York City, worked down at a theme park in Central Florida for several years after graduating with a degree in graphic arts from Pratt Institute. She's very good at what she does—Carl Brentwood has literally millions of followers. She turned her skill for graphic arts into a career in social media management, with spin and excitement—and has her people doing all kinds of video and podcasts and creating major splashes. Right now, Carl seems to be her own pet project, and he's very happy with her. Now, while she was born in New York City, her mother was born in Atlanta and Claire spent a number of her formative years in Georgia. Her mother died a few years back, and Claire went to the funeral and spent some time in Georgia then—and it coincides with the time Eliza Malone went missing. And, she and Murray Meyer have both been in the city for several weeks now. They were first in a hotel on the riverfront, apparently checking out the smaller bed-and-breakfast establishments for Carl's arrival. They've been in the city several weeks—yes, the timeline agreeing with the recent disappearance of Simon Drake and the deaths of Ian Murphy and Lachlan Plant."

"Still—why?" Dallas murmured. "They don't live here. They have no real connections to the area."

"The police interviewed everyone down there associated with Simon Drake—several times, from what I understand."

"Yes, I spoke with people, too. A man and a woman with no real enemies disappeared just about two years apart. So, the answer isn't going to be something we'll grasp easily—no one was cheating on anyone, no one had a jilted lover, no one was rich enough for there to be a big inheritance…so, what the hell happened?"

"That's what you're there to find out, you know."

"Yes, sorry, just working it aloud."

"Quite all right. Now I'll get to the household. Oh, first, I checked out Jamie Murphy. The kid is fairly well exonerated—he wasn't in the city, he was away at school when each of the events occurred—he only came home to bury his grandfather."

"So, the kid is cleared. That's good to know."

"Jamie Murphy is a quite decent young man," Justin said, nodding his conviction.

"Indeed," Monty agreed.

"Anyway, on to Jonah Whitney. Born and raised in Savannah, a friend to both Murphy and McLane, a man who was in the same reenactment Civil War regiment with his friends, recreating battles year after year, lecturing at the fort at times—and very popular, by the way. He's helped bring in physicians who are also historians to teach in the medical tents. He was a banker until he retired in his fifties; he started managing McLane House about fifteen years ago, right when Jedidiah McLane began to feel his age. Ian was about twenty years older than Jonah, Jedidiah about fifteen. He's lived in the house for the last fifteen years, since he started managing it. The man barely had parking tickets. He appears to be a solid citizen. He was married, but his wife died almost twenty years ago. Cancer. By all reports, he was never anything but a good friend to Murphy and McLane."

"Another stand-up citizen," Dallas murmured.

"What's your take?"

"He's friendly, efficient and seems like…another stand-up citizen."

"I made your reservation through him. He said we were really lucky—I'd booked the last room for you."

"That is true. Genie Turner?"

"High school education, married, two children, boy and a girl, adults now, one living and working in Atlanta, the other still in school in Chicago. She's a widower—husband died about eight years ago. Born and lived her life in Savannah. She's been offered jobs at restaurants in the city, but apparently, she had a great fondness for Jedidiah—and likes being the kitchen boss where she is."

"Not even a parking ticket, right?"

"Well, she doesn't drive."

"So, again, nothing. What about Sydney, our young one?"

"Ah! We have an arrest!"

"An arrest?"

Angela laughed softly. "Don't get excited. She was swept up with a few other protestors who got a little carried away during an 'equality' march in DC. She was released almost immediately, but as you know, we can find out just about anything when we dig deeply enough. She's a student working her way through school, gets excellent marks and comments from her teachers, but we're looking at an exact timeline—she came to school and started working at McLane House just a little over two years ago."

"I'm not seeing it, though, of course, more than one person might well be involved."

"Dallas, I know *you* know that children have committed murder, and many under ten have committed some pretty heinous and brutal murders."

"Yes," he said softly.

"But here, I do have a bit more for you."

"Two things. First, Shelley Blake—the performing medium."

"She has lived in Savannah the last twenty years, and she's well-known and popular for her expertise with Savannah's ghosts. Apparently, many people have witnessed unexplainable phenomena during her séances."

"Yep—her knee jostling the table," Dallas murmured.

"Well, before she was in Savannah, she was working for a private tour company up in Gettysburg, Pennsylvania."

"She's not from Savannah?"

"No, she was born in West Virginia, and rather moved around the mid-Atlantic states with her schooling and work. She didn't leave the tour company under the best of circumstances. The manager there now wasn't there when Shelley was working, but read notes on her file. Apparently, Shelley liked to twist history around, telling people her own version of events. And she does have an arrest record—she got into a fight in a bar during a meeting that drew historians and guides from all over the country. The fight was over a great Florida Seminole chief, Osceola, and Shelley was determined they understand he died because the government cut his head off, while the Florida people were explaining he died of disease and his physician took his head later. Anyway, she was let go quickly, and the officer just seemed to think she was young and overserved—she was let go after a night in the drunk tank."

"It still sounds like we're a long way from murder, especially carefully planned murders—four of them, if we're seeing it clearly," Dallas said. "We'll work with this. I have the local detective, Joe Dunhill, the man who contacted Adam, sending out patrols, but…well, they think they're just protecting the safety and sanity of a visiting celebrity. But I'd like to get someone down here with geophysical tools. We can't just dig up a historic square, but Kristi owns the land here, and she's eager to search it, so we can be sure if there is or isn't something there."

"Maybe they'll find me," Justin murmured softly.

"All of us," Monty said quietly.

"I'm just not sure how we keep this on the low—the FBI has not been asked in, and there's no official confirmation that anyone has been murdered—we have a suicide, an accident and two disappearances."

"We can keep it quiet. I know just who to send," Angela said.

"Who?"

"Jackson—and I'll come with him, of course. We'll just be taking a little trip down to Savannah. No one needs know—except for Kristi Stewart, of course. We'll have to find accommodations somewhere close by—I understand that the McLane house is fully booked."

Dallas paused just a moment and saw that Kristi had come out the back door. She was walking toward him, nodding to Justin and Monty, and looking at him worriedly as she took the one empty seat remaining at the wrought iron table.

"I'm sure we can switch some things around here. It's best if you're in the house, or… I have a thought. I'll get back to you."

He hung up. "We're moving forward," he told Kristi. "I have some help coming down—and they'll have the proper tools to look at the grounds without ripping them all to shreds. I'd been thinking we could switch rooms around a bit, but I have a better idea—they could actually go and stay at the Murphy place, as long as you could ask Jamie if that would be possible."

She didn't answer him at first, she lowered her head and nodded, and then looked up at him. "Whatever you think is best," she said, and then added, "Dallas, she was back. This time, when I woke up, she was at the foot of my bed. Eliza—Eliza Malone. She's...not solid."

"Just learning," Monty murmured.

"She's not strong," Kristi continued. "And she didn't say anything that gave me any clue at all as to what happened. She just asked again that we help her and then...then she was gone."

He reached over and took her hands. "And you're all right?"

She flashed a smile to him, and looked around the table. "I didn't scream, gasp, run away or pass out. I think I'm moving right along in the right direction."

"Proud of our girl!" Monty said. "So, how soon does digging start?"

"Not right away," Kristi said, looking at Dallas again. "We've got a funeral to get to."

The services were held right at the funeral home; Amy Simmons welcomed Kristi as soon as she saw her—Kristi and Dallas had made certain to arrive early. Amy greeted her, looking curiously at Dallas, so Kristi introduced them right away.

"You're friends with an old friend of his or something, right?" Amy asked Dallas, frowning slightly. "Mr. Harrison. He donated the money we needed for this service, and for his plot at the cemetery."

Dallas nodded. "Mr. Harrison is a good man," he said simply.

"Well, I know you didn't know Lachlan, but we're very grateful you're here. I understand you're a private investigator?"

"I am, among other things," Dallas said, smiling.

"Well, thank you—and thank Mr. Harrison. Lachlan was wonderful at work, and he was so much fun when we went out at night. And half of the young women he worked with had crushes on him, but he wouldn't give in to…even flirting. Work was work. When we'd go out together, he'd make us all laugh, and, I guess, most important, he loved to listen! He thought he'd found his home finally in Savannah, and he never wanted to leave. Now I guess he won't have to—well, again, thanks to all the people who donated, because who knew that dying could be so incredibly expensive?"

"It sounds like he was a good man, and I'm very sorry for your loss," Dallas told her. "I'll just pay my respects," he said, and left the two of them, walking quickly to the coffin.

He knelt on the pad by the coffin, and looked to be in prayer. Kristi wondered if he was trying to reach the dead man.

"What a…what a beautiful man!" Amy said, looking after Dallas. "He must work out somewhere. He should come to the gym. But he doesn't live here, right?"

"No, he doesn't live here," Kristi said.

"He's staying at your place? I didn't see him in the video—and, wow, Kristi, not the time or place to talk about it, but oh, I loved that video. You're amazing. Well, Carl Brentwood is amazing, too—and Shelley was terrific. Have you seen it yet? His people are good—really good. The video was super—well-edited, creepy, spooky. You're going to be fighting off guests, now, you know. Oh, I was just thinking—maybe we should have had Shelley here instead of the priest. No, no, Lachlan loved the priest. It just seemed that, after this time, it was right to have one day—a service here, and then straight to the cemetery."

"I think you've done a lovely arrangement for Lachlan, Amy, and he'd be very grateful to you. And, no, I haven't seen the video yet."

"You've got to see it! The way it's all up on his site—there's the séance itself, and then the before-and-after interviews with everyone. It's so professional. And the house looks fantastic!"

Kristi smiled; Boyd came up and greeted her with a kiss on the cheek.

"A lot of the old guard seemed to have come out—and Lachlan's clients from the gym. I'm so glad. We didn't know what we'd get. I mean, he wasn't from here."

"I was just telling Amy—this is all lovely. I think he'd be very happy. Excuse me."

She left them, aware they were staring after her, as she joined Dallas where he knelt on the pew before the coffin. She folded her hands prayer fashion—and did say a prayer.

It was too sad and so unfair that Lachlan was gone.

Then she glanced over at Dallas and asked softly. "Anything?"

"No," he said softly, and then she felt his penetrating green-gold eyes on her. "What about you?"

She shook her head.

"We'd best let others come up," he said, rising and taking her hand. He glanced back to Boyd and Amy as they found chairs in the rows set up by the funeral parlor.

Kristi knew many people there, and she greeted them, and when they were seated, she told Dallas who was a tour guide, who ran a restaurant and so on. She fell silent.

"They're talking about you," he told her.

"Who?"

"Well, a lot of people, I assume, but I'm referring to Amy and her friend."

She smiled, lowering her head. "No, I'm old news. They're talking about you."

"And speculating, I imagine."

"Probably."

They looked forward; Amy was speaking with the priest, and it seemed the service was about to start.

But it didn't.

As Amy spoke to the priest, she started to cry, and then she glanced back at Kristi, and pointed at her.

The priest nodded, and Amy excused herself to others as she made her way through them to reach Kristi.

"Kristi, will you say something about Lachlan?" she asked.

"Me?" Kristi asked. "Amy, I called him a friend, but he was much closer to you and Boyd and others at the gym."

"I can't do it. I'll cry. You can just say something short and nice. Please, Kristi, Boyd said he wouldn't get two words out, and the rest of us…well, we can't."

"I—of course," Kristi murmured.

Amy gave off a sigh of such relief that Kristi almost felt guilty for even contemplating refusal. And while the priest rose and started the service, she thought about the young man, Lachlan Plant.

The priest—Father Davies—asked her to come up and she did.

"Lachlan was new to Savannah, and, as we all know, we can be the warmest people in the world, and insular at the same time. But he was just a fine and nice human being, and he endeared all of us to him with his simple love for life and, especially, his love for our city. He was always kind and patient; he was an excellent trainer, but far more important, a friend to those close to him, and a friend to strangers as well. He was a listener—and he loved to hear whatever tales anyone had. We'll never know why things happen the way they do. He was beautiful, he was kind and far too young to be lost. All who knew him will miss him dearly, and pray that indeed there is a greater plan, for such a young man to have lost his life when he was in his prime. He would be happy to see us all here today—he would thank Amy and Boyd and all who helped him. And, of course, he loved Bonaventure—as he loved Savannah. It will now be his forever home. Thank you."

She hoped she had done him justice; the priest thanked her for her words, and asked those present to join him in another prayer.

She fled back to her seat.

Dallas caught her hand and squeezed it.

She lowered her head and breathed deeply, and then it was over, and it was time to head out to the cemetery.

"That was excellent," Dallas told her, smiling, when they were in the car. "No wonder they asked you to speak."

"It should have been one of them, but... Dallas, I don't understand. This whole ghost thing. Justin and Monty—they appear to me just like flesh and blood, and the way they sit out in the courtyard...they're so real. Then there's Eliza Malone, and she's breaking my heart, but you'd think she'd just up and tell us who took her!"

Dallas was driving, and spoke slowly as he looked ahead, following Amy's car in the procession. "I don't think we'll ever fully understand. But this is what I think—the human soul is amazing. I like to believe that when we die, there is a second place we have...and we have different paths to get to it—through whatever our faith may be, but also, through a real path—the path the soul takes. Some stay behind because their will to have something known, to see that someone is protected...whatever, a dozen reasons. And some of us can ride bicycles, or ice skate, or even become contortionists or trapeze artists—and some of us just can't. Eliza has the will to see justice done. She is learning to make herself seen—to you, at any rate, Kristi. And she may know what happened to her—which would make it all very easy—and she may not. The dead do not become omniscient—they can only see in the same manner that we can. One place at a time."

"I really want to help her!" Kristi said.

"Then you will," Dallas told her.

They'd reached the cemetery and followed the other cars through as far as they could to reach the gravesite.

Bonaventure Cemetery was, in Kristi's view, a beautiful place—even if its purpose was to be the final resting place of those who had departed all earthly concerns and cares. It was high on a bluff just east of the city on the Wilmington River.

Many members of her family rested here, including Jedidiah.
Ian Murphy, too, was here, interred in his family plot.

She particularly loved something that frequently happened in
the newer areas of the cemetery. Mourners brought flowers to
their loved ones, but more, too: beautiful fall leaves and other
decorations adorned graves in November; Easter brought lil-
ies—and little toy bunnies. The items seemed to Kristi to speak
of something quite beautiful—a way to keep those loved and
cherished still within reach, and not dead and buried and forgotten, but remembered still in everyday life.

On the site of Bonaventure Plantation, the property was pur-
chased as a private cemetery in 1846 and became public in 1907.
Beautiful roads and alleys beneath majestic oaks, moss sway-
ing in the breeze, extended over the acreage, and all manner of
artful memorial creations stood in memory of those who had
gone. There were contemplative thinkers and angels with and
without spread wings. But Kristi thought it was truly the natural beauty of the place that created the Victorian ideal—a place
to remember those who had been loved and cherished in life.

"The 'Little Gracie' statue is there," Kristi said, pointing to
the sculpture created by John Walz, commissioned by Gracie
Watson's father. "I can't imagine her family's pain. She was supposed to be the sweetest child, charming guests when her father
worked at the Pulaski Hotel. They say she is now a darling little
ghost—you can hear her laughter when she still roams the hall."

"Some ghosts just haunt the minds of us all, because tragedy
touches us all as human beings," Dallas said. He smiled grimly
at her. "Some come to try very hard to reach us, dedicated to
finding the one who can help them."

Kristi nodded and pointed across the vast expanse of the cemetery again. "We have a family plot, beneath that angel over
there, the one with the massively spread wings."

"It's a beautiful sculpture," he told her.

She nodded and said, "Ian Murphy is not far—the Murphy

family plot is here, too. In death, Jedidiah and Ian are still, in a way, just down the street from one another. I never thought that mattered so much before. I always believed the body was a shell, and death took us out of that shell, and so, what befell the body wasn't of much importance."

"The body remains just a shell," he told her. "Or so I believe, myself." He smiled at her and reached for her hand. "The soul is the essence of what we were, what we are…and all the love we shared. But that said, a beautiful cemetery is a wonderful place to remember someone and keep that person close in our hearts."

They joined others at the gravesite.

They stood while the priest said his last words.

Kristi's head was bowed, but while she listened to the prayers, she looked up and around.

And then, across the coffin, standing with a group of mourners from his work, she could have sworn she saw Lachlan. He was wearing the suit Amy had chosen for his funeral. His hands were folded before him.

And he looked across at her, and she was certain he saw her, and recognized her.

To her amazement, he seemed to smile.

And then he began to disappear, until his image had faded completely.

She gripped Dallas's hand tightly. "Yes, I saw him, too," Dallas whispered softly.

The services ended. Amy invited all in attendance to a little get-together at what had been Lachlan's favorite brewery on the riverfront.

"Let's wait," Kristi said to Dallas. "I want to… I want to see if…"

"If Lachlan will reappear?" he asked her, and he was slightly smiling, making her realize he had intended to be the last out already.

And so they waited. Kristi briefly greeted more friends and acquaintances as they made their way out through the cemetery.

There were just a few people left; a representative from the cemetery, the priest and an older woman with whom he seemed to be friends.

Smiling politely, Dallas and Kristi lingered by the grave.

But though they let time pass—with the priest frowning at them as if he was sincerely worried about them—Lachlan Plant did not make another spectral appearance.

"Let's head to the reception," Dallas said finally.

As they drove, he glanced over at her. "Will you call or text your friend Jamie? Would you ask him if it would be all right for a couple of your good friends to stay at his house for a few days? Just tell him you're full up—which you are. I was thinking, at first, of course, and with your permission, we could have doubled up a bit at your house." His smile, as he glanced her way, was sly. "But seriously, if Jackson and Angela stayed at the Murphy house…well, they are two of the original members of Adam Harrison's team, and Jackson still leads us all. They're good. If there is something to find…they'll get it."

"For sure," she said, and added a little awkwardly, "I look forward to meeting them."

"I know they're anxious to meet you. They're driving down, and bringing equipment."

"Oh?"

"You said you want to know what's beneath the ground."

"Yes, yes, I did," she said. She was quiet for a bit, and the silence in the car was heavy. "What am I going to do when you leave?" she whispered.

He glanced her way. "Well, you could come with me."

"That's rather absurd. We barely know each other, I have work here, I own McLane House—and you know, it's going to be booked after that séance! Of course, you could stay here."

He didn't answer; she felt a little heartsick.

No, of course he couldn't stay. She didn't know that much about him, but if he was in a special and elite unit, he was dedicated to his work. And it would mean more to him than a woman he barely knew, just getting over desperate panic at the sight of a ghost...

She gave herself a serious mental shake.

"You'll want to park here—there's nothing closer," she told him.

They got out of the car. A breeze drifted off the river, boats were out and the afternoon was nice and warm. Tourists and locals alike moved down the street, laughing and chatting, some hurrying, some obviously in no hurry at all.

"Sometimes, it used to smell terrible here. There was a paper plant nearby."

"Ah, that smell—but without it, maybe everyone would have moved to Savannah," he teased.

She smiled weakly. "The brewery is just over there."

Amy had set herself up as hostess, greeting everyone at the front door.

"I was afraid you weren't going to make it!" she told Kristi.

"Oh, no. We're here."

They went in and joined the other mourners. People were opting for the brewery's classic ale—or for their famous root beer. Kristi decided an ale was in order.

As they passed people now, Kristi introduced Dallas, and they wound up at a table where a few of Jedidiah's old friends were seated. One, Henry Finley, a retired social sciences teacher, seemed especially intrigued by Dallas.

"I hear you're a private investigator—and that you were here for a close friend of Lachlan's," he told Dallas.

"Yes, sir," Dallas said. "For many, it's just hard to accept that an exceptionally fit young man should meet his end by tripping and striking his head on a curb."

"I thought that myself," Finley said, shaking his head. "And, mind you, I found it damned strange as well that Ian Murphy should jump to his death. Sure, the old geezer said he'd call it quits when it got too bad, but… I have a damned hard time seeing that fellow jumping." He stared at Kristi. "Don't you, Kristi? You knew him! That just wasn't like Ian. He was bright as all hell. He'd know he might not kill himself—that he might end up crippled and in worse shape than ever!"

"I thought it was odd, yes," Kristi said.

"What have you found out about Lachlan?" Finley asked Dallas.

"Frankly? Not much. No one—that the police or anyone else has been able to find—was there when Lachlan died. Of course, the police were quickly there, but there are no eyewitnesses to what actually happened. It's very tragic."

"You had to know Ian—he was smart as a whip, all his life. Why, he—and Jedidiah—and I were all in one company that worked just about every reenactment, Revolutionary and Civil War, that came around. He could talk on just about any subject having to do with the fact the Civil War made embalming popular. Had to get those boys home from the field, you know. He knew about medicine, from the Civil War, and even what little they had during the revolution. Oh, and did I forget the War of 1912 or the Mexican-American War, World War I—"

"Excuse me, I think I'm going to get myself a root beer now," Kristi said, jumping up.

While she enjoyed Jedidiah's friends, she didn't feel like indulging in their arguments and recollections today. She made her way to the bar, but kept running into people she knew. Managing to snag her root beer, she headed toward the rear of the establishment and the little patio they had in back. There was no one out there. The night trade hadn't come in yet, and the mourners were grouping inside.

She leaned against the wall, just breathing.

Lachlan, were you really there? she wondered.

She had almost spoken aloud—she was glad she hadn't.

Someone was nearby, behind an ivy trellis that bordered the patio area.

Whispering to someone else.

"Where the hell is the damned letter? All this, and we still don't have the damned letter."

Kristi stood very still, shivers hitting her spine, and yet, at the same time, wondering why she would immediately believe that someone whispering about a letter would have anything to do with the situation, or with her.

Because it was Lachlan's funeral.

She pushed away from the wall; one way or the other, she needed to know who had spoken. If she didn't, she'd go crazy with the wondering.

She hurried toward the trellis and then around it, ready to either accost whoever was there, or smile apologetically and say she had been looking for a friend.

But there was no one there.

Frustrated, she looked around, and saw that a kitchen entrance that still led into the main bar and dining hall of the brewery was wide-open.

Okay, so maybe the kitchen staff had been asking someone about a letter?

She hurried in, and then came to a dead stop, staring at a harried busboy.

"I—I was looking for a friend," she said.

"Isn't everybody?" he asked her.

"I think he—she—just ran in this way."

"Sorry, miss, I didn't see anyone—I'm running crazy."

"Yes, yes, of course, I'm sorry!" she told him.

"This is the kitchen. It's a delivery entrance."

"I know—I'm sorry. I'll go on through quickly."

She hurried through the bustling kitchen, feeling incredibly awkward. She saw no one she recognized.

Back in the main room, Dallas was still at the table with Henry Finley.

He seemed to be listening very patiently, but he looked up, and saw her coming into the room. He smiled. She joined him. "There you are!" Henry said. "I was just about to tell Mr. Wicker about that time in Culpeper, Virginia, when everything was perfect: private land, Sunday, like the real battle, forces strong, all of us in our wool and the temperature a million degrees—just as it had been, way back when! Guys pretending to be dead all over just because they were so damned hot."

She smiled, and thought she should take a trip into the ladies' room before they headed back—but Henry was still talking.

"Sorry, I'll be right back. And, Henry, I am so sorry, but we'll have to say goodbye soon. I'm needed at the house."

She wasn't needed—they all managed just fine without her.

But between the beer and root beer, nature really was calling.

She dashed into the back, said hi to an acquaintance who was leaving the restroom and walked in, finding a stall.

The minute she closed the door, the lights went out.

She stood still.'

And then she heard a whisper, eerie and rattling.

"Leave it alone, I'm warning you. Leave it alone. Or you'll be next."

There was silence, and still, the pitch darkness.

Scream! she told herself; now was the time to scream.

But the whisper…she didn't know if…

If it had come from the living or the dead.

And if it had come from the living…

Was she now alone with a killer?

CHAPTER TWELVE

"He had some amazing things—really amazing things," Henry Finley said, "like a letter written from a fellow who had just had a leg amputated. He was writing to his wife, wondering if she would still love him now that he wasn't the man she had married. So sad—old Ian had a number of letters like that. He used to collect them back fifty years ago when you could buy items like that for less than a small fortune. Not to mention his buckles, rifles, pistols, magazines and placards. But the letters and the books—he wanted to keep them. After death, you know? He always thought slavery had been one of the worst crimes man had ever perpetuated on man—still is—and the war was god-awful, but he also thought it was incredibly important we not forget it. Hell, look at some of the situations we find ourselves in today—people ready to hop up and grab arms over every imaginable issue out there. His letters—he thought Jamie might want them some day. Or, if Jamie didn't want the library and the letters, he was to give them to Kristi."

"Really? Does Kristi know that?" Dallas asked.

Finley shrugged. "Probably not—but Jamie is a good boy. I imagine he thinks if he defied Ian's wishes, he'd rot in hell, or some such notion. But it wouldn't be fear of reprisal—Jamie loves Kristi and appreciates all she did for Ian, especially after he went away to school. And she's only about four years older than Jamie, but when you're kids, that's a lot. She was his babysitter. He thinks of her as a big sister."

"Did Ian come up with anything special about two years ago?" Dallas asked.

"Anything special? Two years ago, huh?" Finley said thoughtfully. "Interesting, maybe. I haven't got a good recollection of time. But I do remember a while back he was excited about something…thought he might blow the minds of local folk—and maybe historians all around. He asked me to come over. He was going to show me, and ask me what we should do about it—think he'd called old Jedidiah, too. When I called and told him I'd be there the next day, he started laughing. Said he didn't know what he did with the letter he'd found, that he was researching, and that he'd put me off just a bit until he had it in his own two hands again." He paused, and shrugged. "Mr. Wicker, I'm almost eighty-seven, and I was considered to be the young-un in our crew. Well, me along with Jonah Whitney. Don't go getting me wrong—we're good people. Did we like to play dress up and go to battle? Hell, yes. But hey, that's not all. See, studying the past helps let us see where we go in the future. Ian was a huge believer in education—there's a saying, or several sayings. But the gist is that, in America today, it's not supposed to matter how you were born to who—what matters is what you choose to make of yourself. So, Ian thought we were all born equal—what wasn't equal were the opportunities that might present themselves to a man or a woman. He was a huge proponent of education—said he never minded his taxes going to schools, whether he had a kid in school at the time or not. Education was everything."

"I wish I could have known him," Dallas said, smiling sincerely.

"Yeah. Hey, we're here for Lachlan, and chatting up old Ian. But Lachlan loved Ian, too."

"They knew one another well? His coworkers believed Ian might have had talked about some therapeutic exercise, but I didn't know the two were really friends."

"Friends, sir, is when you meet someone, and you like them, and maybe you haven't even known them long, but there's something there. Acquaintances is when you see someone all the time, and you're polite and all—but you'd really not have much to say to one another if you went to lunch."

"Very sage, sir," Dallas said. "But—"

"Sage—hell, yes. I'm eighty-seven, like I told you."

"But was Lachlan seeing Ian as a friend—as well as to instruct him?"

"I don't think that they ever got to the instructing part—they were friends, yes." He laughed softly. "Ian, me, Jedidiah, over the years, we've driven the poor kids—like Jamie and Kristi— to just about mania, we repeat our old stories so over and over again. Lachlan Plant was a new set of ears—he loved listening! Hard to find someone who wants to listen on end to a bunch of old opinionated geezers!"

"The cops interviewed hundreds of people when the deaths occurred. Did you tell all this to anyone?"

"What was to tell? Ian went out his balcony—hard to argue suicide when he said he was going to do it. And Lachlan, well, there was an inexplicable tragedy. Yes, cops talked to me. They asked me if I'd ever heard Ian say he was going to end it his way when the time was right. I don't lie to cops—I told them the truth, that, yes, I'd heard him say such a thing. As to Lachlan—could he have died on a damned curb? Damned strange, but then I've seen a hell of a lot—I did tell you I was eighty-seven, right?"

He saw there was a twinkle in the old man's eye and he smiled. "Yes, you told me, and I think your faculties are all

there, and you like to use your age when you choose to forget
something—or say something over again."

"You got my number, kid."

Dallas smiled and glanced at his watch.

Kristi had been gone too long for a simple trip to the restroom.

"Excuse me, sir, please. I so enjoyed listening to you, and I
hope we can meet again. But I'm going to see where Kristi got
off to—she needed to get back."

"Sure thing. You go find that pretty girl, son!"

Dead—or alive.

Kristi didn't scream; she pulled her phone from her purse and
clicked on the flashlight app and burst out of the stall, shining
the light around.

Someone opened the door and came in.

"Whoa...hey, what's up in here?" a young woman asked.
"There...the switch is there, right by the door. There's the light!"

And Kristi was left standing there, as if she hadn't been bright
enough to know if entering a darkened room, there just might
be a light switch by the door.

She smiled weakly and ran out. Hurrying through the bar,
she saw Dallas was no longer at the table with Henry Finley.
She moved through the crowd to reach the old man's table; he
was in discussion with two of the gym trainers who had been
Lachlan's coworkers.

"Sorry, but, Henry, do you know where Dallas went?" she
asked.

"Looking for you." He eyed her up and down. "You all right?
You look like you've seen a ghost or something. Oh, I know!"
he lowered his voice. "Constipation. Just get yourself a bunch
of roughage, my girl, pretty thing like you, no, you don't want
to discuss or think about it, but...lots of roughage!"

"Um, sure, thanks, Henry." She waved to him, and looked

through the crowd, but she didn't see Dallas. She realized she was still scared—uneasy. The whisper had been close; it had snaked along her spine.

She found Amy and Boyd and thanked them, and walked out onto the street. It was busy with people. The afternoon was waning into evening, and the riverfront was a popular destination, filled with restaurants and bars.

But while she felt safe in the multitude of people, she still didn't see Dallas. Then her phone rang.

"Where are you?" he asked her.

"Outside—looking for you."

"Find you there."

He hung up. Barely a minute later, and he was out on the street with her, slipping an arm around her shoulder. "I was getting worried," he admitted.

She smiled. "I'm fine—but I have had an interesting time."

"So have I—but you tell me. What happened?" He studied her intensely for a moment. "What's going on—what's wrong?"

"Let's get out of here. I'll tell you on the drive."

The drive was only a matter of blocks; she still did her best to tell him about the whispered words she'd overheard out by the trellis—and then the strange threat that had been directed to her in the restroom.

"In the restroom, were you threatened by name?"

"No, not by name. The voice just said, 'Leave it alone, I'm warning you. Leave it alone, or you'll be next.' I was in there, and it was suddenly dark. Maybe—maybe it was meant for someone else. Maybe it was even someone in management, warning a server there, or they thought I was someone else. Now that I'm out of the dark, I'm not so afraid. But when it happened, I didn't know, Dallas. I couldn't tell if it came from someone living, a woman with a throaty voice—or if a dead man was threatening me."

"You should have screamed—loud, like a banshee," he told her.

"I almost did, but… I was too afraid I'd be screaming because of a ghost."

"Ghost or not—scream. Better to look a little foolish and live. Kristi, with what's going on here, you have to be safe." He was silent a minute. "You need to get out of here—take a vacation somewhere unknown for a few weeks."

She was surprised by the way she reacted, but something about his words just hit her wrong. Leave? They were close. The ghost was coming to *her.*

"What?" she demanded. "No, oh, no, Mr. FBI-Private-Investigator-Whatever—you need to solve this thing. We're nowhere, nowhere at all."

"Believe it or not, we are somewhere, Kristi. We aren't just scratching our heads and saying, 'Wow, yes, this is weird.' We are moving forward—I learned a great deal from your friend Mr. Finley. And you were just threatened—someone knows we're close, and that's why I'm afraid for you. And, you…you've made contact. Eliza Malone reached out to you. And Jackson and Angela are coming—and maybe we'll get your wish, we'll find a rotting body!"

Kristi gasped. "It's not my wish!"

"Kristi, I'm sorry—"

"So am I. I'm just scared."

"That's why you should get away from here."

She shook her head and said softly, "No. You need me now."

"And," he said, "you overheard other whispers. Someone talking about a letter. Maybe whoever that was saw you, too, and it sounds like they were flesh and blood."

"They could have been talking about something else, too. I'll never know—they were gone. I didn't see them."

"Just because you didn't see them does not mean they didn't see you."

"I don't see how they could have seen me. And you're in just as much danger as I am, if someone thinks we're close. Lachlan Plant was a big man, fit in every way possible. And they got to him!"

"There's a difference," he said.

"And what's that?"

"Lachlan wasn't a trained agent, looking for danger. And he didn't carry a Glock."

They'd arrived at her house; there was another car in front. Dallas got out of the driver's seat; he closed the door heavily and came around to her side. As he did so, the front door opened, and Jonah came down the steps, an attractive couple in tow.

The man was tall and dark, with a handsome face that gave evidence of a Native American background.

She was pale and blond, tall still, but not so much next to him.

"Hey, super—you guys got here really quickly!" Dallas said.

Dallas greeted the blond woman with a warm hug, and the man with a quick handshake. Kristi watched them all, and while they quickly greeted one another first, Jonah came toward Kristi.

"Nice couple, really cool—I was surprised when they got here, worried I'd made reservations we couldn't honor, but they said they were friends with Dallas, and they weren't staying here, just waiting for the two of you to get back. Jackson and Angela. I guess you haven't met them yet."

"I guess I haven't," Kristi said.

"Come on," Jonah, said, taking her by the arm. "Hey, folks, the queen of our little world, Kristi Stewart. Kristi, Angela and Jackson."

She shook hands with the pair, wishing she wasn't falling into such a tumble of emotions.

"What a beautiful house!" Angela told her.

"Thank you," Kristi said. "We really would be fine with you staying here." She glanced at Dallas. "We could rearrange a bit. I did get a text from Jamie—anything is fine with him, you're welcome to the Murphy house, but no one has lived in it in for a bit now, and it's musty, and it could really use a good cleaning." Again, she glanced at Dallas. "It's just quite—dark."

"Oh, trust me, we'll be fine. We've stayed all kinds of places," Jackson assured her. "I think we'll be very lucky to stay over there, then we'll really see your place, and the Murphy house—how many tourists get to say they've enjoyed that kind of visit?"

"Did you want to go now?" Kristi asked.

Jonah was still out there with them, beaming, happy to have made new friends. "Go now? They may not be staying here, but we've got our teatime and cocktail hour going on here. Why, they were just chatting it up with Granger and his girls, and Carl is in there—I think he's a little shocked himself with the results of his video. Says he can hardly go out on the streets anymore, now that people know he's in town!"

"We are getting to know your guests," Jackson Crow said. "And, I must say, Genie Turner is a talent. Best piece of pecan pie I've ever had."

"Sure—I'm more than happy to handle the evening however you would like," Kristi said.

"Well, come on, then, let's head back in." Jonah set a fatherly arm around Kristi's shoulders, his smile fading slightly as he asked, "You feeling all right? I figured that funeral had to be hard on you—I know you liked the fellow. And him and Ian Murphy dying so close together, and not that long after Jedidiah. It's just got to be a lot—a lot on anyone."

"I'm fine—and happy that it all came together for him. In fact, I feel guilty. I wish I'd been more pro-active in taking care of a funeral for him. It just was all so fast. No excuse—I should have been a better friend."

"Don't you say that, Kristi. You're good to everyone." He winked at her. "Good to that new guy, huh, and he's the one with the friend who gave most of the money for the funeral, right?"

"Right," Kristi said.

Inside, she was immediately greeted with warmth and enthusiasm by Claire Danson and Carl Brentwood.

"The lady of the hour," Claire greeted her.

"Lady of the hour? My heroine!" Carl said. "In fact, I should be jealous—almost half of the hundreds of comments on the video are about you."

Murray Meyer walked up, nodding to her. "I got a call on Carl this morning—there's a major studio with a picture in development about a man dealing with a haunted house—back in the West, 1880s, but it seems that Carl's video made it to the producer, and he's being offered the lead role."

"I'm going to be a ghost!" Carl told her happily.

"That wonderful, Carl, congratulations," Kristi told him.

He grinned. "And it's all because of you."

"I'm sure it's because of your talent and work ethic," Kristi said, "but I'm very glad that you've enjoyed it here."

"We tried to go out today, it didn't work out so well," Murray said. "We had to get Carl whisked away in a car again. But people are careful about accosting us at the house."

"Good. I'm glad it's working out," Kristi said, looking toward Dallas, Jackson and Angela. They were deep in conversation with Granger and Janet Knox. Kristi noted that Lacey was with them, but she wasn't participating in the conversation—she was watching Carl.

Puppy love! So painful.

Kristi excused herself to head into the kitchen and check on Genie and Sydney.

Sydney was busy brewing more tea. Genie was just taking a tray of pastries from the oven.

"You're back—how was it?" Genie asked her.

"I probably should have gone," Sydney softly. "I did meet him a few times."

"It's okay, Sydney, there were a lot of people there. And it was nice, really—Amy Simmons and Boyd Morris did a really nice job on making very awkward arrangements. I'm sure that Lachlan would have appreciated what was done for him—and that they managed to get him into such a beautiful cemetery."

"Well, there was nothing going on here today," Sydney said. "The whole kit and caboodle of our guests were out."

"Sydney, we do make beds and clean rooms," Genie reminded her.

"But these are such tidy guests!" Sydney said.

Genie transferred her pastries from the baking tin to a plate. "And bless them! They eat. I'll never forget when we had those folks we didn't know were here for a meeting of the Beach Body Babes diet group. If I'd known…"

"Not to worry. Their loss. More delicious stuff for the rest of us," Kristi said. "What can I do? Anything?"

"Get something to eat for yourself," Genie instructed.

Kristi laughed. "I just came from the after-funeral reception at the brewery. I'm good, thanks."

"Then, get out of the kitchen," Genie said. "Go—socialize. Those new folks—friends of your friend. They're lovely."

"They are," Sydney agreed. "But where are you going to stick them?"

"Oh, they're not staying here, not to worry," Kristi said. She headed out to the back parlor, and from there, she slipped outside to the courtyard. If Dallas was concerned that any of this mystery could have to do with her household or her guests, it was probably best not to say exactly where Jackson and Angela were staying.

Out back, she looked around, thinking that Monty and Justin might be there.

But they weren't.

And when she headed back in, she discovered that the ghosts of both men were in the front parlor—like a pair of bookends, they were posed on either side of the mantel, apparently fascinated by whatever had been going on between the guests. Only Dallas wasn't in the room. She was about to ask Jackson where he'd gone, but before she could, Granger Knox, who had been seated on one of the overly stuffed antique chairs by the sofa, stood up and looked at his wife. "Appetizers and desserts were delicious," he said politely. "But, Janet, Lacey, I think we need to go out for some real dinner."

Lacey Knox had finally made her way into conversation with Carl Brentwood. She stared at her father as if he had just shot an arrow through her heart.

"Mom, Dad, why don't you two go on? I'm not hungry— I had some of the little sandwiches and one of Genie's eclairs. I mean, honestly, I can't believe you're ready to eat after this."

Granger frowned. "This is a family vacation. I want to go to dinner."

Janet stepped in. "Granger, dear, Lacey is eighteen," she said softly, reminding him that their daughter was of legal age—and didn't have to accompany them anywhere.

"Fine. Stay here—Janet, let's go."

Janet obeyed his commands. She smiled at Claire, with whom she'd been talking, and quickly rose.

"I'll just run up for my pocketbook, darling, and be right back down," she said.

She turned, and headed back toward the stairs.

"I'd go out, but I just don't think that I can do it tonight," Carl said. "I mean, I'm so grateful. I love attention, too, I don't deny that. But I am worn out."

"Genie and Sydney will be going home for the night, but we always keep the refrigerator stocked, if you're hungry later. I'm sure Jonah told you when you checked in that we keep plenty of bread and sandwich meats and cheeses and all," Kristi said.

"Thank you," Carl said. He looked at her almost adoringly, making her uncomfortable.

"Sandwiches…no biggie," she murmured.

"Well, I don't believe this," Carl said, "but I'm heading up for…maybe a nap, and maybe to go to sleep for the night. Evening, all," he said, and he, too, went up the stairs.

"I think maybe I'll go out, wander a bit," Murray said. He smiled at those remaining in the room. "No one gets excited about an agent, trust me!"

"I'll go with you," Claire said.

"Thanks, Claire, but if you don't mind, I think I'd like to wander alone a bit—bask in happiness for Carl, and maybe just breathe a little myself."

Claire appeared to be startled—hurt, even—as if his words had been a small slap in the face. Murray walked out; she watched him go, and then muttered beneath her breath one audible word: "Asshole!"

Then she was gone, following after him.

"Well…see, Lacey—that's what you're looking at," Granger told his daughter, shaking his head. Luckily, before Lacey could answer, Janet came running in with her handbag over her shoulder. "Ready, dear? Bye, all, and, Lacey, if—"

"If I get hungry, I'll get something to eat!" Lacey said, exasperated.

Granger ignored her; Janet smiled weakly and waved, and the two exited.

"They're impossible!" Lacey announced, and flounced out of the parlor and up the stairs, as well.

"Personalities in a house," Jackson Crow murmured.

Kristi laughed. "Well, they're just guests here, but usually, they're very well-behaved." She frowned. She was alone with Jackson Crow and Angela.

Even Monty and Justin had disappeared. But those two seemed to come and go as they pleased, having a special ability none of the rest of them could share.

They could just fade away at will, so it seemed.

"Where did Jonah get off to?" she asked.

"He told me he was escaping," Angela said. "I think he likes leaving social hour to you."

"Yes," she said, and inhaled, looking from one of them to the other. "So, you're special agents. You're really FBI—and you're the...*ghost unit?*"

Jackson laughed. "Something like that," he said.

"And I understand you've recently discovered that you're especially gifted," Angela said.

"Is that what they call it?" Kristi said softly. She looked around again, assuring herself that they were alone.

"Your ancestors are...charming," Angela told her, coming over by her. "You do realize that they are like guardian angels for you? They're very attentive."

"You saw them," Kristi murmured.

Angela nodded an acknowledgment.

"It's so easy for you?" Kristi asked.

Angela glanced at Jackson. "Only because we knew about them, they trust Dallas, they love you—and they chose to be seen."

She nodded. "Then you'll understand when I tell you I know that Eliza Malone is dead."

"Yes," Angela said.

As she replied, they heard footsteps on the stairs. Dallas came into the front parlor, looking around.

"We're alone," Jackson said.

"Someone has been in my room," Dallas said.

"Anything missing?"

Dallas shook his head.

"Sydney was probably in there—she does most of the housekeeping," Kristi reminded him.

But he shook his head. "I told Sydney that I didn't want service. I like to make my own bed and take care of my things. No, someone was in there, looking for something."

"Anything in there that they could have gotten?" Jackson asked.

"No," Dallas said. "My computer is encrypted—I doubt even you could get into it. Okay, Angela, maybe, but only because she knows me."

"That leads us back to someone in the house," Jackson murmured.

Kristi stood and looked at them all, shaking her head. "My guests are just…guests. And I've known Genie and Sydney and Jonah forever. What about Monty or Justin—watching over us?"

"Not unless they know how to go through a backpack and put everything back together so that it was almost impossible to tell."

"I wonder what they were looking for?" Jackson asked quietly.

Kristi brought a finger to her lips; she knew the house well and though the floorboards weren't actually creaking, she could tell that someone was coming from the kitchen.

"Hey, all!" Sydney said cheerfully. "We're heading out for the night," she told them. "Need anything else before we do? Oh, and don't worry about Genie tonight—I'm going to drop her off. It's a little bit later than usual, and she might have missed her bus."

"Sydney, thanks, that's great," Kristi said.

"I can take her, if it's out of your way," Dallas said.

"Nope, I'm fine. Night, all!"

With a wave, Sydney was gone.

"How do they leave?" Jackson asked.

"Out the kitchen door, and they lock up when they go," Kristi said.

"But Jonah lives here?"

"He has a nice little apartment at the far end of the hall—opposite my room," Kristi told him. "It takes away a guest room, but…we still make it anyway. I have actual work—graphic arts in media. Or, at least I had work. I haven't done much of it lately."

"We'd love a tour of the house," Jackson said.

"Okay," Kristi said. "I mean, I can't let you into the guest rooms."

"Of course not," Jackson assured her. "Just the lay of the house—and the yard. We've brought equipment."

"Excellent," Kristi said. "Tomorrow, we'll start looking for Eliza Malone."

After the tour, Dallas had a few minutes alone with Jackson and Angela while Kristi changed out of her heels and dress. He brought them up to speed on everything that had happened, including the whispers Kristi had heard—and the threat she had received in the bathroom.

"Obviously, you're getting close. Have you kept up with the detective, Joe Dunhill?"

"I owe him a call now, but naturally, he assured me we couldn't go digging randomly in the square on the off chance of finding someone who disappeared."

"I checked on roadwork, sewer, electrical…anything that might have allowed for digging up the ground back when Eliza disappeared," Angela said. "There was nothing."

"Then we probably are looking at private property," Dallas said.

"Where, thankfully, we can use equipment—and dig," Jackson said.

Kristi came hurrying down the stairs and into the front parlor. "I told Jonah we were off to get Jackson and Angela settled, and that Carl and Lacey Knox were in the house." She grinned. "He's busy watching *Haunted History*. He loves the show."

"Let's go see the Murphy place," Jackson said.

Since Jackson and Angela had equipment and their bags in their car, they drove the few blocks over to Ian Murphy's house. Angela encouraged Kristi to talk about Ian, and Jedidiah, and the group of men, including Henry Finley, who had all been friends.

"I would have liked to meet Ian and Jedidiah," Angela said. "Perhaps I'll get to see Mr. Finley."

When they arrived, Dallas watched Kristi; she was grave as she stared up at the house, and then she told Angela, "I'm really not sure you should be staying here."

Dallas said quietly, "Not to worry. They both know how to look after themselves."

She flashed him an uneasy smile. "I don't think…oh, well, I'm not going to make sense, but there's just something about the house now. I used to love it—now…" Her voice trailed. "Well, maybe it's just me."

It wasn't just her, Dallas knew. But Jackson and Angela were uniquely designed for whatever it might be.

"Interesting," Angela murmured. Kristi led the way up the walk and into the house. She keyed open the door, and they went in.

Dallas understood Kristi's reservations; somehow, that haze seemed to hang over the inside of the house, as if dust motes whirled in the air, and a fog seeped up from the floor.

"I should have had a cleaning service in here, but…anyway, Jamie wrote me that his room was probably in the best shape. He was here about three weeks ago now, and there is clean linen in his closet and…"

She broke off, frowning.

"What is it?" Dallas asked her quickly.

"I was just thinking. I was here after Ian died. Jamie stayed here, making arrangements, and for the funeral. And there was nothing wrong with the house then. I mean, there's nothing *wrong* with the house."

"But it bothers you now," Jackson said.

Standing in the entry, Kristi shrugged. Then she gasped suddenly. "Dallas! You said that someone had been in your room. The book—the book by the Yankee soldier you were reading.

You brought it back to the house. Maybe someone took the book!"

"No," he assured her quickly, opening his jacket and showing her that he had the book in an inside pocket. "It comes where I go," he assured her.

She sighed softly. "Well, then... I'll show you upstairs, Ian's office and library, and Jamie's room, of course."

She led the way, apparently ignoring the feeling the place gave her. "There won't be any cream for coffee, but there is a single-cup brewer, and I know that Jamie kept coffee here, even after he left. I don't know how much Dallas has told you, but the only person really watching the place has been a gardener. He does have a key, but I'll let him know that you're here."

Kristi walked them around the upstairs; both Jackson and Angela were impressed with the library.

Kristi insisted on helping Angela freshen Jamie's room for the two of them, and then they all gathered in the library again.

"Kristi," Jackson said, "we'll start first thing tomorrow, in your backyard. And we'll make some time to go through the books here, as well."

"As far as the yard goes, you can just tell people that you've decided to look for your ancestor, the great Revolutionary hero Justin McLane," Angela suggested.

Kristi nodded and they all headed downstairs. In the parlor, Kristi hesitated again, standing in the center of the room.

Dallas, Jackson and Angela stood back, watching. But she just stood there, closed her eyes for a moment, and then looked at them.

"I can feel it...like something that comes from the earth, and slowly comes up over us, like a terrible misty darkness."

They waited, but then Kristi shook her head. "Can't you feel it?" she whispered.

Angela walked over to her and gave her a hug. "There's something, Kristi. We'll figure out what it is."

"We will be here. We will find out what happened," Jackson said.

Kristi nodded.

Dallas walked over to her then, taking her hands. "And I'll be with you."

She nodded, and they left Jackson and Angela, walking back across the square to McLane House.

The front and back parlors were empty; Dallas looked out back, and it was quiet, as well.

Since any guest still out had a key to the main house, he made sure to lock up. He thought about the threat that Kristi had heard in the darkness, and when they reached her room, he also made sure that door was locked.

He had barely done so before he turned and found that she was flying into his arms. He caught her and held her close.

Her warmth filled him, along with a strange mingle of emotions.

"Kristi."

"No!" she whispered. "I don't want to talk, not about ghosts, not about the dead, not about being afraid…not about anything."

It was night, and nothing would happen until the morning.

"You're the one who told me…we need to stop, to take time… to… Tonight, I don't want to think anymore, I just want to… be with you."

He smiled, and lifted her chin to his, and kissed her.

She kissed him passionately in return, a sweet blur of fire in his arms, and they were soon entwined together and making love, and he wondered what he would do when the case had ended, and it was time for the next one.

Later, in his arms, she slept, and he rose carefully, walking to the door again, and then to the window to look down into the courtyard.

Justin McLane had been killed well over two hundred years ago. His body, if indeed here, might lie under the concrete and tile in the courtyard, or just about anywhere. Even Monty, or his father, or his wife could lie anywhere on the property.

Tomorrow they would be hunting for unmarked graves.

CHAPTER THIRTEEN

Jackson Crow and Angela Hawkins arrived at McLane House just as breakfast was being served, and Kristi insisted they join for the meal. They made a point of speaking with everyone there. Little by little, the other guests headed out for the day. Eventually, Kristi wound up in the courtyard with Angela, and she finally had a chance to ask her if their night had gone all right. Jackson and Dallas had gone to the car to retrieve the ground-penetrating radar tool that he and Angela had brought.

"Uneventful," Angela assured her. She took a sip of her coffee and added, "But I think that you're right. There is something about the house. It's hard to tell exactly what it might be—by all accounts, Ian Murphy was a very decent man. Not sure why there would be such negative energy there. Only the gardener has been in there. I think we should have a talk with him. He'd be willing to meet with us, right?"

"I'm sure he would be," Kristi told her.

"I know that Dallas wants Joe Dunhill to meet Jackson. Maybe you and I could have a talk with the yard guy while they're seeing Joe," Angela said.

"Yes, certainly, if you think it's important."

Jonah came out. He grinned broadly at them all. "Peace and quiet. The Hollywood types had a big black car drive up and off they went! Oh, and, last night—I guess little Lacey Knox got her wish. Her folks were out, and Murray and Claire were gone...and she and Carl had a lovely little tête-a-tête out here in the courtyard, and after that...well, I couldn't guarantee it, but I think they continued it elsewhere, if you know what I mean. Didn't see anything, mind you, and if I had, it's none of my business. I'm not a hall monitor. But whatever, made for happier people today. Carl went with his people, and the young woman went with her parents. So—what is that thing Jackson Crow is hauling on in over there with Dallas?"

"We're looking for bodies," Kristi said cheerfully.

"What?" Jonah demanded, all humor suddenly gone from his face.

"The séance got me thinking. We think that Justin McLane and Monty and his dad and Trinity were buried hastily in the yard—Justin because he was hanged, and the McLane family because...because the circumstances were just as bad."

Jonah was surprised. "True, but...huh. We never thought to search for them before. And, well, the house could be sitting on Justin."

"Yep."

Jackson and Dallas came around the corner of the house on the kitchen side, rolling the apparatus that would help them explore.

"Can that thing find bones in the ground that long?" Jonah called out.

"It's specialized equipment, Mr. Whitney," Jackson said. "Pretty amazing—it can detect small amounts of bone in soil, and the soil can be analyzed, and scientists can even tell how long a body has been in the ground by the amount of fluids still present—or not present."

"Well, Justin has been dead a damned long time. You think bones could still be present?"

"Actually, it gets far more technical, but sometimes, bones can disappear in a hundred years, and, in others, such as extremely cold situations, they can last almost a million, but then there's calcification, and you're really looking at minerals," Jackson said.

"Never mind, forget I asked," Jonah said. "But good luck to you all. I'll be happy, sitting here, just watching what's going on."

He took a seat and leaned back in his chair, hands folded before him, a broad smile on his face.

Dallas and Jackson spoke to one another about dividing the yard in grids; Kristi decided it was time to text the gardener, Keith Hollis, and ask if he'd mind meeting up briefly sometime during the day.

He replied quickly that he could meet them in about fifteen minutes. After that, he'd be heading pretty far south to the suburbs, and he'd be out that way all day.

He'd sent the address where he would be. Kristi looked up at Angela. "Let's leave the guys to this and head out for a bit. I need to pick up a few things."

"Kristi, you know that Genie and Sydney and I are always happy to do any of the shopping for the things we need," Jonah interjected.

She laughed, and told him, "I will not trust you, Jonah, with my personal shopping." She stood and gave him a kiss on the cheek. Angela rose, as well.

Dallas looked over at them and frowned. "You're going out now?"

Kristi went over to where Dallas was laying out a string along the ground, dividing the yard into an organized grid for searching. "It's our only chance to talk to Hollis today," she said quietly.

He glanced at Angela, who had followed her over.

"I guess it doesn't matter much—this is a project that could go on a long time." He looked at Kristi, and then at Angela. "Be careful," he said.

Angela lifted a brow.

"Yes, you have seniority over me!" Dallas said, grinning. "I still say, be careful."

"We'll be very careful," Angela assured him.

"I'll drive—I know where I'm going," Kristi said as they walked to the car.

"That's fine with me—maybe you could circle the square for me, too, and on the way there and back, show me a bit of what getting around here is like."

The traffic seemed unusually heavy, and it made the short distance to the Ardsley Park area seem long. But Angela was a good companion, and explained a bit more about Dallas, and her own position, and Adam Harrison, as they drove.

"This was an interesting case. A few things coincided—we've actually been asked to look into haunted houses."

"Officially?"

"Oh, yes, there are many houses or buildings out there that are—one way or another—considered to be officially haunted. There's a place in New York that was declared haunted in a lawsuit—it went to court. The buyer felt that he'd been victimized, since the owner hadn't told him about the ghosts. And there are others. Your house is on the record as haunted. Adam had been given a list—and then he was approached by Joe Dunhill."

Kristi groaned. "I don't want to own an officially haunted house!"

Angela laughed. "You might as well embrace it—after that séance."

Kristi shook her head. "I never liked the idea of a séance—maybe because I've always been annoyed with Shelley and her theatrics."

"Her truth is in her perception—or in what makes for good séance material," Angela said.

"I can't tell her the truth," Kristi said. "Or, maybe I can! Maybe I should just tell her that Monty talks to me all the time now—and that he didn't do it!"

"You could," Angela said. "She might even believe you."

Kristi turned a corner and saw Keith Hollis's large work van parked up ahead.

She quickly pulled over to the side of the road.

"That's him?" Angela asked.

"Looks like he's getting ready to start on this yard," Kristi said.

Keith Hollis was a big man, solid rather than heavy, with massive forearms, a crinkled, weather-worn face and a smile that made up for it. He had just been going around to the back of the van, but he saw her park and hurried toward the women instead. "Kristi, you're looking fine. You doing okay?" He glanced at Angela, offering her his hand. Like the rest of him, it was powerful and solid.

"Keith Hollis, ma'am, at your service."

"Angela Hawkins, sir, a pleasure to meet you."

He frowned, looking at Kristi. "So, you've got them staying at the Murphy place?"

"I was full, and they need just a few nights. I mean, not that there aren't a lot of beautiful places they could be staying, but... they're friends and I wanted to offer them a spot," Kristi said.

"You doing all right there?" Keith asked Angela.

"Oh, we're fine, thank you," Angela said.

"I'm the one who was a little concerned, Keith," Kristi said. "I'm not really sure how to explain it, but I keep thinking that someone has been in there."

"I've been in there," he said, and then he shrugged. "You know, oddest thing—naw, never mind, I'm just being odd."

"Honestly, you know when I first went over to Ian's place the other day I felt something odd, too," Kristi agreed. "I didn't see anything out of place, and it didn't look as if anyone had pulled the house apart or anything, but I had the feeling that someone had been in there."

"That's it!" Keith exclaimed. "Yeah, nothing you could pinpoint, and his affairs were all in order long before he died—collections moved right to a museum. There's all the books, but—not that I'm much of a reader, sorry, I just like my hands in the soil—I didn't see any gaps in the bookcases or anything like that. Didn't notice anything moved or missing. So, really, I think it's just me being suspicious. Checked the locks, and the locks are all good."

"I didn't see anything out of place, either, and I don't understand, but it is just a creepy, eerie kind of feeling," Kristi said.

Keith's eyes widened. "Yeah, that's it. Creepy. Hey, I'm a big dude, and I did my time in the Middle East, and I shouldn't feel creeped out, but…yeah, that's the feeling." He shrugged, and grinned at Angela. "Told you, we are an odd lot. Maybe those of us from the historic district most of all."

"Oh, I don't think that you're odd at all, Mr. Hollis—maybe someone has been in the house, and your intuition is letting you know," Angela told him.

He shrugged. "I keep my keys close, ma'am. And I don't imagine Kristi goes handing out her keys either—well, other than that she runs a bed-and-breakfast. But she wouldn't go giving out the key to Ian's old place."

Kristi smiled weakly. "I didn't even know I had a key to Ian's until recently."

"But you don't hang it in the hall and tell guests to go drop in on the Murphy place, do you?" Keith asked her.

She shook her head, smiling. "But honestly, I didn't know about it. It was just there in a drawer in a kitchen. Just to be on the safe side, I might call Jamie and suggest that we get the locks changed."

"That would be fine by me," Keith said.

"You never saw anyone in there, right?" Angela asked.

"No," Keith said. "I never did. But to be honest, I haven't just been hanging around there. I go and do the yard, and I look through the house, just check the pipes—all the stuff that goes on old houses. And then I get out. I've only been inside twice since Jamie left…hasn't been that long that we lost Ian, you know."

"No, not that long," Kristi agreed.

"Well, still, you think that those locks need to be changed, you just call Jamie, and then let me know, and one of us can take care of it," Keith told Kristi. He touched his hand to his forehead, nodding to Angela. "A true pleasure to meet you, ma'am, a true pleasure."

"Thank you, Keith—thank you for talking to us," Kristi said.

"Anytime, Miss Kristi, anytime."

Kristi and Angela headed back to Kristi's car, and Keith moved on to get his equipment out of the van. As they walked to the car, Kristi told Angela, "It's the same—there's some kind of feeling in the house. I mean, it's not like they left a lingering scent of cologne, or anything like that, but when you know a place, and someone has been in it, there's just a sense of it, but it feels like there might be something real, and something underlying. I really don't know how to explain it."

Angela smiled at her as they reached the car. "Don't worry—you don't have to explain it. I think changing the locks might be a good idea, although it may be like closing the barn door once the horse has gotten out."

Kristi was still a minute.

"I don't know. You and Jackson are there now, but I even felt as if someone had been there—or was still there—just a few nights back when Dallas and I went to the house, when we started going through the library," she said.

"Then maybe we need a locksmith today," Angela told her. "Before tonight."

"Before night," Kristi agreed. "Because you think that if someone is getting in, they're coming by night?"

"Well, that, and I don't particularly like the darkness," Angela said, grinning. "And, I especially don't like surprise visits by darkness!"

Kristi smiled, then got in the car. She felt torn in so many directions—she wanted to get back into Ian's library. And she wanted to be at her house, to see what was going on, to see if...

If Eliza Malone had come to her because, somehow, the woman's body had wound up buried in her yard.

"This could take a very long time and not give us anything," Jackson had said when they'd started out.

But he'd been proved wrong.

The ground-penetrating radar tool looked a bit like a lawnmower, with a wheeled base that he pushed slowly over the search area. A small screen on the handlebars showed an image of what lay beneath.

They'd been at it no more than forty minutes or so when Jackson stopped.

He had been working about ten feet to the left of the monument to Justin McLane when he stopped and turned and looked at Dallas.

"There's something here," he said.

"Really? Already?"

Jonah jumped up from the table where he had been sitting and walked back to them—pausing suddenly as if walking over earth he'd walked over a dozen times might change things.

"You found...something?"

Jackson studied the readings on the screen before him.

"I think that we need to call in the local authorities, and some experts in forensic anthropology, since this may not be a recent grave. But you can even see..."

He moved away; Dallas moved forward. Friends had shown him sonograms done when they had discovered they were expecting a baby.

This seemed similar—and completely different.

There was a shape; awkward and indistinct. And, yet, there was clearly something that wasn't just soil under the ground there.

He looked at Jackson. Then he shook his head. "They missed...when they were creating this little memorial area out here. They had to have dug for that monument, and they missed what—what's here."

"It's not a surprise—we always thought maybe the bodies were back here," Jonah said. "But whose body is it?"

"That, I can't tell you. I'm not an expert, and we only recently bought this equipment for the unit," Jackson said. He looked at Dallas. "From here, we need to let Kristi know, get her permission and then..."

"Then we start digging," Dallas said.

"You're going to dig?" Jonah asked. "Dig them up?"

Dallas looked over at him, surprised. "Jonah, if a McLane is down there, don't you want to be able to give them a proper burial? They can go to the family plot."

"They've been here this long. I don't know," Jonah said.

He seemed disturbed by the idea. Why?

Unless it wasn't a long-dead McLane who was down there. It might be a fresh grave, or one just two years there...dug in the night in the far rear of the house, when no one knew.

He kept his smile in place. "I take it there's a shovel in the toolshed?"

"Of course there's a shovel," Jonah said. "I'm not sure you should be shoveling. I mean, you could crack into the bones. Don't people do this more carefully?"

"We're just going to go down and make sure we've found human bones," Jackson said. "Then we'll cover it over and get an anthropologist to supervise, if the bones are old."

"If? What the hell else would they be?" Jonah demanded. He seemed agitated.

It made Dallas all the more eager to work quickly. Kristi knew everyone there, but he did not. His natural sense of logic made a possible suspect group larger—and that included Jonah.

Jackson paced out the area that would need to be excavated, outlining it with strings tied taut to small stakes in the ground. Kristi and Angela came out the back door just as Jonah—unhappily—went to the old outbuilding that now held storage and lawn equipment.

"You found something?" Kristi said, walking toward them. Her features were tense, and she looked as if she was hoping it was so—and dreading such a thing as well.

"There's definitely a skeleton down there."

"A skeleton?"

She looked as if she might fall over. He was ready to rush over to her; she steadied herself.

"Where do we go from here?" she asked.

"If you're okay with it, we're going to dig deep enough to ascertain what we have, and then call Joe Dunhill, and bring in an expert if we think we've found an old grave," Jackson explained.

"Do it," Kristi told them.

Jonah appeared with a shovel; Dallas started digging, following the directions Jackson gave him. It wasn't an easy task; he had to go several feet down.

"The dead should just lie buried, resting in peace," Jonah said. "Hell, what are you going down, six or seven feet?"

Dallas was already standing knee-deep in the pit he was digging. "Maybe," he told Jonah cheerfully.

"Dead should rest in peace," Jonah said again.

"Jonah, it's my family. If they're down there... I want to know."

"I can dig for a while," Jackson said.

"I'm fine," Dallas said, but he paused to wipe his brow. By that point, he was pretty sure they'd discovered an old burial.

A hastily dug grave, just a few feet deep, would be more in line with a clandestine burial at night.

But this grave was deep.

"Careful, you're almost there," Jackson said.

"I'll quit with the shovel. I can use a little whisk broom or something," he said, looking up at Jonah.

Jonah was just staring at him, deeply disturbed.

"I'll get it," Kristi said. She dashed to the outbuilding and re-appeared almost immediately, bearing a small broom.

Dallas went back to work. A few minutes later, he cleared dirt off what was obviously a piece of bone. Careful to crouch at the outside edges of the pit he'd made, he kept moving the broom carefully, exposing, bit by bit, a skeleton.

"It's—it's not..." He looked at her, not wanting to speak suspicions aloud with Jonah there.

"I think it's a McLane," he said.

"Justin... Monty?" Kristi asked.

He hesitated, glancing at Jackson first. "I'm not... I'm not any kind of an expert. But the skeleton is small, and I think it's a woman."

"Trinity?" Kristi asked.

"Trinity!" She heard the name whispered from behind her, and she swung around. She hadn't seen Monty in the yard be-fore, but he was there now, staring past her at the grave. The ghost fell to his knees, bowing his head, and sobbed.

"Should have let her rest," Jonah said.

"My Trinity," Monty whispered again.

Dallas looked at Jackson. "I'll call Joe Dunhill. And..." He paused, looking over at Kristi—and the bowed and sobbing spirit of Monty. "Kristi, the medical examiner seems like a good fel-low. We'll let him disinter this lady, and...verify her identity the best we can. And, then, if you wish, whoever she is, we can see that she has a place in your family plot, and receives a fu-neral, too."

He knew that Kristi was waiting for Jonah to leave.

She wanted to comfort Monty.

Dallas pulled out his phone while the others waited patiently. "We found bones in the backyard. I'd like to see that they're properly attended to—and reverently treated," he told Joe.

"Bones—old bones, new bones?" Joe asked tensely.

"Old, we believe," Dallas told him.

"I'll be right out there," Joe promised. "You're sure—they're old?"

"Pretty sure—there's nothing left but bone," he said.

Finally, Jonah made a disapproving tsk sound, and headed for the house. When he was gone, Kristi quickly knelt down by Monty.

"I'm so sorry, but you knew she was here, Monty, you knew she was here," she told him.

"They threw her in the ground, like trash," Monty said.

"Monty, you and Justin are here, too," she reminded him.

Monty glanced up at Justin, and Justin told her, "There's something different about it. We were soldiers, fighters. Trinity...was nothing but light and goodness. She didn't deserve this."

"None of you deserved it," Kristi said. "No one should be treated as trash. But, Monty, I swear, we'll see to it that she is buried properly. We'll find you, and Justin and Samuel McLane, and we'll do our best to make it right."

Monty nodded, and stood; Kristi stood, as well. As she did so, a curious frown touched her brow.

Dallas was still standing in the hole he'd dug. She reached out to him and said, "Dallas, there is something else there."

She was going to jump down by his side and he quickly reached for her, lifting her down into the pit. She knelt.

How she'd seen the object, he would never know. It was completely encrusted in dirt, and there was barely a glint of anything.

But she carefully reached down, using her fingers to push

away the dark earth covering the object, and then she pulled it out very carefully.

She held a locket.

"It was hers. Open it," Monty said.

Kristi did so, and then after a moment, gave the locket to Dallas.

He looked down at a tiny picture of Monty on one side of locket, and a picture of Trinity on the other. The tiny old photographs were faded and barely discernible, and yet, it was clear—Trinity had worn the locket, keeping her beloved close to her heart.

"It's yours now, Kristi," Monty said.

"We'll bury it with her," Kristi said.

Monty shook his head. "No. She would want you to have it. And don't worry. I will be here, I will be here day and night, until they come. They will treat her gently, oh, I will see to it that they treat her gently!"

Jonah had told Genie and Sydney what was going on, and the two soon rushed out—a little frightened, but mostly intrigued.

"How did you find her?" Genie asked.

"Well, we suspected she was back here somewhere—and probably others, as well. Dallas had been telling me about Jackson and his machines, and I thought it would be interesting to search," Kristi told them.

"Interesting," Genie murmured.

"Creepy!" Sydney said.

They stared at the hole as Joe Dunhill arrived, and shortly thereafter, medical examiner Dr. Perry, who they'd specifically requested, and who was bringing in a friend of his from the nearby university, an anthropologist and a visiting lecturer who had most recently been excavating a Georgia battlefield site. Perry had told them she was an MD and also had her doctorate in biological anthropology—a very impressive woman.

Dr. Perry arrived, along with his colleague, Dr. Colleen Horvath, a very thin woman of about fifty with close-cropped iron-gray hair, bright blue eyes—and tremendous energy. She pumped Kristi's hand, and let them all know she was delighted to help them in any way.

"I'm a field worker—I love young minds, but I already miss being in the field. Of course, I've heard about McLane House, and what happened here." She hesitated. "This is one of your ancestors, and I will be gentle, and take very good care of the remains, I promise you."

"Thank you," Kristi said.

Monty was watching, with Justin behind him, a ghostly hand on his shoulder. Monty had, at least, regained control. His only sad words after the doctors arrived were "She's here, she's here, and yet, still, I cannot see her, I cannot touch her, I can't tell her how very sorry I am that I came home and that Huntington arrived just as I did."

It was inevitable the guests of McLane House should come back to their lodging. Granger Knox was the first to come back, and he appeared to be curious at first, and then disgusted. "Let the dead alone, that's my motto," he said, shaking his head, and returning to the house. Carl Brentwood, accompanied by Murray but not Claire, arrived, and he immediately thought that a documentary on McLane House and the discovery of the bones would be a terrific effort.

Carl cornered Kristi in the kitchen when she'd gone in to bring out a few bottles of water for those who had been in the yard for hours now. He was already holding his digital video camera.

His enthusiasm was electric, but she wasn't particularly in the mood for discussions on a show—not at the moment.

"Carl, please, let's just get her out of the ground," she said softly.

"Oh, Kristi, I am so sorry. I didn't think about what this

meant to you. I guess, I just think it was all so far in the past, but then...you've been through a lot, huh? You were at a funeral for your friend yesterday, and you just lost Jedidiah... I'm so sorry. Truly, I don't mean to be so thoughtless. But you found your great-great-whatever grandmother...wait, she'd have been McLane—you're Stewart. Are you a descendent?"

"A Stewart married a McLane daughter in the years after the Civil War," Kristi explained.

"Of course, then, forgive me. I can't help but thinking..."

The kitchen door swung open and Lacey Knox walked in. She smiled seeing Carl Brentwood, and then frowned—apparently, she hadn't expected to find Kristi, too.

"Hi, Lacey," Kristi said.

Lacey gave her an odd look. "You're all dirty," she said. "You've been grave-digging, I hear."

"Something like that," Kristi said.

"Guess you need a shower," Lacey said, her tone sweet—but something else, as well. With some amusement, Kristi realized Lacey was jealous of her.

"I guess I need a shower," Kristi said, and headed out.

"Kristi," Carl called her back.

She paused.

"Thank you for everything, and I'm so sorry."

"Carl, it's okay. We'll talk about it—just later, please."

She went back out to the courtyard, a six-pack of water in her hand. At the back door, she hesitated. Shelley had arrived; she was standing by one of the courtyard tables, speaking animatedly with Murray Meyer.

Murray seemed angry.

Shelley seemed angry, too.

Kristi opened the door just in time to hear Murray saying, "Well, it's just a little too late now, don't you think? Who the hell ever figured on this?"

Shelley cleared her throat, directing Murray's attention to Kristi in the doorway.

He turned and saw her. "Ah, Kristi, big happenings here today, huh?" He grinned. "If you're going to find a body," he added, "it's best to find a very old one, huh?"

"It wasn't an accidental find," Kristi said. "Dallas had his friends come down because we'd been talking about the fact several family members were supposed to have been buried hastily on the grounds."

"Ah, you went looking. Séance got you going, too, huh?"

"Maybe," Kristi said. "But I guess it's something I've always thought about—I used to talk about it with Jedidiah," she said. In truth, they had mentioned it now and then—but never taken the idea anywhere. They wouldn't have known what do to, really. They hadn't known anything about tools such as the ground-penetrating radar mechanism Jackson had brought, and randomly digging up the yard hadn't seemed like a particularly good idea.

"I suppose such a thing would be natural," Murray said. "I mean, when you know you have relatives in your yard."

"I've been telling you Trinity is here, haunting the place," Shelley said.

Kristi just smiled and walked by them.

There were workers who had come along with the two doctors; they were arranging a grid so the bones could be removed with several inches of the dirt around them. Dallas looked over at Kristi, a frown furrowing his brow. She smiled at him, hoping that would show him she was doing just fine.

Yellow tape and warning placards now surrounded the hole; Joe Dunhill told them not to worry—there were police patrolling the area at all times already, watching out that Carl Brentwood's fans didn't become so overzealous that they encroached on his space, or her property.

They stood and waited and watched, and eventually the bones

were loaded into a box and onto a panel van. Dallas was going to fill in the hole; Dr. Horvath asked that they wait.

"We may want to do a little more exploring in there. You don't have any children staying here, do you? It's clearly marked—no one should be falling into it, especially with everyone in the house aware there is a big hole back here."

Kristi was still unhappy the yard wasn't fenced, but it was certainly too late to throw one up. She thought about the times they'd discovered that kids had been digging in the yard—a set of young adults as well—looking for bones or artifacts themselves because of the house's reputation.

But police were patrolling; her guests were adults.

"Liability is scary as hell," she muttered.

"You do have insurance?" Jackson asked her.

"If anyone is foolish enough to come out here and fool around, you can haul them into court for trespassing and ignoring obvious signs to beware," Colleen Horvath said.

"You're coming with us?" Dr. Perry asked, looking at Dallas.

"Yes, I'll accompany the bones," Dallas said.

"Hey, I hang at the morgue often enough," Joe Dunhill said.

Kristi lingered in the yard while Dallas and Joe climbed into the front bench of the panel van containing the bones, and they drove off, followed by the doctors and the rest of the forensic team in their own cars.

She had the distinct feeling of being watched.

Jonah was in the house.

But she could see him standing at the back window.

Murray and Shelley remained in the courtyard, solemnly watching the strange procession drive away. Genie and Sydney had gone in, but she knew they were in the back parlor, looking out—she had seen them in the back door.

Angela said, "There's nothing more we can do for the time. I'm thinking that Colleen Horvath wants to come back here and explore around the hole, hoping for more artifacts. I'd like to get back to the Murphy place now and start in that library. Jackson?"

"That's a good plan," he said, and then hesitated. "Kristi, I was about to tell you that you're welcome to come with us or stay here, but with this discovery—even if we did find Trinity and her remains are down to bone—things may start happening. If there's a killer operating in the area, this might make them nervous. I think you need to be with one of us. In fact, I think Dallas would want my head on a platter if anything happened to you."

"I understand. Searching in the library still seems important. I just... I need a shower," she said.

"We'll wait," Jackson said.

Kristi nodded and went in through the back door. Genie and Sydney had obviously just moved away from it. Again, she felt as if Shelley and Murray Meyer were watching her—why and for what, she had no idea.

Upstairs, she unlocked her door and slipped into her room, shedding her clothing as she headed for the shower.

Halfway to the bathroom, she paused. There was a piece of paper on the bed. She picked it up, knowing it had not been there when she'd left the room.

It was a page from a McLane House notepad. There were only a few words on it, the letters or full words clipped from a magazine and stuck on.

"Stop trying, or suffer the consequences."

CHAPTER FOURTEEN

"It's actually far easier to give an age for a child, but with just a precursory study, I can tell you this—the bones belonged to a woman. You can tell from the pelvis. She stood about five foot two. Her teeth are good—she was very lucky, she had all of them. The amount of wear on the teeth and other factors suggest the woman died somewhere between the ages of thirty-two, say, and thirty-seven. There are many, many more tests I can do," Dr. Horvath said. "If Miss Stewart wants it documented as pure fact that this lady was her ancestor, we can do DNA testing."

"Cause of death?" Dallas asked.

"I'm still studying the bones for nicks and abrasions," Horvath said. "There are all kinds of things we can do to determine what might have happened. But they do take time."

"Right," Dallas said.

"Cause of death, and method of death," Dr. Perry said. "At this point, we can't tell you either. If there are nicks on the bones, we could possibly theorize about a bullet wound, or a knife to the chest. But if a bullet hit soft tissue, or even if a knife hit soft tissue, that tissue is long gone."

Dr. Horvath had been doing most of the work, but Dr. Perry

hadn't left the autopsy room. He felt Dallas studying him and looked up. "Sorry, she is the expert here. No brain or heart to weigh, no stomach contents... Bones this old, well... But," he said cheerfully, "I am happy to be here, to have her in my morgue, to share in this fascinating discovery. And, luckily, no elderly person died alone last night, and we didn't have a single murder in the county!"

"Yep, lucky," Dallas murmured, glancing over at Joe Dunhill.

"Right now," Dr. Horvath said, "I've taken some samples. They'll go to the lab. We're going to put her away for the night—tenderly and with respect, Mr. Wicker. You may convey that to Miss Stewart for me. We will be extremely careful and respectful, I promise you."

Dallas glanced over at Joe. They were politely being asked to leave, and since Perry and Horvath were going off to do all the paperwork needed for the tests they were requesting, there was really no more reason for them to be there.

Not to mention, Monty and Justin had followed them to the morgue; those two wouldn't be leaving—they would watch over the remains.

"Thank you," he said, and he and Joe headed out.

They stood out on the sidewalk.

"You weren't digging to find old bones, were you?" Joe asked.

"It was no big surprise, though," Dallas said. "There's nothing—nothing at all new on the disappearances—Eliza Malone or Simon Drake?"

Dunhill shook his head. "Eliza Malone's case is still open on the books, but in truth, it's gone very cold. When it happened, of course, we interviewed every coworker, every family member—everyone. We were still left with nothing other than she was having a meeting somewhere around Johnson Square. As far as Simon Drake goes, we're still getting reports of sightings of the man—and we follow every lead, and we've discovered that he looks like half the men in the city. People are trying to help, but we've had nothing concrete." He inhaled deeply. "Man, I'm hoping. I mean, there are cases that go unsolved, but I honestly believe two people were murdered, and the two who have disappeared are dead, as well. That's just—heinous and unacceptable."

"Yes," Dallas said.

"Jackson and Angela—they're Krewe?"

"Top Krewe," Dallas told them. "Jackson is our acting field director. Angela runs the office, chooses and assigns cases and can find out almost anything about anyone."

"We've pulled up everything we could, too," Dunhill said. "What's so bizarre is there is no real victimology. You might kill a politician because he's got an agenda that would wreck you. You might kill a personal trainer because…you're in love with him and he doesn't love you. Or something personal like that. But why the hell would anyone throw an old man out from his balcony? He was going to die anyway."

"But maybe not quickly enough," Dallas said. He looked at the detective. "You had the usual suspects. I'm looking at the more unusual, putting it all together around the fact everything took place in the same general area—and just might have centered on Ian Murphy."

"Eliza Malone disappeared two years ago. Ian Murphy is hardly cold in his grave."

"Right, but what if someone thought he had something then—that he didn't actually have until later? Or had no idea what he had. I've gone through this over and over again in my head, and I know my people have looked at it from every angle, too. Unless we're both just way off the mark, and Ian jumped and Lachlan tripped, and the two disappearances were for monetary and political reasons, it's the only theory that makes any sense."

He was going to tell Joe about Kristi being threatened in the ladies' room, but Kristi wasn't sure herself if the threat had come from the living or the dead.

"Kristi was out in the courtyard at the brewery after Lachlan Plant's funeral. She thought she heard people whispering about a letter."

"A letter? Did she think it had to do with Lachlan's death?"

"Yes, I'm assuming."

"Keep your eye on her," Joe Dunhill said softly. "We have cops going by the house constantly, but they aren't sitting on the property."

"No, they're not," Dallas said.

"What's your next move?"

"We only covered part of the McLane property today—not even half. But with Jamie Murphy's permission, I think we might use some ground-penetrating radar over there."

"Let me know—if it's all right with you, I wouldn't mind being around," Joe told him.

"I'll give you a call in the morning," he said.

He and Joe had barely parted ways before his phone rang. It was Jackson.

"Is everything all right?" Dallas asked.

"Status quo. I got a call from Vickie Preston back at headquarters. She's a historian who recently graduated from the Academy, and she helps Angela with research. After Angela's initial searches, Vickie kept digging. Here's an interesting bit—she found that Lacey Knox was adopted. It was a closed adoption, everything sealed, and she was an infant when it happened. Also, the construction guy—Granger Knox—has political aspirations."

"Very interesting. Thanks."

"There's more, we have a bit on the agent, Mr. Murray Meyer. A very interesting connection there—Meyer is a second cousin to a man named Richard Burr. Mr. Burr was convicted of manslaughter in the second about fifteen years ago—the victim being his wife. He claimed they were both drinking, and she fell. Apparently, there were eyewitnesses who saw them arguing, and the charge the DA went with was manslaughter. Mr. Murray's travel records indicate he was here two years ago—specifically to see his cousin."

"You said a fall—how did Mrs. Burr die exactly?"

"Impact with the ground—she went off a third-floor balcony."

"Now, that's really interesting. Is there anything tying anyone to locations near Johnson Square—or to Ian Murphy, specifically?"

"Not that we've found—they're still looking."

"We can try to draw Mr. Murray into conversation, see what he has to say. Worst thing with all of this, we can't find a reason to haul anyone down to the police station to be questioned," Dallas said.

"One more thing," Jackson told him.

"What's that?"

"Jonah Whitney. His great-grandfather was married to a woman from New York," Jackson said.

Dallas frowned. "And? Sorry, I mean, through generations, we're all married to people from all over the country—and from other countries, as well. We are a land of immigrants—and, of course, Native Americans," he said, acknowledging Jackson's paternal heritage.

Jackson laughed. "And—you're right. It means nothing to most of us. Jonah is just a die-hard Southerner. He may not be happy about it. It might be the family scandal."

Jonah? The man had been best friends with Jedidiah McLane and Ian Murphy. He had worked in the house for years. He seemed to love Kristi...

But it was true that what seemed to be wasn't always what *was*.

"You're with Kristi now, right?"

"She just went up to shower, then we're going to hit the Murphy place, and Ian's library again—the answers may well be there."

"Jackson, this may be overkill, but..."

"Not to worry. One of us will go up and wait outside her door."

"I'll be there soon."

"Just meet us at the Murphy house."

"Will do."

Dallas hung up. And even though Jackson was with Kristi, and Angela was there, he felt uneasy. He still felt a growing sense of urgency to get back.

I will not panic. I will not panic! Kristi told herself.

She had looked at the piece of paper way too long.

She went quickly into motion and began gathering her clothing again. Dressed, she ran back down the stairs, and almost right into Claire Danson, who was just heading up.

"Kristi! Hey, high excitement, huh?" Claire said.

"High excitement," Kristi replied.

"Carl is seeing so many promo opportunities," Claire said.

"And I told him we'll talk later," Kristi said. "Excuse me, Claire."

She hurried past the woman and out back, wondering vaguely if Lacey Knox had Carl Brentwood off somewhere private again, and if her parents even suspected.

But that didn't matter, not at the moment.

She hurried out, smiling as she passed Murray and Shelley, and startled when she saw that Angela was already heading toward the house—and her.

"Angela, I need you," she said simply.

"Of course!"

"Upstairs. Please."

Angela followed her immediately. Kristi led the way back up to her room. Angela entered behind her and closed and locked the door. Then Kristi handed the note to Angela. "This was on my bed when I just came up here," she said.

"Just now—and you're sure it wasn't here before?"

"I'm positive. Dallas was up, and I made the bed before I left—and I locked my door. I always lock the door to my room. Jedidiah taught me if you're going to run an open bed-and-breakfast like this, you must always lock your own door. I don't forget, and I... It's rote for me, but I never forget."

"But Jonah and your housekeepers have keys."

"Yes, but—I swear to you, I'd know if this was from some-one in my household staff."

Angela was silent for a minute. "Do you have an envelope in here? We can check it for prints—they might be in the system. Or other DNA—these letters were pasted on, so some type of transference might have occurred. It's just that..."

"What?"

"It's obvious. It's paper, and it is evidence, and the thing is, someone obviously did this to threaten you."

"And there was the whisper when I was in the bathroom," Kristi said. "It could have been for me, and it could have been... an accident. Or, it could have been...someone dead! I just don't know."

"And they could be unrelated," Angela said calmly. "Take your shower. I'll be right here. You'll be safe," she promised. "We've received a little more information I'll share with you once we're out of here. But enjoy your shower—I'm here, and I promise you, no one will be getting by me."

"Thanks," Kristi murmured.

She collected clean clothing and went into the bathroom, let the water run hot, and long, and thought about the bones in the ground.

Was finding them really going to be the catalyst for some-thing? Had it already begun? Had the note been a real threat? It felt real.

She felt herself stiffen beneath the water; she was suddenly angry. She'd been threatened—by the living, certainly. From what she'd learned so far, ghosts didn't write notes, or create them out of words chopped out of magazines.

She had been an idiot. She should have screamed. The lights had gone out in the ladies' room, and then she had heard the whisper.

Someone wanted her to stop.

Stop what?

Dallas held the letter carefully in his hand, and looked at Kristi, and then at Jackson and Angela.

He was concerned, because she was concerned. But she didn't appear to be scared; she seemed strong, if anything—and mad.

"They were in my room. *My* room," she said angrily.

"I'm not making light of this situation, but this looks like... it looks like something someone who watches a lot of movies might do. I think we will find fingerprints, because I don't be-lieve whoever did this is sophisticated enough to have pulled off a murder that could be made to look as if a fit man fell off a curb."

Kristi frowned. "Perhaps this is something different, but I think we need to look into it," she said.

They were up in Ian Murphy's office with Jackson and An-gela; while the others dug into the rest of the books, Dallas had intended to read the book he'd been keeping in his jacket pocket.

He didn't want Kristi being alone.

She wasn't alone, of course. She was with Jackson and An-gela, two of the most competent and wary people he had ever met. But now, he determined that he needed to find out just who had set the note on Kristi's bed—and why.

He also wanted to talk to Murray Meyer.

"Isn't your social hour about to start over at McLane House?" he asked Kristi.

She nodded. He glanced over at Angela; she was at Murphy's desk, trying to get around the passcode on the computer there.

Jackson had been combing the bookshelves, focusing on the books that had to do with the Civil War.

"I'm going to leave you all to this. I'm going back to McLane House and see what I can discover."

"You want to call Joe Dunhill on the letter?" Jackson asked him.

"Not quite yet," he said, looking at Kristi. "I'm going to take this for a minute. Are you okay with that?"

She nodded solemnly.

"I'm probably going to have Angela and Kristi keep working here, and start with the ground-penetrating radar in the yard," Jackson told him. "It's dark out, but the machine doesn't care."

Dallas nodded. "I'll be back—after social hour, which won't, of course, be anywhere near as charming without the hostess there."

Kristi smiled.

"Ah, not to worry—you'll have a movie star to gape at—and I'm willing to bet Shelley is still hanging around, happy Trinity has been found, and certain she has contacted her many times."

Jackson headed down with Dallas. He waved as Dallas turned the corner to head across Johnson Square and back toward McLane House.

Dallas's return hit the middle of the social hour. He found Carl Brentwood and Claire in the front parlor, talking about future filming in the house, and what a full-length documentary might mean for his popularity as a hands-on, go-places, down-to-earth kind of actor.

Lacey Knox was hanging on his every word.

"Mr. Wicker!" Carl said, standing as Dallas entered. "Anything to tell us?"

"Nothing new," Dallas said. "It will take time."

"Still—it's amazing. Amazing. I mean, we booked this place on purpose," he said, glancing at Claire. "But I never expected anything like this. So much!"

"Carl did find the house, and forgive me, Mr. Wicker, if I seem callous," Claire said. "Being a celebrity isn't such an easy thing, and, well, the more popular we make Carl with fans, the better chance we have at keeping him on a growth chart, so to say. Far too many people fly—and then crash and burn. We have to be grateful."

"I'm grateful you're here," Lacey murmured.

"Good that you're all happy," Dallas said. "However, I would let a little of the dust settle before you come on too strong to Kristi."

"Oh, yeah, I got it," Carl said.

"She has to understand just how important it is!" Lacey said passionately.

She was so young—and so obviously in love.

He considered Lacey. Adopted. But what did that mean? If anything? Just eighteen…certainly far too young to have had anything to do with the disappearance of Eliza Malone. There was no age limit on a person's tendency for cruelty, but the logistics didn't work out.

Not when it came to murder.

"Well, I'll let you get back to it," Dallas said, moving on.

Granger and Janet were in the back parlor, deep in conversation with Murray Meyer over the state of the world. Dallas pulled up a chair, joining them. Murray glanced his way with a little half smile, and then continued addressing Granger Knox. "We definitely need a better system, but who is going to manage it, I don't know. As far as I can see, right wing, left wing, all our politicians have blown it. But now, here is a question. These days, by the very nature of the beast, don't you agree that politics just about corrupt a man from the get-go?"

"Not a good man," Granger argued.

"Good men seem to go by the wayside," Dallas said. "By all reports, the fellow who just disappeared—Simon Drake—was one of the good ones."

"Probably, a guy who shouldn't have had enemies," Murray said.

Granger sniffed. "Just as you were saying, Murray, by the nature of the beast, a politician has enemies. Someone is always going to have a different policy."

"You're about to run for a seat in Congress, Granger, isn't that right?" Dallas asked.

"I am, sir, and I am middle-of-the-road, but mainly, pro-America. Pro the people, and pro the Union and a government that does worry about all the people. The working guy—the man who does his nine-to-five, and hopes to keep a house, and his health, and, well, the pursuit of happiness." He waved a hand in the air, indicating the back of the house. "We're too divided. We fought a great war—borrowing from Lincoln there. And, we did prove that a house divided cannot stand. Hey, by the way, you find out anything more about those bones?"

"So far—definitely a woman. They'll get exact dates and specifications and all that—it just takes time," Dallas said.

Granger sniffed. "They'll find out that it is, indeed, Trinity McLane out there. Stories don't come through the decades unless they're true."

"Truth can often be what we've been taught—what we're led to believe," Dallas said, standing. He excused himself, heading into the kitchen. Genie and Sydney were talking about the bones as they worked on fresh trays of pastries and crudities.

"Hey, you're back—what can I get for you?" Genie asked.

"I think I'll just have a bottle of water, and please don't let me interrupt. I can open a refrigerator door."

"What did you find out?" Sydney asked anxiously.

"So far, nothing we don't know, or think, already. The bones definitely belonged to a woman, and they've been in the ground a long time," Dallas said.

"Creepy, so creepy," Sydney said.

Dallas leaned back against the counter. "Sydney, I'm curious. You have a skeleton key that opens all the rooms, right?"

"I do, sir, of course—for housekeeping, and emergencies," Sydney said, frowning. "But you told me to leave your room alone. I have done so, sir, I swear it!"

"Oh, no, Sydney, I didn't mean anything by that—I know that you're very good at all that you do," Dallas said. "But who has access to the key?"

"There are actually three of them," Genie said, stepping in with a frown. "I keep one, Sydney keeps one and we keep one in the drawer—right there. That way, if they needed it, either Jonah or Kristi would have access. It just sits in there, though—thank God! We've never had an emergency where we had to break-in or anything. A wild crowd usually books at a bigger chain hotel. While we attract families, students, people who love the old and historic—and ghost hunters, apparently."

"Why?" Sydney asked, frowning. "Do you think someone was in your room?"

He smiled. "Just curious," he said.

Dallas glanced out the back windows and saw that Jonah was outside, seated at one of the courtyard tables—with Janet Knox. He smiled at the women, and headed out back.

"Evening!" he said.

"Nice night—nice night to settle over…a big hole in the ground," Jonah said.

Janet smiled. "Jonah doesn't like digging up the dead—I find it fascinating," Janet said.

Jonah shook his head. "No surprise—we knew she was there. Now Shelley Blake will be raising Trinity every time she comes in here—and going on and on about the poor woman's spirit being locked on the grounds—even if she is reburied in a family plot."

Janet laughed softly. "Oh, Jonah—you should have been part of that séance. That Miss Stewart—she did see something, though what… Maybe in her mind's eye. I mean, I do more or less believe that there is more to this world than we can possibly understand, but then again… I don't know. I didn't get to see whatever she saw." She stood and smiled at them both. "Well, let me go see if that husband of mine wants to go out for the evening. Nice to talk to you," she said, and hurried on back into the house, leaving Dallas alone with Jonah.

They were silent for a minute, and then Jonah said, "Well, I don't think that I can stay out here all night."

"You were thinking of staying out here all night?" Dallas asked.

He shrugged, as if unhappy. "No bones about it, and no pun intended. I don't like that we dug up the dead. But we did. When I came out here, that woman was snooping around the hole. She said that she thought that we might see something else—a belt buckle, something. A great artifact—which, of course, she'd have handed right over to us, but…the liability! Damned woman could have fallen in and hurt herself!"

"Okay, Jonah, I guess you're right. You hang in for a while, and I'll get someone out here. My friends and I can switch around through the night. We'll get Dr. Horvath back out here as quickly as possible, and then we'll get it filled in."

"That will be fine," Jonah said.

Dallas left him and went back into the house.

No one was in the back parlor. The Knox family and Carl, Murray and Claire were all in the front room. Claire was talking to Carl about the importance of his appearing to his fans and appearing before them alone.

Janet Murray was being short with Lacey, telling her that they were on a family vacation.

Dallas had barely gotten into the front parlor before Lacey said something angrily to her mother, brushed past him and headed up the stairs.

"Teenagers!" Granger said, shaking his head. "Can't live with them!"

"She's a good girl," Janet argued. "Just..." She paused, glancing over at Carl. "She just has a puppy crush," she said softly to Dallas. "But you mark my words. We will keep her on the straight and narrow, and she'll wind up being even more famous than him."

"Fine—I need a real dinner," Granger said. He nodded grimly to Dallas and headed for the front door. Janet followed him.

Dallas turned and hurried up the stairs after Lacey.

"Miss Knox!"

She stopped, just about to enter her room. "I'm not going with them, Mr. Wicker, if they sent you up here to tell me that I should love and honor my parents."

He smiled. "I don't care if you go with them or not."

"Is that reverse psychology?"

"No," he said. And he produced the baggie with the letter than had been left on Kristi's bed. "I want to know about this."

Angela was deep into her work on the computer.

Kristi was proud; she'd actually helped Angela figure out Ian Murphy's password, which turned out to be Jamie's birthday along with the name Rufus.

Rufus had been Ian's favorite pet, a massive Irish wolfhound. Rufus had led an outstanding long life, especially for his breed, but Ian had never wanted a pet after Rufus had passed.

Kristi's back was actually hurting her—she hadn't realized her own concentration after going through book after book for content.

She stood, glancing over at Angela. "I'm going to run down and see if Jackson has found anything, if that's all right," she said.

Angela looked up, confused for a moment, her concentration had been so intense. "Oh, okay. Let me know if he thinks he might have found anything."

"For sure."

Kristi hurried on down the stairs, and then, at the entry, she paused.

It hadn't seemed so bad upstairs, in Ian's office.

But here...

She felt it again. The terrible darkness, the haze, the fog—whatever it was—that seemed to weigh so heavily on the house. She wanted to run outside, but she paused, as if compelled.

And then, she knew why.

Something seemed to be forming in the middle of the haze and the mist. It wasn't distinct, but she knew... Eliza Malone was there. Trying to reach her.

The woman stared at her, big, entreating eyes clear within the wavering face.

She reached out to Kristi. Her lips moved, but no words formed, and then her eyes looked downward, to the floor.

She disappeared again, swallowed into the haze and the dark fog of dust motes that seemed to cover the room like an eerie, ethereal blanket.

Kristi found energy, and she moved, flying out of the house, and racing over to Jackson, who was working near one of the yard's big magnolia trees.

"Jackson!"

"Yes?" He looked up at her. "You found something?"

She shook her head. "No, I mean, not upstairs. Angela is still working. No, no... I need to know, can you use that in the house—in the basement?"

"Yes, we could use it there. Do you know something, or suspect something?"

"Logically? We all think that someone has been in the house. Still looking for something—or, maybe checking on something. In the basement, some of the floor is poured concrete, and some of it—where wood and coal and all are stored—is just earth, basic ground of the foundation from the time that the house was built. Not logically? I just saw Eliza—and she's not at McLane House, she's here."

The apparatus was apparently fairly heavy, but Jackson didn't hesitate to move it.

"Do you need help?" she asked.

"No, thank you. Just show me where to go."

She hurried back to the house, through to the kitchen and the stairs down to the basement; Jackson followed her more slowly. She hit the light switch.

Overhead bulbs flashed on.

They didn't seem to dispel the miasma, the dark cloud that permeated the place.

Jackson made it down with the radar. "Where do you think?" he asked.

She pointed to an area with a woodpile, a covered barbecue and stacks of charcoal, and then strode to it, tossing charcoal bags and logs for the fireplace off of the pile and letting them fall wherever they may lay. Jackson quickly joined her, making the work much quicker.

"I think… I don't know," she said.

He brought over the radar tool, studied the screen as he moved it slowly over the dirt floor. And then he looked up at her. She couldn't read his expression. Jackson turned away and hurried through the basement until he found a shovel.

And he began to dig.

Not so deep, not nearly so deep as the hole they'd dug to find Trinity McLane.

After a couple minutes of effort, Jackson stepped back.

"Time to call Dallas and Joe Dunhill," he said. "I do believe that you've found Eliza Malone."

CHAPTER FIFTEEN

It was obvious that Lacey Knox was never going to become a master criminal.

Her face immediately flooded with color and she swallowed. "What's that?" she asked, trying to lie.

"A letter you left on Kristi's bed," Dallas told her pleasantly.

"Me? No... I, uh... Why would I do such a thing?" she asked. She was still as red as a beet, and obviously excruciatingly uncomfortable.

"Well, I don't know for sure, but I think you're jealous of Kristi. Carl does show her a great deal of attention."

It seemed that it would have been impossible, but her color heightened.

Dallas pressed on, "Lacey, just tell me the truth. If you tell me, I promise, I won't tell your parents—or Carl."

She swallowed hard, looking around the hallway. "He likes me, I know that he likes me, but every time she comes around, he gets distracted. I mean, she has to be doing it on purpose. Everyone is saying that you and Kristi have something going on, and if so, you have to know what I mean!"

"Would you believe me if I told you that, yes, Kristi and I

do have something going on? I can assure you that she isn't interested in Carl."

"Then she needs to quit being so nice. And so…well, she could dress down a little, you know. I'm sure he thinks that she's elegant and sophisticated."

"She wears jeans most of the time."

"Not that day at the funeral—and at the reception at the brewery, she was all dressed up and really pretty."

"You didn't know Lachlan, did you? I didn't see you at the funeral."

"I wasn't at the funeral. I was just shopping at the riverfront. I happened to walk into that brewery for a root beer, and I saw her."

"I see. Did you turn the light off on her in the ladies' room?"

"What?" she asked, indignant. "No, of course not. That's weird."

"Did you whisper a threat to her there?"

"No. I swear to you, I did not!" she said earnestly.

"Okay, another question. How did you get into Kristi's room? It was locked."

She smiled, as though she thought she was pretty clever. "This is really a family establishment, you know, and I have been around the track. Everyone has a key to the front door. Guests come and go as they please, help themselves to coffee and sodas and water—the master key is in a drawer by the refrigerator."

"How did you know that?"

"I saw…someone put it there."

"Who?"

"I don't know…one of them. Maybe Jonah. I just borrowed it for a minute—I put it right back, I swear."

He didn't get a chance to go further. His phone rang.

Dallas saw that it was Jackson, and picked up right away.

"Get back over here," Jackson said without any preamble.

"You've found something?"

"We found *someone*," Jackson said. "Call Dunhill. Eliza Malone is buried in the basement at the Murphy house."

"I'm on my way, and calling Dunhill," Dallas said, turning even as he spoke.

Lacey called him back. "Hey! Hey—you said you won't tell my parents. Or Carl. You said that you wouldn't."

"Right," he replied, already heading down the stairs.

Dallas arrived at the Murphy house with amazing speed.

He hurried to Kristi first, deeply concerned.

To her amazement, she was able to give him a grim, weak smile—and refrain from falling apart. She wasn't at all sure how, when, or why, but the anger she had found earlier in the shower had given her strength; now she wanted this case solved. She wanted the truth, and she wanted justice for Eliza Malone's death.

Joe Dunhill arrived almost immediately after Dallas, and from there, the medical examiner's office was called, and the basement was soon filled with people as Eliza's body was extricated from its makeshift grave following Dr. Perry's preliminary examination of the body.

Dallas, Jackson, Angela and Kristi remained in the basement, standing out of the way while Perry's workers removed the body.

Dusting off, Dr. Perry looked at them and walked over to Dallas.

"Well, finding bones from years and years ago...that was one thing. You may be working faster than I can handle, and Dunhill wants me to stay with...whatever this is. Now..." He paused, shaking his head. "There's a strange assortment of factors at work here. In a way, she was halfway mummified, and in a way, destroyed by the elements. I'm going to have to get her on the table to see how she died. Her face...her face is almost gone, but one of my assistants found a pocketbook under the body. The driver's license says that she is Eliza Malone. This just beats all—I mean, it's Murphy's house. But I can't see old Ian killing this woman."

"Ian?" Kristi said. "He can't be a suspect."

"This is his basement," Perry pointed out.

Kristi shook her head emphatically. "Ian never killed anyone—I would stake my own life on that. He wasn't well...he battled cancer for a long time before his death. He was in and out of chemo. I'm telling you, Ian didn't do this."

"Young lady," Perry said. "I'm the ME, not a detective. But she has been here two years. And Ian was alive two years ago. And, while I have not begun to determine cause of death, she didn't fall under a woodpile and then bury herself."

Dallas spoke up. "Ian was an old, sick man. It's jumping to conclusions to assume that because it's his house, he committed the murder. He was a friendly man, he had people over, all manner of people visited him here."

Perry shrugged. "Well, the truth is up to you and Joe Dunhill, huh? We'll get her checked in tonight, and the autopsy will be first thing in the morning. You're welcome to be there."

"I will definitely be there," Dallas assured him.

Jackson suggested that they go upstairs; crime scene workers were heading in to start their search for any little clue.

Joe Dunhill followed them, and stood in the entry hall with them. "I need to call Jamie Murphy."

"I called Jamie right away. He's horrified, of course."

"He owns the property. He's going to have to come back home," Joe said.

"He's making arrangements," Kristi assured him. "And," she added, "Jamie is certainly not guilty of anything—he was in California when Eliza Malone disappeared."

"I'm not Perry—and I'm not jumping to any conclusions," Dunhill assured her. He looked at Dallas, and then Jackson and Angela. "Thank you. I didn't have the resources—or the inside access to manage this," he said, nodding to Kristi. "Maybe I should have been a better detective, but…" He paused, frowning. "You don't think Ian jumped off the balcony out of guilt? I'm not saying it's so, I'm just asking."

"No," Kristi said emphatically. "He wouldn't have done it out of guilt, because he wasn't guilty. Whoever managed to get Eliza Malone down here also pushed Ian, I'm convinced of it."

He nodded. "Not to worry—my superiors will give me more support to work it now. They never denied me. They just didn't have much to go on. Now they do." He started out, and then came back to tell them, "There's going to be an officer here tonight. I know you're going through Ian's papers with his grandson's permission, but…we did find a body."

"Of course," Dallas told him.

Joe Dunhill went out—but came back in again. "Reporters," he said with a sigh. "I'm just telling them that we've found a body, we don't know whose yet. It hasn't been proved… I'm leaving it to those with higher pay scales than mine to deal with a news conference." He hesitated, looking at them all hopefully. "I'm really awkward with press," he said.

"We're not here officially," Jackson reminded him.

"Yeah, right. Well, hopefully, I'll say the right thing, and we'll all get out of here without being dragged down by reporters— and tourists with smartphones."

"Here's hoping," Dallas agreed.

Once again, Joe Dunhill left them. They could hear him fending off the press, and promising that there would be news forthcoming—as soon as they had news to give. The flurry died away as the reporters followed him to his car.

Kristi gasped suddenly. "Dallas, shouldn't we have given Joe that note you found on my bed—the threat?" she asked.

"I actually managed to solve that particular mystery," he said.

"Oh?" Angela asked.

He nodded. "The note was put on your bed by Lacey Knox."

"What?" Kristi said, incredulous. "Why?"

"Carl Brentwood pays you far too much attention—and you really need to dress down, you know."

Kristi frowned; she was once again covered in dirt and grime, and her jeans were torn at the knees—and not by a designer manufacturer.

Dallas shrugged. "I got her to admit it. I promised I wouldn't tell her parents or Carl. I didn't say that I wouldn't tell you, and where it goes now is up to you."

"Whatever way you think we should handle it is fine. I don't want to make her even more miserable. But how did Lacey do it?" Kristi asked. "Not how did she do the note—that was obvious. How did she get into my room? I never forget to lock it."

"Apparently, keys around here are easy to come by. It's a nice part of Southern hospitality, and yet, not so good under our circumstances. Lacey went into the kitchen, helped herself to a bottle of water—and the key. She saw someone put it in the drawer the other day."

Kristi was quiet for a moment. "It's the same drawer where the key to this house was kept."

"And very easily taken, as Lacey Knox proved to us all," Angela pointed out.

"It's been a long day and night," Dallas said. "I don't know about the rest of you, but..." He hesitated, and then added, "Jonah is especially worried about the hole in the ground at Kristi's place. He found Janet Knox snooping around—hoping to find an artifact. He's afraid that someone is going to fall in the hole. Cops are patrolling, but they're not going to note someone staying in the house, sitting out in the courtyard—and slipping over to the hole when there's a chance." He shrugged. "Everyone wants a good artifact, I guess."

"And it is nearly midnight," Angela said. "Tomorrow, the news that Eliza Malone has been found will be out—and who knows what that might precipitate, once it's confirmed that she was murdered."

"Someone is going to know what happened already—the someone who buried Eliza in the basement here. There will be something on the news tonight. They won't say that it was Eliza Malone that was found, but the killer will know for sure," Jackson stated. "It could act as a catalyst for more action."

"Let's get back to McLane House," Dallas told Kristi. He headed toward the door and turned back for her. She started toward him, and then paused, looking around.

"It's gone," she said quietly.

"Gone?" he asked, but then he knew what she meant before she spoke.

"The darkness—it's gone. Eliza wasn't dark, but she caused the darkness—she wanted us to find her. She wants justice."

On arriving at the house, Dallas went straight through to the courtyard. Jonah was sleeping in one of the patio chairs.

He walked back to the hole in the rear of the yard; there was no one around. When he returned to the courtyard, Jonah was snoring.

Kristi was waiting for him by the back door. A patrol car went by on the neighboring street, flashing its lights into the yard. Jonah woke up with a start, choking a bit on a snore.

"Hey, hey! Oh, it's you, Dallas," he said.

"Yeah. Hey, buddy. Sorry," Dallas said. "You been out here—all this time?"

"Went in for some supper. I just don't want dingbats like that Mrs. Knox out here, messing around. The cops are doing a good job—they've been waking me up every twenty minutes or so."

Dallas glanced to the back door; Kristi was still watching through the window. "I'll tell you what, Jonah, just let me get Kristi settled upstairs, and then I'll come back down and I'll sit watch—I promise. You can get some sleep. Has anyone else come out—that you know about?"

"Keep drifting off, but the cops are good," Jonah mumbled.

He was clearly very tired.

"I'll be back," Dallas promised.

"Just like the Terminator. Hey, where did you go? You've been gone a long, long time—I mean, before now."

"We found another body," Dallas said.

"What?" Jonah frowned, waking up some. "No, they're here—they're all here. I know it."

"We believe we found Eliza Malone," he said.

That drew another astounded "What?"

"In Ian Murphy's basement," Dallas said. "We had to get the cops out, the ME, you know—and crime scene technicians... I mean, it wasn't a one-hundred-plus-year-old body. I reckon it's been there just about two years. Since she disappeared."

"In Ian's basement?" Jonah said, disbelieving. "Ian wouldn't have hurt a— Okay, it's the South, the man swatted flies. But he was...he was all about life. Until he died."

"I believe you. I didn't know Ian, but from what I've heard, he was a good man."

"A fine man."

"I believe that someone made use of the house—easy enough with a sick man being in and out of his home. Or say, at night, a person could have slipped in and out, knowing that Ian was upstairs, sleeping under medication, and unlikely to hear anything," Dallas said.

Jonah hadn't really heard Dallas's words. He looked ahead, frowning. "Not Ian. It could not have been Ian, not Ian."

Dallas left him sitting there, deep in his own thoughts.

Looking back to the door, he saw Kristi was still watching; she looked as if she wanted to run out and hug Jonah, but she backed away as Dallas neared the door, letting him enter.

"Is he all right?"

"He's watching the yard. I'll go back down and make him come in."

"Get him now—"

"Not until you're upstairs and in the room and I've figured out the way to make sure no one enters while I'm away."

She smiled. "I'm not afraid of Lacey Knox. Honestly, I think that I could take her."

He grinned. "I'm sure you're fierce in a hair-pulling fight."

"Never engaged in them, but...outside, usually, Monty and Justin would be watching the yard, and we'd know if something was going on."

"That was before we found Trinity's remains. Monty won't leave her, and Justin seems to be determined that he has to watch out for Monty."

"Watch out for him—what's a ghost going to do? He was really distraught, and if he was living, I'd be incredibly concerned myself, but...he's dead."

"Who knows the human heart?" Dallas asked her softly. "Anyway...let's get upstairs. We've both had a long day, and you uncovered a crime scene," he reminded her. "How did you find her?"

"I saw her...or, rather, something of her. I was heading out to see if Jackson had found anything, and I stopped by the entry. She was so sad, and she seemed to be pointing down. Dallas, you believe me, don't you? There's no way that Ian was responsible for what happened to her."

"I believe you," Dallas assured her. "Come on, let's get you to bed."

She nodded, and they started for the stairway, but Dallas paused.

There was someone in the front parlor, looking out into the dark street beyond the window. Dallas held up a hand, indicating that Kristi should stay back.

The man standing in the parlor had his hands on his hips; he was just looking out into the darkness of the night. He was silhouetted from the pale glow of the streetlights. Dallas recognized him from his stance.

"Mr. Meyer," Dallas said, walking toward him.

Murray spun around as if he'd been deep in his thoughts—and startled out of them.

"Mr. Wicker," Murray acknowledged. "I guess we're both night owls. Something happened near here, across the square." He hiked his shoulders and let them fall. "There's a breaking news story about a body being found across Johnson Square. They're speculating that it's the woman who went missing years ago."

"Yes," Dallas said. "That's been keeping you up?"

Murray nodded. "I was up working—it's three hours earlier in LA, you know. A lot is done at night, after-hours, friends just talking to friends. Kind of like New York lunches. Anyway, I... You had something to do with it right?" he asked Dallas. "You were here to investigate for the kid who knocked himself dead on the curb, but...you seem to know the cops around here well."

"It was at the Murphy house," Dallas said. "Kristi was good friends with Ian Murphy and his son had given us permission to use his library."

Murray Meyer nodded, looking out at the yard. "I remember when she disappeared. I was here." He shook his head. "I have family in this city, Mr. Wicker. Not family that makes one proud, but family nonetheless. My cousin was in trouble—his wife died. Fell off a balcony. He swears they were both drinking and when they argued, they were pushing each other around, and he swore that while he didn't push her, it was his fault. They shouldn't have been drinking and arguing. He went away for manslaughter, but he's out now, trying to put some kind of life back together."

"He's paid his dues, I guess," Dallas said.

"Yeah, I sent Claire off with Carl the other day and went to see him. I'm trying to get him some work. I suppose I believe him. I have to, I guess. He is my family, and I never knew him to do another mean or cruel thing in his life. This just all...

made me think about the past. I've been lucky—my life is good. And I remember that I was thinking—back when I was here for the trial, trying to help set some things in order—that the woman would show up, that maybe people had been wrong, maybe there was some bad business and she'd run away to Paris or something. Wishful thinking, I guess. And, then, of course, when Genie was picking up some things, she was saying that Mr. Murphy went over his balcony, and that made me think that life was ironic, and... Whatever, it's late, and I didn't mean to drone on about the past and things that haunt me."

"It's all right. They say that every man has skeletons in his closet."

"And some have them in their backyard," Murray said, shaking his head. "Guess it's a good thing Kristi found an ancestor, and a sad thing that another woman was evidently killed because of someone else's...agenda."

"Or the skeletons in their closet," Dallas added quietly.

"All the news about her said that she was an exceptional woman. Well, I suppose it's good to know the truth, or, to at least know... Someone needs to be caught and punished for what happened. Unless the old man did it—and he's far beyond our retribution now."

Kristi stepped up behind Dallas and said, "The old man did not do it!"

"Miss Stewart, I'm so sorry. I didn't mean to offend."

"Well," Dallas said, setting his hands on Kristi's shoulders, "I do believe we'll find out in the days to come. I think we'll go up. Good night, Mr. Meyer."

"Would you like some tea or anything?" Kristi asked Murray.

"No, no, I'm fine, thank you. I was just awake, and Carl is still out with Claire—he discovered that if he went out late enough, he didn't cause any commotion. They won't be much longer. I'll just wait up a bit. If that's all right?"

"Of course," Kristi said. "Turn on a light, if you like."

"I rather like the darkness tonight," he said.

Dallas directed Kristi toward the stairs and she hurried up ahead of him. When they reached her room, he strode to the window that overlooked the courtyard. Jonah was still there—sleeping on guard.

"I have to go back down," he said.

"I can go with you," she offered.

He shook his head. "No, you need some sleep. Tomorrow is going to be hard, and you're the one who has seen Eliza. You need sleep. I just need to figure out how to be there and watch over you at the same time. In the morning, I can get Angela or Jackson back over here. But tonight, I find that I'm agreeing with Jonah. And he's not much of a guard dog while he sleeps."

He turned to her and began looking around the room.

"Do you have any rope?"

"Up here?"

"I guess not," he said, looking around the room, frustrated.

"I have scarves," she said. "Some really long scarves. Would that work?"

"They might do," he said.

Kristi brought him several scarves in an assortment of colors and he began to tie them together.

"I'm really not afraid of Lacey," Kristi told him.

"No, and I don't think you need to be. But Lacey found the key. And that means others were able to find the key, and now we don't know how many copies of a master key might be floating around somewhere."

"Great," Kristi murmured.

He rigged a rope from her scarves, and showed her how to attach it from her doorknob to the dresser, creating something of a bolt. It could be broken, of course—but not without pulling a drawer out of the nearby antique dresser and creating a commotion much like an alarm.

"You understand?" he asked her anxiously.

She smiled. "I got it. I don't know how I'll sleep with you down there, but I'll try. And I definitely need a shower again, but I'll wait until morning when you are back!" She paused for a minute. "I could read," she said. "Somehow, reading what I love and what fascinates me always lets me fall asleep when I'm tired. You still have that book we took from Ian's house?"

"Always on me," he told her. "Our skeleton key thief has been in my room, too."

Reaching into his jacket, he handed her the book.

He smiled and left her. Downstairs, he looked into the front parlor; Murray Meyer was still staring out at the night, waiting.

The man's cousin had been convicted of manslaughter when his wife had gone over a balcony. *Just like Ian Murphy.*

"You're sure you are all right?" Dallas asked him.

He hadn't heard Dallas come downstairs, and started at the words, and then smiled, giving himself a little shake as Dallas apologized for startling him again.

"Now I'm just waiting for my prime client to return. Ah, and there they are!" he said, pointing out the front window.

Dallas walked over by him and saw a black sedan pulling up to the house. Carl Brentwood got out—followed out not by his manager, but Lacey. They were laughing, heads close, as they came up to the house. Before either could use a key for entry, Murray opened the door for them.

"Hey, you—waited up?" Carl asked Murray, perplexed.

"Where's Claire?" Murray asked.

"Still dancing the night away somewhere," Carl said. "Hey, I couldn't make her come back. She's all grown up."

"And you ran into Miss Knox. How nice," Murray said.

It didn't sound as if he thought it was nice at all.

Lacey looked at him, and then at Dallas. "I'm going upstairs!" she said. Hurrying by Dallas, she said softly, "Please."

Lacey had slipped out after her parents had gone to bed. She was, however, eighteen—and it seemed that she and Carl did like one another.

Not Dallas's business.

"Guess I'm going up," Carl said. "Murray, sorry, I didn't know you were waiting up for me. Oh, Mr. Wicker, hey—the gossip was about finding an old body here, but it seems they also found a woman who disappeared years ago? People are talking about it all over town. I guess—oh. You were somehow involved, huh?"

"Somehow."

Carl nodded, and then looked at Murray again. "Thanks, Murray. I'm good."

"I'll see that Claire gets in safely," Murray said.

"Okay," Carl told him. "Well, good night." He headed to the back parlor, and up the stairs.

"I would imagine she'll be back soon. And, of course, she's definitely an adult," Murray told Dallas. "Honestly, I'm just restless."

"I'm actually going to be out in the courtyard, if you need me," Dallas said.

"Thank you," Murray said, smiling. "I might head up soon—hey, I really am all right. Thanks for being concerned—or worried. I swear, I'm not having an episode of any kind, and I'm not going to go nuts and break up the furniture."

Dallas laughed softly. "Sorry—just holler if you need anything."

He headed out to the courtyard and woke up Jonah, telling him to go sleep in his bed.

Jonah agreed.

Dallas sat down to keep vigil over the hole in the yard, the now vacant dig where Trinity McLane had so recently lain.

At first, Kristi sat in the chair where she had so often rested while she'd talked to Jedidiah.

Where she had first seen Monty McLane.

She stared at the strange rigging Dallas had created for her door. No one was entering without creating a hell of a lot of noise—that was for sure—unless she let them in.

She should have just gone down with Dallas; she was never going to sleep.

She looked wistfully at the bathroom door. She really needed a shower. Then again, as the thought consumed her, she had visions of the Janet Leigh shower scene from *Psycho*.

Hm, maybe not.

She looked outside, down to the courtyard. Dallas had taken up a position in the courtyard, at the table closest to the recently dug hole.

He was reading something on his phone, obviously awake and aware. He looked up, as if aware she might be at the window.

Kristi smiled and waved.

She sat again, and then, the feel of the dust and dirt from the woodpile suddenly seemed to be too much.

This killer wasn't going to come after her in her own room, in her own house. The killer was clever and hidden, making people disappear—or die on a curb or go over a balcony.

She was going to have to squash any visions of *Psycho* and bite the bullet; her door was locked, and she had a makeshift extra lock. She was safe.

Leaving the bathroom door open and drawing the curtain only halfway, she hurried in. Soap, shampoo, all applied quickly and with purpose—and with one eye watching out of the curtain toward the bathroom door at all times.

Her shower proved to be completely uneventful.

Clean and much happier, Kristi emerged. She didn't slip into a nightgown, but changed into a knit top and a clean pair of jeans. For a moment, she panicked, looking around the room. The book!

She ran back into the bathroom and found it underneath the

pile of her dirty clothing; she hadn't meant to leave it out of her sight for a minute.

Book in hand, she headed back to the big chair, sat and flipped it open, wondering if any of the incredible volumes in Ian's library had ever been reprinted.

The copyright on this book was 1899—thirty-four years after the end of the war. It had been written by Emory Huntly of the 15th Corp. He had been lucky; he had survived the war and gone on to have five children, and, as of the writing of the book, seven grandchildren.

He had titled his book, *Valor and Lesser Evils, a Soldier's Journey through War.*

Starting at the beginning, Kristi quickly knew why Dallas had liked this book in particular; Huntly managed to give facts and figures, but there was a human element to the book that made it entirely readable. It was also prefaced by the fact that every man who had fought might well have a different vision of what they saw, and what they did.

He'd been from Massachusetts, a farm boy who had followed Lincoln's call to arms with a passion at first.

He'd never been to the South.

As the war escalated into 1862 and then 1863, he saw far too much. Fierce battles in Virginia—he wrote an especially poignant page on the battle at Shiloh.

He wrote a lot about people, battle camps, nurses, orderlies and those who had helped. He watched Union doctors who were true to their oath—determined to save a life, be it an ally or enemy life. He saw cruelty as well—practiced on both sides.

He saw field after field of dead men, their bodies and scattered parts food for the crows, their blood seeping into the soil, helping to irrigate the hate that would live on when the last gun was fired.

Kristi read, fascinated, and realizing more and more that she would have really liked the man, and, as she had always been taught, good men came in all kinds.

The words began to blur before her. She was just getting to Emory Huntly's role in Sherman's March to the Sea.

Sleep claimed her.

It wasn't easy staying up through the night, but Dallas intended to do so. He concentrated on going over files, over everything he had learned through Angela's research and his own interactions with people.

He found a large file the Krewe had compiled concerning Murray Meyer. His reputation as a Hollywood agent was sterling. He was a man who fought for his clients and looked after his employees. During an interview, he said that it was important to get the best deal, and to be reasonable at the same time; celebrity was easy come, and easy go.

Finishing with Murray, Dallas flipped to the information they had on Granger.

The man had started his political campaign, and there was a good deal of information available about his beliefs and platform. Lots of pictures of him at community events.

Dallas had focused on these two men because of the seeming links to the case. Both had been in Savannah several times in the last years—including when Eliza Malone had been murdered.

But what would it have to do with McLane House?

He realized that he needed to speak with Kristi, Jonah, Genie and Sydney again. Kristi hadn't even been living at the house two years ago, and Sydney had apparently just started back then, but Jonah and Genie had been with Jedidiah a long time. Maybe, just maybe, something had happened at the house back then, or they'd had a guest who had perhaps registered under a different name.

Wouldn't they have been recognized?

As he wondered about what might have gone on, he suddenly heard movement.

The sun wasn't quite up; it would be another half an hour or so before Genie and Sydney were due to arrive.

Dallas stood and moved closer to the house. He watched as someone came around the side of the house by the kitchen entrance, moving furtively, heading toward the back, the monuments—and the large dirt pit where Trinity McLane's body had so recently rested.

CHAPTER SIXTEEN

Kristi woke with a start, dropped her book and realized that she had slept several hours in an extremely awkward position. She stood and stretched, and looked to her door.

No one had attempted to break through her scarf alarm-lock, and Dallas hadn't returned.

She retrieved the book from the floor and stuffed it into her over-the-shoulder bag, determined that she would keep it with her at all times—just as Dallas had.

She started down the hallway, then noted that the door to their tiny employee lounge was ajar.

She opened the door. There was someone standing next to the mannequin of Monty.

"Jonah?" she said.

He turned and smiled at her. She walked over to him, and saw that, by his side, the mannequin had been knocked against the wall.

"Are you angry—with Monty?" Kristi asked, frowning.

Jonah shook his head. "Oh, I didn't do that. I came in and the thing had fallen over. I meant to set it right, but I started looking out the window."

"You look tired."

"I am tired," he said, and smiled at her sheepishly. "I mean to watch the pit out in back, but kept falling asleep. And then Dallas came down, thankfully, and I got a few hours of sleep, but—go figure, I used to sleep like a log. These last days… I don't know how to explain this, I just think that we should have left Trinity in the ground. Legend being told and retold is one thing, but bringing everything to light… I don't know." He shook his head painfully. "Now you've found Eliza Malone. I remember so clearly when she disappeared. And before she disappeared, Ian was excited. He told us he was going to have a meeting, and that we were going to shake up history. Ian was in deep with Jedidiah about some piece of information he thought that they could put together, but then…well, everything stopped. I didn't put it together right away—the city was in an uproar when Eliza disappeared, and then after that, well, I never heard either of them say anything about meeting anyone, or searching harder for some little bit of information. Now I'm wondering, but none of it makes sense… Time went by, and age takes its toll. Ian got sick, Jed just got older and older…and then, they were gone."

Kristi frowned, looking at him. "I didn't know any of this."

"Kristi, you weren't living here then. And even I didn't even pay any attention at the time. Now I can't help but feel this jumble in my mind, and be unhappy about Trinity—and horrified that Eliza Malone was found in Ian's basement."

"Jonah, they will find out who killed her," Kristi said, straightening out the mannequin of Monty McLane.

"And maybe Ian," he said softly. "I could never figure him going off the balcony. He had plenty of morphine—all he had to do was go to sleep."

He was looking out the window again. "They're up early," he said.

"Who?"

"Brentwood's crew. Look."

She looked out the window.

Claire Danson might have come in late, but she was wide-awake that morning. She stood on the sidewalk, arguing with Murray Meyer. She was gesturing, indicating the backyard.

Murray grabbed her shoulders, vehemently shaking his head.

Claire pulled away from him, and started walking away from the house.

Jonah looked at Kristi and grimaced with a shrug. "Guess she doesn't want any of our spectacular breakfast this morning. Well, well, go figure. Here comes the famous Mr. Brentwood, running after her, and running after him, the lovely Miss Lacey Knox. Maybe I'd best go down and warn Genie when she comes in that we may not need her to do too much cooking!"

Shelley Blake never saw Dallas as she hurried over to the pit, going past the circling tape and warning cones and letting herself down into the hole.

Dallas waited, and then came and stood over her.

"Shelley?"

She was so startled that she twirled in the hole, tripped and fell on her rear.

"Um—Dallas, hey!"

"Shelley, what are you doing? This was roped off for a reason—it's dangerous, and Dr. Horvath wants to get back in before it's further disturbed."

"I was… I was summoned here—I was summoned here by Trinity. She appeared before me, right as I was waking up. And she told me that I must go to the gravesite."

"Shelley, you do know that I don't believe a single word of that, right?" he asked.

She gasped, indignant. "Whether you believe or not has nothing to do with it being the truth. Trinity—she told me to come here. She said that Kristi, in particular, is continually trying to make Monty McLane into a good guy when he was a jealous killer. I needed to get in here and find proof—I mean, there could be something. A rebel bullet beneath her bones."

Dallas hadn't seen Kristi yet, but he heard her as she walked over to the hole to join them.

"Shelley, come on, you grew up down here. Whatever bullet you might find wouldn't mean anything in the least. It was Christmas of 1864—by then, soldiers were picking up whatever they could find on the battlefield. Rebel gun, knife, bullet, Union gun, knife, bullet. Wouldn't mean a thing."

Shelley frowned. "Well, no, I mean, by then the Union was winning. I mean…if there was a Confederate knife in here… a Union soldier wouldn't be carrying a Rebel soldier's knife!"

"If he found it on the battlefield, he sure as hell might be carrying it," Kristi said. "Shelley, please, I don't mind your acts. I know that Carl and his crew are very grateful. But you must stop this. I'm really sorry, but it's my yard—and my pit in my yard, that my ancestor came out of."

"Out, Shelley," Dallas commanded.

"Yes, but if I found—"

"Found what?" Kristi demanded.

Shelley shook her head. She looked agitated—and nervous. "Oh, never mind. You're right. It's your yard and your hole, and no matter what facts hit you, you're going to believe what you want to believe."

"Come out, Shelley," Dallas repeated, more sternly.

She let out a sound of aggravation and then grimaced. "Um, give me a hand, please?"

Dallas reached down to help her out.

She took his hand; he pulled her up easily enough.

Shelley dusted herself off. "I'm only trying to help," she said.

"Shelley, we have a woman who spent her life studying medicine and anthropology coming back. Let her help, please," Kristi said.

Shelley nodded, and sighed and looked at Kristi hopefully. "May I stay for breakfast?"

"Sure," Kristi told her.

Shelley went in, and Kristi turned to Dallas. "I was just talking to Jonah, and he was upset—he's been upset since we found Trinity. He's more upset now—says that he should have put it together. Jedidiah and Ian had been talking about something groundbreaking that could change history. Then Eliza disappeared, and everyone started talking about her. It was all forgotten. Jonah doesn't know for sure that Ian was supposed to be meeting with Eliza. Now, it seems, he's starting to put things together. And Ian was working with Jedidiah on whatever it was that was going on."

"We're getting closer. I have to get showered and to the autopsy—we don't know yet how Eliza was killed."

"But she was killed," Kristi said sadly.

"Yes, but you have to think of it this way—she wanted you to find her. Kristi, you did. Now—" he paused, glancing up at the house "—I have to go to that autopsy."

"And nothing is going to happen to me here—I'll make sure I stay around a group. Even if every guest goes out, Genie, Sydney and Jonah will be here."

"I'll have Angela come over here, and if, at some point, you decide to go back to the Murphy house, make sure you stay together."

"What about the pit?"

He hesitated; his work made trust a hard thing to come by.

"We'll leave Jonah watching it. After all, he was watching it last night."

Kristi nodded. She smiled grimly. "I missed you last night."

"And, I promise, I missed you."

She could have said a lot more; things were happening—bodies were literally coming out of the ground. But she didn't know how long Dallas would be in Savannah.

Or even if they'd both be alive when all this was over.

The thought crept unbidden into her mind. She forced a determined smile. "Well, get to that autopsy. We need to know the truth. I'll be in the kitchen, helping."

"With your purse?" he asked her, indicating the handbag over her shoulder.

"I have the Emory Huntly book in it. I'm doing what you said—where I go, it goes." She hesitated and said, "I should have started in the middle—I'm just getting to Sherman's March to the Sea."

When they went in, Jonah was in the back room, and he addressed Dallas cheerfully. "Thank you, Mr. Wicker—I have now enjoyed some sleep, and so, now, I promise, I will stay awake for my vigil."

She left them and made her way to the kitchen. Genie was just coming in the side door.

"Hi, early bird—I hear you had tremendous activity last night," Genie said.

"Everyone knows already!"

"There were dozens of pictures up of the cop cars, the ambulance from the morgue, cops right in front of the Murphy place—and they all said that a dead woman had been found, unidentified officially as yet, but presumed to be Eliza Malone. Dozens of friends called me, knowing that Jedidiah and Ian had been friends, and that I work nearby. You know—news. Gossip. Travels faster than the speed of light."

"Yeah. Okay, so—what am I helping you make?" Kristi asked her.

"Eggs Benedict with a Southern flair—we're doing them on biscuits."

Sydney came in soon after; coffee was brewed, biscuits set in the oven as the two of them threw questions at Kristi. She dodged answering as much as she could.

Dallas popped his head in to say that he was going. As soon as he was gone, the questioning began again.

"I wonder that she didn't... Well, dead things and dead people...smell," Sydney said. "Not to be disrespectful."

"She was buried beneath logs and charcoal. I guess that Ian never went to the basement, and Jamie wasn't home enough to get down there much, either. They had to move a lot of wood and charcoal to get to her," Kristi told them. "And it was a basement, and..." She paused, shaking her head. "I don't know," she told them.

When the food was finished, she made a plate to take out to Jonah. Angela arrived as she was doing so; when she returned to the house, Angela was being avidly questioned by Genie and Sydney, and Shelley had joined the conversation.

Shelley was trying to convince her that Trinity had been appearing before her for years, and continued to haunt her, often in dreams.

Angela listened politely.

Kristi picked up a tray to bring out to the back parlor; Granger and Janet Knox had come down, and both greeted her and said that the food looked wonderful. "I thought Lacey would be down by now," Granger told his wife, his tone irritable.

"I—I don't know where she is—sleeping, or she went out."

"If she's asleep, she can get up. The breakfast is half of what we pay for," Granger said.

Janet watched with distress as Granger went up the stairs. She saw Kristi watching her and gave her a big smile. "She needs to be here," she murmured.

Kristi didn't answer. Murray Meyer came down the stairs soon after Granger went up them, asking about coffee just as Sydney brought out the big pot.

Sydney addressed Shelley enthusiastically. "Now, we should have another séance—not that Trinity is free. I'm sure she'd speak right through you!"

"Oh, she would, I'm certain!" Shelley said.

Kristi winced and lowered her head. Murray Meyer was look-

ing at her; he smiled, as if understanding her misery at the concept of another séance.

"I think that with things happening as they are, another séance
may be just a bit premature—especially since Carl is thinking
about doing something a great deal more in-depth—and which
may require a bit of work from you, Shelley," Murray said.

"Ah, it's hardly work, doing what I love—and communing
with Trinity."

Kristi flashed Murray a thank-you smile, and slipped out to
the courtyard. Jonah was just finishing his breakfast, and gave
her a broad smile.

"I can pick up after myself," he told her.

"I know you can. I didn't come out to pick up after you—I
just came out as a way to leave the house."

"I see," Jonah muttered, looking past her to the back door
and the windows. "Dear me, look at Shelley chatting away.
How strange can that woman be?" he asked. He shook his head.
"I've talked with Ms. Danson—she just thinks that the séance
was great publicity for Carl, but I don't think she wants to do
another—she even told me that she saw Shelley moving the
table. Oh, and I think I know what they were fighting about
this morning. Claire and Murray."

"Oh?"

"Murray had been saying that all this was great, but that if
they didn't get a studio in working on a full documentary, there
was no sense doing it. Passion projects don't pay. She's all about
public image—he's all about his percentage."

"Ah, well."

Angela joined them out in the courtyard. Jonah greeted her
pleasantly.

"Should we head over and do some reading?" Angela asked.

"Soon," Kristi murmured. "There is something I want to
keep reading…but I was thinking that I might hop in that hole
and look around a little bit myself. Want to help?"

"You have a scientist coming. And it's not like Trinity would have left a belt buckle or any metal. Why not let that Dr. Horvath do it?" Jonah asked.

"Oh, I will. It should be studied properly. I just need a few minutes."

"I'll join you," Angela said.

"And, Jonah, you have been wonderful, but I know you were up half the night," Kristi said. "You could take a nap. I'll call you when we're leaving."

"All right, then," Jonah said. He stood up and left them.

As they headed back to the site, Angela said, "He is right, although, you did find Trinity's locket. Maybe there's something there, but...who knows if we can find anything."

Kristi stopped walking and looked at Angela. "Well, we may not find anything, but maybe we should let people think that we did find something."

"Tempting fate—it could work."

"Let's see what we do—or don't—find," Kristi said.

Dallas had seen skeletal remains often enough, but oddly, there was something neat and clean about bones, even when one discovered that bullets lodged within them had ended someone's life, or nicks indicated that they'd face the wrong end of a knife.

This was different.

"Sadly, time and circumstances always do a number on a corpse," Dr. Perry told the crew assembled before him, consisting of Joe Dunhill, Jackson and Dallas. "As you can see...the skin over her skull is almost mummified. The stomach and wet organs seeped into the ground, and we may be analyzing the earth and charcoal and wood collected from the site."

What had befallen Eliza Malone's body was sad—she resembled something made for display at a horror house or for Halloween. Her remaining skin was stretched tight and yellowed; her midsection seemed to be hollowed out. In areas bone protruded; in other areas, tight, discolored flesh stretched across bone.

"Quite—something," Dr. Perry said. "She remains, and yet, in ways, there is so little left."

"Are you saying that you don't know how she died?" Dunhill asked.

"Remember—cause and method," Perry said. He hesitated, then looked at them both. "She was struck on the head, hard—right in that same area where Lachlan Plant was struck. That's what I believe. It's a bit difficult to ascertain, because of the condition of the skull and the brain, and the conditions under which the body was found. Her cause of death was damage to the brain—back to method. Just like Lachlan Plant, she might have fallen. More likely, she was struck with something heavy, and, as we have noted, she didn't bury herself in a basement. So, gentlemen, I am going to call the method of death a homicide. The only other possibility is that she did suffer a fall—and perhaps Ian buried her because she died accidentally, and he feared that he might have been blamed."

"I just don't believe that, not with what I know of the man," Dallas said.

"No," Joe Dunhill said. "At some point, she was snatched from somewhere around Johnson Square, and then taken into Ian's house for burial. We know that we have a killer here, on the loose. We have to find him or her." He looked at Dallas and Jackson and added, "Ian Murphy died after Lachlan Plant, and that would hardly allow for him to attack Lachlan on the street. This doesn't bode well for Simon Drake. You—haven't thought of where we might dig him up yet, have you?"

Dallas shook his head. "No, we haven't any ideas on Simon yet," he said. Turning back to Dr. Perry, he asked, "Wouldn't it take a certain medical knowledge for someone to have struck two people just right for them to die?"

Perry was thoughtful. "Yes and no. There are dozens of vid-

eos out there now by doctors and psychiatrists and other interested parties that discuss the properties of the brain. A killer
might have gotten lucky, too, and there might have been other
factors involved in Eliza Malone's death, such as a substance in
her system, something to knock her out before being struck.
She might have even been buried before death. Those tests will
take some time."

A few minutes later, they left the morgue. Dunhill asked
Jackson and Dallas to come to his office, and there, they met
his captain—who seemed to know exactly who Jackson Crow
was and assured him he'd send in an official invitation for assistance from the FBI.

"Always believed in Dunhill. But when you've got nothing
but hunches, no leads, nothing that resembles a clue, then you
have to move on. Joe's a good guy, knew what to do, and where
to go—without really stepping on any toes."

The captain sat in; Joe had a timeline of everything that had
happened. He had lists of people interviewed, and he had a list
of those who lived at or worked at the Murphy place, and at
the McLane house. "Most of what we have on the guests and
employees we have through the FBI files," he said, nodding his
gratitude to Jackson and Dallas. "We've put the cases together,
and we've eliminated those we can't place in Savannah." He went
on, "Our biggest dilemma is finding motive for these crimes,
and thus far...we remain perplexed."

"It may be nothing, but I'd say we might want to look into
anyone with medical training, and I'm going to suggest that we
hone in on Murray Meyer," Dallas said, and explained Murray's family connection to the city. "Granger Knox, a man with
political aspirations, and, although he is not my first pick, Mr.
Jonah Whitney, because he was friends with Ian Murphy and
Jedidiah McLane. He was certainly in the area, and had access
to the Murphy house and the McLane house. Whether we're
looking at Jonah or someone else, we believe that the key to the

Murphy property—and to the rooms at McLane house—were simply taken out of a drawer there and copied."

"That causes a bit of dilemma, doesn't it?" Joe asked. "Someone could have had access to both houses two years ago."

"We know that all three men we're discussing were in the city at the time Eliza Malone disappeared," Jackson said.

"But not at McLane House," Dunhill said.

"No," Dallas said. "And, of course, it wasn't necessarily a man. I believe, however, that if we're right, and if a very able-bodied young man like Lachlan was struck, and then set in a particular situation on a curb, and if a man was hurled off a balcony, it might have taken someone with considerable strength. And someone clever enough to make sure they weren't seen—managing to take Eliza Malone without being seen, kill Lachlan Plant without being seen and get into and out of the Murphy place without being seen. Maybe when Eliza was killed, her murderer purposely placed her in the Murphy house, hoping that if she was found, the blame would fall on Ian Murphy, or someone else who had access to the house."

"There's very little hope we'll find Simon Drake alive," Joe Dunhill said. "I've followed the trail over and over again—it's not much of a trail—from where he was last seen on the riverfront, and on to the Johnson Square area. The oddest thing is that we're talking a number of blocks, and he was seen by Johnson Square, but we've also had some sightings of him by the Colonial Park Cemetery—we've had other sightings, of course, but there are a number of *supposed* sightings of him. I've searched half of Savannah, and…people try, but we don't know what is true and not true."

"I'll walk around the cemetery area and see if…anything looks as if it's freshly dug by the city, or if there is any odd disturbance in the ground around there," Dallas said. "We'll head out now—and put our concentration on Mr. Drake."

Jackson nodded his agreement; they shook hands all around.

When they left the precinct, Dallas said, "I'll take the walk, but..." He had his phone out, and he shrugged. "I want to check on Kristi."

Jackson nodded.

Dallas needn't have worried; Kristi answered right away. She and Angela were fine; they'd explored the pit that morning, and were about to head over to the Murphy place. "Jamie Murphy is coming in sometime tonight," she said. She was quiet for just a second. "I'm not sure whether to have him go on over to his place, or meet me at McLane House. He might be happier away from his place, and if he goes home, he'll have to sleep in Ian's room. I'll have to give him your room."

"That would be fine—I really like joining you in your room. Oh, as long as I have some time to get back and move my things. I'm on the hunt for Simon Drake. You haven't had any visions of him that you haven't mentioned?"

"No, I'm afraid not." She hesitated. "This doesn't bode well for him, does it? Strange day here, by the way. Quiet breakfast, and now everyone is out."

"What did you find in the hole?"

"Nothing—but I'm pretending we did find something."

"What?"

"No, no, we didn't really find anything."

He laughed softly. "No, what are you pretending you found?"

"I haven't decided yet."

"You know that Dr. Horvath wants to get in there and do a proper excavation."

"Hey, remember, my property, my ancestor, my pit."

"True."

"Dallas, it has to be unraveling. It was one thing to find Trinity. It really is quite different—everyone knowing now that Eliza Malone was murdered."

"It's quite different, yes. You have to be careful, even in your house—especially in your own house."

"I promise."

"If you're not with Angela, make sure you are with plenty of people. This killer strikes when victims are alone."

"I promise!"

He smiled. "Okay, well, I'll be back in a bit. Jackson is going to the Murphy place. He's going to drop me off and I'm going to do some walking."

"All right. See you when I see you."

"See you when I see you," he repeated, and ended the call.

Jackson spoke up, "I could hear Kristi. They should be there by the time I get there. You're going to start at the riverfront?"

"The riverfront, and then on to the Colonial Park Cemetery and back to Johnson Square," he said. "On a wild goose chase, but hey—we haven't found Simon Drake. I just wish that I believed we might find him alive."

Kristi and Angela had spent a couple hours working in the pit.

There hadn't been anything to find, at least at first, and when they did find something, it was several smashed bullets. "An expert could tell you what they were fired from," Kristi told Angela. "But what we were saying earlier is true—any soldier might have had just about any kind of weapon by that time in the war."

Jonah came out on the courtyard; Kristi was certain that he was innocent of any wrongdoing, but Dallas's words had struck some kind of chord in her.

Be careful. Of everyone.

She pocketed the smashed bullets, allowing him to see her hide *something*.

"Jonah, can you take over watching?" she asked him.

"Indeed. I had a lovely nap. Thank you."

"We're going to head over to the Murphy place," Angela told him. Looking at Kristi, she said, "The crime scene people finished up last night. Jackson should be alone soon, right?"

"Right."

Inside, they found Genie and Sydney chatting in the kitchen, and Kristi told them that she was going out.

"Jonah is still here, right?" Sydney asked, her voice a little nervous.

"Sure, Jonah is here."

Sydney nodded, relieved.

"You're frightened to be here?" Kristi asked her.

"Shelley said that we may feel Trinity's presence more and more," Genie explained.

Kristi took a deep breath. "If you do feel her presence, she's surely an extremely nice ghost."

"Well, that would be true," Genie said.

Kristi smiled. "Please, guys, please, don't put much belief in what Shelley tells you anyway, okay?"

They both nodded solemnly. They were still unnerved.

"You coming back for social hour? You think our guests will show up?"

"I don't know, but we always have to be prepared. Yes, I'll be back."

As they crossed the square, Kristi told Angela about the book she was reading, and how she was anxious to get back to it. Angela told her that she was reading emails—tedious stuff.

It only took them a few minutes to walk the distance to the Murphy house. Once there, they both sat down to work.

Kristi went through Sherman's March to the Sea, viewing it all through the eyes of Emory Huntly.

He hated that they were ordered to destroy so much, and stated that they had orders not to kill civilians—unless the civilians came at them—and not to destroy little towns or private barns, but to destroy any food that was stored for the winter: *scorched earth*. That was the policy. He wrote, deeply disturbed, about a day when they shot a farmer who had come out to his porch armed. The man had been old—defending his land and his property.

"The worst I saw, however, happened when Savannah had surrendered, and we were occupying the city, Lincoln's gift from Sherman that year. What we did in the cemetery was sad and silly, but we were worn, bitter from fighting and longing for our homes. Savannah had surrendered; the war would not end until April—something we could not know then. Naturally, if citizens came after us, we were to defend ourselves. But men were filled with hate; at one house, we came upon a ragtag enemy soldier, just trying to come home. Perhaps he had deserted; perhaps he was just coming through. But he was shot down; his wife, a gentle and lovely woman, tried to defend him, and thus died as well, along with the old man who owned the house. Such a situation would not have been condoned, but there were only six of us there with our commander, and the deed was done. There was nothing to do but hasty burials, and to forget a scene that we had not intended, and that was nothing less than tragic. It haunted me, as it did the others, and shall haunt me until the day I die."

"Angela!" Kristi cried. "I found it—I found a reference to…a man being shot down, his wife defending him and the man's father dying, as well. This man, Emory Huntly, describes the situation at my house to a T!"

"He uses names, says it was your house—and that… Colonel Albert Huntington killed Trinity?" Angela asked.

"No, he doesn't use names, but just read this passage."

Kristi rushed over to Angela where she sat, handing her the book.

"Well," Angela murmured, "you could make a good argument for Monty. I mean, historically, but—I guess this doesn't really prove anything. There has to be more. Except…"

She set the book down and hit a few keys on the computer. "Here…this is an email from Ian to Jedidiah—dated just a bit over two years ago. 'I'm expecting a meeting soon, with a party who can bring this all to light. I have the book and you have the letter—I believe that between them, we can make the case, and show that history is written by the victors—except that there are a few good men out there who can be victors and still tell the truth.'"

"Keep going—maybe there's more," Kristi said. "I have to get back to McLane House. Someone has a key, and now I know why I thought people were in my room, or trying to get in my room before. It was Jedidiah's room! His papers are still in a drawer there." She paused, frowning. "What difference does this make, though, to the rest of the world? Why would anyone kill over this?"

"The reasons people kill... Money is a big one. Jealousy is another. Family issues...random violence. But for this...we have to keep looking."

Kristi glanced at her watch. "I'm going to run back. It's social hour."

"Jackson is on his way here. You should wait and have him walk you over."

"It's fine. There are still cops on the street, and Genie and Sydney and Jonah are definitely at my house, others, too. Too many people for anything bad to happen. Don't stop looking—please don't stop. I'll be careful, safe and fine," Kristi promised.

But Angela shook her head. "I'll go with you. We'll make sure it's a full house tonight—no killer is going to strike when he's in clear view of a half dozen or more witnesses."

"I hate to make you do this."

"Hey, no problem!"

They headed down the stairs. Pausing in the entry, Kristi felt good. The dark miasma was gone, and with it, any hint of something ominous.

Eliza had wanted to be found; they had found her. And the police and Dallas and Jackson would find the truth.

Two patrolmen were watching Johnson Square. Kristi and Angela politely waved.

They neared the front door when she realized that the streetlights had come on.

Kristi didn't have to unlock the front door; Shelley appeared on the steps. "Okay, give it up, what did you find in the grave?"

Kristi laughed. "Nothing, really nothing."

"Kristi Stewart, you're lying!"

"No, I'm not, really, Shelley. I've got to get in and lend a hand."

Angela smiled at Shelley and entered the house with Kristi. Carl Brentwood was in the front parlor, speaking earnestly with Murray Meyer. Janet and Granger were in the back parlor, evidently arguing over their daughter again.

Genie and Sydney were in the kitchen.

"Hey, we're all under control!" Genie assured Kristi.

"I'll head back, then," Angela told Kristi. "I'm a few blocks away. Have me on speed dial, though I imagine that that Jackson and Dallas will be along soon, as well."

She waved as Angela left, and turned back into her own house, pausing.

So strange, and inexplicable. Even as Angela walked down the street, something within seemed to change.

The darkness had left the Murphy house, but...

Night had fallen. Despite her certainty and bravado, she suddenly felt that sense of darkness, something eerie and foreboding, as she opened her front door. As if...

A darkness was following *her*.

CHAPTER SEVENTEEN

Dallas stood on the riverfront, watching people come and go, some in a hurry, some strolling and laughing, holding tourist books with maps and other information on Savannah.

He turned back in toward the city. It was just a few blocks to the Johnson Square area where Simon Drake had last been seen, and a longer walk to the Colonial Park Cemetery.

He walked around the entire cemetery, looking for any place a pipe might have been dug up, where roadwork might have been done recently, where an enterprising killer might have disposed of a corpse.

Logically, there were plenty of swamps not far from the city; there was the river, where one might weigh a corpse down, and have it disappear for decades, until it began to decompose, or become consumed by creatures, and what remained made its way to the surface.

This killer didn't seem to consider the more logical aspects of getting rid of a corpse. Maybe it hadn't been necessary—Eliza's corpse had remained hidden for two years, and most likely would have remained so if it hadn't been for her spirit trying so desperately to communicate with Kristi. It had been easy enough to make most of the world believe that Ian had jumped, and while it had been ludicrous that somehow a healthy man like Lachlan Plant had tripped and fallen just right and killed himself on a curb, the story had been accepted.

He walked slowly. A breeze was moving, and night was coming. Moss flowing from old oaks drifted along. He admired the beautiful old houses, built in various gracious old styles: federal, Italianate, colonial and Victorian, gingerbread accents on many of the latter.

Around and around the cemetery, and he could find nothing. The cemetery closed at five, but he paused by one of the big trees, looking in—and determined that this made no sense. He was going to walk around again, hoping to find any kind of hint. Dunhill had told him that there had been *sightings* here.

But Drake had been heading toward Johnson Square, and he had definitely been seen going in that direction before he had disappeared.

He leaned against the oak for a moment, and when he opened his eyes, he was not alone. The ghost of a Revolutionary soldier stood by his side, watching him.

"You are gifted. You see me," the man said, smiling.

"Yes, sir," Dallas told him. "I see you."

"You appear at a loss, sir. Lieutenant Max Hudson, at your service, if you believe that there is a way in which I might help you."

"Dallas Wicker, sir, and...you didn't see anyone bury a body around here, did you?"

"Sir, I saw many a man and woman buried here. Soldiers, heroes, bankers, mothers, sisters, wives—yellow fever ripped through our fair city, you know. Most markers are gone, sir, and in the best way, those who revere the past walk over the dead daily as they trail through these grounds."

Dallas smiled. "I beg your pardon, sir. I meant recently."

"Ah, well, no—I don't believe that I've seen activity lately. You are searching for a dead man?"

"A man I believe to be dead, yes."

"Sometimes those who loved this place in life like to wander by. You are a policeman?"

"A federal agent, seeking the truth. I don't even know why this man would have been killed."

"Ah, well, Mr. Wicker, murder has existed since man first coveted what another man had, since human nature came with greed, selfishness and cruelty."

"We don't believe he was killed for love—or even money, Lieutenant."

"Some kill to be merciful—I have seen men on a battlefield kill those they loved, knowing they would die painfully and slowly if they did not. Men have killed for revenge. They kill in the name of God, though what man can kill when the greatest commandments in those religions truly of God say that we must not kill?" He sighed. "I have seen anger take lives, jealousy—and the insanity of drugs and alcohol."

The spirit shook his head and pointed across the cemetery. "There, Mr. Wicker, is a part of this cemetery where many lie who died in duels—thankfully, such events are no longer sanctioned in any way. Great men die needlessly in duels."

"Well, there were no duels fought here, but..."

His voice trailed.

Duels.

No, duels had been fought for honor ... Or a man's perception of honor. A man might kill because he believed that someone wanted to taint his name, take from him what he thought was his due—his prestige.

It all seemed to revolve around Monty McLane, Trinity and Colonel Albert Huntington. But while the tragic story of Monty killing his own wife had been accepted through the years, what possible difference could it make if the truth came out?

"A man might kill to preserve his truth," Lieutenant Hudson said. "Perhaps, if he committed an act that was heinous, and has lived past it—he can let nothing deter the life he has now managed to live."

"But bad things have happened in every decade since humanity began," Dallas said. "Especially in times of war."

"You're talking about the revolution, sir? It was bitter—but I was thinking far more along the personal front. Duelists fought over personal affront, and while that might have been because of political leanings, duels were still a matter of personal honor."

"Personal honor," Dallas murmured.

He thought that he had it down to three likely suspects—Jonah, Murray and Granger Knox. All had been in the city when Eliza Malone had disappeared.

But what might she have anything to do with a man like Jonah, or a Hollywood agent, or a construction contractor?

"Thank you," he told the ghost, and he turned to start walking to the Murphy house.

He pulled out his phone and called headquarters, and Vickie Preston—who could find just about anything anywhere. She was fairly new to the FBI, but had quickly made herself invaluable to the team for her in-depth research abilities.

He was grateful that she answered; darkness was falling, and the young woman could have gone home long ago.

"Vickie, this may not be easy. I'm going to give you names that you've already looked up for me, and I need you to go further back. I believe that we have a guest who is a descendent of Union colonel Albert Huntington—see if you can find out who."

"On it. I already kept trying to trace all the guests at the McLane house," she told him. "Their family trees are all filled with branches, and you know how we work, everything must be verified by more than one source, and—"

"Vickie, you don't need to verify anything. Just go. See if

you can find someone who in any way might be a descendent of Albert Huntington, direct, indirect—anything."

Genie and Sydney had the social hour covered. Kristi checked on Jonah, who assured her he was just fine: he had walked, stretched and enjoyed the afternoon just reading—and no one had dared come near the hole in the ground with him there.

"I'm going to run up to my room for a bit then, okay?"

"Of course, young lady. But come back down," he told her with a wink. "Genie has been on a baking rage all day—she's whipped up pecan pie and peach tarts." He made a face. "And cucumber sandwiches. Now, that one throws me. Why would anyone want to eat a cucumber sandwich?"

"I don't question Genie," Kristi told him, grinning. "Uncle Jed told me never to micromanage, and never to fix what isn't broken. You've kept me along the straight and narrow, so..."

"You can join me out here for a tart!" he told her.

"Will do."

Upstairs, she locked herself into her room—making use of Dallas's makeshift scarf alarm, as well. She set the book on the bed, and paused for a minute, looking around.

For a moment, she took a seat in the big chair by the bed. She closed her eyes, wishing that Jedidiah would appear when she opened them again. He did not.

Monty was still standing guard over the bones of his loved one, and Justin was with him.

Trinity had not risen, as Shelley believed.

Her room was silent—and empty.

She spoke softly aloud to herself—as if she were back a bit in time, as if Jedidiah was lying in the bed and they were chatting and figuring about history, as they so often had.

"So, I have a book that *almost* proves that Albert Huntington killed Monty and his dad and Trinity. It was Ian's book. But with what Angela had found, it seems that maybe Ian was going to meet with Eliza Malone when she disappeared—and, of course, since he didn't really have anything, he'd have never thought that she was stopped or taken because she was going to meet with him. But, Jedidiah, Ian seemed to think that you have something. I have Ian's book, but...what did you have?"

She stood up, looking around the room, and then she dived into Jedidiah's "tax" drawer, where his papers remained beneath a false bottom.

They were a mess.

He'd kept an accountant, of course, so she hadn't been left with a pile of legal difficulty, but when it came to his personal collection...

She started to toss things around a bit carelessly, and then remembered that, like Ian, Jedidiah had collected what he thought to be important for years—including letters.

She tried to sort through the new—the water bills, electric bills and more. With those in a pile, she saw a little wooden box, and in that box, she found a pile of letters, neatly bound together with a fraying ribbon.

She carefully untied the ribbon, and began to study the letters.

Jedidiah had just loved people, stories about people and collecting information on people.

She found one that had a note attached to it.

"Must have verification."

Jedidiah's writing had been scrawled, weak and barely legible. He had found the letter, apparently, and read it just before he had died. He had never gotten it to an expert to have it verified as real.

Quickly opening the delicate paper, she saw that it was a letter written from the Union officer who had also penned the book she had just read—Emory Huntly.

Her fingers were shaking as she looked at it.

"My dearest Amelia, beloved wife," it began.

"I pray for the day that this great conflagration ends; I cannot bear the man I have become. I learned to walk under command with hundreds of rifles aimed at me; I learned to dodge and roll from cannon fire. I watched men die, my friends and my foes, and in death, as I saw men clutch crosses and Bibles and Jewish Stars of David, it seemed not to matter which side they had come to defend. But that is battle—strangers kill strangers, and sometimes, in this tragic case, friends face friends, or brothers look up at their brothers, fathers upon their sons. And yet again, such is war. But today, I witnessed what is not war, what is man's great greed, his cruelty, or, as a few of the men agreed, his desperate need to win, and to appear the victor, no matter what the cost. Savannah is ours, and the house I gaze upon across a beautiful and peaceful square will be ours, too.

"Did we allow this because of fear? Because, after the rigors and horrors of war, we want nothing more than to bide our time here in Savannah, and pray for the end? I don't know, I will never know and I can never speak, except to you, for we have agreed that we were mistaken in what we saw. We told ourselves that the Rebel drew his revolver, stolen, we told ourselves, from one of our dead fellows off the battlefield. But I must tell you, my love, that what you'll hear is not the truth of it; the Reb but came to see his father and wife, and perhaps his child, though the child was not here, and for that small mercy, I thank the Lord. But the truth is that the Rebel was here, and he stepped forward on the porch, knowing that we were there, taking his house. But he came out with no weapons raised, and Huntington—perhaps far too ready for the battles we have fought—drew his gun. And, as he did, the lovely lady of the house stepped forward. Perhaps Huntington never meant to fire, but fire he did. And when the lady went down, the Rebel did scream, a most horrendous cry of agony, and guns began to fire, and quickly they were all dead. It was reported as another incident—many of which we had come across in our march through Georgia—when we were fired upon, and there was no choice, and I believe that my few fellows on that foray for a headquarters began to believe what they were told, for it was all so fast, and then there were the dead...and we buried them hastily. Amelia, my dearest love, I tell you the truth here; I beg you, hide this missive, for as the war continues—and perhaps even in the bitter days to follow—my truth might well mean my death. Pray for me, Amelia. Pray that your loving Emory may come home to you."

Kristi finished the letter, and then sat back on her haunches, staring at it. To her, of course, it was no surprise; the family—with or without being haunted by the ghost of Monty McLane—had never been able to believe that the man, expecting his own death and determined to take a wayward wife with him—had killed Trinity before being gunned down himself.

She carefully rewrapped the letter and replaced it in the drawer. As she did so, she saw one of Jedidiah's old guest books; to this day, their guests signed in, and they kept a record of those who stayed—nowadays asking for email as well, so that they could send them promotions and enticements to come stay again. She picked up the guest book and flipped through the pages, noting that it covered the past four years.

Had a current guest stayed here before? She hadn't lived at the house two years ago, but Jonah had been here, and Genie. And they would have surely recognized a return guest.

She flipped through the pages, going back.

It was easy to look for a Murray Meyer or a Granger Knox—but none appeared. It wasn't so easy to look for a Lacey, Janet or even a Claire—several women with those first names had stayed at McLane House. One of them might have married, re-married, used a maiden name...

She put the book back in the drawer as well, and stood, eager to go down, anxious to speak with Dallas; if not Dallas, at least Angela or Jackson. They could also take what she had—and determine how best to use the information.

She exited her room, pausing again at the door. She hadn't felt it so much earlier, but now, here, out in the hall, the strange sense of darkness seemed to have settled over the very air again, like a mist of something...

Evil.

She gave herself a shake. Maybe Simon Drake was hidden somewhere near, and he couldn't manage to show himself at all, to come to her.

Maybe they did need another séance, she thought wryly.

But she hurried down the stairs.

Peeking into the front parlor, she saw the backs of Carl Brentwood's and Murray Meyer's heads; they still had to be discussing whatever it was they'd been discussing.

The back parlor was empty; Genie's delicious little treats sat on the table, along with a bucket for wine, and the tea samovar and the coffeepot.

Glancing out, she saw Jonah bent over a book.

Curiously, the darkness seemed to be growing.

She headed into the kitchen, and then she knew why.

Sydney was slumped over the table; Genie lay on the floor in front of the sink.

"Oh, my God!" she breathed, rushing over to Sydney, and then Genie, her heart in her throat. Both had pulses; they were alive. She raced for the house phone on the kitchen wall, but there was no dial tone.

Kristi started to race for the kitchen door, and then a scream of pure terror suddenly broke through the darkness and the miasma, and it was coming from the living room.

Kristi grabbed a kitchen knife, the best weapon she could find, afraid all the while that it might be used on her.

The scream came again and again, and then she heard Shelley crying out, "No, no, no...oh, God, help me."

Kristi tore into the back parlor, barely thinking about the idiocy of her movement, just acting on human instinct to help another...someone not in just distress, but pure terror.

Dallas had barely gone a block before he received a call from Vickie Preston.

"You've got something—already?"

"Well, I told you, I've been going back on all these people—when Angela and Jackson left to join you, Angela asked me to keep digging, and so..."

"What did you get?"

"I have two things for you—one of your people started out in nursing school, but then changed their major. I don't know how important that is, but I've also found out who is a descendent of Albert Huntington, and it's quite a connection." Vickie gave him her information.

By the time she finished speaking, he was already running.

Kristi burst into the back parlor, pausing, forcing herself to listen, to wait, to see what was going on in the house.

She looked out the back windows—Jonah was still in the courtyard, slumped over his book.

He must be out—like Genie and Sydney.

What the hell had happened? Had it been something in the tarts? What had Genie put in them? Or had it been Genie? Had she knocked herself out with the others?

She rued the fact that she had left her cell phone in her bag, along with the book. The other house phone was in the front parlor...

"No, no, no… I did all you asked!" she heard Shelley cry.

Moving out to the front room, but holding by the archway in the door, Kristi looked into the living room.

Shelley was in the grips of a man: Granger Knox. He was smiling.

He raised his voice to speak, clearly aware that Kristi was somewhere in the house. "Miss Stewart, I need the letter that your great-uncle had, and, of course, I believe you found the book that Ian Murphy was hoarding, as well."

Granger had a knife. He had it at Shelley's throat.

Kristi tried to remain calm, knowing she had her own knife gripped in her hands—and, afraid, of course, that it could be wrested from her and used against her.

"You know, this just has to be the most ridiculous thing in the world, and so truly tragic! I believe you must be a descendent of Colonel Albert Huntington, but at this point in history, sir—who the hell cares?" Kristi demanded.

"Oh, Miss Stewart, you know nothing about politics," he told her. "How could you know so very much about history, and not realize how a man may be skewered by the past? But actually, no, I'm not a descendent of Albert Huntington."

Shelley, straining against Knox and the knife, begged her, "Kristi, please…do as he says, please, do as he says!"

"Mr. Knox, you're not even a descendent—and you're killing over the possibility that the man be declared a murderer? Seriously, it was war, sir, and many atrocities happened, North and South. And you must realize, Eliza has now been found. The FBI is officially in on this investigation. You killed Eliza—over a meeting with Ian? She didn't even know anything yet. And you killed Lachlan—how could you? What, did you think that a trainer was going to go on the news and declare you…a monster? And Ian! An old man…"

"Ian is the one I should have killed first. But actually, my dear

Miss Know-It-All Stewart, I didn't kill Eliza Malone. Yes, I am responsible for Ian, but...anyway, with Eliza, something had to be done. She was so *active* in stopping crime. Once, when I was trying to find out what the old man had, she saw me entering Ian's house." He paused and shrugged ruefully. "*Illegally* entering his house—you know, breaking and entering—and she was going to call the police. Stop crime in the city right away, you know."

"You're being foolish. Dallas will be back any moment. Jamie Murphy should be landing soon—and two FBI agents are a block away."

He smiled. "I only need a few minutes."

"You'll be caught," Kristi told him.

"Kristi!" Shelley begged.

"I won't be caught. When I have what I want, I'll just help myself to a pecan tart, too, and they'll find me on the floor with everyone else. Now, Kristi, I want the letter."

"You're going to kill me anyway. Why would I help you?" she asked.

"Because you're such a good girl, Miss Stewart. And I'll kill Shelley, too, if you don't."

"Kristi, please," Shelley begged.

"I will kill her," Knox vowed.

"Well, frankly," Kristi said, "she's a serious thorn in my side, and has been for years and years."

Knox moved the knife; a thin line of blood appeared at Shelley's throat.

"All right, you want the damned letter—I will get it for you," Kristi said.

Time, she thought. She had to play for time, because Dallas would come back, because Jackson and Angela were near.

"Do your wife and daughter know about this?" Kristi asked, hearing a noise on the stairway as she spoke.

She spun around. Janet Knox was coming down the stairs.

"That dumb girl we made the mistake of adopting almost ru-ined the whole thing, but…hey, a kid makes you look innocent, you know?" Janet said. She smiled, looking across the room at her husband and Shelley. "Ah, Shelley, longing so hard to be the world's greatest medium! So pliable."

Reaching the foot of the stairs, Janet smiled at Kristi. "I know you don't understand, but we can let Shelley live…she's a bit in on this, you know. I'm the one who came to stay at the house several years ago—as a young, single redhead. Trust me, I'm quite a good actress. And I'm the one who found out that you silly people with your hospitality—just about anyone might have known where all the keys were. But Shelley did help me and, trust me, she knows that if we should be accused, we'll make sure she comes down with us for accessory to murder."

"All right, so Shelley was gullible—but, Janet, you are un-believable. Your husband is a murderer, and you don't care?" Kristi asked.

"I'm a far more talented murderer—I took care of that med-dling Eliza," Janet said. "What was I to do? I arrived at Ian's, and she was making a stink, and she was going to wake the old man up and, at that time, we still needed to know what he knew, and we needed his association with Jedidiah. I should have killed Jedidiah—he was actually the one holding things up. I stayed here, found the key, searched and searched… You see, Miss Stewart, it's not my husband who is the descendent—it's me."

"And I'm going to run for the United States Congress, and soon, the presidency," Granger said.

His wife went on, "And we've known, as we planned this all, that there was just no way Granger could be associated with a Civil War murderer."

"Better for you both to be killers yourselves," Kristi said.

"The letter," Granger said angrily.

"It's upstairs," Kristi said. "And, guess what—I didn't even know about it until very recently. And if you hadn't done all this, I never would have known about it!"

"Get it!"

At the foot of the stairs, Janet Knox edged back, allowing Kristi room to pass by her to ascend.

She felt Janet following her, almost on top of her.

She had just reached the area where the family portraits were displayed when she felt Janet press the point of a knife to her back.

"Drop the knife," Janet told her.

She had seen the kitchen knife in Kristi's hand, held close to her thigh.

"Drop it!"

Kristi was never sure how she managed what she did, but she dropped the knife. And, at the same time, she reached for the Civil War photograph of Monty McLane, displayed so lovingly upon the wall. In a sharp, fluid motion, she managed to smash it hard over Janet Knox's head, and watched as the woman fell flat and screaming upon the floor.

Granger let out a snarl of rage, threw Shelley to the floor and came after Kristi as if he were a rabid dog.

He nearly reached her.

But the front door opened. A whirr of motion was all that Kristi really saw.

Dallas was back.

Flying up the stairs behind Granger, tackling him and rolling down, down, down the stairs with him, until they were on the landing, and Dallas was straddled over Granger.

He lifted a fist furiously, ready to punch the man, but the door flew open again, and Jackson burst in, Joe Dunhill and Angela behind him.

Jackson kept Dallas from beating the man to a pulp, dragging him up and away.

The arrest went to Joe Dunhill. He cuffed Granger Knox

while Angela called for several ambulances. Then Dunhill cuffed Janet Knox.

Kristi remained frozen until Dallas ran up the stairs to where she stood, drawing her into his shaking arms.

EPILOGUE

Dallas stood by the monument to Justin McLane, smiling as he listened to the heartfelt apologies that both Justin and Monty were giving him.

"I might have caused Kristi's death," Monty said. "I left... I should have been here, I should have been able to do something. I don't know... I don't know if I could ever explain what I've felt, what... I loved her so much. It was always agony knowing that she died because of me. I should have returned...and then, so foolishly, I couldn't leave her bones, and..."

"We're so sorry, and incredibly grateful that Kristi is okay... that it's over," Justin said.

"It's all right. Kristi is fine. And the killers have been caught," Dallas said.

He turned around. Kristi was coming out of the house, smiling. She'd just greeted Jamie Murphy, and tried very hard to catch him up on everything that had happened before last night—he'd arrived just in time to find Kristi's house swarming with ambulances and police, and he was, of course, still confused, but Kristi had just sent him off with Jackson and Angela.

For once, the only people at the house were Kristi and Dallas—and, of course, now Justin and Monty.

McLane House guests and staff were still in the hospital for observation.

They'd found out that while Janet had been the descendent of Albert Huntington, it had been Granger who had started out in nursing school.

He had used "Devil's Breath," or a street version of scopolamine, to lace the tarts to put everyone out.

He'd used his anger with his daughter to keep her out of the house—telling her that he'd have a talk with Carl Brentwood and the possibility of them seeing each other in the future if she went with Claire to a professional photographer in the city for her own promo shots. Even though he and his wife were clearly some form of sociopaths, they loved their daughter, in their way.

He later told them where they would find Simon Drake's body—in a sewer near the Murphy house. Drake had been a real danger in Granger's mind—he wanted to gather all the great stories regarding Savannah and publish them in a book about the city. He'd spoken with Ian as he was collecting his research, and Ian had promised to give him everything that he had.

While not confined for observation as the others, Claire Danson and Lacey Knox were at the hospital, too—both lingering by Carl, determined that their love and adoration would help him get better soon.

"Hey," Dallas said, drawing Kristi into his arms as she reached him. He smoothed back her hair. "You're okay, really okay?"

"I'm better than I thought I would be," she assured him. She glanced around Dallas's broad shoulders at Monty. "I'm so sorry that I had to use that wonderful period photograph of you."

"I thank God that I could be of assistance in some small way," Monty said. "Kristi, it's your forgiveness I must ask. My Trinity... I loved her so much. I only pray you can understand."

Dallas felt something clench tightly in his chest, and he whispered, "I think we do understand."

"You can't leave her, you know," Monty said. "You'll never be all right if you do."

"He has to leave. He's with a very unusual and important unit," Kristi said. "But," she added, pausing for a smile, to look at Dallas, and then to say very softly, "I've got it figured it out. I did get to talk to Jonah at the hospital—briefly. I can do my work anywhere. Jonah and Genie and Sydney do fine without me, and I can come back every month for a few days... It is my heritage, and I love the house and all the people—living and dead—residing here. So...if you'll have me..."

Heedless of the ghosts, Dallas drew her into his arms. Their kiss was hot and deep, and very passionate, and still the sweetest he had ever tasted. It naturally spoke the words they hadn't said yet, and when it ended, and he drew away, he did speak those words. "I love you!"

She was smiling, but he searched her eyes before he spoke again. "And...you don't mind. You really don't mind coming with me, living my life...giving up so much of your own?"

"Considering the fact that I haven't worked at all now in quite a while, I may not have any work left here anyway!" she said.

He smiled. "We have some time. There's a great deal to be tied up here," he said softly.

And there was, of course. But he really did understand Monty.

He thought about the time years ago, when he had been in the old forgotten cemetery, when he had seen his first ghost...

When he had learned that the beauty of a soul could linger, and that knowing that could make him a better person to see that justice was done, that some could then go on.

Kristi said softly, "I want your life. I think I could be good at it."

She turned from him then and walked over to Monty.

Dr. Horvath and her team had come back. There had been

a lot more digging, more bones discovered—and DNA tested, though articles found indicated whom the bones likely belonged to.

While the yard was a bit of a mess, good things had come from it.

Monty's and Samuel's bodies had been found.

Fresh sod would be brought in—and Kristi had commissioned an artist to create a beautiful monument for her ancestors. They could be properly remembered now that Monty's name had been cleared.

As Kristi approached, Monty offered her something of a grimace. "As much as I hate to admit it," she said, "I believe that Shelley was right, and that maybe now Trinity can come home—home to you," she added very softly.

The sun was playing softly through the moss that hung from the old oak trees.

"Trinity, it's all right. The truth is known, and he loves you so much. Monty loves you so much, Trinity, it's all right…"

Light dappled over the grounds, through the oaks and the moss.

And slowly, so slowly, an image began to appear. The image of a woman, clad in a lovely blue gown, her pale face beautiful and radiant. She couldn't quite speak, but she mouthed a single word.

"Monty!"

"Trinity!" the ghost cried, and he rushed into her arms, enveloping her.

The sun burst down upon them; a radiant glow seemed to burn.

And then the two were gone.

For a moment, they were all silent.

Then Justin spoke.

"Well, I guess it's just down to us," he said.

Dallas turned to him, grinning. "For tonight, my friend—it's down to you. There's a new hotel out on the riverfront, great spa, incredible rooms... We'll be back tomorrow, of course, but for tonight, well... I thought we might need a bit of a break from... from history. Time alone. Just us. Just for tonight, all right?"

He looked at Kristi, and she laughed, and she was back in his arms.

"For tonight, and forever," she promised him.

★ ★ ★ ★ ★